What Happens in Denver

by

Liz Crowe

What Happens in Denver

Contact Information: info@thewildrosepress.com

Cover Art by *Diana Carlile*

The Wild Rose Press, Inc.
PO Box 708
Adams Basin, NY 14410-0708

Visit us at www.thewildrosepress.com

Publishing History
First Edition, 2021
Print ISBN 978-1-5092-3885-9
Digital ISBN 978-1-5092-3886-6
Published in the United States of America

New friends, a fresh start, a side order of romance—all with a nice cold pint...

He held up his half-empty glass. "To pretentious beer conventions," he said. "And to finding a dive bar where beautiful women drink PBRs."

"I'll drink to all of that." We clinked glasses again. When I brought mine to my lips a little too aggressively, a splash of beer went up my nose while another landed on my shirt. I snorted.

James handed me a napkin, his smile fixed in place. I frowned and took it from him.

I didn't want or need this right now. I needed a damn job. Him and his...tall, burly, not-really-my-type handsomeness was distracting me. I faced the bar again, my throat tight and my head spinning.

"Another," I said, sliding ten bucks across the sticky bar top.

I heard a clunk next to me. I sensed James sliding off his barstool. My hand shot out, seemingly under its own power and rested on his arm. Despite my determination not to, I was hyper aware of the bulky musculature of his bicep. I let go. "Sorry," I muttered.

"Gotta take a leak," he said. He put his lips near my ear. I smelled beer and peanuts on his breath. "Try not to miss me too much."

Dedication

This one's for Annette,
ever the Liz cheerleader and beer advisor.

Chapter One

When anyone ever asks me to give them advice about how to get ahead as a female bar owner-slash-beer expert, which they do, in a near constant yet flattering way, I always say, "Never glance at yourself in the mirror."

"But Andi," they ask, their eyes aglow with eagerness to learn the secret to my success. "Why not?"

"Because you won't look as nice as the people you're serving. You'll always be red-faced, round-assed, flustered, and in a hurry to put out another fire. Plus, self-evaluation takes too much time. As a bar owner, there is no such thing as you-time. Don't kid yourself."

Of course, as is the way with most advice I give out, I rarely take it. So that same-as-always Tuesday night, the night I was told that my bar—okay, the bar I owned with my husband—was now the "Best Beer Bar in America" by who-cares-it's-still-something-I-can-brag-about, I spent a solid five minutes staring at myself in the employee bathroom mirror, wishing I were prettier, better with makeup and hair, or at the very least, twenty pounds lighter.

"Hey! Andi!" Someone pounded on the janky bathroom door. "You all right? Come out. Let's celebrate."

I touched my lips and poked at the freckles that

made a total mockery of me as a grown woman, glowing across the bridge of my nose to the tops of my cheekbones. I pressed my hands to my waist. Felt those squishy extra pounds muffin-topping the jeans I'd wrangled myself into that morning.

I heard a loud "whoop" and more cheering coming from the bar. But I couldn't seem to rouse myself, to move from my position at the mirror, glaring at every single one of my physical faults. I refused to cry. As a result, the tears burning the backs of my eyeballs remained unshed, as usual.

I swallowed hard. I swallowed again. And I kept on breaking my own advice rules by staring so hard at my image in the mirror I thought I might change it.

This is it. I'd made it. Right?

I'd made my decision to drop out of my grad program to follow my handsome boyfriend Matt Rigby into a business he swore would be worth a thousand times more than any degree, only to find myself cast into a world I knew little about and left to flail or drown. While he supervised the build-out of Beer Wenches Inc, or BWI as it'd been dubbed by the various snobs and, later, hipsters who'd taken over my hometown, I'd immersed myself in all aspects of the burgeoning craft beer industry.

I learned how to brew, which was messy. And I studied the intricacies and politics of alcohol distribution, which was crazy complex. I traveled, met, and tasted with as many Southern and Midwest brewers and brewery owners as I could, which took a solid year, considering how damn many of them there were. That was fun, though. After a while, I knew I should take what I'd learned from them and their bearded, tattooed, too-cool-for-school attitudes and make my bar into the hottest, most sought after beer venue around.

I got myself certified as a beer expert—this is a thing, believe it or not—which took several thousand dollars and hours of study, plus a super stressful test wherein I had to identify the what's and why's of off flavors and write an essay about beer and food pairing. When the moment came and I clutched at the oversized scissors with the glad-handing chamber of commerce tool, smiled for yet another camera, and threw open the doors of the renovated warehouse, I crossed my fingers and toes that we wouldn't be closed inside a year.

During this process, I gained thirty pounds. I also got a little too caught up in the craft beer world, a.k.a. I drank until I found myself pouring a pint at eleven in the morning after closing the bar at two a.m. So, yeah, I suffered through a few self-imposed detox sessions.

"Andi! Are you all right? Hey! C'mere, Candace. Will you go in there and check on her?"

"I'm fine." I cleared my throat. "I'm fine," I repeated, louder this time so whoever was milling around outside the bathroom door would go away. I exhaled. Then I opened the door to find half the kitchen staff and a quarter of the bartenders waiting for me. They burst into applause. "Okay, all right. Let's not lose our focus. It's busy tonight."

My eyes were so hot from unshed tears that I wished I could press a couple of ice cubes on them. Instead, I grabbed a clean bar towel, ran it under cold water, and held it to my forehead. Avoiding the front of the house sounded like heaven, so I sat on a low chair tucked into a corner near the break room, happy to watch my people going about their business.

As a boss, I made a point to learn as much as I could about each of my employees. I knew which of my cooks had families and the ages of their kids, if any, and what their spouses did for a living. The bar staff was younger, but I treated them all as family, unless they broke one too many rules. I knew who was dating, who wasn't, who wished they were, and even how many hook ups happened within the four walls of my bar—a lot of them, by the way. I remained aware of it, mainly to ensure that when breakups happened, they didn't affect any of our guests.

Some of this I got from Josh, the at-times hapless, many times hopeless manager. He was great at a few things, one of them being gossip. The dude always knew the inside scoop and had zero qualms ratting out anyone and everyone he supervised, not to mention the back of the house staff. His grapevine listening skills were matched by his whine and complain talents.

I knew better than to trust someone who'd tell me anything I wanted to know about pretty much anyone around us. He was, without a shadow of a doubt, gossiping about me to everyone else as well. So I tried not to provide him with any more fodder, other than what the daily drama of running a successful bar and restaurant did, simply by being a bar and restaurant.

I loved it here. It was the only place left where I felt at home. My house was more or less a docking station where I sometimes ate, slept, and showered. Matt and I had dispensed with the charade of intimacy. Most nights, if he came home, he slept in our closet-sized spare bedroom without me.

But at the moment, my crumbling joke of a marriage didn't matter.

I reminded myself that our bar—okay, my bar— was now The Best Craft Beer Bar in America. And we deserved it. Hell, I deserved it, considering everything I'd given up for it.

A knee-jerk reaction to let Matt know about it passed over me. He was out in Colorado at a beer con. One of the big ones. I'd gone with him the last four years. This year, he'd told me matter-of-factly that he'd be going without me. I hadn't argued. What did it matter anyway? I hated those things, except for the whole getting treated like royalty every year we attended, which wasn't fun when my husband treated me like week-old leftovers once I was alone with him.

The craft beer market was growing tighter by the day with more and more breweries popping up, claiming to have the answers to all the questions beer drinkers didn't even know they had. As long as I got to rotate my forty taps with regularity, I didn't care what wild promises they made about how unique their take might be on the water, malt, hops, and yeast beverages they planned to create. There were already so dang many options. I could be open for the next twenty years before I got through them all, whether they deserved one of my sought-after taps or not.

Subjecting myself to all that glad-handing and BS didn't sound fun to me this year. So Matt went with his main squeeze slash arm candy, the lovely Madison, in tow. Which meant I had to handle all the crap she took care of, like events and social media, which I despised.

Oh, did I forget to mention the woman Matt encouraged me to hire as my marketing manager a few months ago was his girlfriend? Yeah. That.

What did it matter? He got what he wanted. I got

what I wanted. As long as he left me to my life as owner slash manager of The Best Beer Bar in America, who needed him anyway?

My face flamed hot as tears threatened yet again. I kept them at bay. I couldn't recall the last time I'd let one drop, to be honest. Maybe in college. Or maybe the moment I figured out my husband was screwing the woman I had just hired.

My ability to swallow emotion had served me well in this testosterone-riddled world, which was my world now. BWI had grown each year in stature, reputation, and success. The rental hall was never empty. Distributors beat down my door day and night to snag a tap or booze shelf space.

We'd hosted every major brewery, some of them twice for sold-out beer dinners. Our mixology nights with the ever-increasing throng of local distilleries were standing room only events. Now that wine was making a comeback in the face of the beer brigade, I had several wine tastings and dinners planned well into the next two years. I'd even considered studying to be a sommelier, but that entailed way more snobbery and bullshit about "plum notes" and "legginess" than I wanted to endure.

As I said, I got what I wanted. My business. My bar. My employees. Even the sniveling, consummate sucker-upper, Josh. As long as I could avoid mirrors, I was golden. My universe was complete.

****

I pressed the cold cloth tighter to my eyes, hoping to hold back tears. It worked like it usually did.

"Andi? You good?"

I peeled the cloth away from my face and met the

gaze of my head cook, Vincente, son of a professional chef in Brazil. Vincente had immigrated to the U.S. when he was four years old. Now an adult and married to a natural-born citizen, he wore his American status like a badge of honor. He had a three-year-old daughter and another one on the way. His wife was an immigration attorney. They'd met when he'd been attempting to navigate the legal citizen waters at nineteen.

Like I said, I knew my people.

His dark eyes were wide and full of concern. He was a great employee. One of the ones Matt had helped me choose and who'd been loyal to a fault these past years. "Yes, I'm good. Thanks for asking."

He grinned. "Congrats on the award. That's pretty amazing." He turned back to the task in front of him, checking tickets and supervising the food runners.

"Thanks. But I didn't do it. *We* did it."

He gave me a thumbs-up, then got back to work. I exhaled. Even though he must have already heard about it, something perverse in me wanted to tell Matt myself.

I ducked into my small office, a long, rectangular space carved out in the far back of the building. It reeked of old garbage twenty-four seven, but there wasn't a thing I could do about it, other than move it somewhere else. And who had time for that? I grabbed my phone and called Matt after checking the beer con schedule. It was in breakout sessions, none of which he ever attended so I figured I could catch him.

"Did you get my text?" I pressed the device closer to my ear, willing him to hear me over the din of the expo center when he picked up. "Matt? Can you hear me?" Aggravated but too hyped to give up on the conversation, I shut the door, plopped onto the couch I'd curbside-liberated from a fancy subdivision and stuck earbuds in my ears. "Matt!"

A sharp rap on the door forced me to hang up. "Come in." I fixed Josh, the bar manager now peering into the room, with my sternest boss-lady face. "I'm trying to get hold of Matt and tell him about the award."

His gaze flickered to my phone before treating me to a teenager-worthy eye-roll.

"Sorry, boss," he said in his fake-polite voice. "But we've got a situation."

"What else is new?" I crossed my arms and waited for him to elaborate. I'd learned that Josh's "situations" were typically customers—nine times out of ten, women—who were pissed off and up in his face over it. He hated women getting up in his face. This included me. But that was, after all, my job, so it couldn't be avoided.

"A double booking," he said, his face smug. "Madison fucked up the rental hall schedule before she left."

I held out my hand. "Show me."

He handed over the tablet. I glared down at the screen.

"Okay," I said, yanking my hair into a ponytail. This sort of thing made me nuts, because it made my business look bad. But I'll admit it was the kind of problem I needed, anything to distract me from the fact that while I did have a successful business, I no longer had anything resembling a functioning marriage.

No biggie.

Right.

"Tell me who's out there."

He relayed the two unhappy parties—one a simple twenty-person birthday, no food. The other, a more elaborate forty-five person going-away party with food that the kitchen had prepped and ready to go. In short, an utter snafu.

"What's the room look like?" I asked.

Josh rattled off the current situation in the main bar, revealing what I'd hoped. It was only about two-thirds full.

My brain went into full crisis-aversion mode. "All right, tell the rental hall staff to go ahead and set up for the food party. Then grab half the servers and start shoving tables together in the corner of the main room." I'd had part of the bar semi walled-off when we did our original conversion of the decades-empty warehouse. It should suit the twenty-person party perfectly.

My pulse raced and my face flushed, but I was on top of this. *This* allowed me to ignore the hard facts that I'd gotten pretty good at ignoring.

"Got it," Josh said with one of his patented ironic and super annoying salutes.

God, I wished I could cut him loose. Which would, of course, give Matt a reason to gloat, since he hadn't been in favor of the butt-kissing gossip monger from the start.

"Great," I muttered as I rallied my inner super-apologetic bar owner and pondered how to handle all the people collected at the door of the rental hall, thanks to Madison Sandiford.

The woman currently fucking my husband.

Well, not currently.

Okay, probably currently if I knew Matt and his penchant for quickie sex.

I emerged from the breezy hallway, relishing the familiar noise and heat from the place that had become my second home. I observed the busy space, my space, the business I'd left my grad degree for so Matt and I could build it together. Not for the first time, I wondered why I'd done it.

You know, you might consider letting go of all this self-deprecation. It's getting old.

Shut up. It grounds me.

Screw it. And screw him, anyway.

As I prepared my apologies and sorted through how much money I'd lose over Madison's mistake, I almost jumped out of my skin when someone grabbed my arm.

"Jesus, what?" I glared at Josh.

His beady eyes darted around, checking to make sure no one was listening or perhaps hoping someone was. "I'm really sorry, Andi."

"No, you're not. Now get out of my way. We have a mess to handle, and I need you to hold up your end of things."

"No, I mean, I'm sorry about this." He handed me his phone, his face grim, but with the ghost of a smirk playing around his lips.

I grabbed it, figuring it had to do with the problem in front of me. It took me a solid fifteen seconds to read, then re-read, the text message. I blew out a breath, looked up at the ceiling, then stared back down at the words that had just blown my world into a million tiny pieces.

—Tell the staff there's going to be a change when we get home on Monday.— Matt had sent it about five minutes before, which was right after he'd ignored my

call. —*Andi will be leaving. But everyone can rest assured nothing else will change other than who'll be in charge on a daily basis.*—

Josh had responded with —*Who will that be?*—

Matt's response was —*Madison. Don't tell Andi. I will. I owe her that much.*—

When I handed the device to him without a word, he opened his mouth to let fly with more fake sympathy. I held up both hands, afraid that if he said another word, I'd either scream, finally give in to tears, or slug him, maybe all three at once.

"Go," I said, pointing toward the bar. "Get your staff in gear to commandeer that area before it fills in so I can put the birthday party people there. Comp all their beers."

One crisis at a time.

His mouth remained hanging open. I rarely, if ever comped an entire party's drinks. But, all of a sudden, I felt mighty generous. Hell, I might comp everybody's Goddamned beers before the night was over. Four or five or maybe six rounds on the house sounded pretty fucking good. "Are you deaf in addition to being an asshole?"

He sucked in a breath, shocked at my out-of-character rudeness and cursing. I glared harder. He slunk away like the weasel he was.

Work the problem, Andrea. The rest will have to be dealt with later. Emotional triage, kid. It's the only way.

"Right," I said under my breath, furious that I'd gone and channeled my dear old dad who'd run off when I was twelve, taking with him a plentiful store of cutesy aphorisms.

Men.

Fucking men.

I ducked into the small staff restroom near my office, slammed the door, and turned on the exhaust fan so I could scream until my throat ached. Thus purged, I rested my hands on the sides of the sink and met my own eyes in the mirror. Yet again, breaking that cardinal rule.

I yanked the holder from my hair and let the thick, auburn curls drop around my face. The sob ripped at my throat and burst from my lips, surprising me. Leave it to Matthew Rigby to be the one man in the universe—other than my father—capable of turning me into a girlie, weepy mess. Giving up, I bent my knees, still gripping the edge of the sink for dear life, and let the tears flow.

After this second emotional purge, I sat on the bathroom floor and forced myself to think straight. I didn't love him anymore. Madison could have him and his knee-jerk orgasms. But I loved my life, my job, my world. And apparently, he was on the verge of taking that away from me, too. I rose and splashed cold water on my face again, resolute in the face of that hard fact.

There was no way on this earth or any other I'd let him do this to me. My name was on all the LLC documents. BWI was partly mine. If he honestly thought he could just toss me into the street and install scrawny Madison in my place, he had another Goddamned think coming.

In the meantime, I had guests to placate. Beers to comp. A tattered and fraying-by-the-second morale to gather around myself before my staff got wind of the change in the air.

Chapter Two

I kept my focus on the here and now. The straight-ahead and don't-get-distracted. It was the only thing I knew to do at this point. Matt wasn't due back for a few more days. He claimed he was going to "research" some other bars after the Beer Con. I figured him for researching the inside of Madison's thighs, but whatever. I had plenty to keep me busy.

The Tuesday after the "Best Beer Bar in America" thing was announced, a TV crew came in to interview me, my staff, and gather b-roll around the place all day. It was supposed to air the next Monday, the day the happy couple was due back.

The night after all the TV nonsense, I lay awake in my empty bed, staring up at the ceiling. Matt hadn't contacted me since the night Josh had ratted him and his plans out. I hadn't tried to reach him. It was our status quo. But with one huge difference this time. My chest tightened, and my eyes burned, but I'd done my crying already. There would be no more tears shed over that asshole.

I swiped at my cheek, cursed, punched my pillow and squinched my eyes shut. At my mother's insistence, I'd been proactive. I made an appointment with our attorney to go over the LLC documents, if for no other reason than to reassure myself all was as it should be, that he simply couldn't shove me out the door. I was the named President of the company. He was merely a member of the board. We were it. I was the only one who could make any sort of major change to the board structure. At least, that's how he'd explained it to me when he'd set everything up that way himself.

I'll admit to being so caught up in the minutiae, the brewing, learning, touring, and the getting-to-know-you part of the business, I probably didn't listen as closely as I should have when Matt was giving me those sorts of details.

Shit.

Giving up after almost an hour of trying to calm my rattled brain, I sat on the side of the bed and stared down at my unmanicured toenails. My stomach grumbled. I'd not been able to shove much food past my throat since Saturday. Not a bad diet plan, but unsustainable. I flopped back with a groan as the reality of what was about to happen to me bowled me over.

I was about to get dumped…by my husband…for another woman. But what was giving me a real gut punch? They wanted to take my baby away, my child, my only love, that damn bar.

"Nope," I said out loud into the empty room. "Nope. Nope. And…nope." I launched myself up and into the shower, never mind it was four a.m. I forced myself to concentrate on the day ahead. Appointment with the lawyer, eight-thirty a.m. sharp. Check. Run to bank since Josh and I agreed we needed to make a deposit and get more change. Check. Stop in at a new beer and wine shop that had just opened in Germantown. I wanted to meet the owner. Check. Take a breath because lawyer had assured me that Matt and Madison couldn't just stage some kind of a damn coup and oust me as president of my own damn company. Check.

Open the bar.

Help at the bar.

Close the bar.

Check.

I froze between toweling off and putting on panties and sat down on the half-unrumpled bed. But after allowing myself exactly four and a half minutes of self-pity wallowing—God, I was boring. No wonder Matt wanted to screw skinny Madison—I got up and grabbed the top pair of jeans off a tall stack in my closet. I barely noticed that they were a tad loose, somewhat easier to button. Stress non-eating was my M.O. Once I met with the lawyer, I'd be back to filching sweet potato fries and drinking too many shift beers.

I buttoned up one of my nicer BWI, short-sleeved work-shirts, styled after those worn by brewers, with the logo embroidered on the left breast. Then came my usual quick-and-easy makeup routine. Dot the zits with medicine. Slather on some kind of drugstore-level foundation. Top with some powder to keep the shinies at bay. A dab of mascara, which made my already long brown lashes frame my eyes rather nicely, if I did say so myself.

I turned to break my advice chain yet again and studied my profile, sucking in my tummy to give myself a sexier profile before giving up.

"You are in charge," I reminded my reflection.

"He's just making noise. He can't take BWI from you. That's just idiotic," my mother had said the night I found out.

"He's a fucking shithead," Stella, my one

remaining friend had insisted over a bottle of expensive Italian wine two nights ago.

Desperate, lonely, and horrified at myself, I'd called her, knowing she'd come over, get me good and drunk, tell me all the things I wanted to hear about Matt. And she had. Before passing out on my couch, still clutching her glass and mumbling about asshole men.

She was in a lull between marriages but ever on the lookout for Mr. Just About Right. As my only real friend, bless her, she'd provided me with what I'd required, even if it had come with the sort of hangover over-indulging in red wine can provide.

I forced myself to smile. It looked more like a pained grimace, so I bolted to the kitchen before I lost my nerve in front of my own damn self.

I flipped through social media videos of pretty women getting prettier using massive amounts of lotions, potions, powders, and other craziness to "sculpt" and achieve "smoky eye" while I sipped coffee. I'd never have the nerve to try any of their magic tricks with my face, but I was hooked on the makeup videos for some reason. Weird, I know, but one of the few things I'd discovered that could relax me lately.

A few minutes later, I was in the car, giving myself yet another pep talk. I should have paid closer attention to the paperwork. Yes. I should have. But I trusted Matt. He was my husband. He handled that side of things. I did the day-to-day grunt work. The hiring and firing. The marketing. The schmoozing. The PR. Hell, I even fixed the toilets and repaired the ceiling fans when needed.

"Oh shit. I am so screwed." I pressed my forehead to the wheel while the car warmed up in the early morning heat. Where had I gone wrong? When had I turned into this...this jeans-and-T-shirt-wearing...overweight...drudge?

My phone dinged with a text. I glanced at it. It was Josh with a reminder to go to the bank and to stop at the store for more nuts because the food vendor had shorted us. I sighed and answered him, pondering the reality that, if anything, he and I acted like a married couple, managing the bar and its many complexities between us.

Josh was short, a tad paunchy, had a sort of Hercule Poirot-style moustache and beard, which matched his small, dark, ratty eyes. As much as he irritated me, he'd become a crucial part of my daily functionality.

Yeah. Kind of like we were married.

I put the car in reverse. I had a lawyer meeting to make, after which I could concentrate on what mattered. My job. My bar. My life.

The lawyer's office was in a strip mall not too far from the bar. I parked and made my determined way to the glass door. This was a technicality, a bump in the road I had to get past. I'd even initiate the divorce. Save him the trouble. As long as I didn't have to give up BWI.

I set my shoulders and marched up to the desk in the center of the well-appointed lobby. I was asked to please take a seat and told that Ms. Cameron would be with me shortly. I sat and spent a solid fifteen minutes past my appointed appointment time tugging a loose thread at the hem of my shirt until I'd managed to unravel it, making me look even more sad-sack.

Finally, a painfully attractive woman appeared in the doorway behind the desk and called my name. She was dressed in a suit that would be at home on an Italian fashion runway, with sky-high heels and subtle yet obvious diamond earrings. Her hair... Well, anyway. She was perfect-looking. Could easily have done one of those makeup videos I loved so much. I was instantly on the defensive.

I tugged the ratty hem of my shirt, never more aware of my paltry make-up job, my earringless ears, my clunky yet functional shoes. I shifted from foot to foot and forced myself to smile. "Hello. I'm Andi, um, Andrea. Andrea Rigby. We had an appointment."

Duh. Why else would you be here?

My innate self-consciousness around well-appointed—read "gorgeous"—women was taking over again. I set my jaw. I was here for a reason. I needed answers and then I needed to get the heck on with my day.

"Oh, right, yes." She checked her watch. "I'm sorry. I let the morning get away from me."

I blinked at her. It was all of eight-twenty-five. But, of course, I was the night owl. My job meant I stayed up usually past two a.m., closing down the bar and winding down from a day and night of work. I was typically still sound asleep at this ass-crack-of-dawn hour.

"Come in," the model-perfect woman said. "Can I get you some coffee? Water?"

"No. No, thank you." My throat was closing up, forcing me to take tiny sips of air through my nose in order not to pass out. I had a very bad feeling about this whole thing. The lawyer I vaguely recalled from our earliest days setting up the LLC and other stuff had not been this woman. It had been a man, an older guy with a shock of white hair and bad teeth. I couldn't quite square the person I was looking at with the person I'd assumed I would come here to meet, to be reassured, to be sent on my way knowing, while my marriage was a dumpster fire, I would never lose my bar.

Despite my answer, someone handed me a burning hot cup of coffee. I took it and put it on the table next to my chair. It rattled, giving away my stress.

The woman was flipping through some neatly fanned out files on her massive desk. "Let me see…" She frowned at some papers, closed that file, then pulled another one from the stack.

I gnawed on my lower lip, unable to tear my gaze from her, obsessed by the little round morsels of her fingernails, painted brown, like chocolate. I was buzzing from head to toe with hopeful anticipation.

"Ah, here we go." She put two pieces of paper in front of me, facing toward me, so I could see them. I leaned forward, but the words were blurry. I swiped at my eyes, glanced at the woman, who I'd deduced using my keen mental powers, was not the friendly old grandpa who'd set this thing up.

She was tap-tapping her chocolate morsel fingertips on her desk, as if anxious for me to get the hell out. Flustered and pissed for letting her make me feel that way, I focused hard on the papers. It had to be a formality. I was merely checking in on what I already knew about the structure of Beer Wenches, Inc.

But as I scanned the sheets, seeking my own name, I sensed my shoulders tensing, my chest filling with dread as thick as mud. "Okay, um…" I pushed the papers back toward her, pleased when her deep brown eyes flashed with irritation. "This must be the wrong set of contracts."

"No, they're not." She took them, scanned them, and set them in front of me again.

"Yes, they are." I shoved them back at her, anxiety making my ears ring. I was not about to let this over-paid, designer-clad uber bitch push me around.

With a loud sigh, she grabbed them again. "You are here to talk about…" She glanced down. "Beer Wenches, Incorporated, are you not?"

"I am." I sat, my fingers threaded so tightly together I was cutting off my circulation.

She glared at me. I glared back. I could feel my blood pressure rising. It made a *woosh-woosh-woosh* sound in my ears. She knew exactly what was happening, and I realized she didn't have the nerve to say it. To tell me that my husband had come here in his matching fancy duds and divested me of my shares in my own company somehow.

I waited for her to say the words. She flipped back through her file, stalling, I knew. I sat back, released my death grip on my fingers and crossed my legs. This was it. The penultimate moment. I'd know in the next few seconds exactly what I had suspected from the moment I read the text on Josh's phone screen.

Finally, sexy lawyer lady blew out a breath and stuck those same two pieces of paper back in front of me. "I'm sorry. But these are the only articles of incorporation I have for you to review." Her lips, perfectly outlined and the sort of deep red I'd only seen in 1950's movies, curved upward in what was, without a doubt, a smirk.

"So, tell me something. Was he good?"

She flinched. I kept my gaze level. My pulse was calming, now that I knew the truth. The great unknown sucked way worse than the shitty knowing as far as I was concerned. "I mean, Matt, my husband. When he fucked you. Was it, you know, satisfactory? Because frankly, he's gotten a little selfish, if you get me. I would know. I've been faking orgasms with him for years." My voice sounded strong. I wished I felt the same way. I was screaming inside. Melting into a puddle of useless, unemployed, broke, goo.

My vision was narrowing from the outside in. All that was left to me was a teensy pinprick frame filled by the female specimen in front of me. My hearing gave out. Not so much faded as simply stopped, as if a radio had been switched off. I watched her lips move. I heard nothing after she said the words "Capital call" and "non-responsive partner" and "shares surrendered."

I'd been betrayed, more than once, on the marital front, but this? This was so much worse. This was the end of my world as I knew it, to quote my favorite band. The band Matt and I used to listen to in our crappy studio apartment, drinking, smoking pot, screwing our brains out, and drawing up plans for our dream life together.

I felt a giggle crawling up into my throat. I clutched my neck and looked down at the papers once more. To see that Matthew A. Rigby—A was for Allen, a detail that popped into my head apropos of nothing—was now both President and the sole voting partner of Beer Wenches, Inc. My name was nowhere. It was as if I'd died or dropped off the edge of the world. Neither of which was the case.

I shut my eyes, dizzy and sick to my stomach. Where I'd been burning hot, I was now freezing. It was as if a thin sheen of ice covered every bit of me. I might shatter into a zillion tiny pieces if I moved even a fraction of an inch.

"How," I choked out, my eyes still closed. "How in the world did this happen? Did he fake my signature? Do I need my own lawyer or what?" I opened my eyes and glared at the woman, who looked, admittedly, a tad wigged out by my response.

At that, the giggle burst out of me, giving me away. It was my tell, this nervous laughter. And right now, I couldn't control it. I laughed, I guffawed, I slapped my jeans-covered thigh until I realized that I was, indeed, sobbing.

"Never trust a guy in a suit," my dear old dad used to say. He in his ever-present khakis and tieless dress shirt, covered by his white dentist's coat. His always high-and-tight haircut, his wide smile, his large hands—something I always wondered about, how he fit those hands into mouths. He never fixed my teeth. Sent me to a colleague instead, claiming he wanted a more subjective opinion.

Never trust a guy in a suit.

I rose, shaky and weepy, and propped my hands on lady lawyer's desk to steady myself. I had to get out of here. I needed to get to the bank, to the store, to the bar. We'd get to view our little TV feature-ette later today, before it went live on some random channel. I had a press release to write. An ice maker to purchase. Staff to lead.

"I believe you have participated in an attempt to

defraud me out of my fair share of my business. I have the original LLC documents and rest assured I'll be contacting a lawyer today." I was amazed at myself and my ability to rally. I had no idea if I had the original documents, but I'd make it my mission in the next few days to find them. I whirled away from her, playing the wounded wife as best I could, marched myself through her lobby and out into the blazing hot July morning.

I had shit to do. And do it I would. I'd find a lawyer. Figure all this out. He couldn't do this to me. I simply wouldn't allow it. He could leave, divorce me, marry Madison or whoever he wanted. But he would *not* take my bar away from me.

I'd been swindled, emotionally speaking, once already by a man I thought loved me. It wasn't happening again. I had two days before Matt got back from Denver with his new squeeze in tow. It was time to pull on the proverbial Big Girl Panties.

I shot a text to both my mother and Stella telling them I needed my own lawyer, like, right now. Stella responded within seconds, telling me she'd ask the divorce attorney she kept on retainer for a recommendation. My mother said she'd help pay for it. I had my posse in place. And that's all I needed to spur me into action.

Chapter Three

"Wow, Andi, that was so great!" Madison grinned her ultra-bright grin at me, one hand on her bony hip.

I pointed the remote at the flat screen that had replayed the mini-documentary, darkening the screen and the room. Our moment—okay, *my* moment—had been a glossy, b-roll heavy, eight-minute montage about BWI. I'd been featured, in a short interview, during which I blinked too much and giggled like a fool. The shots of me working, when they followed me around as I did a bit of beer pouring and chatting with guests, was way better. It made sense, as it was something I enjoyed and somehow managed not to screw up. The sick irony of the moment, of the way this woman was congratulating me, was so far beyond surreal that I giggled. Again.

Ugh.

I was neck deep in so many emotions, all pointing to me as a huge failure at everything I cared about, everything in my entire world, I allowed myself the giggle in lieu of actually having to talk.

The show *had* been great. It was already garnering tons of replay, retweets, re-posts, the works, now that the documentary had released individual clips of each business they'd featured. I sighed and stared at my email inbox, filling up even as I watched with kudos, congrats, invites to speak, to host beer dinners, the works.

None of which mattered one tiny iota anymore. I'd been unable to find the original contracts. They'd been purged from our home office files as effectively as my name had been from the document itself. The lawyer Stella's lawyer recommended had taken a look at the new LLC paper work and said, in so many words, I was shit out of luck.

I had nothing. Zip. Zilch. Nada. Matt had done an end-run around me, caught the winning touchdown pass and had deflowered the head cheerleader, if the preening woman in front of me was any indication. Last night I'd pawed through our files again, throwing them out of the drawer, leaving them on the floor and couch of the office, consuming half a bottle of bourbon in the process.

I'd woken up on the office couch, random papers, credit card bills, and other detritus of our marriage stuck to my legs, arms, and face. My head pounded and my guts roiled from too little food and too much amber liquor. I'd crawled down the hall to the bathroom, tossed my cookies into the toilet, then climbed into the shower where I'd sat in the corner, letting hot water beat down on me until we ran out, exactly twenty minutes from the time I turned it on. We didn't have a fancy house. All our money went to the bar. We'd agreed on that when we bought it.

We'd agreed on so many things, once upon a time.

I'd loved him. I kept insisting this to myself as if it mattered anymore. I *had* loved him. A lot. Or maybe I'd loved how much he seemed to love me. My low-lying inferiority complex never allowed me to believe it when he told me as much. Of course, he'd stopped doing that over a year ago, if I were being honest with myself.

It was as if this pinnacle, this top-of-the-mountain, beer rock star moment, was the perfect juxtaposition to the long, muddy slide down the other side facing me now. My relationship with Matt had been skidding off the tracks for a while, but my unwillingness to read the wall-writing allowed me to ignore it. I was ever the worker bee, the one who got up every morning and spent twelve, fourteen, sixteen hours at the bar. The distraction of focus—my focus—on the task of making our held together by spit, duct tape, the sheer force of my will, plus terrifying bank loans business a success.

Now, today, after the triumphant "Best Of" documentary, I lifted each foot, rolling my ankles and wincing at the soreness, watching my inbox pile up with reminders of how awesome I was, how incredible BWI was. The screen blurred. As I reached out my hand to wipe off whatever had landed there, I realized that it wasn't the screen. It was my eyes.

Yeah, I was a leaky sieve these days. I hated it. No, I hated him for turning me into one.

But what I really hated most right now was myself. I never should have trusted Matthew Rigby. He was too good-looking, too suave, too successful. What had he ever seen in me, anyway? Other than that crucial thing he needed—a hard working partner who would twist herself in knots to make his business viable.

"Hey, uh, Andi?"

I closed my eyes and let my mind float back to a time when the sound of my husband's deep, sexy voice made me feel happy, protected, loved. When I realized the sound of it had become more fork-on-empty-plate and less romance-novel-hero, I opened my eyes and stared at the wall over the line of beer taps. My mind skipped two, four, ten steps ahead as it always did to the "what next" and the "where do I go from here?"

When I finally turned around and looked at him— really looked at him for the first time in what felt like a while—I understood that this was actually happening. He was divorcing me. He was going to make me leave the bar. He expected me to walk out the door, get in my car and just…go, as if none of my work had ever happened.

He'd felt so strongly about doing this to me he'd initiated what my attorney called a capital call wherein each member of the LLC was expected to pony up cash commensurate with their shares, which in my case had translated to about fifty grand, and for him, a hundred and fifty. When I hadn't responded with money, he was within his rights to say I'd surrendered my shares.

One of my bar regulars, also a lawyer, had set me straight on the whole thing.

There had been no need to fake my signature on any paperwork. As one of the two members of the board, he was within his rights to force the other members to pony up money based on the percentage of their ownership in the company.

While Frank, my bar customer and real estate attorney, was talking me through it, I recalled a brief conversation we'd had about nine months earlier, regarding this very thing.

"We need to raise capital," my handsome husband had said, breezing through the house on his way to the gym on a Sunday morning. I'd been brain dead after a long weekend where I'd had to personally cover for a couple of servers and I'd closed the night before. Problem was, when I closed, I always liked to hang around and chat with my people, share a few shift beers.

A few had turned into a lot with whiskey shots as nightcaps. I'd barely made it home and into bed and recalled catching sight of my phone screen before I fell onto my face, showing the ungodly hour of three-forty-five a.m. I always felt more bonded to my team when I joined them getting hammered. Probably not true. But I'd used it as an excuse more than once.

So, yes, Mr. Rigby had "posted" the capital call by saying those words to me. My grunt, curse, and official rolling over onto my side facing away from him on the couch had been sufficient for him to claim that I was "non-participatory" and allowed him to claim full ownership.

Rat bastard.

But yeah, shame on me up one side and down the other for not paying closer attention.

So now, here we were. At a point in time when he thought he'd be springing this news on me out of the blue, but that I had, thanks to our mutual buddy Josh, known about for a solid week.

"Okay everyone," I said, my voice a tad croaky. "Let's get prepped for today." The group of employees—my people—began to disperse. I stared at the scheduling program on the laptop screen in front of me, but I sensed Matt behind me, staring, waiting, ready to pounce.

"We need to talk."

I turned to face him. He had his hands jammed into his jeans pockets. His wanna-be brewer's beard was trimmed and hipster-perfect. I wanted to rip at it, to scratch it off his stupid face. His deep blue eyes bored into me. The same withering glare that had melted my panties off years ago and kept me in the dark ever since. He glanced over at Madison who hovered, fussing with silverware.

Jealousy surged through me like a thick wave of molasses, clogging my throat, filling my sinuses, making it hard to breathe.

"I loved you," I said loud and clear from across the bar we had built together.

He flinched.

Good. Served him right.

"But I *hear*..." I glanced a Josh who was also hovering in over-eager anticipation of the Big Blowout That Ended It All. "I hear I won't be around anymore and you alerted my staff before you bothered to tell me."

I made a point to stare at the woman he'd been with while he was busy destroying my life. She had the good grace to blush and look down at the floor.

So now, here I was. The jilted wife. The ultimate cliché. The overweight-because-I-had-no-time-to-workout, successful owner/manager of the number one craft beer bar in the U.S. of A. The face of the business, I realized right then with a jolt as I trained my gaze on Matt. The *woman* who had become synonymous with Beer Wenches Inc. Not Matt, the guy with the original idea and the money.

I crossed my arms and pondered him with a sort of clear-eyed objectivity for the first time in a while. My mind spun with memories—him as an adventurous lover, lazy student, semi-talented home brewer, visionary. Not at all the sort of man who'd take the second seat to anyone, not even the wife he claimed to love, once upon a time anyway.

And suddenly, I understood him. Or at least, I got the motivation for this…this ridiculous *coup d'état*. I was getting too much press. I. Me. Lil' ol' Andi Rose with her crazy red hair, freckles, and squishy, unsexy bod. I'd made a name for myself in this world while I'd been working my tail off to push BWI into something resembling a break-even business. In the process, I'd secured a reputation for great food, incredible, guest-focused service, and had a waiting list for my beer taps that could encircle a city block four or five times.

I did that.

Not him.

It had been what I thought he'd wanted from me. The very reason he'd seen what he'd seen in me all those years ago. 'Cause it sure wasn't my Victoria's Secret body or my skill with self-grooming. He'd set me on this path, given me a shove, and I'd taken to it like nobody's business. Like it was my business, my job. Because it was.

Or I guess, it had been anyway.

Furious at this sudden realization, I gripped the back of a bar chair, one of the many chairs I'd put together with my own hands in a mad rush to meet our self-imposed grand opening deadline years ago. After days and nights spent painting walls, sealing concrete, building the bar base, supervising the tap line installation, planning the kitchen layout. I felt dizzy with memory-clogged remorse. But overriding all that was a raw, visceral rage the likes of which I'd never experienced.

I decided to get in front of this, like Stella had advised me to do. To play offense in the face of his onrushing blindsided tackle.

"You're a lying sack of shit," I said.

He frowned. "Excuse me?"

"You heard me. You're a cheater, Matthew Rigby. I want a divorce."

He blinked. I slapped my hand over my mouth to keep from giggling. Again with the giggles. I sucked in a breath. "And I want custody of our kid," I said, my throat tight, my voice pinched.

"Our…what?" If I weren't so mad at him, I'd laugh my tail off at the dramatic look of shock on his face.

I raised both my arms. "This place, you twatwaffle. BWI is *mine*."

His eyes darkened. I sensed, rather than saw, his hot little squeeze move closer to him.

I had always read about what heartbreak felt like. So far, I'd been spared that particular tragedy. But now, I understood it. I mean, I really got it, because my chest felt as if it had been sucked dry by a shop vac, then re-filled with hot coals. I swallowed the urge to puke and straightened.

"I got the loans, Andrea," he said. "My name is on all the paperwork. We agreed that would be best, just in case…"

"Yeah, I remember. In case we failed," I spat out. "And we didn't fail, because of *me*. Because of what I did, here, in this building." I waited for him to drop his little LLC bomb on me.

"We wouldn't be where we are without you." Smarmy douche-canoe had the decency to throw me a bone, one I guess I could take with me when he tossed me under the onrushing freight train. "But Beer Wenches Inc., is mine, legally." He lifted his chin and had the unremitting gall to look like he owned the joint.

Which, of course, technically, he did.

"You didn't meet a capital call. So you lost your shares." He held out an arm. Madison scurried over and tucked her bony bod into his side. "I'm now the president of BWI, LLC and the sole shareholder. I'm guessing you've figured that out by now."

I kept my grip on the chair back, praying my knees wouldn't buckle underneath me. I refused to give Madison the satisfaction.

"Tell you what," I said, my voice strong and loud, covering up my inner quavering. "I won't ask for any support. Alimony. I won't ask for that. Just…" My voice broke. I saw Madison shift ever so slightly away from Matt, who kept one arm wrapped around her waist. I took a deep breath. "You don't even care about BWI," I insisted, not looking at her anymore. "Matt, come on. You're just being…"

"An asshole," I heard someone mutter somewhere behind me. Apparently, we'd drawn a crowd. Great. I didn't want to turn this into a scene. My mother trained such impulses right out of me in her earnest way. Problem was, avoiding scenes was a euphemism for avoiding conflict. Something I had a PhD in by now. His eyes flickered, but I willed him to focus on me.

"Greedy. And for no real reason." I'd decided at some point in the deep darkness of this morning to go for this appeal. I had no legal recourse. My pal Frank the lager drinking lawyer had made that clear.

Matt pressed his lips together, making his I'm-considering-it face. I held my breath and tightened my grip on the back of the bar seat. I wanted to go to him, to take his hands and make him listen to me without the distraction of the arm candy. "Just think about it a minute. I mean…"

A crash of glass behind me made us all flinch. I turned to stare at Candace, one of my original bar hires.

"Sorry," she mouthed as she bent down to clean up her mess.

When I turned back to face my husband and his girlfriend, I knew I'd missed my window.

"We think it's best for you to go," he said. "We'll work out the alimony between lawyers. Having you here will just complicate everything."

"Oh, *we* think that, do we?" My voice was high and screechy. "I sure do wish you'd warned me that the '*we*' I agreed to be was no longer going to include, you know, me." I stared at Madison.

"I'm so sor—" she started to say.

"Do not talk me, you…you conniving cunt," I yelled. Loud. Too loud. Embarrassed, I slapped a hand over my lips. This was it. He was actually doing it. He was firing me. From our marriage, but more importantly to me, from my job. The only real job I'd ever had and the only thing I enjoyed doing.

"I won't leave you high and dry, Andi," he said, letting go of Madison and moving a few steps closer to me. I took the same number of steps back until a wall of humans halted my retreat. "Don't worry about that."

"I don't want *anything* from you," I insisted in a loud whisper. Hands grabbed my upper arms and started pulling me back toward the kitchen. "You're a shitbag human being, Matthew."

I let myself be pulled, watched him stand there in

the front of the house, in his fancy-schmancy suit with his fancy-schmancy new bedmate.

"Oh…my God," I said as my knees gave out.

"Sit. Don't talk. Wait," a male voice said.

I glanced up, shocked to my core to see Josh being my caretaker.

"I know a good divorce lawyer," he said from the doorway, his ratty little eyes full of something resembling compassion. "Wait here. I'll let you know when he leaves."

I sat on the butt-sprung couch across the tiny space from my desk, perching on the edge, like I was a guest, which, I supposed now, I officially was.

I was willing to let the tears flow. They piled up behind the dam of my eye sockets, burning, but not falling. I didn't even have the energy to cry.

Chapter Four

"I'm sorry, but this has to stop."

I squinted at the two human forms standing in my doorway. One of them had spoken words. They were backlit from the late September sun as they marched into the living room and opened the window blinds.

"Ow, cut it out," I said when sunshine blasted into the room, hitting me right in the eyeballs. "I like it dark." I rolled onto my side and dragged a pillow over my head. "Go away." My blanket was snatched off me. "Hey!"

The pillow disappeared next. A hand grabbed my shoulder and rolled me onto my back.

"Leave me alone," I yelped, arm over my aching eyes.

"I will not leave you alone," my mother insisted. She sat next to me. I sensed her there, but I refused to look at her. Or at the squalor all around me. "Andrea Rose, I didn't raise you to be this...this..."

"Loser? Idiot? Fool?" I spat out. "Go, Mom. I mean it. I don't need your help."

"It's been two months, Andi," the other person who'd invaded my space said. I heard her roaming around the room, picking up empty bottles, pizza boxes, half-empty Chinese carry-out containers.

"Beat it, Stella," I mumbled, keeping my arm over my face. I got a big old whiff of myself. Dang, I needed a shower. But it required way more energy than I possessed at whatever ungodly hour this was. "What time is it, anyway?"

"It's get your ass up and get on with your life o'clock," my friend said.

"Fuck off," I said.

"Language," my mother warned.

I sighed and dropped my arm to my side. Keeping my gaze trained on the ceiling, I addressed them both. "I don't require this intervention, but thank you for coming anyway."

Even after the ensuing months between being told I was no longer an owner and had to vacate the premises of the bar I founded and now, my internal clock was set to bar-running time. It was probably ten or maybe ten-thirty. I should be up, ready to head out the door. I needed to do a bank run or stop to pick up something the food vendor had left off our order. We were due for a fresh shipment of swag, which needed to be sorted and put out in the retail area we kept near the hostess station. It was Monday, which also meant I needed to be looking ahead five weeks to book a band or two. We didn't have live music with regularity. It was something I'd resisted for a while. But once we added it twice a month, I was super picky about who I allowed into my space with their amps and instruments and free bar tabs.

"Oh God," I moaned.

Tears flowed.

The usual.

"Get up," my mother demanded again. This time she put some muscle behind it, grabbing my arms and hauling me upright, shoving my legs around so my feet hit the floor. "Come on. Stella's right. You have to move past this. I'm sorry it happened. But it's time to get your life back on track, Andrea Rose."

"I don't have a life, Mom," I said, even as I let her propel me down the hall toward the bathroom. "My life is over."

"Don't be ridiculous. Here." She shoved a towel into my arms. "Get cleaned up. I'll make some coffee."

"Only if you're willing to risk life and limb in this sorry excuse for a kitchen," Stella called from the other room. "If I didn't know better, I'd swear you were trying to find the cure for cancer in your fridge."

I sighed and slumped against the bathroom door. This room was a wreck, too. I hadn't lifted a finger to clean anything since I hit the door after my last, official day at work and had called the cleaning service to fire them. Matt's stuff was already gone. As if he'd had them disappeared by magic. I'd gone on a tear, called everyone I knew to bitch and moan and vent, then, when Stella had appeared with wine and pizza, I'd cried for something like twenty-four hours straight, staying as drunk as I could for that entire period.

I'll even cop to signing in to Matt's Facebook page—we used to be That Couple who shared passwords—and announced that I, Matt Rigby, was a stinking pile of head cheese, a liar, a cheater, and a thief who'd had little or nothing to do with the rise and success of BWI. That I had forced the woman who was responsible out of the building and out of our marriage on a technicality of my own devices.

He sent a furious text right after that. I deleted his number from my contacts by way of response.

I wasn't proud of this. But then again, I was. He deserved it and lots more. If my inbox and text messages were any indication, I wasn't the only one who thought as much. Of course, none of the childishness or glowing messages of support got me what I wanted—my dang life back.

That ship had sailed. And had tooted a puff of smoke right into my face as it pulled away from the harbor.

My mom turned on the water, made a face at the state of the sink and floor, then dragged me into the room with her. "Don't make me get in there with you," she said.

I rolled my eyes, but I got in the shower.

Later, in a bleach-smelling kitchen, we sat at my high table over coffee and pancakes. I sipped and poked at the syrupy mess on my plate without interest. I'd managed to eat some over the last few weeks but for the most part, I couldn't choke anything down.

"So, we need to find you a job," my mom chirped at me. "Right, Stella?"

"Right, Marj. A job."

They both beamed at me.

I scowled.

"Don't gang up on me," I said. "I can go another few months without working."

Not exactly true. My divorce wasn't yet final, so the alimony payments I'd agreed to wouldn't kick in for a while. And since I'd been fired from my job while being fired as a wife, I had no income. Matt kept paying the mortgage and insurance, and I'd put the gas and electric bills on his credit card these past few months. My only expenses had been takeout food and liquor. But that had put a dent in my checking account, since I'd only been paying myself a small salary for the last two and a half years of the almost six since we opened BWI.

Hence the cancelation of all luxuries, like a cleaning service, cable TV, running the air conditioning through the hottest part of the summer, not to mention personal hygiene.

"No, you can't," my mom said. She turned her tablet around to face me. "I think you should go here, to this." She tapped the screen. "Do some networking. It says there will be a job fair, too."

I pretended to look at her device. "No thanks," I said, taking care to cut a perfect square of pancake before putting my fork down, since I lacked the energy to lift it to my mouth.

"Yes, we agree. You should go to the craft beer convention," Stella said. "The one in Denver."

I narrowed my eyes at her. "Since when do you know anything about that, much less when and where it is?"

"Since now," she said, sipping her coffee.

"It's too expensive," I said, shoving my plate away from me. The smell of syrup was enough to make my poor, abused liver roll over and wave a white flag. "And I'll never get a hotel at this point in the game."

I watched them exchange a look. I put down my fork. "What are you guys up to anyway?"

"What would you say if I told you we already signed you up, paid the fee, and got you a hotel?" Stella's voice was chipper, her smile wide.

I tried not to give in to the compulsion to reach across the table and snatch her bald-headed. "I would say you are insane. And you should call right now, get your money back, and cancel the room. That's what I'd say."

"We're only trying to help you, honey," my mom said, grabbing my hand and gripping it tight. I pulled away from her and leaned back, arms crossed, mind spinning with what they were saying. She slid a pre-paid Visa card across the table toward me. I picked it up and saw it was for five hundred dollars.

"For some new clothes for the trip," Stella declared.

"Oh my God, seriously?" I stood up, holding back tears.

"Yep." Stella got up and took our plates to the sink that now sparkled thanks to her earlier ministrations. "We need to punch up your resume, print a bunch of copies, maybe get some business cards printed." She kept her back to me.

"Business cards? Resumes? Are you high? I don't have a job. I've only had one job. I can't... They won't... Oh shit." I flopped back into my seat, pulse racing at the thought of trying to convince a bunch of breweries or distributors to hire me. "They'll laugh me out of there."

"No, they won't," Stella insisted. She slammed the dishwasher door shut and turned, wiping her hands on a towel. "Andi, you got shafted. No one disputes that. But you also started a business—a Goddamned successful business—and you deserve to take credit for it. You have amazing marketing, public relations, sales, and management skills. I can massage your resume. Let's get online and order a couple hundred cards so you can leave them with everyone. Let's get you back *out* there."

I stared at her, then at my mother. They looked so

hopeful it broke my heart all over again.

"It's no use," I said before putting my head on my arms on the table. "There's no point. I'm just gonna…be a store greeter or something."

"Don't be silly, hon," my mom said, patting my shoulder. "Let's get to work. We only have about a week before the convention."

I sighed and cried a bit more. But once the waterworks dried, I figured I might as well try, if for no other reason than to prove to my little cheering squad-interventionist team it was a lost cause.

****

When the time came to pack up my shiny new wardrobe for my trip, I had the first, full-on panic attack of my life. I sat on the edge of the bed, unable to take a full breath while the suitcase lay open on the floor, mocking me with its emptiness. As if sensing my freak out, my phone buzzed its way across the bedside table with a call from Stella.

"Calm down," she said when I answered without saying a word.

Speaking required oxygen, and I needed my reserves to avoid passing out at the moment. I nodded and attempted to do that.

"I'm dying," I squeaked at one point, figuring she might hang up and call 911 for me.

"You're not dying. You're out of practice. Shit, Andi, you've been holed up in your house for months. You haven't even gone outside once. You do realize that, right?"

I nodded again and put my hand to my throat. She was right. I had gone out of my way not to have any human encounters. The thought of having to explain what had happened to me, to my bar and my marriage, seemed well outside the range of my ability. So I avoided any and all situations wherein I'd have to do that.

As a result, I didn't feel unlike one of those naked mole rats, pale, squinty-eyed, likely asexual to boot. I forced my respiratory system to function and dropped onto my back from the effort it took.

"You can't let him do this to you, Andi," Stella said, her voice tinny and bossy in my ear.

I put the phone on my stomach and closed my eyes. She kept talking, dropping little *bon mots* of wisdom about being up and at 'em, not taking shit off any man, the best revenge is success…blah, blah, blah.

I stopped listening after about three minutes, but the sound of her voice soothed me.

I sat up, grateful for her all over again. "Okay, I'm good now," I said, the phone back at my ear. "I'll pack. But wait. Should I take something…nice? I mean, I don't even know… Oh God. I can't do this." I collapsed into a heap again.

"I'll be right over," Stella said.

I wanted to tell her not to. Stella was a good friend. My only friend—a holdover from my life as a happy-go-lucky child. But her style of helping tended to leach over into extreme bossiness. A sort of guilt-riddled, "there are starving children in Africa" comparison game whereby she'd remind me how bad she'd had it in her first marriage. How, thanks to her own self and no one but herself, she'd rebuilt her life post-bad marriage, not once but twice. I sighed and stared at the blank screen and prepared myself for her onslaught.

Chapter Five

By the time the massive expo hall emptied out after the first night of the craft beer convention, all I wanted was a hot shower and a giant cheeseburger. I bent over to touch my toes, trying to work out the deep kinks in my hips as I pondered how I might escape the crowds of increasingly drunken people without anyone noticing me sneaking away like the coward I was.

I ducked out after smiling and waving a few greetings to some folks from the "southeast U.S." section of the giant expo center. They'd all heard my sad sack story or some version of it, anyway. I couldn't face their sympathy or the distinct undercurrent of smug satisfaction at my downfall.

I needed a real drink, if for no other reason than to wash away the slimy, old vomit sensation of failure in my throat. I made my way out, smiling and nodding and generally pretending like I didn't know a soul in here, although I knew many of them well, thanks to my years spent as the hottest craft beer influencer on my personal block. I winced at the thought of my ego, bloated with false pretense when I'd last been in this building.

When I reached the top of a long escalator that would whisk me down to the teeming Denver sidewalks, I blew out a breath. Day one had gone well enough. I'd only had to tell my tale a few times. Most people knew it already. This was a small, insular, gossipy world.

Per Stella's advice, I'd spent the day pretending I was on one long, glorious vacation from the hell of running a bar. I was flipping happy to be shed of it, of him, of my old life, but I still loved them—the beer people—so much. So much that, ta dah! Here I was among them for no reason but to chat and sip and chat and, by the way, are you hiring?

It was awful, but I'd managed it so far.

"Hey, Andi."

"Good to see you again, Andi."

"Damn girl, I thought you'd died."

"Andi! Babe!"

"Wow! Andi! You look…great."

That last one might not be too much of a stretch. Thanks to stress and general unhappiness, I'd lost a few pounds. Brutal, treacherous heartbreak, thy name is fad diet. Maybe I should check into patenting that.

I'd managed to live these past weeks on the savings I'd accumulated by paying myself a small salary while Matt paid the bills. It didn't hurt that I was aces at thriftiness. Besides, my needs were minimal. I would challenge anyone who claimed small business ownership was anything but one long sleepless night, worrying a groove in your brain over how in the hell to make payroll and pay the huge electric bill. Neither Matt nor I had come to the marriage and business with money. We'd had to get loans of all sorts, including the kitchen-table kind he'd secured from his parents. And I watched every single penny going in and out of the place. I was still doing it in my dreams.

I owned my piece of shit car outright, and my mother agreed to pay the insurance for the duration. She wanted to do more, but the last thing I could face was having to ask her—a fellow member of the sorry-ass jilted-wives club—for anything else. If Stella hadn't covered this little junket, I never would have allowed myself to spend the dough. I gazed around me, noting all the averted eyes, the knowing nods, the barely concealed smiles, and wasn't sure if I were grateful or furious that she'd forced me into this torture.

I was here for one reason and one reason only—that job fair tomorrow. I had plenty of copies of my super-massaged and punchy resume and way more business cards than I needed. I had the sweet power suit I'd pulled off the rack at the discount store. I'd even found a pair of low-level designer shoes I could afford using the gift card my mom provided.

The minute I got to my room, I'd pulled the suit and silky blouse that matched from the suitcase I'd borrowed from Stella, since my ex had absconded with all the luggage we owned, and hung it in what passed for a closet. I'd stared at it the night before, wondering if it would make the necessary impact tomorrow and I'd emerge from this horror show with a job.

Because even after today's jittery re-entry into a world where I once reigned supreme, I knew one thing for certain—Matt Rigby's shitty behavior was no longer my driving force. These were my people, these beer folk. My people and I would tug the ragged edges of my life together and sew them up tight. I squared my shoulders and smiled, like the conquering hero-queen I was about to be.

"I can't believe she's here."

"I know, right? She looks good, I'll give her that. What a shit show, and right after the best bar award."

45

"Well, I heard she was fucking the bar manager guy and got caught. But whatever. Rigby's brought in some big money partners. I heard they wanted her out of the way and that's why he did it."

I blinked. My smiled faded.

"Nah, she was doing one of the kitchen guys I think. And that came straight from the horse's mouth. I saw Matt at Great Taste of Chicago three months ago and he told me."

I turned to face the gossipers, willing to believe this wasn't about me but knowing it was. I mean, "Rigby?" That *was* my last name, still. But they must have passed by in the scrum of people headed for the escalators. The snippets of conversation now were focused on the family squabble at Burke Brewing, one of the oldest and most successful craft operations in Michigan.

Face flaming, I swiped at my upper lip. My hands were shaking. My knees, too. I glanced down at myself. I'd chosen business casual this first day, hoping my lack of brands would set me apart. Navy blue capri pants and a simple, sleeveless cream blouse from Chez Stella had served me well enough. But my feet were aching in the cutesy-pie flat shoes. I knew I should have gone with something sturdier. But Stella told me I didn't want to come across as spinster night nurse so I'd left them behind.

Now I felt wilted, like a sad, left-behind rose after prom. What had been sassy optimism not ten minutes ago had morphed back into shitty realism. That asswipe was spreading lies about me on top of everything else he'd done?

Dear Lord but I'd never get past this.

My phone buzzed from my back pocket. I pulled it out, figuring I might as well stare at it a while and avoid all the gossip-hungry gazes around me. Part of me hoped to see a rah-rah-sis-boom-bah text from Stella. But it was just notice from my bank. I'd managed to avoid being overdrawn thanks to the timely deposit of my very first alimony payment.

Yay, me.

It was time for a drink. I shouldered my backpack and forced myself onto the top step of the escalator.

Work the problem in front of you.

A job. You have to find one. It's why you're here, flirting with the extreme outer edges of your credit limits, remember?

"Andi, darlin'!"

I plastered a smile on my face and suffered a bear hug from Hank Fillmore as soon as I hit the sidewalk. His boozy breath encircled my face like a cloud as he yelled over the din. "I am so, so sorry about what happened. What a shit monkey."

"Yes," I agreed. "I don't suppose you're hiring?" Hank was part owner of a newer, successful brewery, also in Michigan. Seemed to be a theme for me today.

He laughed and smacked me so hard on the back I stumbled forward while people streamed all around us. People, I imagined, who were all thinking about the lies my ex was telling as part of his ruin-Andi's-life campaign. "As if you'd want to work down in the trenches with us."

"Well, I—" Before I could say how much I'd welcome setting up camp in the trenches right now, he interrupted me.

"What're you doing for dinner?"

I shrugged, eager to escape him and the memories his presence was shaking loose in my brain, even as my stomach growled, reminding me that a free dinner would be pretty great, regardless of the company.

"You're having it with me, that's what you're doing."

"No, Hank, it's all right. Really." My mind was going fuzzy, not surprising as I'd spent the past three hours sampling beer. I was no lightweight. But some of it was ultra-high content, not to mention disgusting. Not that my opinion mattered anymore. I'd been too nervous to eat that morning, getting ready in my roach motel, convincing myself that I'd come away from this debacle gainfully employed. My lunch hour had been taken up with networking in the VIP area I'd snuck into, using all my powers as FIP—formerly important person.

Hank draped a meaty arm around my shoulders, filling my personal space with the fumes of his day's work once more. I sighed and mentally regrouped.

"Fuck it, Mikey. I'm done. Tag me out, already." The low, masculine voice hit my ears, the words as clear as day, which was odd considering how many conversations were rolling around us as we stood here, blocking traffic. When I glanced over Hank's hand in the general direction of said voice, I locked eyes with a stranger.

And my world changed forever.

Okay, all right, it wasn't quite so prosaic. The voice's owner barely glanced at me. But something about him held my gaze.

Especially since the man in front of him said, "But we had a great morning and I need you to go with me to these dinners. We have to be seen together, the Burke brothers and brotherly unity and all that happy horseshit."

Intrigued, since I'd been hearing near-constant rumblings about these guys and their father's company all day, I slid out from under Hank's arm and jerked my chin in their direction.

"What's up over there?" I asked, still dithering over heading to my hotel versus a decent meal on someone else's expense account.

He squinted in the direction I indicated. "Oh, it's just the Burke boys."

"The what?" I'd figured this out, of course, but these guys were in Hank's backyard, so I also figured he could give me the low-down better than anyone.

"Burke Brothers Brewing, in Detroit. Their old man and uncle founded it in the early nineties. But their dad left a real mess, debts, expansions, empty buildings left and right, so it's languished. One of 'em's the brewer. That one, James. The football player-looking dude. The other one, the sales weasel in the suit, is Michael."

"How's their liquid?" I asked. "Better, I hope. I got a truly shitty batch of the Common right before…well…" My face flushed. I don't know what happened to those kegs of Burke Bros California Common. And that fact made me ever so slightly ill, as if it had just happened to me yesterday and not almost three months prior.

"Damn good, actually. They're clawing their way back, so the rumors go," Hank said, draping his arm over my shoulders again. I was glad for the contact this time. These were my people, after all.

I studied James, the brewer brother, while the two men continued their argument. He was, in a word, ginormous. Tall, with shoulders out to the hinterlands, he did resemble a football player with his bulky biceps and vast chest. His nose had a distinct bump in it, as if it'd been broken, giving him a less-than-perfect profile.

I watched, fascinated for no good reason as he raked his fingers through thick brown hair and around the back of his neck, then through his requisite beard, every time his brother seemed to score a point. He was dressed in brewer-standard dark jeans and a company-branded, short-sleeved, button-front shirt.

Mike, the sales weasel as Hank put it, was in dark suit pants, a bright white shirt, and had the suit jacket hooked on one finger and draped over his shoulder. He was one of those really-handsome-and-he-knows-it types. I would know. I'd been married to one. He seemed to be wearing James down.

Finally, he put a hand on his brother's shoulder. "Just one stop, Jimmy, then you're free until tomorrow."

"Read my lips. Go fuck yourself."

Mike dropped his hand and frowned, which only made his model-perfect face look hotter. "Fine. Go. Resume your hermit position."

"Gladly," James said. "Do I need to do anything to get ready for tomorrow?"

"Yeah. I need you to come schmooze with me."

"You should brush up on your lip reading skills, little bro."

James was an interesting specimen. I couldn't stop staring at him, which shocked me. I'd been so dialed out of anything resembling a social life, much less anything with members of the hairier sex other than hiring, firing, managing, or arguing, it felt like I was exercising a long-dormant muscle. It was a nice feeling if I were honest with myself, but also weird and inappropriate.

James Burke was the polar opposite of what I'd always considered my type, with his bulky, athletic build and growly, bear-like, apparently anti-social attitude. I glanced at his brother and had to acknowledge, had I not gotten my ass burned by Matthew Rigby, I would have been attracted to him instead—slim, sleek, model handsome with a too-quick smile that attracted women to him like one of those super magnets. The two men were locked in a brotherly stare-down, which gave me plenty of opportunity to observe them while Hank schmoozed and hugged all the people who stopped to get a dose of his avuncular greeting style.

When James turned his head and looked right at me, as if sensing my thoughts, I didn't drop my gaze. His eyes were a shade of vibrant green out of place in a man. I blinked, then looked away.

Weird.

Inappropriate.

Cut it out.

But even as I glared down at the sidewalk, I could still sense that green-eyed gaze on me. I exhaled and looked back up, catching him still staring. I frowned, hoping to convey a "don't mess with me, Mr. Interesting All Of A Sudden. I don't have time for nonsense," message. It worked. Or anyways, he returned my scowl, then disappeared into the crowd.

"Okay, doll face, let's blow this pop stand.

Whaddaya say?" Hank's voice cut through my fog. "I gotta get over to the venue and make sure they've got my shit set up the way I want it."

Reluctantly, I followed in Hank's broad wake. "You own this," I murmured under my breath. "You can do this. These are your people."

"What's that, babe?" Hank glanced over his shoulder.

Before I could shake my head or deny I was in the final stages of cracking up, someone hollered at him from across the street.

He waved. "Keep up with me, Andi. I gotta go see this asshole."

I nodded and shouldered my way through the increasing throng, grateful I'd met up with someone still gainfully employed and in possession of the company credit card to feed me dinner.

Chapter Six

The dinner was delicious and interminable as they usually were at these events. It was from a crappy new perspective to be sure. That of the outsider, not the pampered, sucked-up-to successful beer bar owner. I was placed at the far end of the table with the corner poking me in the stomach, reminding me of what a late-add I'd been.

I hated it. It sucked. And only served to remind me how far I'd fallen. But even as I was bitching out Matt in my mind, I pictured something else. A broad-shouldered, tall stranger with green eyes who had seemed about as happy to be here as I was. And yeah, it was getting old, trying to pin every scrap of my unhappiness on what my ex had done to me.

Which had to be the booze talking. Even if it was talking sense.

I looked around the table at the various levels of drunkenness from barely tipsy to practically-lying-face-down-in-his-plate and experienced a strange jolt of determination. I knew how this worked. I had to get myself focused less on feeling sorry and more on fixing things. It was, as they say, time to move on.

When dessert was served, I dug in, realizing this for the last complete meal I'd get for the next day or two. I had myself on starvation rations, trying to hoard all my pennies prior to getting myself employed. But this was on someone else's dime, so I was not going to pass up the opportunity to enjoy it.

"So, Andi," some guy to my left slurred into my ear. "Tell me what happened, honey. All of it." His arm was draped over my shoulders. The fingers of his right hand dangled obscenely near my boob.

I shifted away. "I'd really rather not." I picked up my fork, feigning tears, surprised to find them unfeigned.

"Leave her alone. She's mine," Hank bellowed down the table. I glanced at him, grateful for the save. He winked at me and mouthed, "Nightcap?"

I sighed and shook my head. I needed to get some sleep. I had a big day tomorrow.

Big, job-procuring day. I had to be on the top of my game, un-hungover, fresh as a daisy.

Thus mentally fortified, I rose, seeking a swift escape. I made excuses no one at the over-served table heard and eased behind the chairs. When I stopped where Hank sat, presiding over the feast for favorite people, I brushed his flushed cheek with my lips. He grabbed my hand and tried to drag me onto his lap to the amusement of the table.

I kept my distance, my smile fixed in place. "I'm calling it tonight, Hank. Thank you so much for dinner. Seriously. You're a sweetheart."

He nodded, distracted by one of the younger, hotter chicks at the table now that I'd given him my official rebuke.

Men.

Too predictable and boring.

But for Mr. Green-Eyes Football Player-slash-Brewer Guy.

Stop it.

I hit the bathroom on the way to the steps down to the main floor of the raucous restaurant. Bladder empty, face splashed with cold water, I emerged, ready to summon a ride share and get back to the hotel.

As I made my way past harried servers and over-stuffed tables full of drunk people, I spotted him again. The Burke brother from the expo center. Not the brewer one. The sales weasel one. The one that looked, or maybe just acted, like Matthew Rigby, so much so it was like a punch to my overfull gut.

He was leaning on a miniscule table in apparent earnest conversation with a woman I only saw from the back. When I eased to one side, drawn to their tableau for some reason likely attributable to me being one drunken stage past I-should-know-better, her long black hair hid half her face as I got closer. I ended up jammed into a corner near a kitchen door, unable to move away from them even if I wanted to while a steady parade of servers and bussers zoomed to and fro between us.

Resigned to staying put a few more minutes, I distracted myself by watching sales weasel and pretty lady as their date collapsed in an obvious manner. The woman hadn't touched a bite of food in front of her. Her hands were twisted together in her lap. She kept shaking her head but otherwise hardly moved. Sexy Burke Brother gesticulated and slammed his hands on the table, making up for her frozen state with his dance of frustration.

Fascinating. But for reasons that escaped me.

Until a mere three or so hours ago, Burke Brothers Brewing was barely on my radar, other than a dim memory of discovering that the first beer of theirs I'd put on tap was, in a word, undrinkable. And now, between reliving that moment when brewer brother and I had had what must be described as a significant moment on a crowded sidewalk and being unable to drag my nosy ass away from sales brother's shitty date, I felt like some kind of a fawning fan girl.

While delivering a mental lecture about this being not my business and I needed to get some sleep anyway, I saw his lips move but couldn't hear a damn thing over the din of the place. When his female companion jumped up and threw her napkin down on the table, she almost plowed backward right into me. She wobbled on her teetering high heels, then lurched away and straight into a waiter, whose tray was loaded with salads heavy on kale and entrees heavy on marrow.

I reached out and caught her arm. She was blotto, that much was clear at this close distance. Little Burke Brother—Michael, I recalled—stayed seated, his expression blank during this whole exercise.

Jerk.

A bizarre surge of protectiveness came over me. I took her arm and guided her down the steps. Once we hit the fresh air, she revived enough to peel away from me, drop to her hands and knees, and puke on the sidewalk.

As I held her hair back like some kind of sorority sister, the substantial foot traffic gave us a wide berth, most of them without comment. It was Craft Beer Convention time in Denver. Puking humans were more common than weed stores, at least for a day or two.

While I waited for her to wrap up her worship at the cement altar, I summoned a ride on my phone app, realizing too late I had no idea where she was staying. She probably had a two-star room with a DNA soaked bed and a lovely view of the dumpster, like me. I got a warm, sisterly feeling about her.

I waited while she spit, then rose to her feet.

"Take those off already," I said, pointing to the black patent leather heels. She did. Her eyes rolled around in their sockets. Her lollipop of a head didn't want to stay upright. I plunked us down on a conveniently placed sidewalk bench—gotta love Denver—and waited, not sure which would come first, the ride or the second round of the happy hurls.

Luckily, it was the ride.

After I shoved her into the backseat, I asked where we should drop her.

"Wha… I, um…" She swiped at her lips and chin. "Shh." She giggled. "Don't tell." She hiccupped. "Daddy found out about Michael."

"Yeah, yeah, yeah. Where are you staying? Quality Inn by the airport?" It was jam-packed with the beer distributor flunkies and worker bees, plus me, Her Unemployed Majesty.

"J," she said, nodding in the confident way only gut deep drunks would do. "J dub…."

I gawked at her. "The Marriot?"

"Yep." She hiccupped again. "Who does this color?" She yanked on my hair. "I want it. Gimmie it."

"Ow. Cut it out." I tucked the lock behind my ear. "God does it. He's the only colorist I can afford."

"You're funny. I'm, uh, oh…" She lunged across me. I opened the door and waited for round two to hit the curb. The driver glared at me. I shrugged.

"Too many appletinis for my friend," I said. "She

gets all silly."

Unwilling to play along with her fantasy, I told the driver to take us to my hotel. She could sleep it off, and we'd get her where she needed to be afterward. The route he chose doubled back and took us past the fancy hotel in question, the J.W. Marriot, where the top-level brewers and distributors set up camp for the weekend-long event.

"Wait! Stop! Driver, this is where I get out." The skinny drunk lady I'd snagged away from the asshole at the restaurant knocked on the headrest. The driver slowed and met my eyes in the rearview mirror.

I sighed. "Listen, whatever your name is, I'm sure you're not staying here. I mean…"

"Hang on." She scrabbled around in a miniscule bag for a few seconds while the driver idled near the curb. "Here. Now can I get out?"

She stuck a black keycard into my face. I took it, saw the distinctive logo, and decided I was tired of playing nursemaid to a stranger.

"Wait for me?" I asked as I hauled the floppy woman onto the sidewalk. "I think we'll be back pretty fast."

I attempted to get her to walk on her own while I held her shoes in my other hand, and in this awkward fashion, we two-stepped into the marble-floored lobby. I'd stayed here on a brewery's tab one year, in a giant suite with Matt, where we ordered obnoxious amounts of room service and had equally obnoxious amounts of loud hotel sex.

Ah. Memories. They really knew when to sneak up on a girl with a two-by-four.

I steeled myself for the impending scene and stuck

my shoulder up under her arm, wincing when she turned the full force of her boozy puke breath on me.

"I love you," she proclaimed.

"Right," I responded. "Come on. Let's get this over with."

As we stumble-walked to the massive black granite desk, me praying I wouldn't run into anyone I recognized from my old life as a successful, married, craft beer bar owner, I noted the desk staff dude's eyes, following our slow progress. They were narrowed at first then wide. Then he blinked and shifted into professional mode. He motioned to someone. That someone rushed out from behind the desk and propped up my new bestie on her other side.

"I hate him," she muttered into my neck.

I pushed her head the other way. "Yeah, good plan. He's a piece of work."

"No. I really *hate* him. He's... I want him to..."

"Miss VanAnsel," the person holding up her other side said.

I stopped, which meant "Miss VanAnsel" had to drape her drunk self over the desk staff.

"Let's get you up to your room."

I watched, frozen, as reality oozed over my brain like a warm, runny egg yolk. I had just rescued a VanAnsel.

The slow trickle of recognition made me curse under my breath. The chick in the whatever the hell designer shoes I still had hooked on my fingers was none other than the only daughter of the current CEO and President of VanAnsel Distribution. One of the many large companies I'd targeted as part of my two-tiered approach to the great beer job hunt. Breweries first. Distributors second.

Sloane VanAnsel, her own damn self, had been publicly arguing with the man I only knew as the Little Burke Brother, Michael. I'd seen it all. Including whatever she'd eaten that day when it reappeared on the sidewalk and curb.

As I watched the desk clerk hustle her to the elevators, the girl stopped and turned to face me. "You," she said as she drew herself up the way drunks did when they were about to make a declaration either ill-considered or merely stupid. "*You* are *awesome*." She held out her hand. I blinked a few times like a dolt. "Thank you for helping me."

Still in shock, I stared at her, unable to formulate words.

"Her shoes," the clerk hissed at me and grabbed the girl before she shattered her fragile bird bones on the marble floor.

I handed them over.

"Shh…" the girl whispered before she broke out in giggles. "Don't tell Daddy about Michael." She attempted to straighten her short skirt and run fingers through her hair. She missed at both, which would have been funny under normal circumstances. "'Cause I love him." She crossed her arms and stamped a bare foot.

"All right, let's go Miss VanAnsel. You need some water." The clerk steered the babbling woman to the bank of elevators, leaving me in the middle of the lobby.

The stink of the day's efforts hit me—old beer, stale sweat, someone else's puke, and depression. I turned toward the exit, eager to escape. When Mr. Wankhammer himself appeared on the other side of the sliding glass doors, he did a double take at the sight of me.

But I'd had enough stranger drama for one twenty-four-hour period so I ignored him and ducked into my ride share, in the front seat this time.

"I've changed my mind," I said, without thinking too hard about it. "Why don't you take me to a bar?"

The guy eyeballed me as he fiddled with his navigation app. "I'm gonna need a bit more direction. There are three dozen bars between here and your hotel."

"I want…" I hesitated, but only for a second. "Take me to your best, honest-to-Christ dive bar. I'm talking cracked leather barstools and still smells of smoke, with a maximum of four beer taps, and locals…lots of locals."

He shrugged, plugged in an address, and we were off. My mind spun, trying to come to terms with all I'd seen and done in the past few hours as we stop-started our way through throngs of people and traffic.

I considered it a decent sign regarding my request for a legit local dive when the driver moved away from the streets full of drunk and unrulies, making several turns onto side streets until we reached a stretch of businesses that were either boarded up, bombed out closed or plain-old closed. Trusting a local to find a great bar was one of the best ways to experience an unfamiliar place, so I waited while he turned once more, then came to a stop outside what looked like another empty store front.

"Here you go. The finest dive Denver has to offer."

I peered out into the almost full-dark street, satisfied at the sight of a half-busted neon Pabst Blue

Ribbon sign in a dingy window. "Great, thanks," I said as I got out and sent him a tip with my payment on the app. I stood, taking in the blessed quiet around me, broken only by the odd siren, crash of broken glass, and a random screech of laughter.

Yeah, this was exactly what I needed right now.

Anonymity.

And a dang PBR. Something easy to drink that required no BS to enjoy. Simple and straightforward. That was what I wanted.

I shoved open the door and was assailed by all I associated with bars, plus the added bonus of stale cigarette smoke, long embedded in furnishings and paint. The twangy jukebox was wailing away about somebody's ex-wife or maybe his dog. An ancient television screen flickered above the shelves of no-doubt sticky booze bottles and was tuned to a baseball game. Once my nose adjusted to the smokiness, I caught a whiff of old beer, even older grease, and cheap perfume.

I grinned and strode into the dim light, taking note of five patrons—a man and woman in a dark corner doing dark-corner-ish things and three men with their backs to me at the bar. They were all sitting on the required cracked leather seats, red ones, no less.

Jackpot.

The guys were spread out, so I had no choice but to sit next to one of them, given the number of stools. Revived and already tasting the nachos with cheese-like substance I planned to order to go with my un-complex beer, I took a seat without paying attention to the man next to me. I wasn't here to chat, schmooze, flirt, or otherwise interact. I was here to drink lawn mower beer, eat gross food, feel sorry for myself a while, then leave.

"Your finest PBR, please, good sir," I said to the person behind the bar, going with my gut about their gender, a crap shoot since all I could see of them was a long, stringy ponytail, a gray T-shirt, and a pair of baggy jeans.

"Draft?" the person growled without turning to face me.

"Of course," I said, willing to take a chance on the cleanliness of the beer lines. I'd know if they were bad within seconds of being served anyway and could switch to a canned version of the easy-going lager I was craving.

"On me," a deep voice said to my left. "And another here." I looked over at him, gratitude on my lips. I froze as a fog of what-were-the-odds filled my vision.

It was burly-man brewer Burke brother, right here in my newfound secret Denver dive bar.

"Thanks," I said, staring straight ahead. The beers materialized in front of us, perfectly poured, gorgeous, yellow, and fizzy. "Cheers."

"*Prost*," he said, touching his glass to mine.

We drank. It was liquid gold perfection. Not an off-flavor in sight. I smacked my lips and set the half-empty down on the bar.

"Impressive," he said, still not meeting my eyes, which was good because I'd reverted to full-on, nervous, tongue-tied teenager.

I picked up the glass again, drank more, put the glass down. James Burke, my new-found mini-obsession, did the same. We finished our beers in the sort of awkward silence that caused physical pain.

"One more?" James asked.

"At least," I replied. It was weird. Way beyond weird. Or maybe it was exactly what I needed.

James raised a finger. Two more beers appeared. We drank.

"Protein?" He pushed a basket of peanuts toward me, the word barely more than a grunt. I ate a couple, staring at the game on the screen above our heads.

When he turned to face me, I felt his gaze but didn't meet it. I was woefully unprepared, like a rookie on her first date. Which was dumb. This wasn't a date. This was random encounter land. I flushed. Random encounters sometimes led to random encounter sex, at least on the TV shows I'd binge-watched during my self-imposed retreat from the world.

I chanced a sideways peek. He was staring at me, his chin in his hand, elbow on the bar. He was smiling in a way that relaxed me out of the spiky tension brought on by the thought of random encounter sex. I hadn't waxed down there in over a year. I was pretty sure it had grown cobwebs. And besides I wasn't ready for sex, random or otherwise. Even with this hunky, bearded specimen.

He held up his half-empty glass. "To pretentious beer conventions," he said. "And to finding a dive bar where beautiful women drink PBRs."

"I'll drink to all of that." We clinked glasses again. When I brought mine to my lips a little too aggressively, a splash of beer went up my nose while another landed on my shirt. I snorted.

James handed me a napkin, his smile fixed in place. I frowned and took it from him.

I didn't want or need this right now. I needed a damn job. Him and his…tall, burly, not-really-my-type handsomeness was distracting me. I faced the bar again, my throat tight and my head spinning.

"Another," I said, sliding ten bucks across the sticky bar top.

I heard a clunk next to me. I sensed James sliding off his barstool. My hand shot out, seemingly under its own power and rested on his arm. Despite my determination not to, I was hyper aware of the bulky musculature of his bicep. I let go. "Sorry," I muttered.

"Gotta take a leak," he said. He put his lips near my ear. I smelled beer and peanuts on his breath. "Try not to miss me too much."

"Fuck off," I said, my face flaming so hot I worried about early onset menopause. I put my hand to my neck, then to my cheek, then slammed half of my third beer and tugged a sticky menu toward me. "Do you have nachos?"

"Yeah," the bartender said, again without looking at me. "Wanna double?"

"A what?"

"A double serving of cheese."

"Obviously." I rolled a peanut around in my palm. I should get the hell out of here, go to my hotel, shower, sleep, pretend I'd not had this super bizarre surprise moment.

A hand landed on my shoulder. I shifted away from it.

"Sorry," James said, taking his seat again. "I sometimes lose my sense of appropriate touching when I've had five or six…or seven…or shit, eight…PBRs." He slapped the bar. "Let's make it an uneven nine, my good man."

The guy poured two more beers without a word about overserving or calling us a cab. Living on the edge. I loved it.

The nachos arrived, glowing neon orange under the shitty lighting.

"Oh hell yeah," James said, his voice steady. "I knew I loved you."

I glared at him when he reached across the expanse between us for a chip. "Inappropriate grabbing of food is also discouraged." I shoved a drippy chip into my mouth, closed my eyes, and gave into the horror-show perfection of the warm, empty calories.

"Wow," James said, chin propped on his hand again. "That was super hot."

I grinned and wiped my chin, took another long slug of cheap beer, mirrored his chin in hand position, and shoved the basket of disgusting crap posing as food toward him. He bypassed it to touch his fingertip to the corner of my upper lip, then put said fingertip to his lips.

"Wow. That was super cheesy. You need to brush up, pal. Find something original."

He shrugged and stuck his massive fingers into the mess of chips and orange gunk. "Sue me. I'm out of practice."

I couldn't help but notice he was blushing. It made me tingly, a sensation I hadn't experienced in so long it took me a second to differentiate it. Once I did, I clamped down on it. No tingles for me.

Jobs. Networking. Beer. Shower. Sleep.

I slid off my barstool, eager to escape. As I figured he would, he put a hand on my arm. "Wait, don't go.

Please?"

I stared down at his hand, then into his eyes. "Touching again without asking?"

He grinned, let go of me, and slapped the seat I'd vacated. I rolled my eyes.

"C'mon. Sit. Let's talk. Tell me about you."

I sat and picked up my beer. "I'll listen if you want to tell me about you."

"Ha. Hell no." He held up his glass.

I touched mine to it.

We drank.

"You're really not my type," I said, once the chip basket was cleaned out. I reached in and swiped my finger across a garish smear of pseudo-cheese sauce.

"Okay, I'm about to do something inappropriate. Ready?" He grabbed my wrist and pulled my outstretched finger to his lips.

I was too shocked and polluted on cheap beer to resist. I watched, detached, as if some other woman's cheese-coated finger was about to be sucked into some strange man's mouth. Right before he did it, he grinned and let go of me.

"Give me some credit," he said, taking a napkin and holding it over the finger in question.

"Oh no, you don't," I said, sticking it in my mouth, closing my eyes, and pretending to climax. I mean, say what you will. That scene in When Harry Met Sally was a game-changer. I gave it my all, shivering and moaning and slapping the bar. When I opened my eyes, everyone in the place was staring at me. I grinned and patted my mouth with a napkin, then crossed my legs and threaded my fingers together over my knees.

James stared at me, his jaw hanging open, no

longer feigning nonchalance. Someone out in the darkness beyond the bar lights gave me a slow clap.

"Well, thanks for the scintillating conversation," I said and wished I hadn't the second the words exited my mouth. I heard my bitchy tone and almost apologized for it. But I didn't. Screw this guy and his super annoying…super…hotness. "I need to get some sleep." I picked up my phone and hit the ride share app icon.

He turned to look at me. His boyish handsomeness hit me like a velvet-covered sledgehammer. It set my pulse racing like some teenager's. I sucked in a breath, hoping he wouldn't sense my heart pounding like a bass drum in my ears. "I'm sorry. I'm usually not so…"

"Antisocial? Tongue-tied?" I smiled to soften my words. He matched it.

Holy crap. This man is gorgeous. But in the kind of grows-on-you way I'd never bothered to comprehend. I went for the obvious hotties, like my ex or this guy's brother.

My recently discovered resolve against men and their BS slipped in the glare of his expressive green eyes set in a face reflecting his genetic lottery-winner status. It was different than his brother's, but it was no less awesome. And his nervousness only added to his cute factor.

Yep. Time to go.

No random encounters for this chick.

I slid off the ancient bar stool yet again. "I'll leave you to your meditations."

Resisting the sudden near irresistible compulsion to place my palm along his bearded cheek, I turned and headed for the door.

I made it back to my shitty hotel by one a.m., fell face first into the not-as-clean-as-they-should-be sheets, and blacked out. When I woke to the melodious notes of my phone alarm, my neck was sore from lack of movement. Weak sunlight filtered through the window, which drove the hangover spike deeper into my brain.

With a groan, I rolled off the bed, sat, and pressed my fingertips into my temples. I should have known better than to pass out without drinking any water. It was a rookie move, unworthy of an experienced imbiber like myself. But I had to admit it. The time I'd spent in a shitty bar with James Burke had thrown me for a lusty loop.

I stumbled toward the bathroom, hoping a hot shower would help, even as I recalled from direct experience it would not. As I made an attempt to put myself together for a day on the hunt for jobs via various potions and make-up related magic tricks, my beer-saturated mind kept returning to him, to James. A man I hardly knew existed twenty-four hours ago but who now populated my every thought in a way that irritated, like an itch in the middle of my back I couldn't reach.

After screwing up my mascara not once but twice and struggling to squeeze myself into a girdle, genius-marketed as a figure-shaping garment, I had to sit in front of the anemic flow of air from the air conditioner for a few minutes. I flapped my robe in hopes of dispersing the stubborn sweat beading up on my skin, cursing my lot in life, not to mention my sweatiness.

A quick glance at my phone reminded me I had zero time for nonsense. I pulled on my new blouse and suit, stuck my feet into shoes and almost pitched forward onto the floor they were so high, then hit the ride app. I rode the slow-as-molasses elevator down, waiting for the screen to populate and tell me how many cars were nearby.

By the time I got outside, still sweaty and approaching full panic, my app kept insisting there were no drivers within range. I looked around, praying a good old-fashioned taxi might materialize.

I switched apps and located some guy in a Ford Focus who was twenty minutes away. Not ideal, but at least I knew someone was headed my way. I shifted from foot to foot, already anticipating the high opera my feet would sing by the end of the day.

I flipped through my mental list of supplies. Fluffed up resumes? Check. Bogus business cards that I shouldn't have bought? Check. Spare blouse for when I inevitably sweated through this one? Check. Appropriate, not-too-red-but-not-too-boring lipstick, chosen by Stella? Check.

I glanced at my phone, expecting at least twelve maybe fifteen minutes to have passed. It was more like four. I sighed and slipped my feet out of the torture chambers passing for shoes and waited, sweaty, hungover, with a brand new, football-player-shaped obsession I didn't want filling my brain.

Chapter Seven

I was late, of course. A solid thirty-nine minutes into the event, which meant I pretty much showed up with everyone else. I spent the first half hour wandering around while I pondered how far I'd go to relocate, since the majority of the breweries in here were in states nowhere near Kentucky. Still fragile even after knocking back almost a gallon of water, I started dropping resumes willy-nilly.

I had a decent conversation with Trent Brewing out of Florida and another with Jasper's in Oregon when I saw two newly familiar men enter the room a solid hour and a half late. Flush with possibility, revived after positive commentary about my hirability and skill set, even if there were commensurate noises about being able to afford me, I felt strong enough to wander over and introduce myself. I sifted through the many offers I'd field after this evening's triumph with a smile on my face. Once these guys figured out exactly how affordable I was, I'd have a veritable bidding war on my hands.

The Burke brothers stationed themselves at the one remaining empty table. They both looked rode hard and put up wet…or at the very least hungover as all get out. I hesitated, studying their body language, which screamed "pissed off at the world" or at least each other. Michael set out a few sheets of paper. James headed for the food table.

Deciding to delay the inevitable, I took a detour and scored myself a couple more conversations with breweries who seemed thrilled to meet me. I chastised myself for thinking this wouldn't be worth it. I would emerge from today's effort with plenty of opportunities, even if it meant I'd have to move away from the only home I'd ever known.

By the time I made my way back around to the Burke Brothers table, both men were sitting there. James was stuffing pretzels and cheese in his mouth. Michael was glad-handing, smiling, doing his sales-weasel best.

As I scrambled for an excuse to approach them, I spotted someone else headed their way. It was none other than the lovely VanAnsel Princess, and she looked spitting mad. I ducked back, hiding behind a scrum of eager job seekers. The brothers were engaged in some not terribly friendly-looking conversation, so they didn't spot her barreling toward them.

"Hey, Andi, is that you?" I glanced over my shoulder, annoyed by the distraction.

"Oh, hi," I said, giving the guy a quick smile and wave before focusing my attention back on the unfolding drama.

Sloane looked immaculate in a pair of cream-colored capris and torso-hugging, light blue, V-neck, T-shirt. All trace of the sloppy drunk girl from the night before was gone, replaced with a glossy-magazine-ready vision—perfect makeup, ultra-straight coal-black hair included.

I tugged on the hem of my suit jacket. Women like Sloane had always fascinated me. I honestly wondered how a grown human could exist on a leaf of lettuce and eight cups of green tea a day. There had been a time when Stella was this kind of knee-knocking scrawny, and she always claimed it had been because her husband's celebrity crush was Calista Flockhart, the queen of the skinnies at one time.

When she laid their mantra on me, "nothing tastes as good as skinny feels," I'd laughed until I peed myself. And yet, on some level, I envied her then, and Sloan VanAnsel now, even as I noted her shoulder blades stuck out under the thin T-shirt material like a pair of baby bird wings, which was not the most attractive thing about her.

Something told me her personality was not quite so fragile. I eased closer, wanting to hear her give Mr. Hot Stuff Michael Burke the what-for.

"As far as I am concerned…" she was saying.

But I'd finagled myself into eavesdropping distance too late to hear anything more from her. Sloane tapped her sandal-clad toe. James looked up at the ceiling. Michael kept his gaze pinned on her. I waited for him to speak, but he didn't. Finally, she whirled away from the table and plowed through the crowd, her jaw set and her eyes dry.

Way to go, sister. Never let 'em know you give a rip.

At the last minute, she turned back to face them. I sent all my girl power mojo to keep her from doing anything like yelling. It seemed to work. She kept her thoughts to herself, turned away, and disappeared into the crowd.

I sidestepped her, keeping my head down, too shy to meet her gaze. She stopped in front of a table and took a seat behind it, all business now, smiling at eager prospects, handing out pieces of paper with her family's distribution company logo on the top, unfazed by Michael Burke's stoic attitude.

I gave her a mental high-five, then decided it was time Mr. James Burke met me in a more formal way. I marched myself to their table, waited behind two other employment seekers, then slapped on my most sincere smile when it was my turn in front of them.

"Hello." Michael stretched out his hand.

I blinked. I hadn't expected this sort of greeting. I thought I'd get a bored stare, a quick assessment of my front facing attributes. I did have nice boobs, and since I'd lost some weight, they looked even better. Plus, the redheaded thing really got to some dudes. But someone must have given Burke the younger sensitivity training, because his eyes stayed on my face.

I shook his hand, waiting for James to say something.

"I'm Michael Burke. This giant lunk is my brother, James." He squinted at me. "Have we met before?" He treated me to a flash of his uber-handsomeness with a bright grin and eye sparkle.

I didn't flinch. For guys like him, it was unconscious. I was immune to it.

"No. I mean, not formally. I did see you last night. At Robo's. Your date joined me on my way out." I smiled at him, all innocence and light.

He flushed red.

"Oh, yes, right. Sloane is, uh…"

I held up a hand. "No explanations required. We girls have to look after each other sometimes." I let that sink in. I was enjoying this way too much. I placed a copy of my resume on the table between them. Michael's eyes flickered to it. "Not sure if y'all are hiring, but…"

I wouldn't work for you if you paid me a zillion dollars a day, I finished in my head, keeping my smile as sincere.

James remained silent, just this side of brooding, his eyes fixed on me in a way that made me just this side of uncomfortable. I frowned. What was up his butt anyway? I didn't owe him anything after our mild flirtation last night. He had a damn nerve glowering at me.

Michael picked up my piece of paper and studied it. "Oh, wow. I thought that was you last night, but…anyway. It's an honor. And as a matter of fact, we need a marketing director. Would you mind if I asked you a few questions?"

"Sure thing." I leaned forward, which relieved some of the pressure in my feet. Both sets of masculine eyes shot to my cleavage, then up to my face so fast, if I hadn't been watching for it, I might have missed it.

Why are you messing with these guys, Andrea Rose? Get away from them and go snag the job you came out here for.

"So," Michael said as he glanced down at a list of questions he must have prepared.

"I don't think it would work," James blurted out, surprising me and, it would appear, his brother.

Anger flared, and I let it lead me. "You're probably right. It was nice to officially meet you…both. Give my best to Sloane, won't you?"

I waved at them, then felt like a total idiot for doing so, amused by the way they both stood there with their mouths gaping open. Unable to resist, I looked straight at James and winked. Winked! Like some kind of a campy Hollywood vamp.

Face flushed, heart pounding, I strode from their table and shoved my way through the throng. I needed a bathroom or an exit door or a nice cup of cyanide-laced tea. I found the bathroom first and flung myself into a stall, slamming the door behind me. The metal was cool when I pressed my forehead to it and gave myself a few minutes to regain control.

After a brisk splash of cold water and a breath mint, I was prepared to face the room again. I made the rounds one last time, giving the Burkes a wide berth. A small crowd kept their table surrounded, so I figured they'd forgotten all about me. After another hour, I'd pressed as much flesh as possible and was contemplating a quiet night in the nasty hotel room with little enthusiasm.

On my way out, I spotted a table with the words "VanAnsel Distribution." I stopped, and came face to face with Sloane. She blinked, as if trying to place me.

But I wasn't in the mood. My feet were screaming in agony, my back was sore, and I needed a nap. Pretending my phone screen required my full, undivided attention, I slipped between a few remaining stragglers and headed for the door.

"Wait!"

I froze. Before I could make my escape, she was next to me, hand on my arm, deep blue eyes full of recall.

"Hi," I said, shifting my bag up on my shoulder. I'd offloaded almost every resume I'd brought and dropped my goofy, fake business cards willy-nilly.

There couldn't be a brewery, distribution company, or other affiliated group in here that didn't know about me by now. Except, of course, VanAnsel Distribution. Something in me had resisted that one.

VanAnsel had a massive portfolio of both wine and beer. They sold pretty much every premiere craft brand in the state of Michigan, including Burke Brothers. Like I said, I knew my stuff when it came to beer.

"Hi. I wanted to say thanks, you know, for last night."

"Oh, okay. You're welcome." I forced myself to grin, but it turned into a grimace when I moved my left foot, which had developed a constellation of blisters above my heel. "Ow, sorry."

She glanced down at my feet. "Wrong shoes for today," she said, grabbing my elbow and dragging me back to her table. "Here, take my seat."

"I'm fine," I said as I sat. "I need to—"

But she was already talking with someone else. I used the excuse of sitting to ease my feet out of the heels while Sloane did her thing. She was good. Damn good. In the space of about fifteen minutes, she managed to set up two interviews and, better, to deflect a couple of people who were obviously not suited to life in alcohol sales. They were sometimes hard to spot, humans who needed to avoid life in the service sector, but she figured them out at almost the same time I did.

I rolled my ankles, crouching forward to take pressure off my lower back. I was done in, shattered, over it. I'd given it my best shot though, so hopefully this whole rather strange weekend would be worth it.

"I know who you are," Sloane said, surprising me. She was leaning against the back of the table now, facing away from the thinning crowd. "I mean, I figured it out."

"Oh, well, great." I rose and tried to shove my poor dogs back into the shoes, which was a major no-go with a capital no. I hooked my fingers in them and tried to look jaunty and carefree when I felt wilted and anxious. "So, I'm gonna go…"

I saw the exit doors. I fixated on them, eager to get the hell out of here and away from the picture of feminine perfection staring at me like a microscopic specimen.

A familiar sensation flared in my chest, a combination of jealousy and exasperation and a straight up poor-me-ism burned hot, making my face flush. I glanced away from her, sensing how sweaty I was under my suit jacket. She looked cool, collected, put together in a way I'd never be. Money will do that, I guessed. I let the thought fuel me past the limp-noodle, chest-burning, jealousy tremors.

"Why didn't you drop a resume here?" she asked. A legit question.

"I…I thought I had," I lied, reaching in my bag for one, knowing it for a futile effort. How did she know I hadn't?

She waved a hand. "I don't need to see it. I know how over-qualified you are for a sales job with us."

She glanced around the room. Most of the job seekers were gone. Companies were packing away their swag, job lists, and sign-up sheets, laughing and making plans for dinner. I knew of at least four beer-company sponsored events I could crash. But at that moment, I wanted nothing more than another one of those PBRs I'd mainlined the night before.

I spotted Michael Burke headed straight for Sloane. I rose, compelled by something I didn't understand. "Let's go get a drink."

She raised an eyebrow at me.

"I mean, you know, off the beaten path, maybe?"

"Sure, why not?" She stuck a pile of papers into a leather bag and handed it to one of the three hovering company flunkies.

I met Michael's gaze while Sloane busied around the table, shutting things down. He watched her from a few feet away, hands jammed in his trouser pockets.

Pretty boy needed a reality check, and I was about to provide it. I maneuvered myself so I blocked her line of sight to him.

"Great," I said, making sure he could hear me. "I'll get us a ride."

"Oh no, it's fine. I have a driver."

I tucked the phone in my bag. *Of course, she has a driver, Andi. You're not sisters with this woman. She operates on a whole different realm than you. Try to remember that.*

She smiled at the guys who all looked like they'd carry her out of the place on their collective shoulders if she suggested such a thing. "Okay. We can go."

She smiled at me, but when her gaze lifted to something or someone behind me, the smile faded faster than a Polaroid picture.

"Sloane," I said. "Don't."

Her eyes, a shade of cornflower blue that really ought to be forbidden to women who already looked as good as she did, flashed. Her lips pressed together into a thin, almost but not quite unattractive line. Her lightly tanned skin reddened.

"Hey, um…could we…talk?"

I turned and positioned myself so I was shoulder-to-shoulder with her. I couldn't explain to myself why I was doing this. What in the hell did I care about this woman anyway?

"We have someplace to be," I said.

She glanced at me, her face a mask of conflict. I nodded at her, tilted my head toward Mr. Wonderful. Not subtle, not in any way at all. She nodded and turned to him. "No, Michael. I think we're done talking."

"But…"

"You heard her," I said. I treated him to a blatant up-and-down checking out that would get me reprimanded by any half-decent HR department. But I owed him at least one, recalling the way he'd ogled my tits earlier. "Beat it, hot stuff."

His frown deepened. "Listen, Andi, I don't think you understand…"

I held up my hand. "We have plans. Go on now, scoot."

He made as if to do the opposite, to march around the other side of the table and confront Sloane despite my mother-hen clucking. I shifted to my right, doing everything short of tucking my charge in behind me.

"You heard her," Sloane piped up. "Scoot."

"Come on," James said as he strode up behind Michael and shoulder-bumped him aside. "I'll catch you later?" he said to me.

As if.

"Highly unlikely. Bye-bye now, boys. Bye-bye." I flapped my fingers at him, something I'm fairly certain I had never, ever done under any circumstances.

I am losing my ever-loving mind.

I watched the men head for the door, James' wide shoulders in his brewer's Tee next to his brother's covered in a crisp blue dress shirt.

"They're quite the pair," I said under my breath.

"Something like that. Our ride's here. Let's go."

"Wait. Let them get all the way out."

She heaved a sigh. "You're right."

"I know I am."

Chapter Eight

"How soon can you start?"

I was sipping my second dirty martini at the end of this extraordinary day when Sloane VanAnsel dropped this little question bomb into our midst. I sucked in a breath at the wrong time, sending the olive-infused booze down my windpipe. Sloane handed me a napkin so I could conclude my coughing fit, which, I'll admit, I dragged out longer than was needed to give me time to formulate an answer.

Finally, I sipped some water, then picked up my martini glass again. "I don't know…"

"Don't be silly. I know you need a job and would prefer it to be away from your home base. Louisville, right?" She sipped her Vesper martini. Admirable. Anyone who could drink anything combining gin and vodka in one glass impressed the hell out of me.

"I'm not limiting any options by geography." I put down my empty glass.

Sloane had asked her driver to take us to some "off the beaten path, half decent bar," so we ended up here, a perfect mix of classic and hipster but far enough into the Denver suburbs to be away from the beer throng.

I turned the glass stem around, my mind wrapping itself around the concept of what was happening right now.

A job.

I was being offered a job.

"I mean, all I have to offer right now is sales, but if you agree to take it, I can offload some dead weight on the staff, consolidate their portfolios, and give you a decent bunch of accounts to handle." She barely raised a finger, and the bartender scrambled over to her. "One more round," she said, smiling at him.

"I don't know," I said. "Martinis are like tits, you know."

She raised a dark eyebrow at me.

"One isn't enough? Three is too many?"

"Eh, you'll be fine. Drink some more water."

"I need to eat." I picked up the single page menu between us and scanned the options. As I suspected, not a nacho chip or fake cheese food sauce in sight. "Would you share something with me?"

She looked away from her phone screen. "What? Oh, sure. Get whatever." She refocused on her device. "It's on me."

Our drinks showed up. I ordered roasted Brussels sprouts and fried green tomatillos, figuring I'd end up eating them all myself. I'd been here before with a skinny friend. We sipped a few seconds in silence. Sloane sighed and put her phone on the bar top.

"Let me guess," I said. "Mikey Burke is at it again?"

She side-eyed me, then leaned forward on her elbows. "Back to my original question…"

It was my turn to sigh. "I don't know, Sloane. I guess I didn't picture myself starting at the bottom. But then again, I didn't picture my husband dumping me and taking my bar away either."

My eyes burned. I swallowed hard. I didn't know

this chick well enough to cry in front of her, at least not yet.

"I watched you today. You dropped resumes at every damn table but mine, and that includes at least seven distributors, only one of which is bigger than VanAnsel. So don't feed me a line about not wanting to be a lowly salesperson."

"Okay, fine," I said. "I'm not sure why I avoided VanAnsel, okay? You happy?"

"I will be. When you take me up on my offer. I can have your book of business ready in a week."

I frowned at her and took another sip, feeling the forbidden third gin drink slide into my bloodstream, making me feel powerful in a way I knew was false. But what the hell. I went with it. "Oh yeah? And what will you be paying me? Who'll be my direct boss? What are my chances of advancement?"

"Yeah," she said, giving me the full force of her gorgeous face and no doubt killer negotiating skills. "Fifty-five base, plus commission and benefits. We have a damn good insurance plan. You'll be reporting to my Uncle Art. He's sales director. You could run the department but, you know, family." She waved her long, elegant fingers.

I stared at them mesmerized by the short, perfectly polished nails. "Right. Family."

The food arrived. I put my napkin in my lap and dug in. I'd skipped breakfast and only had time for a few snacks at the job fair food table. This was one body that didn't run on lettuce leaves and tea, and I was hungry enough to eat all this green stuff plus one of the steaks passing by on raised trays. But this would do for now.

Sloane stared at the options and kept drinking her martini.

"Go on, have some," I insisted.

"I'm fine, thanks though." She glanced at her smart watch. "Listen, I'm due at an event back at the hotel. Can we conclude our business so I can feel like this stupid trip was worth the headache?"

"Tell me about him," I said.

We were only here, together, right now, for one reason after all. My empathetic, knee-jerk reaction to her drunk-ass situation last night and my need to drag her away from a guy who reminded me of my ex had all combined to turn me into this overprotective weirdo. Obsession with both her and the Burke brothers had provided me with a nice diversion from my never-ending pity party. I wasn't so sure about jumping into the deep end of the pool with them and moving my Southern girl butt up to Michigan.

"Your accent gets thick when you drink," she said while playing with the curl of lemon peel in her glass. "It's cute."

"Hmph," I muttered, self-conscious as hell about my wide hips, the shelf of my boobs, the sweat beading up under my jacket. "If y'all think you can distract me from my mission…" I plunked my elbows on the bar's edge and looked at her. "Y'all are sadly mistaken," I said, going from subtle Louisville drawl to deep, hillbilly Georgia.

She frowned and ran a fingertip around the glass's edge. "He's… Well, he's not anything to me, not anymore."

"I will say I'm a little confused about how you could be dating the owner of one of the breweries you

85

rep."

"Technically, that's not a problem." Her phone buzzed. She turned it over and looked at the screen. Her face reddened. She put it back down and closed her eyes for a second. "The problem is my father."

"Ah, of course. Uppity Mikey Burke and his sticky beer fingers coming after the crown princess."

"The…what?"

"Never mind." I sipped, until I realized the glass was empty.

"Want another?" She pointed to it.

"God, no," I said, pushing the glass away and picking up my water.

"Okay, listen, Andi," she said, pulling her hair up and fastening it with something she must have conjured out of thin air. Women like her had that sort of magic. "I really have to get going. So I'll ask you one more time. When can you start?"

She pinned me with her bright blue stare. Her face was open, guileless. I wanted to trust her, to close my eyes, pinch my nose shut, and jump right in. "Can I tell you in a few hours? I need… I should talk it over with…"

Right. And who would I be talking it over with? It's not like I had anything holding me to Louisville. My mom was there, of course, but she was healthy and independent.

I could practically hear her and Stella yammering in my ear to take the job already. It was something I could do with my eyes closed, having been on the opposite side of the table from legions of sales reps for the last six years.

Sloan motioned for the check, tucked in a credit

card, and signed when it was returned to her.

"You're really loaded, huh?" I almost slapped a hand over my lips, but the words were out there in the air between us before I could stop them. "I mean, what do you do if you're not managing the sales team at your...at VanAnsel?"

She stepped down from the high bar chair and tucked her tiny purse under her arm. A few tendrils of hair had escaped, turning her bun messy, and yet, somehow, still perfect. I shook my head, the ill-considered third martini sloshing around in my guts.

"I used to work in Chicago at a PR firm. I worked my way up from assistant and was about to get promoted with my own clients. Then my mother..." Her voice broke. "My mother got ovarian cancer, and I came home. She recovered, but since then, I've been working in various capacities at the family business."

"And how does Sexy Boy Burke fit into the story?"

She clenched her jaw, looked up at the ceiling, then back at me. "We met in Chicago. He wasn't involved with the brewery at the time. He didn't want to be. He was a securities trader, a good one. He was...is loaded."

"Nice," I said. "It fits his type, I guess."

"Thanks to some really bad business choices his father made, he had to leave that behind, too. Ended up in Detroit, running the brewery with James."

"So did you meet at a bar or the gym or what?"

She flushed deep red. "We met at a club. A private club. Anyways, we were a good fit, at least for a while. When we both ended up back in Michigan, things got too complicated."

"Ooh...a private club. Do tell." I leaned my face in my hand, or I aimed for it. Instead, thanks to my third boob drink, I almost gave myself a black eye on the table's edge. "Jesus, I told you my limit was two."

She was smiling again. "I've never really had a friend... I mean I had sorority sisters..."

"Of course," I said, giving her a girlie finger waggle. I was getting good at those.

She rolled her eyes. "Yeah. So, they were a passel of bitches, mostly. Anyway..." She checked her watch again. "Thanks, Andi. I mean it. For last night. I don't... I somehow always manage to do or say or act stupid whenever I'm around him." Her eyes got bright. I averted my gaze, unwilling to see her cry. I wasn't quite there yet with her. "I'd really like it if you'd come to work for my company. I can help you get settled. I know where to find you a decent condo or whatever you need."

"Oh, I won't be buying anything for a while."

"Fine, an apartment then. I know all the places you should and shouldn't live. I mean, I grew up in Grand Rapids."

I studied her, intrigued by the fact she honestly seemed to think having her as my BFF would convince me to move to Michigan, to the same state where James Burke lived and worked. But I couldn't confess that to her yet. It would be way too strange.

Besides, I barely understood it myself. How could I explain to her I was terrified of being in such close proximity to him? That I didn't trust myself around him for reasons I couldn't iterate?

I closed my eyes. "Is Grand Rapids close to...ah..."

"The Burke Brothers brewing facility is based in Detroit. It's about two hours away."

I glared at her. "That's not what I was going to…"

She patted my shoulder and put her lips near my ear. She smelled like subtle perfume with a slight hint of gin in her breath. "Yes, it was. I get it. Don't worry. You need a job. A fresh start. I need to offload some crappy sales guys. And I could stand a friend in my corner. Win-win." She spread her hands. "Let me know later, okay? Promise?"

"Sure. Okay. Promise."

I stared at the line of unlabeled liquor bottles, wondering how in the world the bartender could manage, using the teensy little tags hanging from the necks of them all. They blurred on me as I stared. I drank more water. The bar filled up with handsome men and their lovely dates or wives or whatever. The feeling came back, the burny-angry-pissy-poor-me feeling.

Damn you, Matt.

No. No more of that.

I had a job offer, a decent one, and someone willing to help me get settled, even if our connection might be even more complicated than it appeared on its surface. I needed to stop stressing over what might be with a guy I hardly knew and who, likely, had forgotten me entirely already.

"One more?" the bartender asked, no longer bowing and scraping since my beautiful companion had left.

"Nope, thanks." I finished the water and put my tender feet on the floor, then limped my way to the door and out into the still-warm Denver evening. It was only seven. My flight wasn't until noon tomorrow. I should go celebrate the success of this junket. But the thought of pouring any more liquor into my system on top of what was already there held little appeal. A girl should know her limits, after all.

I glanced down to see if there were any ride shares nearby. I'd hardly paid a bit of attention to our ride here. It had been so great to be off my feet and in a nice, climate-controlled SUV.

I slipped out of my shoes and started strolling toward what looked like a cluster of restaurants down from the one I'd just exited. A breeze lifted the ends of my hair and cooled my face. I took a seat on a bench under a picturesque tree, knowing I was tipsy but also knowing I had done what I'd come here to do.

I had found a dang job.

Chapter Nine

"May I join you?"

I opened one eye, already knowing who it was and figuring it for some kind of effed-up karma. "If you must."

I moved my shoes down to the sidewalk and shifted as far to the left armrest as I could. James Burke plunked himself right in the middle of the thing.

"Do you mind?" I crossed my legs to avoid having our thighs touch. I wasn't in the mood for flirting or otherwise. I'd just done something great for myself for the first time in over a year and didn't feel like sharing the victory.

No matter how good-looking said potential victory-sharer might be.

Or how close he was sitting to me.

"Don't you have a Burke Brothers beer dinner to handle?" He didn't. I knew, thanks to my new-found stalkerish behavior. I'd discovered the brothers weren't hosting one this year. Odd. This would have been a great way to showcase their new quality-problem-solved brews to their fellow professionals. But it was their brewery, not mine.

"Nope," he said, putting his hands behind his head and stretching out his long legs.

"Nice manspreading, dude," I said in my prissiest voice.

"Nah, not really." He glanced at me, then bent his knees and opened his legs out to each side, jamming me even farther into my corner. "Now *this* is nice manspreading."

Without even thinking about it—and thanks to my three martinis—I twisted around and plopped my legs on his lap. He grinned, grabbed my left foot and dug his knuckle into my arch. I tensed, until my poor battered foot relaxed.

"Oh…my God…yes." I closed my eyes and let him do what he would, no longer caring that we were making a spectacle of ourselves.

After a few moments, he switched to my other foot. I shivered and sighed again, stretching out like a cat until I realized my hips were practically on his lap.

"Oh, I'm sorry," I said, shifting away until only my feet were there. He shot me a look that made my face flush hot. "Okay, I'm good. Thanks much." I rotated and put my feet back on the sidewalk where they belonged.

"My pleasure," he said, his voice soft and low.

I glared at him. "Don't flirt with me, pal. I'm not in the mood. And you're not my type."

"So quick to judge," he said, stretching his arms back and his legs out again.

When he closed his eyes, I allowed myself a quick, up-close assessment, which was a bad idea, in my weakened state. I've established that the guy could pass for an NFL player with his wingspan, immense shoulders, and ever-so-long legs. His beard was neatly trimmed off his neck and cheeks. The matching dark brown hair was thick and a bit on the long side, which made me have to curl my fingers into fists to keep from touching it.

Oh boy. Where did *that* come from?

It came from the bottom of your third martini glass, you silly girl.

I jumped to my feet. James opened his eyes, slow and easy, as if knowing I was about to make a panicky bolt for it and figuring he should go slow, to treat me as if I were a rabid animal trapped under his front porch. Forcing myself to relax and smile, because I was in control of this, after all, I picked up my shoes and made a point to look at my phone screen.

"Don't stare. It's rude," I said, my finger poised to call for a ride.

"Can I buy you a beer?"

I sighed and looked at the darkening sky, never more aware of how badly I did want to sit with him, to have a beer and a chat. But I was determined not to develop bad habits, like the one that had landed me with Matt in my post-grad years.

I would not—could not—allow myself to do anything more than drink and enjoy his company, then I'd get my sorry tail back to my hotel and pack. I had a lot of things to do after all. I had a move to plan.

"Andi?"

I flinched. I'd been standing here too long, not answering him. My inner polite young lady kicked in. "Sorry. Um, sure. Okay."

"Don't get too excited about it."

I glared at him. "Fine. I won't. Catch you on the flip side, Jimmy."

I was a solid fifty steps down the sidewalk before he caught up and fell into step with me. He kept his hands to himself, which I appreciated. I was too jumpy by half and needed my personal space honored. I gave him a mental half-point. He stuck his fingers in his jeans pockets, and we walked a while in comfortable silence.

"This place looks nice," he said, stopping in front of a fake Irish pub, complete with flapping banners of green, white, and orange flags. I rolled my eyes. He held open the door and made a grand sweeping gesture with his other hand. I heard cheesy music floating out onto the cooling air, clinking glasses, laughter. I cocked my head and stared at him, this utter stranger trying to convince me to drink yet more beer with him in a city far from our respective homes.

Yeah, it had random encounter sex written all over it.

A tiny, somewhat atrophied part of my brain started yammering and banging around in its cage, telling me to go for it. To jump aboard the James Burke train and ride to my heart's content. I blushed and ducked into the cooled interior, forcing the bigger, stronger, grown up part of my brain to smother that horny little minx with a pillow. This was neither time nor locale for such nonsense. I wasn't in a good place, emotionally. Plus, I smelled like stale flop sweat.

I marched to the bar, found a chair, and sat, not bothering to see if he followed. The bartender was quick with his coaster and water, which I appreciated. By the time James was seated, I'd already ordered for both of us.

"What'd you get us?"

"An Irish stout, what else?" I waved a hand around, indicating the general décor.

James grimaced. I smiled sweetly at him and

sipped my water. When the beers were placed before us, James chuckled. The rich, dark liquid was served in brandy snifter-style glasses, indicating higher alcohol content. Not an Irish stout, in other words. I'd taken one glance at the options and ordered a couple of Imperial stouts from a famous brewery not far from where we sat.

I held mine up, he touched his to it. We both took long sniffs first, then sipped at the same time. I grinned as I took my second, more important drink and let it linger on my tongue. Like any good stout, it was well balanced, not overpowering either in malt or hops but a near perfect blend of crucial ingredients. We smacked our lips at almost the same time, then both laughed. I permitted myself to relax ever so slightly as the rich brew coated my throat and the hefty booziness warmed my chest.

"Damn," James said, turning the glass around on the bar top. "Well done."

"Indeed," I said. Part of my research-slash-obsessive behavior the last twenty-four hours included digging into the recent Burke Brothers Brewing Company issues, which included two entire batches of popular brews being recalled with much fanfare and bad beer press. "So I have to ask. Why'd you go all asshole on me at the job fair?"

James closed his eyes and sipped again, doing his best to buy some time I surmised. He set the empty glass down and wiped his lips with a napkin before turning to face me. I kept my face neutral, although I'll admit I was this close to reaching out to touch the soft curls along his jawline. Since entering the booze community years ago and becoming an expert in craft beer in particular, I'd been surrounded by bearded guys and never once felt such a compulsion to caress a man's facial hair.

He pursed his lips, almost comically, as if thinking hard, which dashed cold water on my overheated brain. "If you must know, Burke Brothers Brewing is a total cluster fuck these days."

Shocked, I set down my beer and touched his arm despite my inner warnings not to. He glanced at my hand, then up into my eyes. I patted him like a grandma and moved back into my own space. "Sorry to hear it."

I raised my finger for the bartender's attention. This was none of my business. I had my own life to reorganize.

Before I could put in my beer request, James spoke over me. Irritating, if something I'd become used to, working in the man-centric alcohol world. "Let's try the New England IPA. The one from Trader's," he said.

I scoffed. "Don't tell me you like that juiced-up nonsense, or you'll be in danger of losing all my respect."

"I think one should remain fully cognizant of trends," he said with a shrug. "Protein?"

He pushed a bowl of peanuts toward me. I smiled at the echo of our first meeting over PBRs the night before. I peeled a couple and ate them, conscious of his gaze on me.

"Besides, that juiced-up nonsense as you call it is taking over. We've never had more requests for hazy, fruity beers. Even sours. It's weird. But I'm getting over my *Reinheitsgebot* snobbishness. Can't have that anymore and expect to make money unless you're macro. Here, catch."

He tossed a peeled peanut at my face. I opened my mouth and caught it.

"I still believe if you can't make really great beers from all the grains and yeasts and hops available now, you're a big fat faker." I'd always been a bit of a snob when it came to the so-called German purity law. Not so much a law, of course, but a set of guidelines for making beer that declared "beer" was only "beer" if it was made up of four ingredients—barley, hops, water, and yeast.

"Really?" He turned so he faced me all the way, his knees within centimeters of my leg. I tried not to flinch away. A move of pure self-preservation, of course. "I wouldn't have thought that about you."

"Why not?" I nodded thanks when our drinks arrived. "Wow. Seriously. Haze me much?"

The beer looked more like a glass of pulpy orange juice with a foamy head than anything. I took a sniff. The combination of yeast and hops needed to make this particular style created a distinct, fruit-like aroma, which had become part of its wide appeal to people disinclined to jump into the craft beer thing full force. It smelled like a shandy, which was beer and fizzy lemonade mixed together to tone down the alcohol during hot summer months.

I took a sip. The sharpness surprised me. I'd tried a few versions of this style before and had been underwhelmed. But this was something else altogether. I had a second sip, letting the liquid sit in my mouth a few seconds to allow my tongue to experience it. The sharpness was a tangy, hoppy tingle by the time I swallowed.

"Okay, this one's good," I said, enjoying my third

sip like a normal person without over-evaluating it.

"Told you so," James said as he held his glass up to the light. "It's damn expensive to make. Takes a shit ton of hops and extra time in fermentation. Plus, if you don't get it packed up super tight and keep it constantly cold, it'll go bad on you." He smacked his lips after his third taste. "Damn tasty though. I gotta call Stacy, pick her brain a little."

"Stacy? You don't mean Stacy Renner do you?"

"I do. You know her?" He'd turned back to face the bar by now, which made me both sad and relieved. "She's the one who basically invented this recipe. Everyone else has been trying to recreate it with varying levels of failure, in my humble opinion."

"I love Stacy," I said. "She was just starting out when I opened my bar in Louisville. Apprentice brewer to some giant asshole at a local, lager-centric place that folded, thank the good Lord. She was amazing. So energetic and creative."

James was staring at me again. I cleared my throat and put my half-empty glass down, regretting the double whammy addition of these beers on top of my existing alcohol level.

"I wonder how many other people we have in common," he said.

"Tons, I'm sure. Okay, I should go." But I was frozen in my seat. I was, in a word, drunk. Ergo, I wasn't a hundred percent certain if I could navigate my way to the front door.

James kept watching me while I drank my remaining half glass of water. When I couldn't spot a bartender anywhere near us, I rose, reached over the bar, and located the beverage wand. After refilling mine, I held it up to him.

"I'm good, thanks." His lips twitched. I could tell he wanted to laugh. "You're kind of amazing, aren't you, Andrea Rose?"

"I said, don't flirt with me, mister…mister… beardy…hot stuff."

Wow. Stop talking now, maybe Andi? Get the heck out of here, perhaps before you really act a fool?

I smoothed the front of my blouse, exposed since I'd given up on the jacket buttons hours ago. I wasn't sure how to take his words, but hearing them spoken in his deep, throaty voice landed in my brain like a bum firecracker, exploding and making a giant mess of my already rattled psyche.

My hand shook when I reached for my water glass. I stopped halfway to it and curled my fingers into a fist. I should be flattered by the attention this handsome man was showing me, the compliment he'd paid me. Part of me was. Another, more brittle and growly part was rising up and demanding that we hightail our kind of amazing selves right on out of here before we did something stupid.

Flustered, I jumped down to the floor, landing so hard the soles of my abused feet cried out. About the time I realized I was pitching forward, poised to flop not quite so amazingly onto James' left side, he turned and caught me. Now, don't go misunderstanding me when I say "caught." He must have been preparing to slide off his chair as well, to bid me a fond, chaste, farewell. The way we ended up was way more awkward tangle of limbs and faces than perfect, *"Oh my, thank you good sir. Forgive me. I feel faint,"* style of whoopsie daisy rendezvous.

Liz Crowe

"Um…sorry," he said when one of my arms ended up on his shoulder and the other was tucked under me against his torso. My nose ended up pressed into his chest. A lovely, strong chest if I do say so. And he smelled nice. But this would never do.

I pushed away and almost tipped in the other direction. He grabbed my arm, legit alarm on his face. I sympathized, and for a hot second, I felt bad for him, having to watch me crumple like a drunk college student.

"Whoa," I said once I righted myself between our chairs. He was still so close I caught the lingering scent of his skin. I shook my head. A giant error since the room did a super-duper nauseating three-sixty on me as a result.

"Oh," I said, exhaling and inhaling with purpose, forcing myself to be sober, which worked as well as it always did. "Sorry," I said before I hiccupped.

James let go of my arm and grinned.

"Oh shit. This is bad. You don't know me and hiccups." Basically, once I started, there was no stopping me until I passed out. Annoying, but there it was.

"Let's get you back to your hotel." He tossed some cash on the bar and cupped my elbow enough so I could lean into him and get my drunk self to the door. "Okay, here we go," he said, propelling me forward into the dark night.

We waited a few minutes for the ride he'd called. I observed him from my swaying, all-the-way-sloshed point of view, closing one of my eyes at one point, to force the three Jameses to merge into one.

For some reason, I glanced down and noted with

interest that I'd shed my shoes again. I wiggled my toes to reassure myself they were, indeed, mine. Yep. There they were, in their plain, unpolished glory. I hiccupped again. James grabbed my arm before I swayed too hard to the other side without saying a word.

I was also suddenly, keenly aware of the girdle I'd been shoved into all day. It was within minutes of cutting off my circulation at my midsection. I tugged at it through my blouse.

"Ow—hic!" I slapped a hand over my lips and giggled.

"Here we go. Can you ride in the back, or do you need the front seat?"

"Back's fine," I whispered, before another loud hiccup gripped my diaphragm.

He poured me into the back seat, tossed in my bag and shoes, then climbed in next to me.

"Sorry," I said.

"No worries. You've had a long day. And trust me, I've experienced my fair share of drunken saves by others. I don't mind." He smiled. I felt my lips turning upward in response but worried I resembled a sloppy clown. When his hand came toward my face, I ducked. "Chill, Andi. It's all right."

I closed my eyes, determined to be sober so I could at least invite the guy up and into my room like any normal woman would. I felt his fingertips on my face, tucking hair behind my ear, tracing my jaw. I shivered but kept silent, my eyes shut tight.

"I have to wonder about a man who'd dump you and take your business away from you," he said.

I opened my eyes at this and glared over at him or, at least, where two of him shimmered in the dark car's interior.

"Well, I guess you don't really know me. I mean, I can be a pretty hard-ass bitch." This firm tone was followed by not one but three loud hiccups in a row. I groaned and turned away. "When I'm not making a total fool of myself."

"I have no doubt you can be tough," James said. "You're also gorgeous, in case you were wondering."

"Don't flatter me, Jimmy. I'm immune."

"It's James. And I'll bet you are."

I ignored him for the rest of the ride, a long one since we had to go all the way out to the airport. Of course, I managed to pass out first, so when the car stopped, I missed it altogether.

"Up you go," I heard a deep, sonorous voice in my ear about the same time I felt hands under my arms, lifting me to my feet.

"Oh, shit, wow, I'm good. I mean…ugh." I wiped the spit off my cheek, already past the point of worry about being graceful, ladylike, or in any way attractive.

While James reached in the backseat to grab my bag and shoes, I took a quick minute to sniff my armpits. He caught me doing it, of course. It was fated.

"Don't stare at me," I mumbled, grabbing my bag and shoes out of his hands.

"I recall. It's rude. Sorry." His grin was wide, and at that moment, I wanted nothing more than for us to go upstairs, climb between the iffy sheets, and cuddle.

I sighed. At least I wasn't hiccupping anymore. But otherwise, I probably looked—and smelled—exactly how I felt. Shattered, squashed, strung out on lust, and drunk.

I inhaled. This was time for a rally, not a collapse. I

stuck out my hand. "Welp, thanks a mil for the ride and the beers, James. I guess I'll see you..."

I would be seeing him, all right. I was about to take a job with a distribution company that repped his damn products.

What had I been thinking? I felt myself listing to the left again.

"Yep, that's what I thought. Come on. I'll get you upstairs." He held out his hand. I gave him the bag and shoes, willing to relinquish those but not to take his arm. I could walk, thank you very much.

I couldn't of course. Funny thing about dumping a couple of high ABV beers on top of three martinis. It rendered one almost immobile. I filed this away for future reference as James slid his arm around my waist.

"Lean into me," he said. I sensed myself leaning away instead. He rolled his eyes. "Give it a rest, Andi. I'm just going to help you upstairs, not run over your dog."

"I don't have a dog," I said, indignant even as I realized I was damn lucky he was helping me because right now the ugly chairs in what passed for the lobby of this place looked mighty good for sleeping. We rode the elevator to the sixth floor. He held out his hand. I pulled the key card from the side pocket of my bag, somehow, not sure how.

And, just like that, we were in my room, re-made and icebox cold from the blaring air conditioner. He dropped my bag and shoes on the floor and handed me the key.

"Well," he said, looking nervous. "You okay to get...you know..." He gestured to the bed, the giant, crouching object in the middle of the room.

I took his hand. "Come on, don't pretend you didn't want to…"

I went up on my tiptoes—kind of way up, which was new for me, and yeah, I liked it—and pressed my lips to his. He flinched, for a hot second and a half, maybe two before he responded. His warm hands were on my waist, then my back, then in my hair as we shared what could only be termed a serious, rookie liplock.

The thing about kissing was, the first go at with someone new was typically a disaster. I was a realist. I understood that, the same way I understood our first hookup was about to go down, in a classic, drunken fashion.

He pulled away, though, and took my hands, which were resting on his oh-so-firm-and-fabulous chest, and put them down at my sides. "Sorry, but I'm not so much into…this."

"What?" I crossed my arms or tried to. They ended up on my hips so I took the opportunity to strike an indignant pose. "You're not into me? You're a liar." I swayed to my left. His hand shot out as if to steady me, but I righted myself. "Come on, Jimmy. You can't tell me you weren't looking for a little of this tonight."

I started unbuttoning my blouse, not very well, mind you, but still. I was single-minded. I hadn't had sex in…oh God. It had been two years. Matt and I hadn't touched each other a solid year before he dumped me.

My eyes were burning hot. My face flamed. My entire body shook with mortified determination.

"Fuck!" I gave up and flopped into a chair, legs splayed, head spinning. "I'm sorry. I don't usually…"

"Cuss?"

I glared up at him. "Thass right, I don't," I slurred as a fresh set of hiccups burbled up my throat. "My mama raised me to believe it was lazy talk."

James crouched down next to me, his hand on my knee. "Don't get me wrong, Andi. I am into you. Big time. You're as cute as hell with your lazy talk. I want to stay. And that's why I have to leave."

I sensed the passing-out moment lurking around my edges. "Phooey," I said, surprised by such a dumb word.

James raised an eyebrow, chuckled, and touched his finger to my lips. "You're amazing. I'm gonna go now. You sure you're okay?"

"Go on, git." I slid deep into Louisville accent-ism. I'd likely been giving him the full, syrupy treatment from the start tonight. "Ugh." I put my head in my hands and felt his palm on my shoulder, comforting and solid. "Please go. I'm gonna sit here and die of embarrassment." I hiccupped. "Crap."

"Don't die," he whispered, his lips so near my ear I smelled the beer on his breath. "We still have some talking to do." I'd swear he brushed those lips against my cheek because I felt the rasp of his beard. But I was done for the night. And he was one of those nice guys, unwilling to take advantage of a drunk-off-her-ass date.

Great. A nice guy. How was I supposed to resist that?

The door clicked shut. Forgoing the shower, the tooth brushing, the water I should have consumed to alleviate tomorrow's guaranteed misery, I stumbled to the bed and fell face down on the pillow. My mind was a jumble of memories of Matt and my former life but, more promisingly, of what my life was about to become.

If I survived the looming hangover, of course.

Chapter Ten

"Mom, stop already." I paused the frantic box construction project for a few seconds and lifted my damp T-shirt to expose my skin to the fan. The temps were in the low nineties, even in September, which figured. The bungalow I'd once owned with Matt had an ancient central A/C system, and I went well out of my way not to use it too much. I'd rather sweat through a couple of hot nights in the early fall than crank it and worry about it breaking for good.

At the moment, my mother was fiddling with the ancient thermostat, muttering about it being hotter than Hades in here.

"Seriously, Mom, it's fine. The heat's going to break tonight, and I don't want to use the A/C."

"Fine." She stepped away from the thermo and flapped a magazine at herself. "Lord, have mercy."

"Yeah." I got back to my task. "I don't have a ton of time. Can we focus?" I waved around the room full of flat boxes and unpacked crap.

"Yoo hoo!" I sighed at the sound of Stella's voice. We'd had our teary good-bye party two nights when I'd been feeling super positive about this whole thing. Today, not so much. And ergo, I was not in the mood for her right now.

So much not in the mood.

"I brought some wine."

"Stella, I told you I had to get all this done in two days. We had our farewell dinner the other night."

"Yeah? So? I can help. Let me open this." She waved a couple of chilled bottles of Pinot Gris. I'd give her this much. She knew I hated Chardonnay. I think it was all the barrel-aged beer I'd been drinking the last few years as that craze spun itself out. And also why I was finding myself enjoying Stacy Renner's version of the New England IPA. It was a break from the norm, and breaking from the norm was now my jam.

"Jesus." I stared around at the chaos reigning in my living room. I'd managed to get the bedroom and small office packed up the night before, thanks to a few energy drinks. My guts were still roiling from them, not to mention the encroaching anxiety about this whole moving to Michigan thing. Complete radio silence from my rescuer hero man hadn't helped. I'd figured he would have called or at least texted me in the last few days while I got my life sorted out, packed up, and ready to roll in his general direction.

It was probably a good thing I didn't have his number. It kept me from reaching out. Since he'd obviously been full of baloney with his "we still have talking to do" and the flattery BS he'd been feeding me.

"Take a break," Stella insisted, handing me a red Solo cup full of chilled white wine. I glared at her. She waggled the cup. "Come on, you know you want to."

I took it and sat on a nearby packed box. Panic raced up my spine when I stopped moving. I quelled it with a healthy slug of the crisp, cold booze. I watched my friend and my mother assemble a bunch of boxes and start layering in newspaper between the contents of my kitchen.

When I looked down to note my plastic cup was empty, Stella sloshed in another healthy portion, then held hers up in the air in front of me.

"To Andrea," she said. "To her new life in Michigan. And to the handsome, beardy hunk waiting for her there."

"Shut up," I said into my drink.

"What's this about a hunk?" My mother eyeballed me. I glared at Stella. She shrugged and sipped between dropping spatulas and hot pads into an almost full box.

"Nothing," I said, getting up to join them.

"I knew there was something else that made Michigan appealing," my mother said.

"No, there isn't. Please, Mama. Just…fill another box for me, okay?" I held out the tape gun, begging her with my stare not to bring it up again.

She sighed and took it.

"So, this woman, this Sloane person. She's the one who helped you find a decent apartment," Mom said.

I finished my second over-pour and set the cup down with a burp.

"Andi, really."

I smiled at her. I adored my mother. She'd been through such hell with my father and his abandonment. She'd done a great job raising me on her own. But her constant adherence to outdated mores and politeness rituals in the face of harsh reality sometimes made me want to pitch her out the window on her prim, Southern lady tail end.

Ignoring her instead of being bitchy felt like the best response. So I dragged an empty box into the small laundry area off the kitchen and started putting away the cleaning supplies. I could hear Stella chattering

109

away, filling dead air like only she could, while my mother answered back, since she was genetically unable not to. When my phone buzzed in my shorts pocket, I snagged it, unable to stop my pulse from racing at the thought it might be, could be, him.

Andrea Rose Walker Rigby, get a grip upon thyself this instant.

I took a breath and snuck a peek at the sender. Sloane again. The woman was over-programming me to death. But if I were being honest, I was grateful for it.

"The lease is finalized," she said in her latest missive.

She'd taken it upon herself to negotiate it, thank heaven, since I'd been busy trying to find a tenant for this place. I'd been tempted to sell the two-bed, forties-built, un-updated pile of memories until I realized I'd be letting go of an anchor to my hometown. It was close enough to the University that it had been a snap to rent. My mom was going to act as landlord and manager, which meant she'd be showering whoever lived here with homemade cookies and pies and letting Stella handle anything remotely confrontational.

Not a bad system. I was lucky to have them.

I answered Sloane, and within two hours, we had my entire house packed away, ready for removal, for relocation, for the change I thought I wanted but for the army of butterflies whamming around in my guts. I skipped the pizza Stella had ordered, unable to fathom putting food into my roiling stomach. As I was tossing the boxes and napkins into a spare trash bag, I realized… This was it.

I froze, staring at the bare kitchen, a place I'd once loved to linger over coffee in the mornings.

"I'll be here first thing with food and coffee," my mom said, giving me a tight hug and trying not to cry. I knew because she and I made the same face when that happened. She sniffled and waved me away when I tried to tell her I'd be fine, we'd be fine, all would be fine.

I wasn't quite sure I believed it anyway.

Stella grabbed her as she was headed to the door and wrapped us both up in a third hug-it-out layer.

"Okay, I can't breathe," I said after a few seconds. "Let go already. You're coming up to see me in a month, remember?"

We stood in the small foyer, sniveling.

"Go," I said, wrenching open the door. "I can't stand y'all another second."

They left. I stood on the wide, wood-planed front porch and watched until their taillights were no longer visible.

****

It took the four moving guys less than an hour to load my paltry belongings into the back end of their massive moving truck. When they'd opened it and said they already had one household packed and my stuff would balance their load, I was skeptical, but it all fit like a furniture and box puzzle. They slammed the doors shut. I stood on the lawn, watching as they drove away.

"Okay," I said, turning to face Mom and Stella who were shoulder-to-shoulder, their eyes brimming with tears. "God damn it. Y'all sent me out to that stupid event in Colorado to find a job. So I did. Stop making this harder than it already is. I'll see you in…" I glanced at my phone. "Three weeks, okay? I'll have plenty of room. The dang apartment I found is bigger than this house."

I busied myself, pretending to check all the rooms to make sure I hadn't left anything behind. As if I'd do that. I stood in the middle of my empty bedroom, smelling my life disappearing from the space. Someone else would live here and, hopefully, make a better go of it than I had. Plus, they'd be covering the mortgage payment so bonus points to me.

I swiped at my face and squared my shoulders. Moving on. That was what was demanded here. And move on, I would. I had a solid six and some change hour drive ahead of me. Sloane said she'd meet me at the apartment tonight with dinner. I was covered. I had to get going.

The tears surprised me with their ferocity. I'd gone for so many years biting them back, unwilling to shed even the angry kind, it was as if these last few months had torn down the floodgates. I sat in the middle of my empty bedroom in the back of my empty house, about to move my empty life, and cried like a toddler in need of a nap.

"Oh, honey." Stella sat on the floor with me, arm around my shoulders until I had myself under control.

"God, I don't know where that came from," I said, using a bit of toilet tissue I'd left in the bathroom to clean up. I stared at my image in the bathroom mirror.

"*You are gorgeous.*" James' voice wafted through my brain, unwanted and, yet, comforting. Not that it mattered. I was obviously off his radar. And no wonder, given what a glorious, delicate, dessert blossom I'd been, coming at him like a spider monkey—a drunk, horny spider monkey.

"Where's Mom?"

"She left already. I told her to go. That I'd get your tail in the car and pointed in a northerly direction." She pulled my hair up and used the ponytail holder on her wrist to corral it for me. "So...this is me, getting you in the car and pointin' you in a northerly direction."

I turned to face her. "I'm sorry, Stell. I've been a bad friend."

She shrugged. "Sometimes. But so have I."

I nodded. "Yeah. Sometimes." I gave her a fierce hug. "You take care of yourself, okay?"

"Oh, you know me, hon. I've got plenty of time and ex-husband money to spend."

"Right. Okay. This is me, really going this time."

Chapter Eleven

It was odd having Sloane hover my first week. I'd never gone out of my way to make adult women friends. Stella and I had grown up together. She'd left for two years of college, during which she achieved her stated degree, that of M.R.S. to a R.B.T.—Rich Banker Type. He'd been husband number one of course. She was grooming number three—a neurosurgeon no less—best I could tell, but she was always a little cagey with me when it came to the men in her life.

Sloane VanAnsel was in a different league altogether. She had a Master's in business administration, same one I almost got, but that was where our similarities ended. In undergrad, she'd been president of her sorority, played club volleyball, graduated with a four point, the works. She was the only child of a big-time, wealthy couple who doted on her, she insisted, to the point of absolute smothering, which was why she'd bolted for Chicago three days after her graduation brunch.

We did some late-night bonding the first week, over wine or beer and various forms of carry-out. By the end of the week, I was bloated and nervous and certain I never saw her put a bite of food into her mouth. She gave me the low-down on what I was walking into, pulling no punches about the old-boys-ass-slapping network she was trying to help shake up by adding me and one other woman to the sales team.

"Where's your office?" I'd asked the first night when I'd been inhaling pad Thai while she sipped her wine.

"Don't really have one," she'd said. "I sort of, I don't know, float, I guess. I'm still consulting a couple of clients in Chicago, so I try to get over there…some."

Her face flushed. I swallowed the Michael Burke question. I'd decided to pretend neither he nor his brother existed.

The next night, we shopped for my apartment together. I was loath to spend too much, but I needed a couple of decent lamps, a shower curtain for the second bathroom, and more cleaning supplies, so I pulled out my precious plastic, mentally adding up every item she would toss into my cart without a second thought.

"Listen," I said after a set of two hundred dollar sheets found their way into the melee. "I can't afford these, but thanks for the recommendation."

She frowned but stopped doing the shopping for me. By the time we made it to the checkout, I'd given in to her insistence on throw pillows "for ambiance" and a new duvet cover in addition to the items I needed. We chatted more about the workplace I was scheduled to join the next day over some sour beers—one of their repped products—and falafels that night. Or rather, I ate a pita full of falafels and half a container of hummus with crunchy vegetables while she played with the wine-shaped beer bottle.

"You should know a few things about the Burkes," she said out of the clear blue sky, startling me and making me almost drop my glass.

"Oh? And why is that?"

She sighed and stretched out on the floor. We'd taken to eating at the coffee table, sitting on the floor instead of the perfectly good, if small, dining room table. But I didn't mind. I was starting over, remember? All new Andi. And so what if the new Andi ate sitting on her living room floor? It felt glamorous, somehow. Even if Sloane never ate a dang bite.

I observed her in all her glamorous glory on my fake Turkish rug. She was and would probably always be the only grown woman I knew who could pull off leggings in the way they were meant to be. The navy-blue pair she had on now were the super expensive brand, the one with the symbol like the Greek letter omega. I could never say the name right. They were ankle length and when she lay flat, with her arms behind her head, her hipbones stuck up so much she looked skeletal. But I wasn't in a place to give lifestyle advice, so I kept my opinion to myself.

"Do you know the history?"

"Of what? Burke? No. I don't." I gathered up my detritus and poured us another helping of the famous Belgian style brew.

She kept her gaze trained upward to my rotating ceiling fan. I tried not to be jealous of her slender frame, her perfect make-up, her well-pampered feet with their pink painted toenails. She was my friend and had been nothing but helpful to me so far.

"Their dad, Carter, and his brother, Jeff, founded it, in nineteen ninety-seven when all the famous craft breweries were getting started."

I leaned against the couch, complete now with its ambiance-lending throw pillows and my mom's favorite, red and cream-colored quilt. Cradling my glass to my chest, letting the beer warm, which would release the more complex flavors rendered by the ancient, open fermentation process, I settled in for some Sloane-level tale-telling.

"Jeff was the brewer, like James is now. Carter was the business manager and the money. Or rather, his wife, Amelia was—is—the money. She's a Belanger. They're one of those old furniture money families. She's a straight up country-club, tennis whites, gin for lunch kind of lady."

"Hmm." I closed my eyes, determined not to give a damn about this family or their gin-sloppy mama. And of course, unable to stop…giving a damn, that was.

"Those original Burke brothers did everything right, up to and including finding the right distributor. My father and his brothers were converting over from soda and wine to wine and beer when the craft craze began. I'm talking late nineties, early two-thousands. They glommed on to Carter and Jeff, along with all the Grand Rapids area locals who are big names now."

I nodded. I knew all these names. But Burke's products hadn't hit Kentucky as hard and fast as the others. Hence, I wasn't as familiar with it, although the name held plenty of cache amongst beer know-it-alls such as myself.

"Jeff died young of a massive heart attack. He keeled over on the brewing floor when he was in his mid-fifties."

"Wow," I said. "I had no idea."

"Yeah, so by this time, James was in Germany at the Brewing Institute. He didn't even come home for the funeral, which was odd, since Jeff and James had been super close. Loved to brew together, all of the above." She sighed and lifted both her legs straight up into the air, then bent at the waist, and dropped her legs until her toes touched behind her head. "I already told you about Michael. He didn't want to have anything to do with the brewery, mostly because he despised his father. I mean, I'm talking serious hate."

Her voice was pinched. Not surprising, considering the yoga pretzel thing she was doing. "James ended up in Detroit three years later and jumped right in to work with his dad. He got married about that time. Michael had just graduated with his MBA from Northwestern." She executed some kind of awe-inspiring move I found hard to imagine, much less describe with her legs and arms. It kind of made me hurt to look at it.

"Suffice it to say, James' wife was hand-picked by Mama Belanger Burke. The wedding was in all the papers, a social event, two old money names, blah blah. I don't know. It's the sort of thing my parents want for me." She rolled her eyes. "It lasted seven years or so, I think. No kids. A seemingly amicable split but for the fact that the ex-Mrs. James Burke moved to California and married some tech ga-jillionaire. Gosh, when was that?"

She was upright now but had one leg bent back behind her and the other one bent out in front of her. I don't even know how. I looked away.

"Wow, not that long ago. I guess she and James split up in January of this year, and she was out with her new guy, having another fancy wedding in…June? Yes, June."

I blew out a breath. Mr. J. Burke was on the rebound, was he?

"Of course, by this time, the shit had really hit the

fan at the brewery."

I leaned forward. This was the part I needed to know. Why had James called it a cluster fuck and discouraged his brother from hiring me? I would have been a great fit for that job.

"There's all manner of rumors flying around. But the bottom line, I think, and my sources are pretty good, is Carter squandered a shit ton of the brewery's money setting up some kind of a separate brewing space. Expansion, he called it. He claimed he wanted to use the excess capacity for contract brewing, although not many breweries use contract services anymore. So anyway, he bought an empty auto supply factory and had it converted at enormous expense. Then he had James hire a bunch of new brewery staff and put them on a twenty-four-hour a day brew schedule. That's when the problems started."

"Bad oversight. Poor quality." I nodded and sipped, already feeling closer to James than I wanted, thanks to this unfolding soap opera.

"And how," Sloane said. Yoga moves complete for the day, she sat cross-legged and picked up her beer. "This is one of my favorite styles," she said, taking a long sniff then a quick drink, like a pro.

"It's a good one. Not my favorite, but close."

"Right, you're a hop head, right?"

"Kinda. I was for a lot of years until brewers went nutso with the hops, tossing them in by the pound and making their beer too astringent to drink. I'm a fan of the New England versions these days. Don't hate me." I pretended to shield myself from attack.

"NEIPAs are amazing phenomena. Really got a lot people into craft beer. I'd give anything if we repped

Traders'. Do you know Stacy? She invented that whole thing."

"I do know Stacy." I smiled and blushed, recalling the last time I'd said those words.

"I'd never diss a trend," Sloane said. "The only people who can afford that kind of smack-talk don't actually run businesses around beer."

"Truth." We sipped. I was dying for more Burke family gossip but wasn't about to ask lest I give away my core truth. I wanted to know everything I could about James and his family and his family's business.

"I asked Uncle Al to give you some of the better on-premise accounts," she said, startling me again. "But he's got to move a few things around first. Not sure when it'll happen."

"I, um…" Every inch of my skin flushed hot. "I mean, I don't want to rock the boat or anything."

"I said when I hired you I'd be using your coming on board as an excuse to clear out a couple of the dead weight guys. We can't afford to keep carrying them. Uncle Al knows. He just doesn't like firing people."

"It's not easy to do. I speak from real life experience."

"I know you do." She sipped, then set the glass down. "Tell me about it, Andi."

I sighed and swirled my beer, trying to decide what, if anything, I wanted to share with her.

"I mean, you know, when you're ready." She jumped up and started putting away her uneaten meal.

"I'm sorry. It's just…"

"No, no, it's fine. I'm sorry. I'm too direct sometimes. I think everyone wants to spill their guts the same way I do."

Guilt filled my chest. Sloane took my glass. "Don't feel bad. You asked me about Michael and I told you. I don't mind talking about him. Especially now. Since it's over." She poured the remaining beer, then handed the glass back to me. "We're strong women. People misunderstand us, you know? Call us bitches when we're only trying to get shit done. It's hard to win in this business."

"I do know." And I did. How I'd managed to save this chick from a man I considered an evil asshole was anyone's guess. She did not strike me as someone who required saving. "You're okay? With it being over, I mean?"

She shrugged and resumed her position on the other side of my scarred coffee table. "What are my options?" Her gaze flickered. Her smile faded. She wasn't okay. But like she said, what were her options?

My admiration for her ramped up higher. "I'm okay, too. I mean, I still feel like I got double divorced. From my marriage *and* my life—or rather, my bar, which was my life." I sighed. Sloane stayed quiet so I kept going. "I loved Matt. I had it bad. I'm talking worship of the ground he walked on, at least some part of my life. Partly because I couldn't imagine what he saw in me. He wasn't romantic. If anything he was an anti-romantic. But we had a good life. Or so I believed."

Tears threatened. I fought them and won.

"I don't miss Matt. Not one bit. But the bar…" I bit my lip. "Those stupid four walls, with its never-ending employee drama, kitchen craziness, promotional strategy nightmares, clogged sewer lines, double booked bands. *That* I miss."

"It's a hard life, running a restaurant."

"It was. I resisted having a full kitchen at first until I was forced to accept the only way I'd expand my customer base was opening for lunch and dinner and, eventually, the bane of all restaurant workers' existence, the dreaded Sunday brunch. Holy cow, those people were awful. But we did it. Every Sunday. Full Bloody Mary bar, a singer with a guitar in the corner, the works. To this day, if anyone suggests I go anywhere near a Sunday brunch, I'll poke their eyeballs out with my bare fingers."

"Bummer. I like brunch."

I rolled my eyes. "Yeah, well, it's not breakfast. It's not lunch. It's both. Plus it's an excuse for rookies to day drink. A bad combination all the way 'round."

"I've made a note never to ask you to brunch."

I smiled. "Yes, please and thanks." I sucked in a long breath. "I'm nervous about tomorrow."

"Don't be," she said, finishing her beer with a loud smack of her lips. "You're gonna kill it. You're the best damn hire I've ever made. Remember, you report to Al. He's my uncle. A super nice guy, maybe a little too nice, too easy. And you should know I am totally grooming you for his job."

I watched her make her way into the kitchen, dump her uneaten food into the trash, rinse her glass, and put it in the dishwasher. My new place was no Buckingham Palace, but it was in a half-decent suburb of Grand Rapids, a thirty-minute commute in rush hour, Sloane claimed. And it had two bathrooms. I hadn't had two bathrooms in my entire life. Too bad there was only one of me, now.

Nope. Nope. And N.O.P.E. Pity parties forbidden.

Even the private ones in your head.

When I joined her in the kitchen, Sloane was staring down at her phone screen. Her arrow straight black hair hid her face, but when she swept it back, her face was red, her lips pressed together in a thin line.

"Let me guess," I said as I put my glass in the dishwasher. "Michael Burke requests your attention." I didn't care what she did, but I did care that she looked completely wrecked, when she'd been so funny, strong, not to mention super flexible, a mere half hour ago.

Men. They were experts at turning strong women into mush, weren't they?

She leaned against the kitchen counter.

"Do what you want to do, Sloane. If you want to talk to the man, talk to him. What's so wrong with—"

"You don't understand," she snapped. "Sorry. I…I have a headache."

No wonder. You've eaten the caloric equivalent of three cherry tomatoes today.

But I held my tongue. I was doing the same thing I'd done when Stella was in her super skinny stage—overcompensating by eating for both of us. Not a great plan if I wanted to fit into my new work wardrobe.

"Our dynamic is hard to explain," Sloane said. "We, um… We're kind of good and bad for each other at the same time. I don't know how else to describe it."

"I only have one question at this delicate stage of our nascent friendship." I leaned against the sink, our shoulders touching. "This private club, where you guys met. Is it one of those, um, you know…"

She smiled, and at that moment, she was hands down the most beautiful woman in the universe, even with the extra sharp cheekbones and thin neck. If I'd been inclined, I would have kissed her.

I wasn't, though. So I didn't. "Well?"

Her smile turned wicked and her blue eyes sparkled. "It's not BDSM if that's what you mean. It's more like a club where really rich guys take other really rich guys, and sometimes their dates, to drink, talk, make deals, and see the classiest strip show in town. There's a huge bar, great service, classic cocktails, top shelf wine and beer."

My mouth must have been hanging open because she reached out and pushed my chin up until my lips met. "Don't be so shocked. It's pretty common."

"You were…a stripper?" My voice was squeaky. I cleared my throat. "I mean, I get giving a big old up yours to your annoying parents, but still…"

She didn't even blush. "No, I was the date of one of the rich guys. Actually, my PR company sent me with him. We were trying to get him to move his company's business to us. He was really good-looking, too." She gazed out into the middle distance. "Boring as hell, though. I met Michael that night. We, ah, hit it off, right away, if you get me."

"I do get you," I said, fanning my face. "But sheesh, you sure are shocking this hayseed country girl with your big city stripper club talk."

"It was an amazing few months. He was trying so hard not to be an asshole, like he had been doing for so long with other women. And I…I gave him a hell of a hard time. I mean, when we weren't fucking our brains out. Which we did, a lot." She glanced at her phone again. "Then it got complicated. I didn't want to continue it, and once he figured out I hadn't told him my real last name…" She shrugged. "He was pissed. I don't blame him. Anyway, it's over."

"Something tells me it's not," I said, busying myself with my already tidy kitchen.

She didn't reply.

"Will you be around in the morning? I mean, when I get there?" I tried to keep the tremor out of my voice.

She was smiling at her phone again. I snatched it from her, surprised at my cheek but going with the whole we're-strong-chicks-sticking-together thing.

"Hey," she protested but only a little.

I looked at the screen. It took me a minute to figure out what I was looking at. But when I did, I handed it straight back to her, my face white-hot. Her lips were twitching with amusement at my reaction to the sight of Michael Burke's erect willy.

"Impressive," I said. "But dick pics? Really?"

"Yeah, it is." She grinned. "He only did it because I dared him. We're all kinds of fucked up. I don't know why I can't let go of him."

"Well, I see one reason why not. Some things speak for themselves."

She blushed. We giggled like teenagers.

"Wanna see it again?" She pulled out her phone again.

"Nope. No, thanks. I'm good. Yep. Seen enough." I held up both hands. "I'm pretty sure it's gonna remain etched on my retinas for my lifetime. Whew. Lordy."

"You sound Southern again."

"Yeah, it's the beer and horrified shock at seeing your man's peen. To be expected."

"I'm gonna go."

"It's for the best, I think."

We giggled our way to the door.

Chapter Twelve

Four Weeks Later

"Morning," a male voice said.

I smiled in its general direction.

"Hi Andi," another one called out.

I nodded.

"Hey there, Red," yet another one said. I ignored him. I'd made it clear Red wasn't my name, but this particular old-timer got away with it no matter how many times I complained. It, and the not-so-low-level sexual innuendo that washed through every sales meeting and most every encounter I had with my colleagues, was getting way, way old.

"Oh, hey Andi, can you come to my office a second?" This voice made me pay attention. It was the one belonging to my boss, Mr. Al VanAnsel, brother to Grant, who was father to Sloane, my unexpected new friend.

I followed my boss out of the break room where I'd been reading the news on my phone and drinking coffee, pondering the day ahead. I suffered the random killer glares, rude gawking, the various and sundry BS I'd come to know as normal for my working life as a sales rep for VanAnsel Distribution. I managed fine, although some days it wore me down to the point where I had to take an hour-long shower and self-medicate with a bottle of wine and a pint of super expensive gelato.

There was no hiding the fact I'd flat out taken accounts from a couple of their former colleagues. Never mind I wasn't the one who'd fired them or hadn't done the crappy job they'd done to deserve getting their asses canned. In short, I was still the target of a fair bit of vitriol from a lot of guys. It manifested in subtle ways. I wasn't openly harassed. But the way they'd decided to assimilate me involved unapologetic, ribald language. Plenty of dick jokes, in other words, plus a whole hell of a lot of unnecessary discussion about their sex lives—or lack thereof.

I complained once to Al. If I said a word about it to Sloane, she'd be all over it, but I'd decided to give these guys some time to get their need to prove something out of their collective system. Then I would holla to HR, big time. Because I liked the job when I wasn't in the VanAnsel building.

I'd jumped right into the groove, channeling what I liked and avoiding what I despised when I had received beer and wine rep visits. I was great at reading body language. Years of bartending experience hadn't hurt. I'd already impressed a lot of people and had positive placements one month on the job.

None of this endeared me to my fellows. But if they didn't get it through their heads I wasn't going to be intimidated by them, they were working on borrowed time.

"Have a seat," Al said, gesturing to the two cushy leather chairs opposite his desk.

I sat, my mind already skipping ahead to my long list of calls. Truth be told, I was having a blast, chatting up store managers, beer and wine buyers, bartenders, parlaying my own low-level celebrity status to prove to them I knew what I was talking about. The few times I'd been rejected, it had been with a caveat to come back in a week or two, when they had an open tap or more shelf space.

I had this thing. I was *all* about it. Thoughts of James had faded to the point I thought I might even be able to forget him or at least ramp down my obsession level.

If only the guy hadn't been such a good kisser.

Sloane had been absent since my first day. She'd texted me that she had to be in Chicago for a week or two. But after a couple of days, I didn't stress about it. I got a handle on things, even if some mornings, when I had to play nice with the boys, it felt tenuous and irritating.

A spike of anxiety flickered in my chest when Al took a seat behind his desk. He usually sat in the chair next to me when we had discussions. This felt formal, ominous.

I sat up straighter and smoothed my skirt across my thighs. One thing I did regret was, being all power-suited meant I had to endure the girdle-slash-body shaping device torture every day.

I focused on my boss and prayed the boy's club hadn't gone behind my back and started making up a bunch of lies. Although I wouldn't put it past them.

"I had a call from James Burke yesterday," he said.

I blinked fast, sure my overheated imagination had forced these odd words from his mouth. "Oh?" I managed a voice break in this one syllable.

"It would appear that he wants to sell with you. Today."

"But…I'm not… Burke's not…" I slumped back in the chair.

"You know, we like to keep our top suppliers happy."

I sat, speechless, my pulse doing a loud dance in my ears. On autopilot, I took a quick assessment of what I was wearing. I'd forgotten to pick up my dry cleaning after a long day on the road, so I'd had to do the fabric softener trick with a stale silk blouse, plus the suit I'd dragged out the closet was missing a skirt button, and I was about half convinced the jacket had a stale beer stain on it I'd forgotten to deal with.

Ugh. Yeah. I reeked. It hadn't mattered much when I knew I only had a few stops this morning, plus a crap ton of computer time and paperwork in the afternoon. It was a tight day. I had zero time to accommodate this…this…intrusion. This demand from above.

Anger shimmered around my consciousness. My skin was all tight and tingly. That burny sensation was flaring in my chest. Confusion made my vision wonky. I took a shaky breath and focused on Al as he worked to accommodate James' demand. He'd really knocked over a whole set of dominos with this nonsense today.

I looked up at the ceiling. I was going to see James again. He was going to be in the car with me, for the better part of the day, selling with me, chatting, in close proximity to my stale, smelly, anxious self.

I turned my phone over and tapped out a quick text to Sloane. —*I'm selling with James today. His idea. Or demand. Or whatever.*—

She was quick to respond. —*WTF?*—

I smiled. I loved this girl, I swear it. She was like a prettier, scrawnier version of me.

—*IKR*— I typed out. —*Just thought you'd like to know.*—

—*I'm back in GR*— she said. —*Spending the day on myself. Chicago was a shit show.*—

—*Ok.*— I wondered what someone as rich as she was did when spending a day on herself. I'm sure I couldn't begin to imagine it. I put the phone on my lap. My hands were shaking. I clenched them both into fists and rested them on my legs, waiting to see what happened next.

"Hi, James!"

I looked up, alarmed at Al's loud tone. I gripped the chair arms, closed my eyes, and counted the seconds.

One. Two. Three…

"Al! Great to see you again."

Holy crap on a cracker.

He was here.

For real.

Al was staring at me funny. I licked my lips, took another long breath, and rose.

"And there she is," James said. "The superstar saleswoman herself."

I held out my arms. "Here I am. You should know you've thrown a monkey wrench into my day, James."

He shrugged and jammed his hands into his pockets. He was wearing a pair of dark indigo jeans and a long-sleeved, button-down Burke labeled shirt with knife-edge creases in both arms. His hair looked damp. His beard was trimmed close. His green eyes danced with amusement at my obvious displeasure.

I drew myself up, lifted my chin, and met his gaze. "But, you know, I'm flexible. Al, we all set?"

"Yep. Here you go." He handed me a printout of Burke products we had in stock.

I took it and crossed my arms, keeping my gaze on James who hadn't moved from his position in the doorway. "I hope those samples of Common and the brown ale are good ones, not that shit you guys were peddling earlier this year."

"Touché. And no. I bought all of it back and destroyed it. You have nothing but fresh product. Plus, I have a surprise." He produced a Burke labeled cooler from out in the hall. "You'll never guess what I've been working on."

Al and I watched as he opened the lid and pulled out a growler emblazoned with the Burke logo. He held it up, Vanna White style with a wide grin.

"My very own New England IPA. A small batch to be certain, but something we could use to tempt our more recalcitrant accounts?" He put the growler near his face, keeping up his showman charade.

I tried not to smile at him. "Great. Okay. Let's get started. I have a whole afternoon's worth of paperwork to do today once I'm done with you."

James put the growler away. I brushed past him, irritated beyond belief but, of course, at the same time shivery all over at the thought of being around him. I was grinning like a goofball when I hit the warehouse and started loading the four Burke Brothers products we sold the most into my cooler, dumped in ice, and turned to face two of my jerkier colleagues.

"Nice work," Rick said.

"Thanks," I said. "Have a good one."

"You're just a newb," the other one—Calvin—insisted.

"I realize that, Calvin. You have a swell day, now. Take those orders." I gave him a soft punch in the arm. I was done letting these creeps try to mess with me. They could take their rent-free, he-man-woman-hating club and hold meetings elsewhere. I was ejecting them from my head.

I was going to sell with James today.

Get a grip, Andrea Rose. This is nothing. He only wants to...

What?

I stared down at the printer in the large room that served as our group office. It was spitting out the day's orders for the warehouse staff. Deflated, I dropped into a nearby chair, not caring if James was wondering what had happened to me. He had manipulated this whole thing, this "selling day." I was, once again, letting my life be determined by some guy.

No, it's not like that, I insisted to my inner feminist. *I can enjoy his company and still crush the dang patriarchy in this place.*

Hell, Al handing me, the "new girl," one of the biggest stars in the VanAnsel sky meant a lot. All I had to do was take it and run with it. Show him and all these jerks I knew exactly what I was doing in this job. I knew how to sell, when to sell, what to sell. I was no mere order taker.

Refreshed by the pep talk, I got up, made sure my tablet was configured correctly for the day, and headed out to face Mr. Burke and his New England IPA growler teaser. We'd use that all right, but only at one store I was thinking of. A guy who was susceptible to anything resembling brewery royalty-slash-rock stars. But who also needed a little more convincing to put

Burke products back on his shelves.

I had work to do. And I wasn't about to let James in my car with me all day distract me.

Much.

Okay, possibly a little.

"Ready?" I kept my tone light as I headed down the carpeted hallway between the warehouse and main offices.

James was still leaning in Al's doorway, chatting, which allowed me the observation that the man wore a pair of jeans well.

Stop it, Andi. Be business-like. That's all this is about.

He turned mid-conversation and smiled at me, which made me falter.

I recovered and breezed past him, tugging my cooler along behind me. "Let's get to it, Jimmy. We've got beer to sell." I didn't look back, but I'll admit I put a bit of sway in my hips on the way out the door.

He caught up with me by the time we got to the car. My third-hand Toyota was clean, and it ran okay, but it was, without a doubt, flirting with its use-by date. The trunk hinges squealed as I opened it, making me wince. When I reached down to grab my cooler, James was already lifting it. I waited until he placed his in there, alongside an expensive-looking leather messenger bag.

"I hope you brought some marketing materials." I pointed to the bag. "I don't have anything for you. If you'd bothered to give a girl some notice, maybe I could have. I mean, I know your pricing, but…"

I slammed the trunk shut. I was both re-aggravated and re-irritated by his presence. The fact was I'd gotten my life in order these past weeks and had plans for the coming ones that involved joining a yoga studio and solidifying my spot as a legit member of the sales force at this company. Him swooping in here today and upending everything, demanding to sell with me and not the guy who usually did, was already messing with my life and its turn-around plan on a lot of levels.

I didn't want to be excited about seeing him, being with him all day. I most definitely didn't want to acknowledge my excitement about his requesting to sell with me.

I was, of course, excited about both of those things.

He got into the passenger's seat. I started the car and entered the address of the first stop in my company phone, praying the beer buyer would be there today. Nothing to do now but get on with it.

I took my designer knock-off sunglasses from the console and slid them onto my face. It was a gorgeous Michigan October morning—sunny, bright blue sky, chilly enough for a jacket but not cold, not yet. Sloane had warned me that Michigan winters hit hard and lasted long, but there was no sign of it so far.

I looked at my selling buddy. He was looking at me. I sighed, happy my eyes were hidden, put the car in gear, and peeled out of the parking lot without a word.

Chapter Thirteen

Okay, here's the thing about selling beer. It's way more convoluted than it should be. It involves a middleman, something that has been the law of the land since the repeal of Prohibition. Which, as we all know, was the Great Failed Social Experiment that gave us Blind Pigs, Speakeasies, and huge, powerful, conglomerate breweries, many of which made ice cream or pottery during those supposed off years.

In short, the government believed keeping innocent Americans safe from the evil purveyors of the devil's juice was crucial. Hence the three-tier system of distribution was born.

Breweries, wineries, and in some states, distilling companies sold their products to wholesalers, a.k.a. distributors like VanAnsel, who in turn spent their days finding placements for said poison at both "off-premise"—grocery and package stores—and "on-premise"—bars and restaurants—locations.

It meant more jobs. It also created a natural animosity between producers and sellers. No brewery or winery ever believed their precious liquid was represented fairly by any distributor. The salespeople at which had way more than one company to represent. Now, thanks to the relative success of a few good craft breweries, everybody's uncle's cousin's best friend from college who brewed a few batches in their kitchen believed they'd be the next famous big deal brewery. Which meant we had way more product to sell than shelf space or tap handles to put them on.

In my former position as manager slash beer and wine buyer slash chief toilet cleaner at BWI, I was in the best space possible in this three-tier arrangement. I was the end user. The decider. The one with the checkbook who would, or would not, purchase entire kegs or cases based on my knowledge about my drinking audience. I'd taken a few chances on some new companies and had about a seventy-thirty record when it came to selling the stuff at my bar. But the more these reps came at me with their new breweries and bizarre new brews, the harder that record was to maintain.

I understood the pain all beer buyers experienced when they spotted me coming through their doors, trip-tripping in my fancy high heels and selling suits, tugging my ubiquitous cooler, ready to sell, sell, sell!

I developed a unique style, based on my experience on the other side of the equation, leaning into "*what* is selling now?" and away from "you *need* to sell this now!" So far, it was working. But then again, I hadn't gained much traction with Burke's products yet. Having Mr. Burke himself riding around and selling with me might be the sales boost I needed. Of course, there was that stumble Burke Brothers had taken—those bad batches James himself bought back. No small expense for them, and something breweries rarely, if ever, did.

Oh, the whole "buying back" thing was confusing. The wholesaler or distributor, i.e. VanAnsel, pays the brewery for product up front. Real money was already spent on every ounce of booze sitting in their warehouse. It behooved them to get the stuff sold, and fast, at a serious markup. And the end user, i.e. used to be me at BWI, also added their mark up.

So the beer customers enjoy? It had been sold twice over before they got their mitts on it. In other words, it was twice removed from the people who actually made it. Thanks to government oversight and a need to tax the living hell out of it coming and going.

"So what happened, I mean, with the crappy batches?"

We sat at an intersection where traffic was backed up way more than usual. I glanced at James. He had one hand balled in a fist on his thigh, the other one gripping his phone. His expression, as he stared at the thing, was an odd combination of stressed and flat out furious.

Well, too effing bad. He'd put this day in motion, not me.

I waited, tapping my fingertips on the cracked leather steering wheel.

"I'm sorry, what did you say?" he asked.

Determined not to reveal my irritation, I kept my voice level. "I was wondering what happened to the Common and the brown ale, you know...the bad batches."

He blew out a breath and looked at the roof of my car, no doubt taking in the clever duct tape repair of ripped fabric. "Um..." He ran a hand through his hair, making it stand up funny and forcing me to bite the inside of my cheek not to reach over and smooth it. "My father..." He sounded choked.

The traffic inched forward. I inched with it.

"It was Carter's fault," James said after a few silent seconds. "He'd been brewing it in some facility he'd set up, not at our production brewery."

"Oh," I said. I knew some of this, thanks to the Sloane News Update I'd received. I made a mental note to text her later with this bombshell addition. The shitty beers that had cost them in ingredients and labor up front and then twice as much to purchase back only to pour them down the drain—thousands of gallons—had been brewed at the strange facility James and Michael's father had bought and outfitted on the sly. Weird.

"What other facility?" I kept my eyes forward. I had a terrible poker face. He would have figured out in a hot second I already knew about it if I'd been facing him.

"The one in Southfield." He said this as if he already knew I knew. I risked a glance. He was frowning at me. "Sloane knows about it so I assume you do, too. I'm surprised it didn't make VanAnsel's employee newsletter."

The traffic moved again. I focused on inching a few feet ahead as if I were engaging in micro-neurosurgery. My neck and face flamed, giving me away.

"Anyway, it doesn't matter. Michael and I are on top of things now."

"Well, that's good."

The interior of my car filled with tension so thick I could feel it coating my face, pressing against my chest. I decided to let go of the topic. "I'm not sure we'll be able to meet with the right people today. I kept my original schedule but added three extra stops for your products. Two of them took all your beer off their lists, and I haven't convinced them to add you back. I hope the owners are there since at these two places, they make their own beer selections."

"Great. Do I know them?"

"I don't know if you know them, but you will, after today." I took another quick peek at him. He was staring at his phone screen again. His face had gone an alarming shade of red. "Are you okay?"

"What?" He met my gaze and made a concerted effort to change his expression, to erase the stress, to seem, if not happy, at least not about to bust an aneurism. "Oh, yeah, I'm fine. Sorry. Just…you know, owning a business." He made a show of turning his phone over and putting it on his leg. "I'm sorry. I'm being rude."

I pressed my lips together. "I'd rather you be honest. I need to know if there're problems I'll have to deal with downstream."

At that moment, the traffic scrum broke free, so I scooted through the intersection before the lights changed again.

"Tell me about our first stop," James said.

"Don't change the subject."

"I'm not. I'm focusing on the day's work."

"Fine." I pulled into the parking lot of the semi-luxury grocery store, a chain founded in Michigan that had done successful expansion into contiguous states. It was a crucial placement and one I'd been cultivating for the last three weeks. Careful conversations, "stopping by to say hey and drop off something new for you to try no pressure," style of establishing my bona fides as the one-time owner of a famous beer bar turned sales grunt—that sort of thing.

"Don't mess this up for me," I warned as I gathered my work phone, tablet, and the sell sheets I'd created for the beers I planned to sell today.

"I wouldn't dream of it." His voice was calm, his face no longer beet red. He pulled sell sheets from the bag at his feet. "Let's do this, partner."

I caught myself before I rolled my eyes, matched his smile, and got out.

Two-and-a-half hours later, I pulled into a new restaurant that had opened in the suburbs. Our last two stops were the most crucial. But I needed refueling.

"Let's eat while we're here," I said. "And it's on you. That's ride-along etiquette."

"Good call. I'm starving."

I grabbed some promo packets I'd made featuring a few new products. This place struck me as a "craft beer lite" kind of place, ripe for ciders, shandies, and other gateway styles, two of which I could easily provide. I'd never been here but had been trolling the local papers for new places to visit and had spotted this one. I hadn't planned to stop here today, but since lunch was on Burke Brothers, I decided I needed a cheeseburger.

Plus, I wanted to pick James' brain about what was going on over at his brewery. It was obvious there was a crisis he was trying to manage from afar, if his attention to his phone was any indication. I figured we'd have a beer and a meal and he'd spill it.

We sat at the bar and took the menus and water that were provided to us by a smiling young woman. She did a triple take, which I figured was for the hunky beer rock star at my side.

"Wow. Are you...I mean...sorry. I'm not trying to stare," she said.

I kept my focus on the menu. It was the typical mix of basics—burgers, club sandwiches, Caesar salads, upcharge for proteins. They had decent vegetarian and vegan selections, too, something that was becoming more a requirement and less about popularity. I scanned the beer list, noting our biggest competitor, Trident Distribution, had a lock on their taps with a bunch of beers I wished we had. Interesting.

When I felt a poke in my side, I startled. "What?"

James jerked his chin toward the woman who was still standing in front of us.

Confused, I frowned at him.

His grin widened. "You have a fan."

"I have a…what?"

"I'm sorry. I don't mean to bug you at lunch. But are you Andi Rigby?"

I turned to look at the bartender. I heard the lilt of her accent at the same moment I realized she wasn't ga-ga over James Burke. She was ga-ga over…me.

"Yes, I am. Have we met?" I held out my hand.

She shook it, and her face lit up. "Actually, yes. I used to live in Louisville, and my boyfriend, Travis, worked for you. We were there a lot."

"Oh, right," I said, recognition washing over me. "I'm sorry. You're Jennifer, Jen, right? It's strange seeing you out of context. My bad."

"It's okay. I'm so happy to see you again. You… I mean, we heard what happened." Her lips turned downward, and her eyes dimmed. "That sucked. He was an asshole."

I held up a hand. "Yes, well, it did. And he is. But it's over now, and I'm here."

I was doing everything I could to quell the onrushing angry, burny sensations. Whenever I was faced with my past, confronted or slapped upside the head, or as they say now "triggered" by anything that reminded me of where I'd been relative to where I was now, it flared up, filling my chest and throat with regret.

"Right," Jen said, perking up and reading my signal loud and clear to drop the subject. "So, welcome to Grand Rapids. What can I pour for you?"

I smiled. "I'll have…" I squinted at the list again.

"We'll have the Traders Haze, please," James said, taking the list out of my hand.

"Hey!"

"Calm down. I know you wanted one."

"You know what they say about telling someone to calm down, right?" I sipped water while Jen got our beers. He was right of course. But I wasn't about to let him know that.

The beers were sublime, a perfect match for the giant grilled chunk of cow flesh coated with a slab of melted Wisconsin cheddar I ordered for my lunch. James ordered the same. We chatted with Jen until she had to go manage other customers.

"So," I said, leaning on my elbow and looking at my date for the day. "I want to know more about this secret facility of yours."

James frowned into his beer. "Hell, Andi, that's old news. There's a lot more to worry about now."

"Oh?" Intrigued but also more than a little worried about him and his blood pressure, I waited for the follow-up details.

"Yeah." He ran a hand down his face, picked up his glass and drained it, then set it down with a loud thunk.

Jen turned her head at the sound to register the

empty. Impressed, I watched her finish with the three guys she'd been serving, then make her way down to us. She smiled at James. He smiled back. A lick of jealousy hit the center of my brain.

"I'll have the Golden Lager this time," he said. "Traders."

"You know Stacy?" Jen asked him as she took his empty and turned to fill a fresh glass.

"Yep."

I sighed. We all knew Stacy. I was about to propose we all go visit her, since Traders Brewing Company was only an hour away to the west. Jen put the beer down in front of James with an extra sparkle in her eyes. Or so I thought.

Not that it mattered to me. He was allowed to flirt with as many bartenders as he liked. And flirt he did. They chatted about Stacy, about Burke's new efforts to concoct a New England IPA, the works. She was a pro, Jen was. By the time she had to rip herself away from the handsome man at my side, I was experiencing a strange sensation that I eventually identified as seething. It wasn't pretty.

Our food arrived via a kitchen runner. "Dig in," I said, not looking at him. "We have to make an appointment in about forty minutes."

"My brother wants to sell us," James said out of the clear blue sky.

Once I decided I wasn't going to choke to death on an inhaled French fry, I grabbed his arm, re-aware of the firm musculature of his biceps. Dang this dude was amazing.

But no, that wasn't why I'd touched him.

"Holy crap," I squeaked and let go of him.

143

"Yeah, that about sums it up," he said, turning his full pint glass around on the coaster.

Unsure what to say, what to ask first, I took a sip of my beer. James' food sat in front of him, going cool and uneaten. "You're not doing it, right?"

He sighed and looked at me. I had to work harder than ever not to touch his face, to smooth his sticking-up hair, to do something, anything to ease the unhappiness. "I don't know. I mean, I always thought I wanted to break from Burke. To go off and brew funky, sour, old ales and not sweat about who bought them. But when those bad batches came through, it opened this giant Pandora's box of shit I couldn't deal with by myself so I made Michael come help me. He's been great, if a bit of a hard-ass. But now?" He shrugged, picked up a fry, then put it back down. "I can't help but think the work we've been doing together this past year and a half has been nothing but a way for him to position the company for this—for a buyout. And I don't want that. Not anymore."

That was the other thing happening, daily, it seemed. There were so many tasty little morsels of small breweries with great products and no money to find a niche for them, bigger breweries were moving in, sniffing around and snapping them up with, at times, obnoxious amounts of money for the lucky owners. To date, only one of the bigger Michigan breweries had done this, but they'd been smart and spun it as a partnership, done to gain access to said big brewery's national distribution networks.

It was a new trend and one that had craft beer purists flaming hot. I never believed it my place to judge. I mean, these guys showed up at your door with six suitcases full of cash and the opportunity to use their well-established sales networks nationwide. Who in their right mind would turn it down?

I didn't hold to the popular-amongst-beer-snobs credo that once it happened, they could no longer touch your liquid because you'd "sold out." No one who'd ever actually run a business, sweated payroll, insurances, taxes, and more on a day-in-day-out basis would ever scoff at the offer of a massive cash infusion.

But I understood that partnering and selling were two different things. James had said "sell."

"That's what's so weird about it."

"Hmm?" I sipped and kept my opinions tight to my vest for the moment.

"I really wanted to quit. I was within days of bolting. I was sick of Carter and his tight-fisted, ignorant, grasping BS. We'd butted heads on so much for so long, I walked around with a constant headache. Once I figured out that my own father, the man who'd founded the brewery that had my name on the building had little or no interest in sustaining the high-quality standards his brother insisted on because it cost too much money, I was done. No lie."

"Huh. And how long ago was that?"

He stuck a fry in his mouth, chewed, swallowed. "Three years ago."

"You've worked with your dad how long?"

"Five years, almost six."

"That's a short honeymoon."

"Not with Carter Burke. He's a piece of work. Obsessed with turning as much profit as possible, slicing employee benefits not to mention employees. Why do you think we were at the job fair? We really do need a marketing director. Or I guess, I thought we did. I guess I don't know shit anymore." He had both hands clenched in fists, resting on either side of his plate.

"Is the food bad? I can bring another." Jen was back, leaning over the bar to give James a close look at her cleavage.

Oh God, stop it, Andi. The woman is just doing her job.

"No, no, sorry. I'm not as hungry as I thought I was." James pushed the plate toward her. They stared at each other long enough for me to clear my throat as a precursor to hitting them with a water hose.

"Well, y'all's tab is on me," pretty sexy Jen insisted, taking both our plates. Mine was almost empty, natch. Being the strong, healthy gal I was and all.

"Thanks," I said, glaring at James' profile.

He was watching the bartender as she made her way to the kitchen with an expression akin to a drowning man eyeballing the last lifeboat.

I sighed. I guess I'd had my shot at him in Colorado and I'd outdone myself, getting stinking drunk and making him have to pour me into my hotel room before he left.

When she returned, Jen handed us each her business card.

"Great to see you again, Andi," she said.

I smiled sweetly. "So, how's Travis doing?" I recalled they'd been together a while. As in they might be married by now.

"We broke up. He's still in Kentucky. I had to get the hell away from him. You know how that is, right?" Her grin matched mine. She patted James' hand. "Hope your day gets better."

"Yeah. Me, too." He ogled her a bit longer before turning to me.

"Is it a sale or some kind of a partnership?" I asked, determined not to let him drop the subject. I had less than zero business obsessing over James and his budding love life.

"A straight up sale. Diego Brothers and their consortium of breweries. They want the brand, the buildings, the equipment, all of it."

I whistled. Diego had gobbled up at least half a dozen breweries, but none of them as big or as much a part of the founding fathers group as Burke Brothers. "Do you think that was Michael's end game?"

"I don't know. I didn't think so. I mean, I was the one who asked him to come back to run the place. We forced Carter into retirement and took over the board of directors once the truth came out about his secret brewing facilities. That was a ton of fun. Jesus. Cost us almost a quarter of a mil in lawyers. But we managed it. Carter's out. He has ownership shares and zero voting ones. Our mother still votes, of course. She'll never let her shares go, and all the attorneys we paid told us not to try and dislodge her. She's entrenched. It was her money that started the whole thing, and she made sure the original articles of incorporation included her as board member for life."

I raised an eyebrow. This was more words strung together that had come out of his mouth than I'd yet heard. It was odd. And also, wonderful. His voice was low, melodious. I realized I'd been fixated on his lips, so full and lovely in the middle of that dark brown beard, a bit too late. He'd stopped talking.

I blinked fast and pretended I hadn't been staring at him and having sex fantasies about his lips.

Whew. Get a grip, sister. This man is not yours to ogle or fantasize about. And he's opening himself up, probably could use some advice.

"Anyway, Michael told me this morning, via text, the coward. I still don't know any more details than what I've told you, and if he knows I told you—a VanAnsel rep—he'd likely kill me anyway, so I guess you're gonna have to pinkie promise me you won't say anything." He propped his elbow on the bar and stuck out his little finger.

Surprised, but with a girlie thrill, I hooked mine into it. "Deal. Not my business anyway, right?" I tried to slide my finger out of his, but he held me in place.

"Hang on. We have to consummate this." He pulled our fingers close to his lips, kissed them, and grinned. "Go on. Your turn."

Embarrassed, I did the same, quickly, and tugged out of his grip. "You're a little strange," I said, but I heard the hitch in my voice.

"So I'm told."

I stood and was reaching for my bag so I could leave some stuff with Jen when he put his hand around my upper arm. Despite all my heroic efforts not to, I got all shaky at his touch. I truly must have been losing it. I should get myself laid, stat. As I was pondering this unlikely scenario, I realized he was pulling me closer to him.

"I wanted to see you again," he said, those fantasy-inducing lips close to my ear. "So much so, I drove out here and initiated this ride along. But I... You're... I don't know what I expected, but I get the feeling I've fucked it all up somehow."

"Let's start with you letting go of me. In case you missed the memo, it's no longer politically correct to go grabbing women you work with and whispering in their ears at lunch." I'd been glad-handed, rough-handled, and groped plenty in my working life. Up to and including the way Matthew Rigby had done the ultimate bait-and-switch with me. I'd lost too much, thanks to my inability to understand it when a man was doing something for me or something to me in order to help himself.

James frowned and let go of me. "Oh shit, I'm sorry. That was a total Michael move. Honestly, I usually don't…"

"It's fine. Chill. I just don't like to be, you know, manhandled, as it were." I sounded like a total priss, but I didn't care. It was the truth. Working for the past weeks in the testosterone hot pot at VanAnsel had made me more than a little prickly. My hands shook as I put the sell sheets on the bar. I took a long drink of water and gave the eager Jen a friendly wave, indicating I'd like her attention.

She trotted back to our end of the bar. "Can I get you anything else?"

She kept her focus on me, but I could sense the sizzly *thing* between her and James. We women have a sexual attraction radar built into our psyches.

"I wanted you to have these. You know, in case you ever have an open tap. No pressure."

She glanced down at the papers. "Oh, yeah. Sure! We could use a cider or two. I'll call you, okay?" The universal signal for "Don't sell to me. I'll let you know if I ever need anything but probably won't" was loud and clear.

"Gonna hit the head," James said.

Jen's gaze followed his oh-so-followable rear view as he made his way to the restrooms.

"Thanks so much for lunch and beers," I said to her. I felt her pain. Truly I did. We were compatriots, founding members of the James Burke Fan Club. I was determined not to see her as a rival.

I forced my smile wider. "Great to see you, hon." I patted her hand, the same way she had done to James, establishing my…what? My older female dominance?

Whatever it was, it was exhausting.

I headed for the ladies', figuring I should splash some cold water on my face at the very least or dunk my head in a sink full of it, perhaps. I emerged to discover James leaning forward on the bar, in an obvious come-hither pose to the equally engaged Jen.

I sighed. "Come on, lover boy. We have work to do."

I ground my back teeth all the way to our next-to-last stop of the day. I'd run through every possible emotion since showing up at work to hear that the man had demanded to take over my day. Surprise, panic, anger, frustration, happiness over the way he and I seemed to be able to sell ice cubes to Eskimos before lunch. And then a sick stew of jealousy over his flirtation with the bartender. Now I'd circled back to anger—more like raw, visceral fury, the kind I could crunch between my teeth and feel the grit from on my tongue.

But he wasn't going to know that. No way, no how. I had no reason to reveal how much he'd thrown me for about six different loops in as many hours. I was self-aware enough to understand what was happening.

I liked him.

To date myself and my penchant for awards shows at the same time—I really, really liked him.

Which would get me nowhere, fast. I had to muscle through these next two calls, dump him out at his Porsche or whatever, and move on with my life. I was itching to call Sloane. I needed her style of no-nonsense advice, like, right now.

We hit another traffic clog on our way across town, which meant I had to fill the air with something resembling conversation. "So, did you ask her out?" I groaned to myself. Where did that come from?

"No, why?" He didn't seem put off by my nosiness, but he was staring at his phone screen again. "Shit. I never should have told you anything."

"We pinkie promised, dude. I don't know about you, but that means something to me." I meant that. I'd not breathe a word to anyone.

Well, maybe to Sloane.

Maybe not.

God, this was a mess.

"I don't want to do it." His voice was firm.

I smiled to myself. "But it'll give you the out you wanted. Sour, nasty old alcs, remember?"

"I know, but that was when I had to work with my dad every day. I'm not anymore. So, it's not so bad. As long as Michael gives me some freedom to do experimental stuff, I'm good where I am."

"I get that," I said. "Okay, we're here. Now, listen, this is one of two placements we need to get back for you, but they're two of the most stubborn, know-it-all store owners in the universe." I peered out the windshield. "This one is the easier of the two, but Gloria is a hard-ass. Don't try to flirt with her. It's a guaranteed way to get us tossed out on our ear. Follow my lead."

"Got it." He saluted. At least he had the decency to blush at his dorkiness.

We got our coolers out. I fluffed my hair and put on some lipstick. James handed me the sell sheets. We headed for the door.

Exactly fifty-five minutes later, we were back in the car, James wearing a shit-eater of a grin while I gripped the wheel and tried to catch my breath. "How... Why... Oh hell, never mind."

"What can I say? Gloria loved me."

"Dear God, man, she was about to ask if she could have your baby by the time we got out of there." I rubbed my temples. "I don't get it. I've watched her eat other guys alive for trying to pull flirty moves."

I froze when his hand landed on my thigh. Thanks to how quickly I'd dropped behind the wheel, my skirt was hiked up higher than usual, so his palm touched bare skin. I stared down at it, my vision narrowing.

He snatched his hand back almost as fast as he'd bestowed it on me. "Sorry. My bad."

"Right. Okay. So. Let's go see if we can repair things with Palio as neatly as you did here."

"Is he gay?"

I burst out laughing. "No, but thanks for asking first. This guy's a real beer rock star groupie. So we're going to use your star power, not your, um..."

"My hot ass? My sexy, smoldering gaze? My—"

"Spare me."

"Let's do it. I'm on a roll." He rubbed his hands

together.

In short, he did. Do it, that is. By the time we were headed back to VanAnsel from our last stop, we'd not only placed some of my existing brands in new locations, we'd managed to get Burke's California Common, the brown ale and their double rice IPA on twice as many shelves as I'd thought we would. We were like a couple of giddy teenagers after getting away with a house party.

"Okay, I'll admit it. You're a natural," I said.

"I think we're a pretty good team."

We had been, especially at the last stop. The fawning over James and his as-yet-to-be-released New England IPA had been non-stop, but Palio was a stubborn so-and-so. He'd taken a lot of convincing to put the Burke Brothers standards back on his shelf. James and I had, by then, developed a decent give and take between us so the buyers or owners didn't feel so much assaulted by a sales pitch. It was less stiff, antisocial beer-snob and more casual, cool-kid conversation.

James had outdone himself. The perfect balance of humble and apologetic about his brewery's past screw-ups and honest about what he and his brother were doing to put it right. At one point, when he'd been rhapsodizing about how much he loved working with Michael, how much better everything was already, I'd heard something in his voice—sincerity bordering on real emotion—a clear signal to me that he'd fight the buyout.

I just hoped it didn't split their brotherly team. I could tell they were close, but this issue could rip that apart.

"What? I got something in my teeth?" He lowered the visor to look in the tiny mirror.

"No, no, sorry." I started the engine. I had to admit it. I didn't want the day to end.

His phone buzzed with a text. He glanced at it. The shit-eating grin was back. "Well, I didn't ask her out, but she's asking me, the brazen hussy." He waved the phone at me.

"Good for her. We twenty-first century women have to take matters into our own hands. If we waited around for you guys to make a move, we'd be clearing cobwebs off our hoo-hahs."

"Your...what?" He chuckled. "Is that Southern for 'ask me out, James, quick, before my vagina gets old'?"

I blushed so fast and so hot I thought I might pass out. "No. Shut up. Leave me alone. Oh Lord." I put a hand to my face. "I have no idea why I said that."

He laughed again. "So should I say yes?"

"Say yes to what?" I slammed the car into reverse and nearly backed straight into an oncoming car in the parking lot. "Shit. God damn it."

"Nice mouth, Scarlett. I thought cussing was lazy talk."

"Go fuck yourself, Rhett." We glared at each other until I was overcome with giggles—nervous ones, but it broke the tension.

He grinned, and it had to be the most wonderful thing I'd seen in a long time.

"You have a great smile." I cleared my throat. "I mean, nice work today, with the smile...and the smoldering gaze...and the ass."

"Why, thank you," he said.

"Okay, I think I can do this without killing us

now." I backed out of the space and headed toward VanAnsel.

"I have a better idea," he said after about ten minutes of silence.

"Better than what?" I signaled to get off the expressway. I was already pondering my night ahead—a hot bath, after a cold shower, Chinese take-out, a bit of movie binging, then early to bed. I needed to shake off everything about this day so I could move forward, let James go about his business while I went about mine.

"Go out with me."

My foot hit the brake as we approached the top of the exit ramp with a little too much energy. We jerked to a stop, our heads rolling forward, then thumping back against the headrests.

"Sorry," I muttered. I kept a death grip on the steering wheel.

James stayed quiet. I pondered the pros and cons as quickly as I could. In the pro column—I was dying to go out and have a nice, quiet, possibly romantic dinner with the man sitting next to me. A con—I shouldn't get myself any further entangled with him. His company was about to undergo a huge trauma.

I knew I wasn't ready for this. I wasn't sure I'd ever be ready. I couldn't trust my own judgement anymore.

As if sensing me waffle, he leaned forward so he could look me in the eye. "Come on. You know you wanna."

I stuck my tongue out at him.

He grinned and sat back.

"Okay, I will. But just dinner."

"Well, of course. What else would it be? I mean, what do you take me for?"

I pulled into the parking lot and drove around back near the warehouse entrance. I turned off the engine, took a breath, and looked at him. I was going with brutal honesty. I didn't have the energy for anything more.

"I take you for a handsome, charming, talented, recently divorced guy used to getting his way, including with women. And you have to know, James, that I'm…I…" My throat betrayed me, closing up so tight I could barely suck air. "I can't get involved with anyone right now. I'm not in a good place with myself yet, you know? I have some work to do still." I bit my lip. "Jeez Louise, do I sound like a sappy soap opera or what? Sorry. Never mind."

I opened my door, eager to escape these close confines.

Time to detach.

He met me at the trunk. After he'd lifted both our much lighter coolers out and set them on the asphalt, he took one of my hands. Shocked at the quick contact, I didn't resist when he held it between his, warming me in the cool afternoon air. "I'm sorry if I came on too strong earlier. It's been a bizarre day. But you should know I've been thinking about you a lot since Denver. I thought I could, I don't know, maneuver my way into your life somehow. But—"

"But we turned your scheduling lemons into lemonade sales," I said.

He held onto my hand. I didn't protest. My chest was hot and tight, but it wasn't bad this time. It felt nice, comforting, like I'd taken a drink of expensive bourbon.

"Let me buy you dinner, Andi. You and me, talking. Nothing more or less. I promise."

"Fine," I said, pulling my hand away. "I have some paperwork to do." I lifted my chin, indicating the building behind him. "Do you want to come in? You could work in the break room if you need to."

"Okay," he said, smiling that slow, easy, wonderful smile.

I gave myself a mental shake. *Dinner. That's all. Nothing more. You aren't ready for more.* "More" will only get you in deep doo-doo with a man you hardly know.

"Fine," I repeated.

He handed me my bag and pulled the cooler handles up.

"I can do that."

"I know you can. Let me help you. It's tough for you. I get that. But letting me pull the damn cooler handle up is not a negation of your strong, independent womanhood."

"Sheesh, you're bossy."

"*You* are."

"You."

He started toward the employee entrance, our coolers rolling behind him.

I grinned in spite of myself.

"Come on, already. Let's wrap this up so we can go. I'm starving," he called over his shoulder.

"No wonder. You didn't eat a bite of lunch."

"I was nervous," he claimed as he held the door open.

"You? Nervous? Hardly."

He shrugged as I passed by him into the warmth of the back hallway. The warehouse was deserted. All the trucks were on the road with their deliveries, following up on our orders and placements.

"You do it to me," he said as he followed me into the warehouse.

I took my cooler from him and dumped the remaining ice into a big sink. "Don't sweet-talk me, Mister. I'm—"

"Immune. I remember." He dumped his cooler's contents. "Let's finish this while we work. Whaddaya say?" He held up the growler that contained a couple short pour's worth of his new experimental brew.

"Okay," I said, pointing toward the glassed-in office. I could see a few guys milling around inside. I wasn't in the mood to take any shit off them, so I figured I'd bring James with me, to forestall any nastiness. They'd control themselves in front of our local rock star. Or, at least, I hoped they would.

James wandered over to the office and pulled open the door.

I tugged him back. "No, let's go to the break room with it."

"But there's room in here."

"I don't want to go in there. Not right now."

"Hey guys," he called into the room without taking his eyes off me. We stood together, awkward as all get out, holding the door open and apparently arguing about if we were going in or not.

"Hi."

"Hey James, what's shakin'?"

"Hello."

I tightened my grip on his arm. "I don't want to go

in there right now."

He nodded, let go of the door and followed me into the main building. I led him to the break room, got a couple of clean glasses, and emptied the growler into them.

"Damn it," James said as he held his up to the light. "The flocculation's breaking down already. It's not holding the haze."

I sipped mine. "Still tastes good. I think the key is keeping it super cold. It doesn't travel well at all I've heard. Gets unstable and funny looking."

"Yeah. It's a challenging style, but it was damn fun to make. Only took fourteen days."

"Nice."

We clinked glasses.

"Are those guys assholes to you?"

"It's nothing I can't handle."

He glared at me.

"I'm fine."

"Then why are my caveman hackles rising?" His eyes flashed.

I sighed. "I'm good, James. I don't need anyone rescuing me. I've got this. They're gonna learn their lesson or they'll be fired. VanAnsel has a zero-tolerance policy about harassment."

"What?" He rose, his face flushed. "What have they been doing to—"

"Hey guys!"

I turned to see Sloane in the doorway, looking amazing as usual in a gray, pinstriped skirt and long-sleeved light pink blouse.

"Hi Sloane," he said, sitting down and deflating.

"Try this," I said to her.

She sipped my beer and smacked her lips. "Wow. Nice first try, James."

He flipped her off but with a smile. "Thanks, PR Barbie."

She returned the bird with a sweet smile. "Yoga tonight?" she asked me.

"Oh, um…" I glanced at James. I'd forgotten I told her I'd go with her. "Can we go tomorrow night?"

She looked from me to James and back to me again. "Sure. But you listen to me, mister." She pointed at James. "You'd better take her someplace really nice and expensive. I recommend Five on Fifth."

"You got it," he said, making a thing about pulling out his phone and poking at the screen. "Reservation made." He rose. "I'm gonna go talk to your dad. He here?"

"Of course." She let him peck her cheek on his way past her.

"I can pick you up at your place at seven thirty, Andi. Text me the address."

"Sure." I watched them together, easy, jokey, comfortable, and pictured myself in the middle of it all before giving my imagination a firm shake. *Not happening. Not at all. It's dinner. Nothing more.*

"Oh, and Sloane, I recommend that you ask your hot shot sales lady over there about how her co-workers are treating her," James said.

I frowned at him as he ducked out the door.

"What? What's he talking about, Andi? Spill it." Sloane sat and took a sip from her ever-present water bottle.

"It's nothing. Let's talk about it later. I need to get some stuff done before my…date." It hit me then, like a hard poke in my guts. "Holy crap, Sloane. I'm going out on a date with him, aren't I?"

"Yes, I'm afraid you are." She attempted to look at me like a stern auntie, but her lips twitched with amusement. "God help you. You, too?"

I crossed my arms. "We won't be going to a fancy strip bar for our first date."

"Your loss." She shrugged.

"Tell me I shouldn't go," I said, reaching across the table and grabbing my friend's arm. "C'mon. You know you want to."

"Nope," she said with a wan smile.

"You feeling any better? After pampering and all?"

"Not really," she said with a sigh. "I went out with Michael again. We do that sometimes when we're in Chicago together. I don't know why we can't make it work once we cross the state line, but something just…happens to us. I don't know. It's like it's all fantasy and fun over there, but when we have to face reality, we get all bitchy and angry."

"Huh," I said. I didn't have a decent handle on the younger Burke brother. Hell, I barely had a handle on the older one, so I didn't feel equipped to offer advice.

"It was fun, though." She propped her chin in her hand on the table. "He's so…"

"Okay, gotta go," I said, jumping to my feet. "I'm still processing the fact that I know too much about your man's equipment. I don't need any more details."

"Have fun. Do you have a nice dress? Five on Fifth is full-on dressy."

"I'll come up with something." I wondered how James would pull that off. I was pretty certain he didn't travel with a suit and tie.

My phone buzzed with a text. I glanced down to see it was James. My face flushed.

Oh dang. I needed to get that cold shower, and fast. I was mentally scanning the contents of my closet when I opened the message.

—*Sorry, can't pull off Five on Fifth, although if we make it to date #2, we will def go there.*—

—*No problem*— I replied. —*I'm the opposite of high maintenance. Name a good pizza joint, and I'll be happy.*—

—*No, I'm not sinking that low. That's fourth and fifth date territory.*—

—*Fine. Surprise me. But at least tell me how I'm supposed to dress.*—

—*Somewhere between work and formal.*—

—*Not helpful.*—

—*You'll figure it out. I'll see you at seven-thirty.*—

Chapter Fourteen

He was a solid ten minutes early, which was uncool, considering I was running twenty behind.

"Jesus," I muttered when I peered out my window to see his car in the lot. "Great. He's one of those guys."

The prompt kind.

I fluffed out my hair and stared at myself in the mirror a few seconds pondering the options. I'd engaged in my typical, low-key makeup rituals. A bit of foundation, a touch of powder, a hint of blush, and mascara. Between my freckles and natural coloring, I'd never truly conquered the whole facial perfection thing, my obsession with makeup videos notwithstanding.

And my hair? Well, that was a whole 'nother issue. I owned a blow drier but rarely broke it from its cabinet lair. It was easier to let my natural waves-almost-curls dry in the air. I spritzed it with some product Sloane's way-expensive hair fairy had insisted I use if I continued to insist on the whole *au naturel* thing. It did cut down on the frizzies.

The color was on the wheel between auburn and brown. In some lights, I could pass as not a redhead until my freckles came into view. I'd always worn it long, but said expensive visit to the Grand Rapids hair salon had resulted in a nice layering thing that framed my face and kept me from looking so drab.

My phone dinged again.

—U standing me up?—

—Nope. I'll be done in a few. Ur early. Cool jets— I texted back.

I'd chosen a pair of black denim jeans I found in a consignment shop that fit me almost too well. They were serious, curve-hugging, attention-grabbers, and I knew it. My ass was pretty awesome. I turned to admire it.

I'd topped the jeans with a cream, cashmere turtleneck sweater that highlighted my matching awesome rack. I'd bought a pair of second-hand, sky-high, black leather boots I loved. Although now that I had them on, I felt kind of Dominatrix-y.

I snapped a photo and sent it to Sloane. *—How's this?—*

—Nice. Don't forget your whip and nipple clamps. I'll bet he loves being topped.—

I groaned. *—Should I not wear them?—*

—Definitely wear them. He's gonna shit bricks. Send me a pic when that happens, k?—

—Bitchy.—

—Nah. I've got ur back. U look fantastic, my friend. Don't ever think different.—

—Where r u tonight?—

There was a pause before I saw the talky bubbles. *—I'm with my mother.—*

—Ok.—

—Send me updates— she insisted in her next message. *—I want to know EVERYTHING!—*

—I'm not sleeping w/him so just chill.—

—Y not?—

—I'm not ready for that. Not yet.—

She didn't answer. After one last lingering study of how much I thought the boots made me look slutty, I grabbed my purse and coat and headed out. A date. Look at me. I have a bona fide, real live date.

James stood in the lobby by the front door, arms crossed, one ankle over the other, looking like some kind of a romance book hero. I paused and took a breath.

"You pack a spare set of clothes or what?" I kept my voice light.

"Nah, did some shopping. You like?" He held out his arms to show off his new duds—khaki colored, slim-fit trousers and a blue button down topped with a soft-looking sweater. He'd even gotten a new pair of skids. Chelsea boots if I wasn't mistaken. And thanks to my new friend Sloane, I'd become versed in such things. Who would have guessed? Me. I used to assume everyone either wore designer suits and wing tips or jeans with branded T-shirts.

"You look all right," I acknowledged.

As I made my way down the steps, he stood up straighter and his gaze took me in, in all my high-boots glory. He whistled, low and loud.

"I'll take that as a compliment."

"You should. You're stunning tonight, my dear Scarlett." He crooked his elbow. I slid my hand into it.

"Cut the crap, Rhett. I'm not in the mood."

He opened the door, and the cold night air hit me square in the face, taking my breath.

"Holy…wow," I gasped.

He glanced at me. "What?"

"It's as cold as brass balls out here, that's what."

He laughed. "Oh honey, you haven't seen anything

yet." He opened the door of his truck and handed me in.

I sat in the warm, leathery-smelling interior, a smile stuck to my face.

"So you know I've been married." His first conversational gambit threw me, to say the least, considering we'd not even made it out of my parking lot.

"Yep. So what? So have I."

"Ah, Sloane. God bless her."

"Well, what do you think? She'd not tell me? It's a pretty significant life detail."

"I guess so. We've both been to the puppet show. Seen the strings, as it were."

I threaded my fingers together in my lap. This was headed into weird territory. I stared out the window. "Is that snow?"

"Sure is." He flipped on the windshield wipers. "Welcome to Michigan winter, Andi Rose. It's gonna be a doozy."

"Winter, eh? It's only the third week of October last I checked."

He glanced at me at a stop light, the red coloring one side of his face.

"What?" I asked.

"Nothing."

We rode the rest of the way in silence. I didn't recognize the restaurant, which was odd. I'd made it my business to know all the places where I might peddle beer and wine.

"Hang on," he said, as he was getting out. "I'm going full chivalrous tonight."

I waited, and he handed me down from the truck's passenger's seat. I leaned into him, closing my eyes against the stinging wind that drove tiny drops of what must have been ice daggers into my exposed skin. He tightened his arm around me as we walked toward the door. Fake fire pits danced in the brick patio entry. I tried not to like it, any of it. But I did.

I floated along on a cloud as we were seated, marveling when my date pulled out my chair. That hadn't happened to me since…I don't know, prom? And that kid only did it because he thought it might get him laid.

Oh, wait…

But I refused to let worries about "later" and "laid" ruin this for me right now.

We ordered a couple of beers, my choice this time. I went with Neapolitan stouts from a brewery in Saugatuck.

"Good call for a night like this," James said as he studied the wine list.

"I thought so." I sipped water, nervous beyond belief.

"This place changes its menu every season. They're into the winter stuff—root veg, soups and stews, roasts. The lamb shank is dynamite. Do you like lamb? Oh, cool, marrow's on for an appetizer."

"I…"

"You okay? You look a little flushed." James flapped his linen napkin at my face.

When I pressed my palm to my cheek, I figured I was redder than a summer strawberry. *Great. Way to play it cool and calm, Andi girl. Never let 'em see you blush.*

I cleared my throat. It was only James. We'd spent an entire day together, working in tandem, doing quite well, and enjoying each other's company. What was my problem now?

"I love lamb," I blurted. "But I always feel a little guilty eating it, you know? Like I never eat veal anymore either. I've never had marrow but would try it."

Our beers arrived. We touched glasses and sipped.

James smacked his lips. "That is such a great brew. All three flavors at different points. Amazing."

I sniffed, tasted, then took my second, bigger drink. He was right. I hadn't had one of these in so long. As soon as I'd seen it on the menu I pounced. I got the initial hit of chocolate from the malt the brewer had used, then the secondary sweetness of fruit, and the vanilla finish. Truly a sublime experience. "I can't believe they haven't won gold at the beer world cup for this."

"They've won silver, twice."

We sipped. Silence fell between us. James cleared his throat.

I looked down at my hands, clenched together in my lap. "I'm sorry," I said at the exact same moment James said, "Maybe we shouldn't have…"

We smiled.

"You go," he said, picking up his pint glass again.

I exhaled. "I don't mean to sit here like a lump. I don't know what's wrong with me. Well, other than I haven't been out on anything resembling a date for a solid decade and a half."

James's grin widened. "I hear it's like riding a bicycle."

"It's not, I assure you. Sheesh. I'm a nervous wreck." Going with gospel truth felt right, so I did it.

James rested his arm on the table, his palm upturned. I stared at it longer than was probably polite, then put my hand in his.

There is no universe in which would I be considered petite. I was, as I've said, a solid, average female. Size twelve on a good day, a fourteen otherwise. I hated exercise with a burning passion but forced myself to take walks that sometimes went two or three miles when I had something I needed to work out in my head.

I stood five-foot-five flat-footed and my curves were real—something I highlighted with close-fitting jeans and shirts once upon a time. I tried to do the same with skirts and blouses these days and had adjusted to life in my selling shoes, which lifted me to five-foot-eight or so. My hands were unremarkable, short nails for practicality, utilitarian, nothing special.

But when I put one in his open palm and he closed his fingers around it, I felt like…I don't know, something akin to a princess in an exotic, far-off land, with tiny, delicate fingers being caressed by a strong, handsome prince.

Woo doggie. I've gone around the bend and back again.

I blinked and tried to smile.

He held tight to my hand, his grip firm. "I've said it before. I'll say it again. Chill out, Andrea Rose. Relax. Sometimes I wonder if you even know how."

"I can relax," I said, stiffening and then forcing myself not to do that very thing. What was happening right now? It was like riding a wave or facing an onrushing summer storm. Unstoppable and terrifying and yet, somehow, inevitable. All I could do was go along for the ride and see where it took me.

He gave my hand one more squeeze, then let me go. "So, how do these apps look to you? I'm thinking we go with the marrow and the roasted carrots and balsamic. But would you prefer the risotto balls?"

I put the hand he'd been holding in my lap, teenager-y thoughts roiling through my brain—*OMG, I will never wash this hand again!* I picked up the menu and made myself read it.

"Sounds good to me. Oh, hey, let's do the whole roasted garlic."

He peeked around the menu at me. "Well, I was going to suggest that, but…"

"But what?"

"You really haven't been on a date in a while, have you?"

"Thanks for reminding me." I blushed again and made a show of hiding behind the menu. He meant he didn't want to order it because we would be kissing later.

Oh Lordy. What am I doing here with this man?

"So, tell me about your ex-wife," I said, once we'd placed our orders—root vegetable lasagna for me, lamb stew for him.

He raised an eyebrow as he drained his beer. "Oh, right. I almost forgot. Sloane told you."

"Of course." I sipped, put my beer down, and patted my lips.

"She's so helpful."

"Don't be a jerk. She's my friend."

He smiled and motioned for the waiter. "Another?" He pointed to my near empty glass.

"Sure. I'd like an IPA. I hear there's a brewery in

this state that makes a good one."

"Yep. We'll have two Galena LionHearteds, please."

I stared at him. "I was talking about the Burke Brothers one. You know, the one you brew?"

He shrugged. "Ted Galena's is better. I'm mature enough to admit that."

I was so completely tongue-tied I could barely stand myself. Where was my famous, witty repartee when I needed it? Vanished, along with my common sense. I'd swear I could've sat and stared at James Burke all night long. He was so handsome. A word I didn't use lightly. Matt Ribgy was hot, steamy, compelling in a sexy way. As if he knew every female in a two-mile radius would happily leap into the sack with him.

James was boy-next-door good-looking. The cute kid you've known since grade school who ends up the quarterback of the high school football team, dates the head cheerleader, is nice to everyone he encounters, goes to the state college and then to law school.

No, no, not law school. He'd be too nice to be a lawyer. He'd be an engineer or something safe and nerdy, able to provide for his beautiful wife, two kids, and a dog in the suburbs. All the neighborhood ladies would flirt with him. He was miles better looking than their husbands. But he only ever had eyes and hands for his gorgeous wife.

The guy who could rock a suit, a pair of jeans, or the ratty shorts he'd wear while he mowed the lawn. He never gained or lost a pound, could change the oil on the car, make simple plumbing fixes, and change a diaper.

But, of course, he had or did none of these things. James Burke was a business owner and a Master Brewer, a legit one. A chef who used hops, water, malt, and yeast instead of flour, salt, and eggs to concoct his masterpieces.

"Someone told me once that staring was rude." James leaned forward, his elbows resting on the table.

I blinked, busted. But who could blame me?

I handed him the wine menu. "Order us wine for dinner, will you? Or should I?"

He handed me the menu. "I could, but why don't you pick, now we know what we're eating?"

"Sure thing." I studied the options. There weren't many, but they were impressive. "This one," I said when the waiter returned with our beers.

"Great choice," he said.

"I know."

We clinked glasses.

"To first dates," James said, his green eyes doing that mesmerizing thing again.

I blinked and steeled myself against it. "Sure, okay." I sipped, smacked my lips and stared at the amber liquid in my glass. "I've been off IPAs a while and have forgotten how…"

"Perfect it is?" He was staring at his glass, too.

We had to look like idiots to the other diners but I didn't care.

"Yes," he said. "This is hands down the gold standard of IPAs. Balanced but leaning into the hops in a way that makes your tongue tingle and your throat warm. It's an art, this beer. Ted and his crew deserve every bit of kudos and success they get."

"Do you ever get jealous?" I asked, setting the beer

down so I didn't drink it too fast.

It was higher in alcohol than your average quaff at seven percent, which was another one of its perfections, in my opinion. The sweet spot of six to eight percent was something many brewers shot for but couldn't manage. I wasn't a fan of high booze beers, although I understood their appeal and popularity. As a result, I usually only went for the four to five percent stuff out of necessity. Most people didn't understand how challenging it was to craft a beer that hit this combination of boozy malt and sharp hops. I did. And I almost wished I hadn't ordered wine now so I could have another.

"Of what? Of this?" He held up his almost empty glass. "No, not really. Ted Galena, Carter and my Uncle Jeff were among the pioneers of this crazy business in Michigan. They helped each other out, lent staff, fixed equipment, and sometimes traded out yeast or hops in the early days. Beer people were all buddies, then."

"I guess. But I have to wonder how sincere the friendships were. I mean, being buddies is all well and good until there's a brewery opening up every dang morning in your backyard, determined to be the next Galena's or Burke Brothers."

He leaned forward. "I don't mind that, either. Healthy competition encourages higher quality." He shrugged. "Besides, it looks like I'm not gonna be in the biz as a brewer for Burke Brothers much longer."

"Don't say that!" I ducked my head, realizing I'd spoken way too loud for a nice restaurant. "I mean, you're going to figure it out, and you and Michael will make a go of it. I'm sure you will."

James sighed. "I always had this naïve idea the

town with a bunch of breweries and brew pubs is a town that's content. I mean, breweries provide jobs and a space where people can gather and be social or intimate or enjoy lunch and a brew with co-workers. It's our job to be the constant for people in a sea of chaos that is their lives."

"Wow," I said. "Those are some deep thoughts, Jimmy."

"No, no, listen. When I was thinking about leaving, it was over this very thing. Burke's had gotten so…I don't know…"

"Hugely successful?"

"Big and corporate and too production-minded was what I was reaching for, but thanks." He winked at me.

I blushed like a schoolgirl, but I was into this. I wanted to understand him, so I could maybe provide advice about what to do in the face of this potential life-changing decision he needed to make.

"I wanted to be the local, you know?" he went on. "The unassuming place where you could always go for a really great beer and a burger. Nothing more. My father made it clear that was not our mission and I'd be well-served to understand it. I got it. I know *how* to run a huge production brewery. I just don't always like it. Am I making sense?"

I sipped some water and gathered my thoughts. "So, then, maybe you should consider selling. Take your proceeds, which I assume will be vast to excellent and open your new place, somewhere not in Detroit."

His expression grew pensive. The worry line between his eyes begged for me to smooth it out with my fingertip. I sat on my hands lest I give away how much I wanted to touch him.

His lips twisted. "But in a perverse way, since Michael's been back and we've been working together, I've been a lot happier. I think—or I thought—he felt the same way. We were going to hire a new Tap Room manager and work on getting that place back to basics. We were also going to scale back on some of our generic, everybody-makes-them brews and try some new things, limiting them to the Tap Room so it became a special experience to go there." He leaned back in his chair. "But I guess I thought wrong about him. He has other plans."

"Do you know for certain? I mean, have you actually spoken to him since he sent you the news flash today?"

"No," he admitted. "I'm ignoring him right now if you must know."

Our food arrived, which was a relief, since I was about to lay into him about making assumptions before having conversations and would probably come off as way bossy.

I let the lasagna distract me a few minutes. It was melt-in-your mouth delicious, an ideal blend of rich, root veg, light sauce, and about a pound of goat cheese. "Want a bite?"

He nodded so I shoveled some into his mouth in the most unsexy way possible.

"My turn." I pointed to the lamb stew. He held a spoon of it to my lips but hesitated. "What?" I could smell the rosemary and thyme combined with the rich meat.

"Nothing," he said, bringing the spoon closer.

I took the bite and had to close my eyes at the wealth of flavors rolling around on my tongue. I sipped my wine, pleased by the pairing, which was more complementary than complex.

"My ex-wife was the daughter of one of my mother's friends. She and I were railroaded into the whole thing. It wasn't bad. But it wasn't good. And it ended. No big deal." He picked up his glass and held it in both hands.

I tried not to act shocked at the U-turn in our conversation. I had asked him earlier. I figured he'd dropped the subject on purpose. "You were married a while. That is kind of a big deal."

"Eh." He shrugged, but his expression didn't match his nonchalance.

I didn't want to push. But something told me to keep asking questions. Knowing what I knew about his family, probably no one ever had asked him anything. Just taken his blasé "no big deal" explanation at face value. "She hurt you."

He frowned. His full lips pressed together. "I would've stayed with her. Tried to make it work. But she'd checked out of our marriage months before we split. I figured that out pretty fast."

"I'm sorry."

"Don't be. I've rallied."

"Feels to me like you're rebounding."

He laughed out loud at that.

I glanced around noting people looking over at us.

"With you? God, I hope not. You are a lot of things, Andi, but a woman I'd rebound with isn't one of them."

"I think I'm insulted."

He leaned forward again, pinning me with his incredible green stare. "Don't be. It's a compliment. A serious one." His eyes flashed in a way that made me flush hot. I wanted to look away, but I was incapable of it. "You are so damn cute when you blush."

"Shut up," I said. My hands flew to my face. "I hate you."

He chuckled again.

We ate, discussing nothing heavier than where I should go to get a decent winter coat and boots, even though I had a ton of questions I wanted to ask. It was nice, comfortable, without stress. We both cleared our plates.

"It's nice to eat a meal with a woman who actually eats. My ex ate like Sloane does, which is to say, very little."

I picked up my wine glass. I'd chosen a Russian River pinot noir—a rich, fruity and spicy accent to both our entrees. It was perfect. I knew my wine, almost as well as I knew my beer. Between it and the beer we'd started with, I was feeling no pain.

"Pro tip for your next date, Jimmy. Don't compare how *she* just ate to how your ex would never eat."

He held up a hand. "Say no more." He picked up his glass. "You, Andrea Rose, are hands down the sexiest, most gorgeous, perfectly sized woman I have ever met in my entire, useless life."

"I'll drink to that."

Our glasses dinged nicely. We drained them.

"Dessert?" the waiter asked.

"God, no. I am full to bursting."

"I'll take the check," James said.

After he paid, he pulled out my chair and we headed into the biting wind. It wasn't snowing anymore, so it wasn't like it was picturesque. More like

177

to-the-bone freezing. We hustled to his truck, and he handed me into the passenger's seat. It took a few minutes for the cab to warm up. My teeth chattered the whole time.

"You need a better coat. Winters here can be brutal."

"Sloane keeps telling me."

"So what's up with those two, anyway?"

"Who? Sloane and Michael? I have no idea. Other than a whole lot of kinky sex." I blushed again, grateful for the darkened truck cab interior.

"So I've heard." He was quiet for a few moments. "I don't know what we're going to do."

I looked at his profile, saw how he clenched his jaw. "You need to talk to your brother. You guys have to be on the same page about it."

"I knew he didn't want to leave Chicago, his job, his life he'd built independent of the family business. But I didn't think he'd do this."

"Maybe he didn't. Maybe it's as much out of his control as it is yours."

"Bullshit," James spat out. "He knows what he's doing." He parked near the door of my building. "I don't even know how to ask. We weren't close growing up. Our father saw to that. He put us in direct competition for absolutely everything." He chuckled. "We took it to heart. Dude slept with my high school girlfriend after I went to college."

"Were you broken up with her?"

"Um. No."

"Ah."

The truck interior was warm and toasty by now. I dreaded the thought of having to leave it. I dreaded leaving James even more.

Which meant I really needed to get out of here.

He turned off the engine. "I'll walk you to the door."

I waited for him to come around and help me out. The freezing cold wind slammed into my face, taking my breath away. James tucked me into his side, like he had when we'd walked to the restaurant. I decided it was my favorite place to be in the whole world.

He hesitated, but I pulled him into the small foyer on the main floor. He held me close, ran his fingers down my face, around the back of my neck, then through my hair. We didn't speak. I couldn't have if I'd wanted to. When his lips met mine, I didn't consider protesting. I had my arms around his neck in a second. I'd not kissed a whole lot of guys in my life, but this one was turning me inside out. I never wanted to kiss anyone else, ever again.

He broke away, smiling, keeping our bodies pressed close. He kissed my nose, then my forehead. "I'm gonna go now," he said, his voice lower than usual, raspy, and sexy-sounding.

"Okay," I said, initiating my own kiss this time. By the time we broke apart, we were both breathing heavily. "This is you, going."

I let go of him, let my hands trail down his chest, relishing the firmness under his shirt.

"Yeah," he said, letting me touch him for a few more seconds before he stepped back, putting some distance between us. "Wow."

"Back at ya." I grinned. "Wow. Oh, and thanks for dinner," I said, cocking one hip, doing a little mating dance and hating myself for it.

"My pleasure." He tucked his hands in his pockets and looked so stinking cute I wanted to drag him into my apartment and rip off his clothes. I backed up toward the staircase. "You're not driving to Detroit tonight, are you?"

"No. Staying with a friend."

"Oh. Okay. Cool."

We waited. It was obvious what we both wanted, but something about it scared me into action. "Bye, James. I'm going upstairs now."

He sighed. "Okay. Good call. Speaking of calling… I'll call you, okay? Probably in the next fifteen minutes."

I melted even more. This guy. Where had he come from anyway? Was he real? Or was I just making him up?

"Sure. I'd like that." I headed up the steps, got to the top, turned, and looked down at him. "What're you waiting for? Go on. Call me."

"I was just admiring the view."

I shivered from head to toe. "Go on. Get out of here." I went into my place, shut the door, and leaned back against it, grinning like a crazy woman.

He called me not in fifteen minutes but closer to forty. I'd taken a bath, sipped some water, and wandered around my apartment in a haze of lust and fairy tale endings. I had a job I liked. A new friend. A place to live. And could it be? A legit boyfriend? And what a boyfriend. Not jumping my bones, demanding we hook up, but kissing like no man had a right to and still be single.

When he did call, I was on the couch, wrapped in a blanket, reading a book. "Hey," I said, unable not to smile. "What're you doing?"

"Andi." He sounded out of breath.

I sat up straighter, immediately on alert. "What's wrong? Where are you?"

"I'm headed to Detroit. I have to… It's… Shit. I need you to call Sloane."

"What's wrong? Is it Michael? What happened to him?"

"It's not Michael. It's my…our father."

"Your father?"

"He's dead. Heart attack. Died in his office at home."

"Oh no, James. I'm sorry."

"I can't find Michael. Will you call Sloane for me? See if she knows where he is?"

"Yes, I will. Do you need, um, want me to…"

"Well, I was going to ask but didn't want to assume anything."

"I'll find her. We'll drive over. She'll sort us out a place to stay."

He sucked in a breath. "That would be… I'd really appreciate it. Thanks."

"Of course. Drive safe. I'll let you know when we get there. And if she knows where Michael is."

"Thanks."

"You're welcome." I waited. "I'm going to hang up now."

"Hearing your voice has made this…easier." His voice broke, which just about killed me.

"Go on. Stop flattering me."

"Can't do that, sorry."

"All right, but I am hanging up now. I gotta get hold of Sloane."

I hung up and stared down at the phone in my hand for a solid five minutes before I called Sloane. Something in me resisted going deeper into James' life, even if he needed the support of friends during a tough time for his family. It both appealed and repelled me at the same time. I was, in short, gun shy. I knew it. But I closed my eyes and recalled his voice, his arms around me, and those killer lips.

I made the call.

Chapter Fifteen

The Sloane Organizational Machine leaped into action after a brief phone update about the Burke family troubles. Conveniently enough, she was with Michael when I called, and so she could break the news to him herself. Once he left for Detroit, she said she'd be over to me in about a half hour.

"But…" I was going to point out that it was almost eleven thirty already and what in the world could we possibly do at that hour, but she'd already hung up.

I shed the robe and tugged on a flannel shirt I'd kept with the BWI logo on it. Then I heated up water for tea, assuming we would talk tonight and would head over to the east side of the state in the morning.

I opened the door when she rang, ready to spill all about my date with James.

"Where's your bag?" she asked.

"My what?" I backed up to let her enter, already concocting excuses for not going with her, ignoring the echoing sound of James' distraught voice in my ear. I couldn't do this. We weren't together. It wasn't my place.

"Your suitcase. I have our hotel booked. Let's go." She snapped her fingers at me.

I took a second to study her. She was free of makeup and flushed, but no wonder since the winter wind had only gotten stronger since I'd come indoors.

Her hair was yanked back into a ponytail and looked wet, like she'd gotten out of the shower before coming over here. She was wearing jeans, pretty yet practical boots, and a mid-length, black down coat. "Sloane, have you lost weight?"

She frowned and headed into my kitchen. "Off topic. Go pack. Please."

I stood my ground. This had been bugging me for the month and a half or so we'd known each other, and something about this moment, five minutes past midnight on a night I'd had a date that blew my mind and scared me half out of it at the same time, seemed like the time to say it. I marched into the kitchen where she stood, warming her hands over the tea kettle.

"I'm worried about you," I said.

"No need. I'm fine. Let's go."

I sat at the small table between the kitchen and living room. "Why in the world would we go now? What can we do? It's not like they need us to help make the…arrangements or whatever. We'll be in the way. I have to work tomorrow. I'm behind on a ton of paperwork, thanks to…" I bit my lip.

Her shoulders slumped. I waited, determined to get to the bottom of why she was being so manic. It was sad, sure, but best I could tell, neither Burke brother would miss their father much. She stayed silent. I got up and took the few steps over to her. We stood together, looking at the teapot. When it began to whistle, I moved it from the burner and flipped off the gas.

"I want to be there for him," she said, her voice barely a whisper. "Even if we…"

Before I knew it, she was sobbing, her face pressed

into my shoulder. I patted her back, unsure what to say or do. Their relationship was so odd. I had no idea how to react.

"We broke up tonight. For good. I think." She sniffled and drew back.

I handed her a tissue. She dabbed her eyes, then clutched it in her hand.

That brought me around to my original question. "Sloane, you're too thin. I think you might have a problem. You know, with your weight."

She blew out a breath and poured herself a glass of water. "I've paid plenty of therapists to tell me the same damn thing. I just...I don't know. When things start spiraling, I stop eating. It's like the one thing I can control in my fucked-up life." She blew her nose and stared out my window.

"So you get upset about Michael and you stop eating." I didn't phrase it as a question.

She turned, her lips turned downward. "No. It's not just him. It's my parents. I've never been... Food and I have a complicated relationship, okay?"

"Do you have any uncomplicated relationships?" Rude, but true, so I decided not to feel bad about it.

"Well, yeah. I mean. I like to think our friendship is straightforward. It's the nicest, simplest relationship I've had since grade school if you must know."

"I'm glad to provide simplicity for you. But seriously, Sloane..."

She held up a hand. "I've had enough brutally honest conversations for today, okay? Just...pack and let's go."

"I still don't get why..." But even as I spoke, I was heading to my room, pulling down my small suitcase, and filling it.

"Be sure to bring funeral wear." I looked up to see her standing in the bedroom doorway. She'd unzipped her coat but was still wearing it.

"How quickly will they get this sorted out? Where I'm from, we'd have a couple days of visiting with friends and family, then a funeral, then a food-and-drink-fest."

"Michael said he wanted it done by Wednesday if not sooner. They have to respond to the buyout offer by end of the week."

I pulled my gray suit from the closet and packed a pair of dress shoes in the bag with my other stuff—a couple of dressy/casual pants and sweaters with the usual necessities. "I can't stay over there through Wednesday. I have a job, remember?"

"I know your boss," she snapped. "I'll write you an excuse."

I glared at her, anger building in my chest, shoving aside the worry about her health and concern about how this was going to add to James' stress. As if fielding a buyout offer he thought his own brother machinated wasn't bad enough?

"I'm sorry, Andi." Sloane's eyes shone with fresh tears. "I didn't mean to be a bossy bitch." She sat on the edge of the bed and swiped at her damp cheeks.

"It's all right." I patted her down-covered shoulder. "You do it well. I'm impressed."

She nodded and blew her nose. "Anyway, I'd appreciate it if you would stay. Do you have anything pressing this week?"

"If I want to hit my monthly sales target to get the highest commission, then yeah, I do. But I'm okay. If

I'm back Thursday, I can manage it."

"From what I've heard, you're already in the top commission tier. Don't be modest."

I shrugged. "I'm an over-achiever. What can I say?" I shut my suitcase and put it on the floor. "I'm still not quite sure how we can help."

"Having familiar, friendly faces around will help them. Both of them."

"I thought you said you guys broke up for good." While I didn't want to open fresh wounds, I couldn't wrap my head around what the big rush was about.

"We did. But Michael looked so… Well, he asked me to come. To help manage his mother. I know how to do that. So, I'm going and I'm asking you to come with me."

"Manage his mother?" I followed her out into the living room, grabbed my purse and phone, and waited while she tapped out something on her device.

"You'll see what I mean soon enough. And besides…" She shot me a sly look. "I'll bet, after tonight, James will be thrilled to have you around."

"Nothing happened tonight, Sloane. I told you I'm not ready for anything, um, physical. Not yet."

"Good for you." She tucked her phone away and zipped up her coat. "I'm guessing that's James' speed, too, since his divorce and all."

She smiled, allaying my fears about her physical state for a moment. She was, once more, the beautiful woman I'd impulsively rescued from ignominy in Denver who'd befriended me and set me on my current, upward trajectory. She was asking for my help and support. I'd be a pretty rotten friend if I refused.

"Okay, I'm ready. You driving?"

"Yep."

My phone buzzed with a text, but I waited until we were ensconced in her fancy SUV before I looked at it.

—I hear you're headed my way. I'm glad. Thank you.— James had sent.

The smile spread so wide over my face, I covered my lips to hide it.

****

I wasn't sure what I expected when we got up the next day to meet what remained of the Burke family at a fancy, suburban funeral home, but it wasn't at all what happened. After the huge suite at the downtown Detroit hotel welcomed us when we arrived at near three a.m. on Saturday morning, I'd fallen into a cloud-like mass of duvet and pillows and slept like a stone for five hours, not really caring what Sloane did with herself.

She woke me by flipping on every light in the room and with the smell of coffee.

"Arise, sleeping beauty," she said. I rubbed my eyes and groaned. "We have to meet everyone at the funeral home in an hour."

I scrabbled for my phone and peered at the time. "At nine a.m.? On Saturday? Lordy, you people are anal. It's not like Carter's going anywhere."

I rolled onto my back. I'd never been a morning person. My ideal schedule skewed late. I was good well past midnight, as long as I could sleep until ten or so the next day. It had served me well in Louisville, in my former life. I was still adjusting to new hours as a salesperson so staying up so late and chatting with Sloane to keep her awake while she drove had been no sweat. But now?

"Five more minutes," I called, dragging a pillow over my face.

"Nope." Sloane snatched it away. "Come on. Hit the shower. I ordered breakfast. It'll be here when you get out."

I sat on the side of the bed and tried to get my bearings, to sort through what was going to happen today, but I was too groggy.

"Coffee," I muttered. Sloane handed me a cup as I walked past her. "Thanks." I took a few sips then headed for one of the two bathrooms.

Somewhat revived, thanks to the six shower heads, I wandered out, hair in a towel, body wrapped in the softest robe I'd ever worn in my life. "I want to keep this. Think they'll notice it missing?" I stroked the lapels as if it were a cat.

Sloane sat at a rolling, white cloth-covered table in front of an untouched plate of fruit.

I dropped into a chair across from her and uncovered my plate. Eggs, toast, a couple of slices of delicious-smelling bacon. "Yum. Thanks." I dug in. My experience with Stella had prepared me for this kind of thing, me eating everything in sight while my friend merely watched, eating vicariously. I was beginning to think that Sloane's food complication, as she'd called it, was a lot more dangerous than Stella's. But it wasn't my business.

As if sensing my thoughts about her, my phone rang with a call from my Louisville friend. "Hey," I said, still munching the last of the toast.

"Hey, yourself. Go on, ask me."

I sighed and tucked my feet up under me. Sloane had abandoned her lonely fruit plate and was staring out the tall window onto the gloomy gray morning. I was determined not to obsess over the way her shoulder blades stuck out through her sweater or how fragile her neck seemed from my perspective.

"Ask you what?" I pulled the towel off my head and ran my fingers through damp hair.

"Ask me what I'm wearing right now."

"Honey, we've discussed this. I'm not into you."

"Very funny, bitch."

I could hear shuffling around in the background, like fabric or sheets. "Are you calling me from bed next to the brain doctor?"

"Maybe."

"Okay, what're you wearing?"

"Not a stitch, except this."

"Except what?"

"Hang on. I'm sending a photo."

When it appeared, I whistled and put the phone back to my ear. "Congrats, Stella. That is easily the biggest rock yet."

"Don't be mean."

"I'm not." I wasn't. I sincerely hoped the third time would be her charm. She deserved one. "When're we having ourselves a fresh wedding?"

"Not sure yet. I wanted to share this moment with you. Hey!" She dissolved in giggles.

I sighed. Stella had always been that friend who overshared to the point of embarrassment. But she'd had a shitty life growing up. No love, barely any attention, so she craved it like a junkie as a teen and adult. It hadn't always served her well.

"I'll let you go. Tell Doctor Fabulous I said congrats and he'd better treat my friend right."

"I will. Thanks, Andi. Hey, how was the date?"

I'd kept her appraised of things at work and had told her about the impromptu date, of course. It was how we rolled. "It was…nice. Thanks. I need to go. I'll fill you in more later."

"Oooo, is he there with you? Naked? His peen as big as we—"

"Bye, Stell." I hung up, unwilling to let on how the night had ended or what I was about to do today. It would require way too much explanation, and I wasn't sure I had it in me right now. I barely understood it myself.

Sloane hadn't moved from her perusal of downtown from our penthouse perch.

"I have a question," I said as I headed for my suitcase to cobble together something to wear. I stared at the contents, unsure what would be appropriate for supporting-my-friend-while-she-managed-her-ex-boyfriend's-mother while also "being there" for James.

"Hmm?"

"How rich are the Burkes anyway? I mean, James and Michael are always dressed well. But he drives an older truck and doesn't give off an old money vibe. I don't get it."

Sloane turned from the window and picked up her coffee cup. "It was Belanger money—their mother's family's—that got the brewery started. The original Burke brothers were solid, middle class, semi-blue collar, best I can tell. I do know Amelia—that's his mother's name—was pregnant with James when she married Carter."

"Scandalous," I said as I studied and rejected one clothing option after another.

"It was at the time, plus, considering her family's old money standing... The Burkes were upstarts, nobodies, not exactly who the Belangers pictured for their only daughter. Wear those."

I held up the navy blue work pants.

She nodded. "With your cream sweater."

"The one I wore last night?"

"Yes. It'll look nice with the blue. It flatters your complexion. Do you have heels that aren't the stripper boots you wore last night?"

I held up one of the two pair I'd brought with me. I only owned them because she'd taken me on a quick shopping spree before I started work, stocking me up with "the basics—we'll get to the fun stuff later."

"Perfect." She checked her watch. "Hurry, though." She put her phone to her ear. "Hi."

I waited, hoping to hear more, to get a handle on where she was in her head with regard to Michael Burke. But she headed into her room and shut the door. I got dressed, fluffed out my hair, which was dry-enough, and did my basic makeup routine, all of which took ten minutes.

I knocked on Sloane's door. "Hey. I'm ready."

It took her a minute to answer. She emerged in slim black pants and camel-colored sweater with matching boots. Her eyes were red, but they had been all morning.

"What exactly are we doing today?"

"Providing moral support," she said as she tucked her phone into a different, understated, designer bag. "Follow my lead."

I nodded, my chest tight, face hot with anxiety. I wasn't ready for this. Yet, here I was, so much in the middle of this particular family incident I had no way out.

****

"Sloane! Thank *God,* you're here."

The sound of a strange, female voice hit my ears. I knew who it was, of course, but part of me didn't want to acknowledge it. I'd heard enough about Amelia Belanger Burke from Sloane to have concocted a decent imaginary image of her. I gave myself a mental high five for not being too far off.

James' and Michael's mother was petite, slim, with a classic blonde bob and icy, blue-gray eyes, almost the same color as Michael's. She wore a suit that matched her eye color, with a hint of a camisole peeking up from the jacket's V-neck, and gray, suede pumps to match. She exuded a distinct aura of expensive perfume with a slight edge of gin and tonic.

Sloane stiffened when she heard her name called. I only knew because I was standing behind her and saw her freeze in the doorway. I watched as she shook her head, took a deep breath, and walked up to Michael's mother. "Amelia. How awful for you. I'm so sorry. How can I help?"

I scurried in her wake, eager and yet horrified at the thought of meeting James' terrifying mother face to actual face. The two women clutched hands, air-kissed European-style, exchanged the fakest set of smiles I'd ever seen, then let go of each other.

"And who is this?" Amelia peered around Sloane's shoulder and fixed me with a glare I could feel slicing into my skin. "Sloane? Is this a friend of yours?" The unspoken "and you brought her here, today, why?" portion of the question hanging in the air like cartoon bubbles over our heads.

Sloane turned and tugged me forward. "This is Andrea—Andi. She is a friend of mine. But also—"

"Andi." I head James' voice about a split second before I felt his arms around me, which gave Mrs. Burke the answer to her question.

I closed my eyes, determined not to give a rip that he was hugging me so obviously, and in front of his mother. I held onto him a few seconds, then disengaged for propriety's sake.

James held me at arm's length. His eyes were bloodshot. He was still wearing last night's date outfit, and he reeked of whiskey. "Thank you for coming."

I heard his mother sniff, like snooty old ladies did in black and white movies. My hackles rose.

Michael wandered up, looking dapper and put-together in a dark suit and shirt with French cuffs. He nodded at me and put his arm around Sloane's shoulders. She stiffened even more and moved away from him.

"Well now, I suppose, since we're all here together, we should decide how we're going to handle the next few days," Amelia began.

"No big party after," Michael insisted.

"Don't be ridiculous, Michael. I've already booked the club."

"Okay, then we are agreed on cremation?" Michael looked around at all of us.

"I'm having second thoughts about that," his mother said.

"Too bad, Mother. It's what he wanted." Michael's voice was so dry I got thirsty listening to it.

"Fine." She waved her hand at her youngest son

and glanced around the room, as if seeking a waiter with a tray of drinks. James stood by me, gripping my hand, saying nothing as his mother and brother argued over every possible detail.

Finally, Sloane, who'd been tapping on her computer tablet the whole time, interjected, "I have all of this down. Amelia, why don't you let me go with Michael to talk to Mr. Hunt. You should rest."

This, I deduced because I'm good that way, was the funeral director guy. Not a stretch since the name of the place was Hunt's Funeral Home. I leaned into James, exhausted from the residual tension.

"I don't need to be coddled, young lady." Amelia narrowed her eyes at Sloane, then did a blatant up and down of the younger woman's appearance. "You look different. Have you picked up weight?"

"Mother," Michael's voice was a low, frightening growl of a thing.

"What?" Her gray-blue eyes widened in fake innocence. Then she trained them on me. I tried not to shrink away from it into James' side. "And you, my dear. Where on earth did you come from? James? Are you really looking to add a bit of ginger to the family genes?" One side of her upper lip lifted ever so slightly as she treated me to the same once-over she'd given Sloane.

James opened his mouth, closed it, then opened it again. "You're tired, so I'll let the rudeness slide. Let's get this over with. Michael, we'll talk to Hunt with Sloane. Andi, are you okay to…"

I blinked, realizing he was asking me to stay and entertain his mother.

"I'm leaving," Amelia said. "I'll see you tonight at

the house. Family dinner." She made a point not to look at either Sloane or me.

"We'll get back to you on that," Michael said.

Chapter Sixteen

The next two days were a blur. Sloane and I only had to encounter Mrs. Burke face-to-face once more, thank the good Lord above. The brothers spent time Saturday recuperating from what we learned was an all-night bender the night before. They reported for the family dinner, although James claimed it was the last time he planned to subject himself to his mother's form of torture via dry pot roast with a side order of guilt.

Sloane and I conducted some retail therapy after the morning's fun—her more than me—before she insisted on paying for massages and facials at the hotel spa. I managed to pry out of her what she might enjoy eating and dedicated myself to getting as much of it in front of her as possible. Who knew Detroit style pizza was so damn good anyway? She ate more than I'd ever seen her eat before, which meant she took some bites of the thick, buttery-crusted 'za as opposed to staring it down as if it were her mortal enemy.

On Sunday, she worked out for a couple of hours while I slept in. James and Michael took us on a tour of the brewery in the afternoon, ending with an invite out to dinner.

"Like, a double date?" I elbowed James.

He smiled, but it didn't reach his eyes. The whole elephant-in-the-room thing about the buyout offer was making everyone anxious. I wanted to ask Michael about it, to cut to the dang chase, as it were. But I wasn't comfortable enough with him.

"Yeah, like that." Michael's obvious misery matched James'. The dark circles under his eyes reflected the crisis the brothers were facing. I decided to keep my nosiness to myself...for now.

"Okay, then, let's go. We have to be at the memorial at ten a.m. tomorrow so I suggest we make it an early night." I glanced at Sloane. She was staring at Michael. I sighed. This should be super fun.

They took us to Slowe's Barbeque, which went a long way, but not quite all the way, to convincing me that the best barbeque in the world didn't originate in my home state. We ate like pigs, even Sloane, considering she took maybe five bites of food. After our third round of beers, things began to loosen up.

At one point, while I was in the bathroom feeling a few stages too many past tipsy, I sent a group text to Stella and my mom. "I'm in Detroit with James and his brother. Their dad died so I'm going to the funeral tomorrow."

—*FAMILY FUNERAL!*— Stella shot back. — *That's even bigger than going as plus-one to a wedding. You know that, right?*—

—*I'm sorry to hear it*— my mother chimed in. — *Do you have a dark dress?*—

—*You'd better bring hunky brewery man to my wedding as your plus one, Andi Rose*— Stella texted.

—*Yes, I have the right dress, Mom, thanks. And I don't know about the plus 1 thing, Stell. When is your wedding?*—

—*Soon! Very soon, and it's going to be bigger and better than the first 2!*—

I reapplied some lipstick, or at least tried to, but my ankle didn't want to cooperate while I was standing at the mirror, and when I fell off the new boots that Sloane had picked out for me to buy, it sent a dark red smear of color across my cheek. I glared at it a second, then burst into giggles.

Once I'd cleaned up and headed to our table, everyone was standing and waiting for me. Michael had his arm around Sloane. She looked radiant in a way I'd never seen before.

"What's up?"

James pulled me close, kissed my hair, and declared we were going to play darts and drink a few shots in honor of Carter Burke.

I leaned away from him. "More drinking?"

"Hell to the yes, more drinking. It's the only way to truly honor the man. He stayed buzzed most weekdays from the moment he got home to when he crawled into bed. And on the weekends… Well, it was a real boozy free-for-all in our house, eh, Mikey?"

Michael and Sloane weren't paying a lick of attention to us. They were staring too hard at each other for anything else to matter.

"Let's go, lovebirds," James said, smacking his brother's shoulder so hard the man almost stumbled. "I know the perfect place."

The perfect place, as it turned out, was a near replica of the dive where James and I had first met. Stale smokiness, greasy food, and macro beers abounded, along with the loudest damn juke box I'd ever heard. Ergo, perfection.

We had our first round of whiskey shots—bourbon, in honor of Miss Kentucky as I was dubbed for the night. I protested. Bourbon was not meant to be guzzled. But I was overruled, even by Sloane who'd only quaffed about half as much beer as the rest of us at dinner.

We had ourselves a boys-versus-girls darts tournament, during which I was once again regaled as Ringer Queen when I bullseyed almost every round. At my last three shots, half the bar cheered for me. I turned, executed a sweet curtsey, if I do say so myself, and grabbed my beer. I held onto the rail around the dart boards so as not to face plant.

In short, I was, once again, drunk off my ever-loving ass with James.

"Hey, hey, hold on," James said, grabbing me as I tried to make a break for the ladies'. "Don't go, Andi." His smile was wide, his eyes glassy. He hadn't pawed me or kissed me or anything so far. We'd been sort of more like buddies. I wasn't sure if I liked it.

"I'm not leaving for college, Jimmy. Just to take a pee."

He laughed and let go of me. "What's up with those two?" He jerked his chin to a dark corner where his brother and Sloane had decamped.

"Who the hell knows?" I brushed by them on my way to the bathroom. "Putting on a show, there, Ms. VanAnsel," I said.

She broke their liplock and looked at me.

"I know. I don't care anymore." She hiccupped, then giggled.

"Marry me," Michael said.

We both stared at him. I wasn't sure if I'd heard him right. Sloane burst out laughing so hard she doubled over. I waited, way too interested in this show than in alleviating the pressure in my bladder.

She stood up, shrugged, and said, "Okay. Sure. Why the hell not. In the meantime, let's dance." She grabbed his hand and pulled him onto the makeshift dance floor that was essentially the empty space of sticky concrete floor in front of the blaring juke, which had gone from honky-tonk to blues and was now blasting eighties-style disco. Michael made it look good. No real surprise there.

After I peed, I splashed cold water on my face, realizing all I'd accomplished was turning myself from a sweaty drunk into a damp one. I emerged and was immediately dragged out to dance. Other patrons joined us, and within a few minutes, we'd scooted almost all the tables and chairs out of the way and had ourselves a makeshift dance party.

At one point, gassed and dying of thirst, I flopped into a rickety chair. James joined me, bringing blessed relief in the form of two ice-choked glasses of water. I drained mine fast, letting a trickle of water escape in my haste. It cooled my neck anyway. When I set the glass down, James decided to lick it off.

Now this was more like it.

Dizzy from him, and the booze, I leaned my head back when he pulled my legs onto his lap. His lips made their slow, teasing way up to mine.

And so, here I was, wanting to jump the bones of this man while I was seeing serious double.

Not good. Not good at all.

I broke our contact with reluctance, holding his face between my hands, the rasp of his beard oh-so-pleasant against my palms. He smiled, but it was the smile of the seriously inebriated. I knew that look. I'd seen it on my own face in the bathroom.

My God. How long ago had that been? What time was it anyway?

I grabbed my phone and attempted to focus on the numbers. "Holy shit," I squeaked dropping my feet to floor and lurching toward Sloane who was hanging off Michael's shoulder and giggling. "We gotta go."

"What? Why?" Sloane pushed Michael off her. He tried to look suave, almost landing on his drunk ass.

It made me giggle, but I got hold of myself. "It's almost three in the dang morning, y'all. We have a fu—fun—funny—fuck…a funeral to go to." I snapped my fingers, trying to pretend I was sober and thinking straight.

James barreled into me from behind, flipped me around, and dipped me so low I could smell the stale, sticky bar floor.

"Get off me!"

But he pulled me upright and kissed me again.

Oh boy. He was a class-A champion. I'd almost forgotten.

No. Not really.

"You're right," he declared when he ended that lovely moment. "She's right. Andi. Is. Right." He tucked me under his arm and motioned for his brother. "Mikey. Find us a ride. We need to get out of here. And don't give me any BS about wanting to go to the hotel with PR Barbie over there either. You and I need a few Z's before this debacle tomorrow."

"Quite a speech, my brother," Michael said weaving his way over to us. "Impressive, for one so…so…drunk." He had his hands on James' shoulders now. "Fuck me running. I'm polluted. Sloane!" He roared.

"Jesus, I'm right here. What?" She was busy putting her shirt back in order. "You flipped open my bra, you ass. Now I can't get it re-fastened."

"I hereby declare this to be a bra-free zone. No bras. All the time." He reached for her, but she slapped his hands away.

"Ugh. Stop it. Andi, can you help me?"

I pulled up her shirt in the back and hooked the tiny undergarment back together.

"You're right. We should go." She leaned on my shoulder. "But first, I want everyone in here to know..." She held up her left hand. I squinted at it.

"Is that what I think it is?" James bellowed as he grabbed Sloane's hand so he could eyeball it.

"Yes, my brother, it is." Michael put a hand on James' arm. "I have asked the fair Sloane to become my bride. And she has agreed, indeed. And so, since I am savvy in the ways of women and know that putting a ring on it is of tantamount importance, voila! I have ringed it... I mean put some ring on it. Oh hell, you know what I mean."

"Mikey, I hate to interrupt while you're breaking your arm patting your own back but this..." He held up Sloane's hand. "This is not a ring. It's a Goddamned paperclip."

Sloane jerked her hand back and held it close to her face. "It is, but I'm counting on my sweet-cheeks lover man over there to replace it, like, by noon tomorrow or this deal is off." She tossed her hair and flounced toward the door, coat and purse in hand.

James laughed and slapped Michael on the back. "Well played, brother. Well fucking played."

Michael gave a courtly bow, which ended with him on his hands and knees on the disgusting floor. James helped him up, even though they didn't have a sober synapse between them.

"Dear God in heaven help me, but I love that woman so...*fucking* much." He pointed at Sloane who seemed to be the one amongst us with enough non-drunk brain cells to call for a ride. "And you!" He swung around James' large torso to point at me.

I pointed at myself, looked behind me, then mouthed "Me?" at him.

He pointed at my tits, then up at my face. "You are going to marry this son-of-a-bitch, right?"

"Whoa, there Mikey. You're jumping my gun a bit. I just shed myself of one marriage, remember?"

I flinched, my warm, happy bubble bursting into a zillion tiny ones.

"Tracy was a class-A bitch. A carbon copy of Amelia. You're well shed of her, but this!" Michael ran to me, hugged me close, and didn't let go for an embarrassing period of time. "You and your..." He stared right at my chest. "Your gorgeous eyes and this awesome hair." He picked up a strand and held it to his nose. "And your fucking beer savvy and your sales *cajones*." He sighed and gave me another squeeze. "Mmm..." he muttered.

I started giggling.

"Stop fondling my date's tits, you freak show." James dragged him off me, but they were both smiling. I was glad to see it regardless that it was mere hours before we all had to present ourselves at the memorial service. These guys needed the outlet. If nothing else, I was glad to have witnessed it.

"*Vamanos*!" Sloane yelped from the door. "Ride's here."

"My beautiful bride," Michael called. "Your chariot awaits." He stumbled toward the door.

"Crap," James said, rubbing his eyes. "We're gonna pay for this for real, aren't we?"

"Yep. Come on. If you play your cards right, I might let you touch my boobs before the night's over."

"Hubba. Hubba," James said, planting another kiss on me that was a skosh sloppier than his usual, but I was hardly one to talk.

I didn't remember a single thing about the ride back to our hotel, other than Sloane hiccupping and James snoring. She and I got out and made it to our room.

"Water. Lots and lots and lots of water," I said, draining one of the six dollar bottles before refilling it from the wet bar tap.

"He wants me to marry him," Sloane chirped from the couch. She was lying inverted in what I assumed was a yoga pose until she tried to execute a backward somersault and ended up on the floor with a loud bump and giggle. "Andi! Look!" She held out her paperclip ornamented hand. "He loves me. I knew he did, you know. I fucking knew it."

I handed her a water bottle. "Yeah, yeah, great. Drink this. We need to pass out for a few hours and get through the damn service, then come back here for a nap.

"He loves me…" she said again.

I left her on the floor, cooing away, and dropped onto the bed, fully dressed, asleep before my eyes fully closed.

Chapter Seventeen

My head was clanging, echoing with my own heartbeat, and had been since I rolled onto the floor at the harsh sound of the wake-up call from the front desk. The few short hours between the call and this moment had passed at a snail's pace. A painful, hungover, miserable snail.

The agony assaulted me in fits and starts, in between bouts of trying not to throw up and wishing I were dead so I could stop feeling how bad my brain ached. Sloane seemed normal, but she hadn't had quite as much to drink as the rest of us. Although I had to attribute the unhealthy pallor of her skin to something other than excitement about being paperclip engaged.

Anyway, we took showers, got dressed, and drank more water. I attempted to choke down coffee, but my stomach wasn't having it so I quit before we all regretted it.

Michael and his mother had compromised and put on a combination memorial service and reception at the Downtown Detroit Club, which, I'd learned, was an old money country-in-the-city club that the Belangers had belonged to for four, count 'em, four generations. Carter had only been a member by association while his sons were full members, being the half-Belanger silver-spoonies that they were.

Sloane had filled me in on this arcane nonsense.

She'd also told me to expect at least two hundred and fifty people to stream through the club's main room Amelia had rented. It would boast a full bar—natch—and an expansive array of finger foods. I didn't get it. But I wasn't a rich person whose family had always considered her husband beneath her.

I wasn't exactly shocked to find out, from Sloane again, that Carter and Amelia Burke had barely been on speaking terms the last five years. I guess it stood to reason she'd be throwing a massive party upon the occasion of his death.

We located James and Michael straight away, standing at the table where their father's mortal remains were contained by a fancy urn. They looked worse than I felt, which was saying something. James waved when he caught my eye, before turning his attention to the line of people waiting to express their condolences. I sighed and sat, groaning when the movement jarred my neck, sending shockwaves of fresh pain into my skull.

I looked around at one point, amazed. I mean, I knew to expect people. Carter Burke had been in business close to thirty years, and his wife's connections went even deeper. But this was…serious people. The room, which had been expanded by taking out dividers, was so full it was hard to move. Luckily, all I wanted to do was sit and feel sorry for my sorry-ass self. No moving required.

Sloane had rallied, of course, and was chatting and working the room like a normal person. Impressive, I thought, right before I gave in to the temptation to rest my clanging head on my arms on the table. I might have taken a brief nap. I was a stone-cold expert in the ways of over-indulgence behavior.

I figured I was in the still kind of drunk stage. Because the thing about hangovers was, they were unavoidable, albeit somewhat controllable with plenty of hydration and other precautions none of which I had taken.

The only real cure was time. Nothing else works. But there were stages. As established, I was in "still drunk." Soon, if I didn't get some actual sleep, as opposed to the passing out I'd done earlier, I'd be in dehydrated/angry stage. Which would morph into eat-a-slutty-cheeseburger-stage to soak up the residual poisons in my system. Then more sleep. Then I'd be cured. Like I said, only time would heal.

I felt a hand on my shoulder and looked up, blinking like a mole who'd been dug out of its hidey hole. James. Holding what looked like a plate chock full o' carbs. My mouth watered. Okay, so I would skip a stage.

"Thanks," I said when he plunked it down in front of me.

He brushed my temple with his lips. I smelled residual booze on him still and realized I was likely wafting about in here with similar perfume. Nice. "Can't stay, but you looked miserable so I thought I'd bring something to…"

We said, "Soak up the poison," at the same time. It was cute. But my head hurt too much to care.

Michael barked out his name from somewhere. He sighed. "Duty calls. Catch you after?"

"Unless I figure out a way to escape to the hotel."

"I wouldn't blame you if you did. It's not like you know anyone in here except the immediate family."

I stiffened. It wasn't like I didn't want to be here,

to provide moral support and all. Okay, that was a lie. I still wasn't sure why I was here other than to provide Kentucky-accented comic relief when I wasn't being snarked at by his mother. "I'll stick it out a while."

He took my hand and actually kissed it.

I shook my head. "Cut the crap, Jimmy. Go and do your thing."

At that opportune moment, Mrs. Burke her own self floated by. She, too, smelled of booze, in her case, gin.

"Very courtly, James," she said, sneering at me, huddled in a chair in a corner, enduring the suffering of an ill-planned drunk fest. "We must talk more, Miss…" She held out her hand, palm down.

I stared at it way too long to be considered polite. Then I stood up, took it, turned it to the side, and gave it a firm shake.

"Must we?" I smiled.

She blinked, processing my rudeness. I muffled a groan, imagining how hard my mother would smack the back of my head for being such a bitch to a poor widow.

Poor widow, my hind parts.

Her nostrils flared, which impressed me for a second before she whirled away. "James. Come with me," she commanded.

He gave me a thumbs up and mouthed "nice one" before trotting behind her, doing his duty as a loyal son.

"It's the booze talking, ma, I swear," I whispered under my breath before picking up a croissant. Before I knew it, the pile of bready products had disappeared and I was hoping no one would notice me picking up the plate and licking it. I pushed it away instead and drank another glass of water.

Eager for more hydration, I risked standing. After a mild wobble, I wandered over to the bar and got a refill, only tempted for a few seconds by the thought of a Bloody Mary. I knew better.

After the carbs and water solution, I was point-five percent better. But I'd take any improvement.

The room seemed to get more crowded, the murmuring so loud it hurt my ears. An odd laugh broke through the polite undercurrent of "so sorry for your loss." I leaned against the wall to take some pressure off my feet. Michael and James stood half a head above most of the crowd, guarding the Carter Urn, still shaking hands and nodding, smiling and trying not to look as bad as they had to feel.

Sighing, I shifted from foot to foot, looking for Sloane. She was tall in her heels, and I expected to spot her moving about, doing her special work-the-room thing. This was her crowd, a rich crowd, well out of my league. I sought James again. He was busy hugging someone. Someone very pretty and thin and not Sloane. I launched myself away from the wall and into the fray, headed straight for him.

"Andi," he said, looking startled.

"Hi," I said, making a point to stare at the woman standing way too close to him. Never mind they'd shared a bed for almost seven years as a married couple, because I knew, without being introduced, this was the former Mrs. James Burke. The notorious Tracy-now-married-to-tech-millionaire. The woman James would still be married to if she hadn't ended it.

I stuck out my hand, praying I didn't reek of booze even as I knew I did. She glanced at James, who kind of looked like he had an electric pole jammed up his butt. She took my hand, her expression strained.

We women could spot from ten miles away when our man was being targeted or otherwise claimed. I edged closer to James' other side, so he was bracketed by us. When he grabbed my hand and threaded his fingers in mine, I felt somewhat less like an interloper.

Tracy could give Sloane a run for her money in the classy and cool category of beauty. She was blonde, something I hadn't imagined her being. She was tall, five seven or eight. Her cream-colored boot heels put her almost on eye level with James. Said blonde hair was golden and flowed down her back and across one shoulder in elaborate, natural-looking-yet-not curls. She wore a cream suit to match her boots, which should have been jarring, but she did live on the West coast so maybe she'd forgotten how we plebes showed respect for the dead in our drab blacks, grays, and navy blues.

The jacket had oversized lapels, was nipped in tight at her waist, and matched the pencil skirt and boots. She wasn't stick thin like Sloane. She had decent curves. Okay, they were well in proportion to her height—perfect, in other words. I became aware of the large shelf of my boobs, protruding from me like the prow of a ship, coated with breadcrumbs. I brushed at them, my face flushed while Tracy remained too close to her ex-husband's other side, her brown eyes studying me. They were a magazine-ad-worthy couple. That much was clear.

"I wanted to make it work," James had said at dinner, looking like a sad, kicked-in-the-face puppy. It hit me then. This…person, this woman, had cheated on James with her current husband. My chest filled with

righteous indignation. As if sensing me getting riled up, James let go of my hand and draped his arm over my shoulders.

"I'm Andi," I said. "Andi Rigby."

"Nice to meet you, Andi," Tracy said before sliding to our right. "Michael, darling, it's so lovely to see you. I hate that it's under such horrible circumstances."

I watched her work, impressed despite the roil of fury in my head. Michael accepted her hug. "Tracy. You're looking appropriately...rich." He was smiling at her in a familiar way. A way I wanted to scratch off his face. "How's life with the boyfriend—I mean, husband."

"Oh, sweetie, don't be mean." She hooked her arm in his, nonplussed by this dig. "Where's your gorgeous gal? She and I are long overdue a catch-up."

James eased away from her. I looked up at him. He was watching her, his eyes narrowed. I'd swear he was quivering like a downed live wire.

When Tracy looked square at me, I almost flinched.

Almost.

Instead, I lifted my chin and tucked myself in closer to James' side.

"Besides, looks like James has replaced me already," she said.

I disentangled from James, needing some space and air. This whole too-comfy scene was making me doubt myself, from James' mother's near caricature evil-bitchiness to his ex-wife's judgy staring, I felt oafish, down-market, and out of place. Not to mention I smelled like a dang distillery.

"Nice to meet you, Tracy. Excuse me," I said with as genuine a smile as I could muster, a nod to my mother's politeness training if nothing else.

"Likewise," she said, her smile brief as she trained her attention back on James. Some women could not let go. It was clear as day to me. She didn't want him anymore, but she preferred him to remain single.

Exhaustion smothered me like a hot blanket. I wanted out, away, back in bed, preferably in my hometown, and done with all of this. It was not my scene in any way, shape, or form. Guys like Michael and James worked hard, but they could walk away from the brewery tomorrow and never have to work another day of their lives. Me? I was still thousands of dollars in debt on credit cards and only beginning to get sorted into my new life.

My throat tightened. Tears burned my eyes. I felt transported back to the moment I faced reality about my former marriage and the only life I'd known. I moved farther away from their little triangle of awesomeness.

James moved with me. "I'll come, too. I need a break."

"No, no, stay. You have mourners to greet." I turned before he could see how upset I was. It wasn't fair to him. Not today. I'd deal with myself and be fine. But I had to face one harsh reality, the one where I did not fit into his world. It was less self-pity and more acceptance. I'd be fighting my whole life if I tried to insert myself into the Burke family, not unlike Carter with his in-laws' ever-present disapproval. And as pleasant as that seemed on a purely physical level—James' kisses foretold of other, more interesting skills—I'd honed my self-preservation instinct to the point I'd be remiss if I ignored all the red flags this weekend had thrown me.

Too early, much, Andi girl?

Quite possibly. We'd had all of one actual date, several kisses, many of them sloppy from booze. Why was I thinking so far ahead? Why not have fun? Enjoy him and his…kissing and whatnot?

I observed him a few more minutes. He seemed relaxed since I'd absented myself. He and Tracy and Michael were laughing, most likely recalling some fancy vacation or dinner or party they'd attended together.

Time for me to go. I refused to dig in any deeper with James. I swallowed the urge to cry over lost opportunities and sought out Sloane. I was done. I needed a nap, and I was going to get one. Nobody would miss me, least of all yon tall, handsome brewer who was staring at his ex-wife like a dying man in the desert eyeballing a water park mirage.

"Oh, thank God, there you are," I said when Sloane rushed past me. "Wait…what…"

She pushed through the scrum of people between the bar and the closed, double entry doors without stopping. The right one hit the wall behind it with an admirable whack when she stiff-armed it. She was marching through the lobby of the club, leaving me no time to ogle the ornate, high painted ceiling or the ginormous chandelier in the lobby.

"Sloane! Wait!" I lurched along in my heels, my arches screaming in agony, my calves locking up in sympathy.

She jumped into the back of a waiting SUV in front of the club. I stared at her, confused. But we were leaving, which was my goal.

"Come on," she said, her voice tight. She motioned for me to join her. "I'm done here."

I climbed in and shut the door.

"Hilton," she barked out to the driver. "Shit." She yanked off the paperclip ring, tossed it to the floor, and attempted to mash it into oblivion with her high heel, one of those fancy, expensive ones with the red soles. "Goddamn it," she said. "Goddamn that…bitch."

"Yeah, I'm totally feeling you." I patted her shoulder, surprised, since Sloane had managed Amelia way better than I ever would, or could, or should. I figured them for equals in the snooty-rich-lady department. Difference being, for Sloane, it was a mask she slipped on and off as needed. While, for Amelia Burke, it represented the sum total of her personality. "What happened?"

Sloane blew out a breath. I tried not to overreact to how red-faced she was. "My so-called impromptu engagement? Yeah, it's got nothing to do with me. It's all about the fucking buyout. *My* father pulled *his* mother into the whole mess. They're forcing us together, so Burke won't fire VanAnsel."

"Wait. What does their relationship with VanAnsel have to do with the buyout? And how did you find out?"

"Oh, you'd be surprised what you can learn sitting quietly in the bathroom stall."

"No lies there. But still…I don't get it." More like, I didn't buy it.

Michael Burke was ass-over-tea-kettle in love with her. I could tell. Another thing we women knew when we saw it. He might be a little emotionally constipated, but I could read him like a dang book. Sloane was brittle and as high maintenance as they came, but so was he. They were a great couple, and they both knew it.

"My father is behind the buyout offer. He approached Diego Brothers in secret, proposing the purchase as a way to anchor Burke products to VanAnsel. He pulled Amelia into his scheming. So she told Michael to propose. I don't know the details, but I know my fucking father is ruining my life, yet again. And he's bringing Michael and James along for the ride this time."

My mouth dropped open. This was not at all what I'd expected to hear her say. She glared at me, her eyes bloodshot, her face mottled red.

"VanAnsel gets a portion of Diego's book of products as part of the buyout. More famous beers and wines to distribute in Michigan, but more importantly, the Burke family ownership shares are weakened while at the same time, they have no way of dissolving their distribution deal with us." She shook her head. "My father's had it in for Carter for years. They hated each other's guts. Michael's been rumbling about cutting us loose. He's not happy with our track record, now that he has full access to the sales data."

She sniffled. I handed her a tissue from my purse. "I convinced him to give us more time. And with you and Sandra on board, we're going gangbusters. Better than ever." She blew her nose. "Now that Carter's dead, my manipulative shithead of a father is worried he can't push the deal through. Carter was willing to take it—he needed the dough—but Michael and James don't want to. So I guess he's using his only daughter to shore up his odds or some shit. I don't know."

My mind was rolling around like a bunch of rogue marbles. I couldn't capture a single thought other than the one whamming the front of my noggin. Michael didn't do it. Michael didn't betray his brother, like James thought he had.

"So, in order to get Diego to stay at the table, VanAnsel and Burke have to be a package deal," I said, realizing how huge this was for her.

"Sure, and if we're married, breaking up the partnership gets super awkward. Based on that guarantee, Diego increased their offer today. Fuck."

She threw the tissue on the floor where it lay next to the sad, stretched out paperclip ring. "What an asshole. Using me...and making me think...I...he... Ugh!" She flung herself away from me and stared out the window. "Story of my life. It was why I left, went to Chicago to have my own damn life. Why he had to be at the club that night, looking so..." A tear slipped down her cheek. She wiped it away. "I'm done. With him, with my father, with all of it."

I decided it wasn't the time to share my own epiphany with regard to the Burke Family. She had enough on her mind. But something was bugging me. "Sloane, I don't mean to beat this horse or anything, but this buyout... Do you know how much money they're talking about?"

She pressed her forehead to the window. "It's a huge number. Plenty to cover the loans Carter ran up to open the other facility plus some decent walk-away money for James and Michael. Not that Michael needs it. Damn man is richer than God, thanks to his investments and real estate shit."

"And James?"

She side-eyed me. "I never did tell you about him, did I?"

"Well…" She'd told me a lot, but nothing relative to his financial position. I merely assumed it was solid, stable, well-funded.

"After their Uncle Jeff died, and James didn't come back for the funeral for whatever reason, his father cut him off. He was on his own for the bulk of his time in Germany getting his Master Brewer's certification. When he came back, Amelia convinced Carter to hire him as the head brewer. He did but only paid him a pittance, as retribution or something for being so selfish and leaving the country, for not coming back out of respect for his uncle. To this day, as far as I know, Michael doesn't know why James stayed away."

She leaned back and shut her eyes. "To say James' relationship with his father was dysfunctional is the ultimate understatement. They fought every day about everything, according to Michael." She took a breath. "Michael's way of dealing with his parents was to leave for MBA school and stay in Chicago. Until, of course, James convinced him to come back because Carter was running the family company into the damn ground. I'm guessing once Michael was put in charge of the board and the books, he started paying James a decent wage. But as far as I know, it's the only money he has."

I stared at her. There was so much I didn't know. So many complications. I felt even better about my resolve to avoid James and any potential relationship with him. I shut my mind to the surge of recent memories—the bars in Denver, the ride-along day, the date, these past couple of days.

Nope. That's going nowhere, and I don't need the headache or potential heartbreak. I was a rebound, despite his insistence to the contrary. He had too many issues between his mother, his brother, and his ex-wife. It was time for me to execute my own extraction from this mess.

"I never should have come here. I'm sorry for dragging you along." She grabbed my arm. "I was just in…I don't know, rescue mode or something. But not anymore." She let go of me and crossed her arms.

I spent a few seconds worrying about how prominent her cheekbones were. This woman, my new friend, who'd been so good to me, a virtual stranger to her, was about to lose her shit. I could tell.

"Sloane, let's get some rest, then have a decent dinner—pizza, your favorite. Then let's go home."

"I refuse to stay here another night." She was folding and unfolding another tissue, her fingers working it over and over. "I have to get away from this…from him."

"Okay, fine," I said, disappointed when the precious potential nap faded from my immediate future. "I'm so behind at work it's ridiculous."

We sat, staring straight ahead, both of us, no doubt, thinking of our respective Burke Brother. Both of us, no doubt, letting them go in the name of self-preservation.

Chapter Eighteen

Three weeks later

To claim it was challenging to ignore James Burke in the weeks after that horror show weekend was putting it mildly. The man was as stubborn as my grandaddy's mule.

He called. He sent texts and social media messages. He even snail mailed me a dang postcard. In the third week post-Carter funeral, he sent a bouquet of roses to my office, which was the last straw.

"Oooooh, somebody's putting out," Rick called as he strolled past my cubicle. I didn't give him the pleasure of a response.

"Hey, Todd, would you send fifty buck's worth of out-of-season flowers to a chick you'd just been dating?"

"Hell no. That's for after a special night. Preferably early in the process. I'm not very patient."

I pondered the note. It was hand-written or should I say hand-scribbled in a left leaning scrawl.

Andi. I don't know what happened at the funeral, but whatever it was please accept my apologies and these damn flowers. Now, go pick up your fucking phone.

Cheers,

James

Still resolute, if wobbly around the edges, I took

the bouquet into the break room and tossed the note in the trash. There. That would do it. Let everyone else enjoy his floral largesse. I had no time for it. We were approaching holiday season, which meant working triple time to fill orders.

I, for one, was enjoying the rush and distraction of being busy from six a.m. until whenever, falling into bed bone-tired around midnight and rising again to start it all over. I had a full schedule today, including stops at some of my more important buyers.

Orders for Burke products were at an all-time high, too, I'd noticed on the sales reports. Score one for Andi, at least that one time.

The boys at the office had lightened up as well, today's vile comments excluded, so I felt less stressed being around them. I'd even engaged in some light, ever-so-slightly sexual banter to prove I didn't give a rip what they said to me. I was encouraging bad behavior, but right now, at this juncture in my life, I needed a job, not to cause a huge stink in my workplace. The lesser of two evils and all that.

Besides, it had caused a few of the more vocal guys to reevaluate me, resulting in the current détente. My ever-present worry about this whole buyout thing and how James was handling it, not to mention how it would affect VanAnsel if it went south, provided me with enough stress.

As I was pondering sample options for the day, Al stuck his head around my cubicle wall. "Hey, Andi, do you have a minute?"

"If you're going to tell me James Burke is here and wants another impromptu selling day—"

"It won't take a second."

I sighed. The man was my boss. What was I going to say? No can do?

Unlikely.

I got up and followed him. I'd already entered selling mode in my head and was formulating pitches and scripts to go with my sell sheets. I wasn't guaranteed sales at several of my scheduled stops, so I needed to be on my game today. I wanted top tier commission, bad. What I didn't want was a private meeting with Sloane's Uncle Al.

When he shut the door behind me, I experienced a flare of panic and started flipping through my recent orders and encounters, seeking something I'd done wrong.

"Have a seat," he said, taking the seat next to me this time, not behind his monster of a desk awash in sales reports and year-end forecasts.

"So, Andi," he said, hands on his khaki-covered thighs. "While I'll admit I was skeptical when Sloane said she'd hired you out at the expo, you've been a real asset to our team so far this year."

"Thanks," I said, wary and waiting for the proverbial other shoe to drop.

He plucked a random sheet of paper from the pile. "Your numbers are impressive." He made a whistling sound. I didn't have to wait long for said shoe. "The thing is…I need to ask a favor." He leaned back. Puzzled, I waited some more. "It's about… Well, quite frankly, it's about this whole Burke Brothers thing."

"What thing?" I knew. I wanted him to say it.

"I know you know what I'm talking about."

His eyes darkened. He looked, for want of a better word, predatory. I shifted in my seat, wondering if this particular expression was one all the men in this company were asked to perfect before they were hired.

Albert "Al" VanAnsel was a younger, better-looking version of Sloane's father. He had a slap-happy, easy-going manner, and kept it up while running our sales meetings, which bugged me. He needed to be less everybody's favorite beer drinking buddy and more the boss. But right now, he was neither.

He was scary.

"The buyout?"

"Exactly." His expression relaxed into something I recognized—testosterone-addled satisfaction, which was beyond weird, not to mention inappropriate.

I was all kinds of confused, but more importantly, I was on edge, nervous in a way I hadn't been in weeks.

"What can I do about it? Their sales are way up."

"Yes, yes." He made a tamping-down gesture with one hand.

Before I could react, that hand was on my knee, which today was covered in gray, woolen work pants. But there he was, touching me, and with some kind of bizarre intent. I stared down at his hand, then up into his face. He made no move to get his meaty palm off my leg. "You and James are…close, are you not?"

One of his dark eyebrows raised, and I would swear on a stack of bibles he leaned closer to me.

I forced myself not to move. "We are not."

He frowned. "I hear otherwise."

"You're listening to the wrong gossip." I picked up his hand and put it back on his own knee, patted it, and stood. "I declare this meeting over. Unless you'd like to move a little closer to a harassment complaint?"

My pulse was racing. My heart pounded in my

223

ears. I could barely breathe, but I was not about to be intimidated. Those days were over.

He patted the seat again, his smile wide. The predation gone, at least, for now. "I'm sorry. I'm too old school. I forget we can't touch anyone these days."

Against every better judgement I possessed, I sat, staying as far on the far side of the chair away from him as I could manage. I wouldn't allow him to intimidate me, but hell if I knew how to get away. That hashtag-me-too empowerment only took me so far. Apparently, I needed to devise escape plans from the VanAnsel higher-ups and their closed-door meetings.

Fury flooded my chest, neck, and face as my flight instinct kicked in, urging me to bolt. I remained in the chair, but at great cost to my nerves.

"Listen, Andi, we all know VanAnsel's future growth and success is tied directly to those boys agreeing to the buyout offer."

"Do we? Know that, I mean. It's not exactly public knowledge. I only know because Sloane told me before she decamped to Florida. And I'm not exactly sure I—"

"It's public enough." He talked over me, as usual. "So, here's the thing. Since Sloane's decided to avoid everything and everyone for whatever reason, I need you to find out more about where James and Michael's heads are relative to the offer. They only have until December thirty-first to respond."

I stared at the man, shocked, horrified, and yet somehow, not surprised at the same time.

"Okay, so you want me to do what, exactly? I mean, you know, I don't think I can, um…" While dithering and stalling, I made a pretense of checking my phone. "Hang on a sec, Al. I need to take this."

I winked at him like we were already in bed together on this deal. I'd read somewhere that turning on your phone's recording device before heading into a sketchy private meeting with your boss or a co-worker was becoming standard practice. I stepped into the hall and tried to recall if I even knew how to use the recording device on my phone.

It took longer than was wise, but I found it. I ended my fake call, hoping I'd managed to pull it off, touched "record," put the screen to sleep and stuck the phone back in my pocket.

"There, sorry." I shut the door and sat back down, crossing my legs and looking as sexy as I could manage. "Now, what was it you want me to do again?"

"I need you to get close to James, use your…you know…" He made a sweeping motion with his hand up and down my body.

"My what?"

"Your connection with him. Your…wiles, whatever. Pillow talk, that kind of thing."

"Ah, I see. You'd like for me to have sex with James and, afterward, find out if he and Michael are actually going to sell their brewery. So VanAnsel can reap the benefit. That about cover it? Do you want to recommend a specific move for me? Oh, I know. Blow jobs. Every red-blooded boy loves one of those." I smiled, keeping my voice neutral as if we were talking about sports or the weather. I'd blown the whole "record them saying something bad" thing of course in my haste to run my ever-loving mouth.

Al's face flushed. His eyes narrowed, and his lips thinned. "There's no need to be—"

"Honest? I mean, that is what you're asking me to

do. 'Getting close' being a clever euphemism for it. If I'm not speaking truth here, please enlighten me." My voice had an edge to it now.

He heard it and made an obvious attempt to soften his expression.

"Andi, hon…"

I glared harder, praying the phone was picking up every word.

He rubbed the back of his neck. Sweat popped out on his forehead. Good. He should feel rotten for suggesting this to me, for a million reasons, not the least of which it was well over the border into sexual harassment land. And he damn well knew it.

I touched the edge of my phone. Even if it wasn't recording anymore, I already knew what I was going to do next. But I waited for Al to shove his foot farther down his throat in case I needed more evidence. It didn't take long for him to oblige me.

"It's not a big deal, Andi. On your next date with James, see if you can find out if he and Michael have made a decision. I don't care how you do it. We need your help with this." He leaned so far forward I could smell his coffee breath.

I held my ground. Didn't flinch or move. "Or…else?"

"No, no, don't be ridiculous. It's a favor. Nothing more. If you can't do it, tell me. I won't bring it up again." He rose and walked around behind his desk, looking strung out and rattled. I allowed myself a moment to feel sorry for him. No doubt his big brother Grant, a known bully, had forced him into this most awkward conversation. I'd liked Al, until today. "You know what, forget it."

I froze, wondering if he was doing some reverse psychology thing on me.

He met my gaze. "My brother and the rest of the board are sweating bullets as you might imagine. This whole damn thing was Grant's idea, and he pulled Amelia Burke into it, trying to appeal to her need to fuck with her lame-ass husband. Then Carter goes and dies, and now we can't get a handle on anyone's motivation anymore. Amelia won't answer calls or emails, says she's allowed some time to mourn." He made a scoffing sound. "If mourning him means her regular tennis foursome at the club every day, followed by several rounds of drinks, sure, okay, she's mourning."

I cleared my throat. "For the record, Al, I think the whole thing is disgusting. I mean I get how competitive things are. I'm the one with boots on the ground dealing with it every day. But to try and force a buyout on the…on James and Michael, just so you can increase your own portfolio? That's about as greedy a move as greedy gets." I stood, having made a snap decision.

For the well-established record, I wasn't great at those. The last one had me dropping out of my MBA program, marrying a guy well above my pay grade, looks-wise, and then running his bar for him. And we all know how that ended.

I took a deep breath, smiled at my boss, and said, "I quit."

"What? Wait, Andi, don't…" His face turned an alarming shade of red.

I held up my hand. "No, I'm not waiting. This place is a cesspool of male-chest-beating bullshit, and I'm sick of it." The swear word tumbled out of my mouth so fast I almost didn't hear it myself.

"You can't…"

"*Au contraire*. I can. And I am." I pulled my phone out of my pocket and turned off the recording. "You might think about contacting the company law brigade. We have a little something to discuss." I waved the phone, then walked out his door, down the hall and into my cubicle. I stared at the stacks of sales reports on my desk, the three half-empty coffee cups, the snap I'd printed of me and Stella at one of her previous wedding receptions.

This was not the place for me. But I had an idea about what might be.

I'd been half-pondering this move for over a week, once I'd gotten past feeling like Little Red-Headed Orphan Annie at the memorial service. I'd been watching the Burke Brothers product list grow and realized something important about their need for a cohesive marketing plan that didn't toss new styles into the ether, willy-nilly.

Not to mention the memory of James' earnest desire to turn his family's successful production brewery into something better, something more special, more connected to the community.

I would—could—should—be that person. And I was about to tell them as much. Right about now.

Well, right about as soon as I could drive there, anyway. I smiled to myself as I left the company assigned laptop, phone and business cards on my desk and headed for the door.

This was nuts. Idiotic. I'd only been at this job a couple of months, but they'd been eight weeks of hell, trying to navigate through all the slap-happy, boy's club crap. I was over it. If they were lucky, I wouldn't claim harassment, although they totally deserved it.

I was wavering already by the time I got to my car. It was such a piece of crap. I needed a new one and had planned to start shopping after January, since I'd be in a much better financial position by then.

It all hit me at once. I'd signed a year lease, beginning my life over, here in this conservative but nice west Michigan city. Shaking but resolved, I got behind the wheel and started the engine so I could get the cab warm, then sent a text to Sloane.

She'd left for Florida a week after the memorial service mess, claiming she needed time to recuperate and recharge and accept that she and Michael would never be together. I was wary about the running away thing. I'd encouraged her to confront her father and Michael's mother. To tell them she wouldn't be their pawn anymore. Then she should go back to Chicago and live the life she wanted to there. Her mother had recovered. She suspected her parents had overplayed the cancer diagnosis to get her home anyway.

But something in my strong, sassy, over-organized friend turned into little girl mush at the thought of confronting her father.

"Hey. Can you talk?" I asked. I waited a solid five minutes, but no little bubbles appeared to tell me she was answering, which was beyond strange. Sloane was one of those immediate answerer types.

I hit the call button and put the device to my ear. I owed her this much. She'd hired me. She needed to hear from me why I'd up and quit.

"Hello?" Her voice was low and scratchy.

"Hey, Sloane. It's Andi. Are you okay?"

"Um, hang on a sec." I heard shuffling around noises, fabric on fabric sounds, the tinny sound of a television that abruptly stopped. "Okay. That's better." She sneezed.

"Do you have a cold?"

She blew her nose. "Something like that."

I sensed those imaginary red flags waving madly again. "Is that all? Really?"

She sighed. "Don't hover, Andi. I get enough of that from my mother."

I hesitated.

"I'm sorry," she said. "I'm being bitchy. Yes, I have a bad cold."

"Well, okay. Um, I quit today."

"Quit what? Drinking? Smoking? Men?"

"My job."

It was her turn to be silent. "Why?" she asked after a few beats.

I looked up at the car's ceiling, found a bit of loose duct tape, and started unraveling it. Nervous, of course. This was a strange conversation to be having with her. "Well, it's related to the Burke buyout thing."

"Oh?" She sounded like she couldn't care less and was humoring me, but I needed to talk to someone, so I blurted out the whole story, ending with me threatening Al with a harassment suit. I winced as I said it.

"Oh shit. I've really messed up, haven't I? I should go back, tell him I'm sorry. Beg for my job back." A tear slid down my cheek. I was shivering, but it wasn't from the cold. My knees were knocking together as the adrenaline rushed out of my system.

"Don't you dare." Sloane's voice gained some strength. "Don't give any of those assholes the satisfaction. You said that most of the sales guys were sexist shitheads anyway, right? Well, now you can be rid of all of that. Jesus. I can't believe they thought you'd even consider such a crazy thing. They must really be desperate."

"Yeah, I guess." I sniffled. "I'm such an idiot sometimes."

"No, you'll be fine."

"Sloane, allow me to remind you that I don't have a giant trust fund to fall back on. I need to work to do all those silly things like pay rent and eat."

"Don't overreact. We'll find you something else. Why don't you come down here for a week? We can sit in the sun and recover together."

Florida? Now? It sounded so far outside the realm of reality for me I sensed giggles bubbling up in my throat by way of hysterical response.

"I could use your company." She sneezed, then sniffled. I sensed some drama behind it. "Please?"

"Okay, tell you what. I'm headed over to Detroit first. I have to tell Michael—and James I guess—something important."

"And what might that be?"

"Sloane, you and Michael should—"

"That's not an answer to my question."

"Fine." I set my shoulders. "I'm going to tell them I'll be their sales and marketing director. I'll do it for a half decent salary and benefits and will guarantee them improved numbers, but they have to reject the buyout."

Sloane sucked in a breath. "You are so fucking gutsy. I love that about you."

"Well, they could easily laugh me right out of the building."

"But they won't. I can't believe Michael has any intention of selling, but he's getting a ton of pressure from all sides. I told him his mother was in on it, but I haven't talked to him since."

"I haven't talked to James since that night either. I'm not about being anybody's rebound."

"You wouldn't be. You and James are, like, soulmates. So well matched. He and Tracy were a thing he did to get his mother off his back. Or to please her. He's that kind of a guy. A pleaser."

"I don't judge you about Michael. You don't judge me about James. Deal?" But I was smiling when I said it.

"Only if you promise to come down here to hang with me a few days. Build that into your compensation negotiations. Michael Burke loves a hard negotiation session." My face grew hot. "Don't blush. I'm done with him. I can't…be what he wants me to be and what my parents want me to at the same time. I'm only fulfilling their expectations. Not mine."

"Fair enough," I said, putting the car in gear. I needed to get my tail over to Detroit. "But Sloane, I can't afford a plane ticket, so you'll have to suffer along without me, I'm afraid. And do not dare tell me you'll buy me one. I owe you enough already."

"Nah, I'm not buying you a ticket."

"Okay, whew." Part of me was disappointed. For as long as it took for her to speak again.

"You can take our private jet. It's at the Willow Run airport, west of Detroit Metro."

I pulled onto the expressway and pointed myself toward Detroit. "You're full of *caca*."

"Nope. I'm not. I'll call the pilot and tell him to

make sure it's ready. What time, do you think?"

"I don't know. Let's make it tomorrow. I mean, I have to pack. I don't have anything suitable for sunny lounging."

"Fine," she said, sniffling again. "It's an open invitation. If you need to do some stuff to get sorted in your new job as VP of sales and marketing at Burke, do that. But plan on spending some time down here with me before Christmas."

"I will. Thanks, Sloane."

"No, I'll be thanking you. I need…well, I could use some company." Her voice sounded weaker by the minute.

"I never said VP."

"Don't downplay what you have to offer those boys. They'll be damn lucky to have you. You want the title and at least eighty thou."

"Dollars?" I put a hand to my throat. It was an amount of money I couldn't imagine in one place.

"No, hon, pesos. Of course, dollars. Jeez. Don't underplay your worth."

"Okay. Got it."

"I mean it, Andi. Don't you dare drive all the way over there to beg them for anything. You're offering an ultimatum. And one I know they'll leap at, lucky to have you and to have a viable excuse to tell their mother and my father to pound sand."

I had to admit I hadn't even thought about what I'd ask for in compensation. But it wasn't that high. Not even close. I squared my shoulders and gripped the wheel again. It was starting to spit snow, and I was still uncomfortable driving in it. I needed to get where I was going, do what I'd decided to do, and make it worth my effort.

"Keep me posted." She sneezed again.

"I will. Eat an orange or something. Take care of yourself."

"Right. See you soon?"

"See you soon."

Chapter Nineteen

I drove all the way to Detroit sans news radio, my typical go-to when I was in the car. I didn't notice. I was too busy having multiple conversations in my head with Michael Burke, none of them ending the way I hoped. Once I got past the Detroit airport, which put me within about thirty minutes of this impromptu, whacked out, huge mistake of a meeting, I exhaled, trying to unkink the knots in my neck and arms from sitting so stiffly for so long.

When I was within ten minutes, I sent a voice text to Michael.

"Hi. It's Andi Rigby. I'm about to be at your doorstep. Can we talk?"

He answered so fast it was as if he were waiting for my message. "Of course. Tell Melinda you're here to see me. She'll show you to my office."

I got to the brewery, parked out front in a visitor's spot, turned off the engine, and sat a few seconds, gathering my nerve. After a quick makeup and hair check, plus a swipe of lip gloss for no reason whatsoever, I got out. I wished I had on nicer clothes. This day, which had begun something like ten years ago, was to have been an in-and-out-of the-car kind of a day, so I'd chosen wool trousers and a simple, now wrinkly and somewhat damp, white cotton blouse. So yeah, I was dressed like a waiter. But there was nothing for it now.

I put on a dark jacket, leaving the heavy coat behind. I was plenty warm thanks to the encroaching panic over the fact I had no idea what I was going to say once I got inside the place.

And what, pray tell, would I say to James if I saw him?

Oh God. I hoped I wouldn't see him. But then again, I wanted to so badly I could almost conjure him with the sheer force of my will right here in the dang parking lot.

I stuck my phone in my purse and looped it on my shoulder. The Burke Brothers' main building housed the Tap Room, a rental hall, kitchen, and the original brew house James used for his experiments. It was a three-story brick building, repurposed from a car parts factory. The production brewery where the big work was done—meeting the massive orders from a dozen different states plus Michigan—was tucked in behind it, invisible from where I stood. It was a masterpiece of modern brewing techniques combined with the classic, German basics.

I recalled from our tour a few weeks ago that massive fermentation vessels filled one entire room, a bottling and canning line filled in the middle while the brew house itself was up several levels from the main floor. At least the tops of the mash tun and kettle were up there. The vessels themselves took up the equivalent of three floors beneath. It was impressive, spotlessly clean, and well-organized.

The memory of the way James had touched each vessel, stroked the various parts of the canning and bottling lines, smiling like an indulgent parent at the people scurrying around, brewing, fermenting, storing, and packaging the beer, was one of the main reasons I was here today. This was important to him. I knew I could help implement the changes he wanted to make and still increase revenue.

Michael's jobs included oversight of the tap room and rental hall staff via four different managers. He handled sales, marketing, accounting, and HR issues as well. From what Sloane said at various times when she was waxing poetic about him, he had the respect of all employees. He was fair, honest, and open.

He and James ran the place on an open-book policy. They shared the financials with anyone who wanted to see them. He'd done this for transparency and to get every single employee invested in whatever they did to contribute to the final bottom line each month. He was in his element, and she believed he was happier here, now that he and James were in control.

On the other side of the equation, their sales staff was slim. Carter hadn't believed in having in-house beer ambassadors—industry jargon for sales support and retailing. Their social media was hit or miss, inconsistent at best, invisible at worst. They didn't get out in front of problems with positive public relations. It made sense on some level. Once upon a time, the damn stuff sold itself. Burke Bros was one of the originals and had a lock on the market for years. Those days were way over.

I pushed open the doors to the tap room, smiling at the overfull tables and loud, satisfied noises. Man, did I miss this. Nothing gave me a charge like watching a room full of happy customers, consuming the beer or wine or booze and food they'd paid my staff to prepare and serve.

I made my way around to the side of the pick-up window and ducked into the hallway I recalled from the tour. The admin area was up a level, accessible via a single set of metal stairs behind the kitchen. Michael had kept it austere but quirky, typical of even the most successful and well-funded breweries. Framed photos of their earliest label art, Christmas lights, plants, and in the case of the HR manager, a huge, slobbery dog made up the ambiance of the administration floor. A far cry from the way he'd worked at one time, I imagined.

"Hello," a woman seated at a nearby desk said. "You must be Andi. Michael's waiting for you. He's back there." She pointed to one side, toward his office.

It took up the entire front of the building on this floor, overlooking the parking lot on one side and the original brew house on the other. It was big enough for his executive-style desk and a small conference table, plus a sitting area with two cushy leather chairs, a small rug, and a bookshelf.

I stood outside his half open door, panic skittering up and down my spine. I could hear him, conversing with someone. Oh God, please don't be James. But it sounded one-sided like he was on the phone.

During a lull, I knocked and pushed the door open. Michael sat at the desk, fancy shoes up on top of it, leaning back in his huge chair. The phone was to his ear. I started to duck back out, but he waved me in and put his feet on the floor.

"Yeah, that's about the sum total of it. I really appreciate you considering this, Jack. I know you won't regret it." He paused. "I'll send all the pro formas to you by end of the day. Okay, thanks again. Bye." He put the phone on his desk and rose.

I was struck all over again by the sheer, physical perfection of the man. He looked nothing like his brother, and the more I got to know them, the more differences I found. Burke the younger was slim hipped, long-legged, his shoulders weren't nearly as wide as James'. His thick hair was jet black and carefully styled to look not-styled. His face was chiseled, male-model worthy not unlike Sloane's.

He was clean shaven, with thinner lips than James, and an aquiline nose. He was dressed, as always, in an impeccable, dark suit, a white shirt with French cuffs, and a silky blue and red tie. He looked like a banker, but his smile put me at some ease.

"Andi!" He came around the desk and gave me a brief hug. I tried not to giggle at the memory of him clutching at me so he could mash my boobs against him at the bar that night, drunk off his ever-loving ass. "To what do I owe this pleasure?"

He motioned for me to join him at the leather chairs-rug-and-bookcase area. I sat on the edge of my seat, hands on my lap, attempting to stop the butterflies from bursting out of my stomach and landing in a big mess on the nice rug.

He sat and poured us both a glass of water in heavy crystal glasses. He might have been keeping it funky up in here, but he didn't stint the niceties, either. I sipped, grateful for the hydration. I could hear hollering and banging around beneath us in the smaller brewery.

Resisting the urge to peek over the side through the bank of windows, I gripped my knees and focused on the goal. "I'm here to give you an ultimatum."

One dark eyebrow raised, Michael sat back in his

chair and crossed his legs. "Color me intrigued. Please, fill me in."

"I want to help you. I'll serve as your…" I hesitated but only for a second. "As the Vice President of Sales and Marketing for Burke Brothers. I'll do the job you need done, and I'll do it for less than you might pay another MBA."

He smiled and leaned forward, elbows on his knees. "I'm still listening."

I took a quick breath. "I'll do the job for eighty…five thousand, plus benefits, including dental. I'll need carte blanche to hire a decent sales staff and for travel expenses. In my first week, I'll write a clear, usable marketing plan that incorporates past sales, realistic future projections, and current capacity. I understand this business from top to bottom, and the bottom line is…" I paused to breathe again. "I want to work for you. But I have one condition. You can't sell out. I mean, I won't work as a contract employee for Diego Brothers. Some breweries need that kind of arrangement—the money, the connections, the distribution networks. But you don't need any of it, and I know this for a stone-cold fact." I finished, breathless but trying not to look like it.

"Do you?"

"I also know that VanAnsel is chomping at the bit for you to take it. We both know why."

His expression darkened. "Sloane told me. The night she also told me take my marriage proposal and shove it up my ass." He sighed, and his shoulders slumped. "How is she, by the way?" His face took on an eager, almost boyish expression. "She won't talk to me, and I don't even know if she's… Well, she has a problem with food."

"I know. And she's fine, or at least, I think so. She's in Florida. She wants me to jump on her family's jet and join her there." I shook my head. "I love that girl. I swear I do, but sometimes she loses track of what reality means for the rest of us."

"It's a nice jet." He sat back again, almost slouched all the way down in the chair, and played with one of the buttons on the leather arm rest. "We've used it before."

I cleared my throat. Taking the pause to also clear my mind of that God-awful text he'd sent her. The last thing my future boss needed to know was that I'd seen his willy standing at attention. And had been duly impressed by the dang thing. "Look, I'm really sorry about Sloane. I don't get you guys at all, and I'm not about to start trying. I will say, without the risk of breaking our Girl Code, she's torn up and has been since the memorial service."

He frowned deeper. "I haven't spoken to my mother since then either. It's gonna make for a super fun Thanksgiving."

I licked my lips. Thanksgiving was two weeks away. I had vague plans to go home and spend it with my mother and Stella but was already making other plans—the kind that involved a moving truck and figuring out how to get out of my Grand Rapids lease.

"I'm curious about something, Andi." He sat up straight, back in Mr. Charming Banker mode. "I know why Sloane's ignoring me. Despite my explanations to the contrary, she honestly believes I let my mother and her father convince me to ask her to marry me. It pisses me off she thinks I'm that easy to push around. But whatever. It's done now." He paused, and my pulse raced faster. "What I really want to know is why you've been ignoring my poor hapless brother for the past three weeks like you were getting paid big money to do it."

I sucked in a breath. I had half expected this. James and Michael would have each other's backs when it came to women. I went with brutally honest. "I'm not a good fit for him."

"Bullshit."

I tried to relax and paste a smile on my face. "Is my potential employment here conditional upon me talking to James?"

"What makes you think you're not good for him?"

"I don't fit in with your family, Michael. And when I saw how comfortable he was with Tracy at the memorial service, I guess it just hit home for me. But it's fine. I'm nowhere near ready for a relationship. I may very well be ruined for them, if you must know the truth."

"I'll repeat myself. Bullshit. I've never known a woman more suited to James on every level. Tracy was…" He waved a dismissive hand. "She was a cheater, for starters, and a climber. She was the polar opposite of what he needed or wanted. But James is a pleaser."

I smiled at his use of this word. He and Sloane had obviously discussed this before.

"He's only happy when everyone around him is happy. It was a losing battle growing up in our house, I assure you. My mother shoved Tracy at him at a moment when he was feeling unmoored, fighting with Carter every day, frustrated beyond belief. And lonely. Never discount the power of suggestion over a lonely grown-ass man."

He rose and walked to his desk, pulled out a folder, and brought it back to the chairs. "All I'm saying is, give him a shot. Don't discount him because you think he's rebounding. Tracy wasn't half the woman you are, Andi. And in that vein, I have an employment contract here, ready for you to sign."

I flinched at the abrupt change of tone. Then again at what he'd actually said. "An employment contract? For me? Already?" My voice was high and squeaky, more mouse than big talker VP.

He handed it to me and tucked his hand in his trouser pockets, looking sheepish, which was odd, considering he was such a master of the universe type. "I've had it since Denver. Ever hopeful, that's me." He handed me his Mont Blanc pen. "I think you'll find the terms agreeable."

I took the pen and opened the folder. There it was. In black and white. Vice President of Sales and Marketing. Starting salary…I blinked at it. "Michael, this number is…"

"Fair market value for you." He sipped his water.

I heard a shout, then loud laughter from below that I recognized as James's voice. I shut out the sound and read through the rest of the contract. It included something odd toward the last page.

"I own a couple of rehabbed houses not far from here. I'm offering one of them to you for a decent rent."

"You…want to rent me a house." My mind was spinning, my hands clammy.

"And I'll buy out your lease in Grand Rapids." He leaned forward, fingers clasped together in front of his knees. "I need you here, bad. This is where you belong.

Not slinging half-ass, bullshit beer for those VanAnsel douchenozzles."

I looked up at him and closed the folder. "And regarding my one condition?"

"I'm not selling. Once I understood the machinations behind it, I was certain. James is with me. He's looking to expand the original brew house so we can sell a specialty line to the hard-core beer snobs. They need love, too. And they'll spend big bucks." He smiled, and something in my chest relaxed its hold, allowing me to take my first full breath in twenty-four hours. "You coming here today has only solidified my decision. I can't tell you how happy I am you're as stoked about working for me as I am to have you in charge of our sales and marketing."

I felt giddy, dizzy with all of this. "But…what about James?"

Michael smiled, re-opened the folder, and turned the last page. "I have a feeling he'll be okay with it, too."

We shook hands.

He grinned and dragged me into a hug.

"Risking an inappropriate touching complaint, here, boss," I said into his shoulder. But I didn't mind.

"Sorry," he said, letting me go but holding onto my arms. "But you're basically family. You just don't know it yet."

Chapter Twenty

Thanksgiving Day

"Dear God, woman. What's in here? Your bowling ball collection?"

I stood at the top of the front steps, admiring the tidy little porch where I could sit and read and have coffee, once the weather warmed up. James had one of the blue totes labeled "LPs" and was headed up the short sidewalk.

"Nope," I said, pulling my hat farther down to cover my freezing ears. "My vinyl one."

I was being short with him, but I was still half-irritated that he'd shown up out of the blue at my new house to "help."

I'd put Sloane off a couple of weeks, needing to get settled before I took my BFF Florida vacation. I wanted to sever my ties in Grand Rapids as efficiently as possible. The VanAnsel HR guy had been short but sweet with me, regarding my leaving. I had one paycheck and a hefty commission left to me. Should they simply use the direct deposit as usual? That sort of thing.

I could tell he'd been warned about me and my ability to throw a huge mess in their laps, were I so inclined, but I'd decided to let it go, at least for now.

I'd hired a couple of guys from the rental truck place to help me load everything once I had it packed in a twenty-four hour, no-sleep, beer-fueled frenzy. This included the unloading of my POS car, since I planned to lease something new using my last commission from VanAnsel as a down payment. Michael had indeed paid my way out of the lease. It was a done deal by the time I got back to my place, the same day I'd hauled off and told him to hire me and to reject the buyout offer.

Michael had given me an employee list with asterisks next to those he knew could use the work, so I had two brewery employees, ready and waiting for me at my new place, a fully renovated two-story house in the Woodbridge neighborhood, near Midtown and within a fifteen-minute drive to my new job. They weren't the only ones waiting for me. Mr. Awesome Himself was chatting with his employees, all of them shivering on my new front porch when I pulled up in front of the house behind the wheel of the truck.

Between us all, we made short work of it. I stared at the truck's empty interior once the last stick of furniture had been removed. I was feeling a tad burny in the chest again, thanks to James' proximity. I wished I could name the emotion underneath the physical sensation. It was some odd combination of sadness and anxiety mixed in with a fair bit of anticipation. I knew he'd stick around, help me unpack, then try to kiss me. My level of inner confusion about whether I wanted or didn't want him to was epic.

I'd lain awake the night before, my last in the nice apartment in Grand Rapids, the place I'd come to escape the horror of my life, thinking this would be the solution. My life married to Matthew Rigby and running BWI felt like it had happened to someone else, in another lifetime. He'd been replaced whole cloth with the man currently standing on my porch, sipping coffee I'd ordered in advance from a local place Michael had recommended.

The surreal bubble I'd been operating in for a week, which included a signing bonus from Burke that exceeded every penny I'd made at VanAnsel and then some, wouldn't allow me to think too hard. But now that I'd done this thing—moved myself all the way up from Kentucky, then across Michigan from Grand Rapids to Detroit and was prepared to recreate myself as a Vice President of a major brewery—reality was starting to poke its way in. Colors that had been muted for a week were becoming too vibrant. The smell of my stuff combined with the subtle odors of James' shampoo or soap filled my sinuses. The sounds of downtown, even on a holiday like today, were harsh, hitting my eardrums with the force of a pair of crashing cymbals.

As I was climbing off the back of the truck one last time, unsure what to say, how to act, what to do around James, I watched a small delivery truck pull up behind the rental. It said "Hygrade Delicatessen" on the side. A kid hopped out, grabbed a massive cooler, and began rolling it toward the steps without paying any attention to me.

"Cool. Our Thanksgiving dinner is here," James said. He signed something on the kid's computer tablet, then took the cooler handle and rolled it inside. "Pull up a box, guys. I've got the goods."

I heard a whoop of response as I climbed the steps.

"Hey, would you mind grabbing my cooler from my truck?" James asked from the open front door. "I brought beers, too." He winked at me, then disappeared into the—into *my*—new house.

Berating myself for feeling ungrateful, I headed back down, opened the back of James' truck and pulled out the Burke labeled cooler. Once I had it in the house, I noted my dining table was set for a lovely turkey sandwich feast. Candles and a small bouquet of flowers included.

Mr. Awesome was at it again.

James and the other guys had found either chairs or boxes and tucked napkins into their shirts. Chest tight with a bizarre mix of conflicting emotions, I opened his cooler and pulled out three growlers and four pint glasses. I swallowed the need to say something snarky and ruin a perfectly nice moment, passed the glasses around, and took a chair that had been left available.

The men chose their beers and poured. I waited, unable to take my eyes off the man at the far end of my small table. His thick, chestnut brown hair was in its typical, messy state. His beard could use a tidy-up, but his green eyes shone, and his full, too kissable lips were turned up in a constant smile at the sight of the guys digging into the feast.

At one point, he met my gaze. "Happy Thanksgiving," he said, holding up his glass of Burke's famous porter.

My imagination was running rampant, forcing unwanted images to cross my brain—James and me and other people enjoying Thanksgiving year after year, his beard going gray, my face more lined.

I shook my head. *Jumping ahead. Fantasies. None of this will happen. It can't. You made up your mind about him, remember? You're about to be this man's employee. Get a dang grip.*

I poured myself a healthy portion of the Burke IPA—a classic style, not the trendy New England one—and lifted my glass to match the other three.

"Here's to new beginnings," James said. "And friendships."

We all clinked and sipped.

"God, that's good," I said, smacking my lips.

"But not as good as LionHearted," James said. "I know."

"Dude, Galena isn't gonna know what hit him once I'm in charge of your brand."

The other guys cheered and whooped.

James sat perfectly still, watching me.

"Wait until you try this sandwich, *amiga*," Tomas said, passing me a giant, foil-wrapped bundle. "*Es muy delicioso.*"

"I don't doubt it. I've heard about this place."

"Hearing of it is nothing compared to eating it," my other helper, Dante said. They took big bites of their mile-high turkey Reubens. I unwrapped mine and did the same, grinning when a sploosh of dressing shot out and hit the table in front of me. James was licking dressing off his arm, and the other two guys were in some similar stage of fighting through the mess.

But I'd be damned if it wasn't the most delicious combination of turkey, dressing, cheese, sauerkraut, and thick rye bread I had ever put in my mouth. I took another bite, then another, only putting it down to combine the amazing flavors with James' IPA. As I drank it, I was formulating how I might convince him to change up his hops mixture, to give it a bit more punch.

"I told you," Tomas said. "Didn't I tell you?"

"You told me, all right. Thanks, James." I lifted my glass again. He did the same.

My helper crew stayed long enough to unpack the kitchen and get the bulk of the furniture set up. I still had to wait for a guy to connect my internet, but we assembled my Smart TV in one corner of the high-ceilinged living room, and Dante who was some kind of electronics savant set up my turntable, receiver, and wireless speakers on the table I'd bought at a consignment store for that express purpose.

"Use the hotspot on your phone," he said. "Until you get your house wireless connected."

I nodded, recalling the company phone I now used, complete with company paid bill. The surreal bubble surrounded me again, muting sounds, while I watched the men bustling around, trying to get my household set up.

At six that night, we dug into leftover sandwiches. While we were eating, my doorbell rang. I jumped, startled by the sound of it.

"Might want to get that," James said as he patted his belly.

I made a mental note to be more aware of the Burke brother tendency to take over, to smooth the path in a slightly imperious way, and opened the door.

A young woman stood there, holding a small, square box. "Andi Rigby?"

"Yes." I glanced over my shoulder, but James had his back to me.

"I have a delivery for you. Please sign here." I signed the screen with my fingertip and took the box. It said "Zimmerman's Bakehouse" on it and was covered in cartoons of people eating pie.

"Ah, *mijo*!" Tomas said when I walked back into the dining alcove. "You went all out."

"Yeah, well, nobody does pecan pie like Zimmerman's. They're in Ann Arbor but deliver all over."

"Huh. You'd better not let my mother hear you make that claim about pecan pie." I said it the proper way—"Pee-Can" and not "Pee-Kahn."

"Next time I see her, I might throw down that challenge," he said.

"Hmph," I muttered, put out all over again and for no decent reason. Other than the obvious one—he'd implied he'd be seeing my mother—which sent my poor, rattled imagination spinning out of control.

I found a knife and four small plates in my newly sorted kitchen and handed them to James. After I started a pot of coffee, I stood, staring out the kitchen window to the tidy backyard, marveling at how far I'd come.

And how far I still had to go.

Resolved not to allow my base desire to let this whole scene work its magic, the kind James was probably counting on working, I took a deep breath, grabbed mugs and headed to the table.

Mouth-watering pie consumed and gourmet coffee drained, Tomas and Dante looked around and declared their work done. James and I stood on the porch in the cool dusk and waved goodbye. My imagination took hold of me again. I sensed myself rushing forward, picturing us waving good-bye to…whom? Kids headed out after our family dinner? Friends, after a group potluck gathering?

None of the above, that's what. I clenched my jaw.

251

"You can go, too," I said, heading back into the house.

"I'll help clean up," he said, following me.

"Not necessary." I dumped all the deli stuff into a garbage bag. He ignored me and started loading cups and plates into the dishwasher. The kitchen was at the back of the house. The dining room was between it and the front room, with a small first floor room next to it. I planned to use it for a home office.

The eighty-five-year-old structure had been renovated but not so much it lost its charm. The big wooden doors, crystal knobs, and pocket door between the dining and living rooms were original. But the dark granite counters and mid- to high-end stainless appliances in the kitchen, plus the newer claw foot tub, tile floor, and decent-sized sink vanity in the bathroom reflected stellar updating work. The three upstairs rooms had been combined into two so one of them could pass for a modern main bedroom. The ceilings were vaulted, with skylights in the bedroom and bath. All the original hardwood floors shone with a high gloss refinish.

It was, in short, the nicest place I'd ever lived in my entire life.

Michael was charging me a fair rent, so it was also the most I'd ever paid to live anywhere in my life, including the mortgage payment I paid every month on the bungalow in Louisville. So it didn't feel like charity, although I'd done some research and understood I was living in one of the hottest neighborhoods in a reviving city. Michael had jumped in early, his prescience with real estate almost as keen as with other people's money. He owned two houses on this block and three more scattered between here and the university.

"Rich as God," Sloane had told me once about Michael Burke. I had no reason to doubt it.

"Nightcap?" James said, jolting me out of my reverie.

"Um, sure." I put the garbage on the back porch to carry out to the alley.

I needed him to leave.

I wanted, more than I'd ever wanted anything, for him to stay.

As I was walking through the kitchen, I heard the opening strains of an Aretha Franklin album wafting through the house.

Oh, James. You sure know what you're doing.

I leaned in the wide doorway between the dining and living rooms, watching him as he flipped through the box that held my records.

"Here, let's finish this one off." I held up the growler of porter. We emptied it into our glasses, clinked, and sipped, then stood, staring at each other, awkward as all hell.

"Do you come here often?" James asked with a grin.

"Don't be a jerk." I flopped onto the couch, my back and legs singing out in relief. I kicked off my shoes and put my feet up on the rickety coffee table with a sigh. "Oh dang, this feels good."

James hesitated, then sat, not at the opposite end of the couch but not bumped up next to me either. "You make me nervous, Andrea Rose."

I side-eyed him, then took a drink of the rich, dark lager. We sat in silence, Aretha filling the air with her special brand of beautiful sounds for a solid five minutes.

"I don't make anyone nervous, James. And you don't have to say things like that to convince me you're a nice guy. I know you are." I waved around the room indicating the mostly put-together household and the dining room where we'd feasted. "This is all I needed to give me final proof."

He put his empty glass on the table and rose at the precise moment the song ended, and another one began. *"You Make Me Feel Like a Natural Woman"* was my second favorite of her songs. I stared at James' outstretched hand, battling with myself until I decided to go for it. I put my hand in his. He pulled me up, into his arms, and we danced in my new living room to one of the best songs ever written or performed.

I was stiff at first, unwilling to enjoy the sensations of his arm around my waist, my palm resting in his other hand, and the distinct thump-thump of his heartbeat near my ear. To his credit, all we did was dance. When the song ended, he lifted my chin and stared at me a few seconds. I readied myself to resist while knowing I wouldn't. But he let go of me and walked over to the turntable instead.

I watched from the middle of the room, quivering with anticipation and anxiety as he changed the record. I rolled my eyes when the initial riff of *"Your Love"* hit my ears. James grinned and started boogying around the room and me while I stood there, staring at him, wondering what he was trying to prove.

Finally, he snagged my hand and forced me to join him, swinging me around, under his arm, dipping me not unlike he had that crazy, drunken night before his father's service. We danced to three more songs on the compilation album he'd chosen, laughing, sweating, singing at the tops of our lungs until I flopped into a chair.

"Uncle," I gasped.

"Oh, no, you don't," he said, yanking me back up so we could dance to *"Boogie Shoes."* It was one of my favs to dance to and sing. And for the first time in years, I was legit happy in the company of a man.

The song ended, and I stood, hands on my hips, breathing heavily, mirroring him across the room.

"You know this isn't a rom com, right? I'm not gonna stumble over my own feet and fall into your arms." My voice sounded harsh, but I was antsy again, nervous about how much I wanted him to kiss me, toss me over his ample shoulder, and carry me upstairs like some kind of cliché. I sensed my angst shimmering in the air between us like heat over asphalt.

He grinned. "One more dance. Then I'll leave, I swear it."

I sighed and crossed my arms. I wasn't trying to be a bitch or play hard to get. I was honestly conflicted as heck over this guy and this situation and our future working-together relationship. Not to mention the little factoid about him being out of my league.

"I don't want to like you," I said. "I don't want to be your rebound."

"Hold those thoughts." He flipped through my LPs again. "Ah ha, I knew you'd have this one. I feel like I'm looking at my own collection. Well, except for these Journey ones. Can't say I was ever into those guys."

"It was a moment of weakness," I said, not moving from the spot in the middle of the living room. I was quite literally freezing in the overheated room we'd been bouncing around in for the past hour. The chill was moving up from my toes, to my legs, arms, chest. By the time he turned to face me again, grinning like a crazy person, my face felt ice cold.

What was this, anyway? I can't claim that Matt ever affected me this way. He'd made me hot all over, non-stop, for years, until we'd hit a wall and everything had gone cold and not in a good way.

This cold I was experiencing right now, this was the kind of cold I knew could only be remedied one way. Only one thing would warm me. And that thing was standing at my turntable in my new living room, in his tight jeans and slightly damp T-shirt, holding an album cover.

I closed my eyes to keep from bursting into tears when I heard the strains of *"At Last."* James pulled me close, warming me like I knew he would. I was gasping when he finally, *finally* lowered his lips to mine. He started slow, a soft brush of contact while we swayed to the music like a couple of horny teenagers at homecoming.

He slid his hands up my arms, across my shoulders, and tugged out my ponytail holder so he could bury his hands in my hair. I opened my lips to him, sensing him groan deep in his chest as I did it. I had to go up on my tiptoes to wrap my arms around his neck, wanting this moment to last a lifetime…or at least long enough to get us the hell upstairs and onto my bare mattress.

Bad. Wrong. Don't do it, Andi. Do not…

He trailed tiny kisses down my neck, setting me on fire everywhere he touched. Cliché much? Yep. But some men were capable of making them the God's honest truth. He lifted my sweatshirt up and over my head in one smooth movement, reached around and flipped open my bra.

"Dear God, you are exquisite, Andrea." He cupped my breasts, bringing my nipples to stiff peaks with his thumbs and kissing my neck the whole time. I leaned back, wanting him to touch and kiss me all over.

I was in serious meltdown, way more than I'd been with Matt. My ex had been explosive, aggressive in a way that had blown my mind for years. By way of comparison, this man, James Burke with his football player bod and killer, full almost pillowy lips was a slow-goer. A builder-upper. A tension-maker. His rough hands on my naked skin, teasing then retreating, stroking then stopping, all the while kissing some part of me was turning me into a writhing mess.

I reached for his jeans. He stopped me.

"I'm not done yet," he said, his voice low, raspy with lust that lit a match to the smoldering fire in my belly. "Not by a long shot." He cradled my face in both hands. "I'll say it one more time. You aren't a rebound. You are a woman who scares me but one I want to make love to so badly I'm about to jump out of my skin. Will you let me? May I make love you to, Andrea Rose?"

I must have shed a tear, because he touched my cheek and put his fingertip to his lips. "I don't make women cry, at least not out of sadness." He kissed me then, firmer, faster this time, his tongue taking over my mouth like he owned it. And heaven help me, I loved it. He picked me up, like he had in my overheated imagination, and headed for the stairs.

He tossed me onto the bare mattress so hard I

bounced, bit my tongue, and giggled.

"That's better," he said, his voice back to that low, growly tone. He unbuttoned, unzipped, and pulled my jeans down and off. Then he stood, hands on his hips, staring down at me, his green eyes gone dark, his face flushed.

I glanced down at my panties. "Ugh. Sorry. If I'd known you were going to work so hard to get into my pants today, I would've worn my sexy undies."

"No, wait. I want to hold this in my head, take a mental picture so I can revisit it when we're not together." He knelt on the floor, slid his hands up my calves to my thighs, around to my butt, and tugged the grandma panties off.

"Yes," I said, still propped up on my elbows, watching him while every nerve ending I possessed danced with happiness.

"Yes, what?" he whispered, his breathing heavier every second.

I sensed his desire coiled in him, needing an outlet. My skin flushed hot in response. "Yes, I'm a legit redhead."

"I see that." He parted my thighs.

I shivered all over, ready for this, ready for him, ready for anything and everything.

"Lie back, Andrea Rose. Let me work."

Eyes closed, I did what he told me to do, already halfway to climax.

"James," I gasped when he tossed my legs over his shoulders and his lips landed right where I wanted them. "Oh...my..." I said, tilting my hips. "That is...nice...and...yeah...there...right there. Oh my sweet Lord."

The orgasm barreled up my spine and burst into my brain.

"Fireworks," I said, sighing and shivering all over.

"Hmm?" he muttered from between my legs.

"Nothing." I propped on my elbows again. "You have on too many clothes. Be more naked, now please."

He grinned, rose, and stripped out of his clothes in seconds. I waited a beat, barely able to breathe at the sight of the carved marble perfection of his chest and abs. I slapped a hand over my lips at one point, adoring the fact he had chest hair. I couldn't wait to get my hands on it, on him. All of him.

He frowned and looked down at himself. "What?"

"Nothing. Get your ass back down here, pretty please." I wasn't about to tell him I could now confirm that he was as well-endowed as his brother. We could call him perfectly proportional, I think.

Yep. We sure could.

He dropped down next to me and turned me so we were facing each other, our bare skin touching at several pleasant junctures.

"Andi," he whispered, running his fingertips across my cheek to my lips and down my neck to the tops of my breasts. "I want to make you happy."

"Okay, I'm game." I kissed him, letting my tongue explore his mouth, smothering the voices in my head reminding me about Tracy, about how elegant everyone in his life was, how rich and perfectly put together. Sounds filtered in and out of my ears. My breathing. His breathing. The low, sexy noises he made in his throat. Small, happy whimpers from me. And behind it, an insistent, pulsing almost alarm-like sound I was convinced I'd conjured in my head.

I wanted this. Bad. I deserved this, no question.

But the alarm pushed me to go fast, to find the finish line, to break through the barriers I'd put up for years around my body and my heart.

"Wait," I said, breaking away as he was taking a lovely journey down my torso after teasing me to yet another climax with some amazing finger dexterity. "Hold on. Do you hear that?"

He looked up from my neck, his eyes dark, his lips wet. "Hear what?"

"That." I rolled to my other side and stood. "Is it your phone? It's blaring like a fire alarm."

"Oh. Shit. Hang on." He tugged on his underwear and ran down the steps. I waited at the top.

"What? Goddamn it, I'm a little bus— What did you say?"

My breath caught in my throat at the panic in his voice. I threw on my clothes and headed downstairs. James stood in the dining area, hand over his eyes, phone to his ear. "Okay, okay, calm down and let me think."

I put a hand on his arm.

"Hang on a second. Let me ask Andi." He pulled me to a chair and sat me down.

"What is it?" My body and brain were clanging with worry.

"It's Sloane. Her mother called Michael in a total freak-out. She's not answering calls or text messages. She stopped two days ago. Have you talked to her?"

"I… No, I haven't." I picked up my phone. Nothing from her. I sent a quick text, asking if she was okay. I was headed there in a week and was looking forward to a bit of sunshine therapy before launching into my new job. I waited, staring down at the message, showing as delivered but without any answer bubbles. "Why would her mother panic now? She's been down there almost a month."

"I don't know. Here. Talk to Michael. I need some water." He shoved his phone at me.

I attempted to quell the flat-out dirty thoughts I was having at the sight of his tight ass, covered only in his boxer briefs as I put the device to my ear.

"Andi, thank God. Can you get away? I can meet you at the jet. I mean, are you, um…"

I blinked, not quite processing what he was suggesting. "Get away for…what?"

"We have to go to Palm Beach. A delivery guy brought some groceries to the VanAnsel house where she's been staying, and his manager called Sloane's mom. She was…she looked… Oh fucking hell."

I snapped to attention. "She looked like what, Michael?"

"I think the exact description was 'a walking skeleton.' She could barely talk when he arrived and almost fainted while he waited for her to sign the receipt. We have to get down there, Andi. She needs us."

"No, Michael. I'm afraid she doesn't."

"She— What?"

"She needs me. You have to stay here."

"No, Goddamn it. I want to help, too—"

"Nope. Sorry, this isn't your Prince Charming rescue moment. She needs to rescue herself. With my help of course. I'll call you when I get there."

"But…Andi…wait—"

I ended the call.

"James, can you give me a ride to the airport? I'll pack a bag."

He stood in the kitchen doorway. "Of course. Want me to—"

"Nope. No Burkes allowed. Sorry. I have to stage this long-overdue intervention by myself."

Chapter Twenty-One

I'd never flown on a private jet before and had zero clue as to the boarding etiquette, but I jumped down from the truck cab, pulled out my suitcase, and made for what looked like a small terminal. We ran into Michael the minute we walked in.

"I'm going," he said.

James pulled him away. "No, you're not."

"Fuck you, Jimmy. She needs me. I have to go. I have to do *something*!"

"Andi will handle it, Mikey. She'll send us updates. If she needs you, she'll let you know."

"Goddamn it." He dropped into a plastic chair, head in his hands. "God*damn* it."

James sat next to him. "Go on," he said to me. "I think that's the pilot."

He pointed to a guy in a uniform who was heading toward us. I hesitated, nervous as hell all of a sudden. Maybe I was overstepping. Maybe Michael *should* come, too. I opened my mouth.

James got up, took my arm, and steered me toward the pilot-looking guy. "Go," he said in my ear.

"Wait." I turned to him, put my arms around his neck, having to go on my toes, something I knew would never get old. So swoony. So romance hero-y. "I'm sorry. I mean, talk about coitus interruptus."

He wrapped his arms around my waist and kissed

my nose, then my lips with the perfection that was the stuff of all my James-induced clichés. I sighed when he stopped.

"I demand a rain check," I said, surprised to feel tears threatening. But this time, I didn't berate myself over being a sap. I let myself have every single one of those feels. I'd earned them. I pressed against him, memorizing the sensation of his body against mine and knowing, now, I didn't have to deny myself anymore.

"You got it. Be sure and let me know when you get there, if you need anything or…whatever."

"I don't know what I'm going to do."

"I think being there is a good start."

"I hope so."

"Ms. Rigby?" The pilot was hovering. "We should get in the air. There's a cold front moving through, and I want to get away before it hits."

"Oh, right, sure." I zipped up my coat and grabbed the handle of my suitcase. "Up in the air we go."

"Wait, Andi." Michael had gotten up and was standing next to James. "Will you give her this for me?" He handed me a heavy cream envelope. "Please?"

"Of course." I tucked it into my purse.

James touched my cheek. "Safe flight, Scarlett."

"Oh Rhett, fiddle-dee-dee. I'll be fine," I said using my best deep Georgia accent. Before he or I said something we couldn't take back, I turned and followed the pilot onto the tarmac.

I'd never flown anything but cattle-car commercial and that not very often. I had no clue what to expect from this whole private jet thing. It was nice. Okay, it was cushy. The pilot pointed out a small fridge stocked with booze, water, and juice. There was a fruit bowl and a plate of great-smelling cookies on a table surrounded by four huge leather seats.

"Go ahead and take a seat. Buckle up. We'll be in the air in fifteen." He saluted me.

I saluted back, then winced. *World's biggest rube, much, Miz Andi?*

I grabbed a water bottle and sat, trying not to hyperventilate. The few times I had flown, I'd not enjoyed it. My innate nervousness at being thirty some thousand feet off the ground never allowed me to relax. I buckled up and opened the water, trying to play it cool until I remembered I didn't have anyone to impress.

We taxied and were, indeed, airborne inside of fifteen minutes. I gripped the cushy chair arms on ascent, blew out long breaths as the pilot banked, giving me a terrifying aerial view of the dark Michigan landscape beneath me. Once he'd reached flying altitude, we hit a ton of turbulence. My stomach lurched, and I was afraid I'd go horking up my lovely Thanksgiving meal.

"Hi Andi, this is Nick up in the cockpit. We'll be out of rough air in about ten minutes. Do me a favor and leave the seatbelt on a while longer."

"Aye-aye," I said under my breath. As if I'd unbuckle it.

I got busy getting right with my prayer life. "Dear Lord, don't let me die on this dang rich-person's play-toy airplane." But we were coasting smooth as silk within fifteen minutes. It was pitch black out. I sensed myself fading. The physical and emotional exertions of the past twelve hours caught up with me, and I dozed, my head lolling and rebounding as I floated in a twilight zone, worried about Sloane but recalling the moment I'd decided I wanted James to make love to me.

"Holy crap," I yelped when the plane bumped down onto the tarmac, jarring me awake. We had arrived in the sunshine state. I wiped drool off my chin and finished the water, then fished out some gum so I wouldn't insult the competent pilot with dragon breath. I checked my phone. It was only one in the morning. How in the hell was I going to get to the VanAnsel house from here, anyway?

I sent James a text, confirming we were wheels down and I had no idea how to get to Sloane's parents' house.

—*No problem*— he answered. —*There's a driver there for you. He'll have a sign with your name on it.*—

Of course there would be a driver holding a sign with my name on it. The Burke brothers left nothing to chance. I only chafed a few seconds at this, berating myself even as I did it. They were only trying to help. It was how they operated, both of them. I'd better get used to it.

The driver was at the foot of the steps down to the tarmac as promised. He took my bag, and we walked over to a waiting SUV. Very movie-starlet treatment, indeed.

"I have no idea where we're going," I said when I jumped into the front passenger's seat. The man looked alarmed. "I can't ride in the back. I'll puke."

He nodded, got in, and we were off. It was chilly here, in the smack middle of the night, but it wasn't Michigan-level cold. I flushed when I thought about how nice it would be to have James keeping me warm and focused straight ahead, thinking through the possible scenarios I'd face.

It was a solid forty-five-minute drive to the Palm Beach gated compound where she'd been holed up for a month. I clenched my jaw and forced myself to stay awake, knowing I'd insisted on coming here alone for a reason. Sloane needed me.

Seeing Michael in full-frontal savior mode would only set her back. We had to get hold of this thing controlling her and wrestle it to the ground. She also needed to move her tail back to Chicago for real. If she was earnest about leaving Michael behind, steps had to be taken in that direction.

I shot a quick text to Stella, explaining the situation and asking how she'd snapped herself out of her obsession-to-the-point-of-unhealthiness with her weight. I didn't expect a response, considering the time. My phone buzzed with a call from her in a few minutes.

"Hey. Where are you? Why are you asking?" I could hear something that sounded like a bar or party.

"My friend, Sloane. I told you about her, remember?"

"Yeah, vaguely. What's up with her?"

"I'm not really sure, but I've flown to Florida at her mother's request because she's been hiding out here for a month after a final break up with her, um, guy friend. She hasn't answered any calls or messages for a couple of days, which is totally unlike her. I know she uses control over food to pretend she has control over other areas of her life, but I'm afraid… I mean, I don't know."

"Well, I can tell you that if she's inclined to think that way, it'll never really stop. I still sweat every bite I take and haven't touched carbs in a decade. I've trained myself to think they're poison so I probably couldn't put a bagel near my mouth even if I wanted to."

"Okay, so what do I say to her? I don't want to be a nag, but I have a feeling I'm walking into a pretty shitty situation. I want to help but don't know how."

"I'll send some links about it." There was a brief pause. "I ended up in rehab over it."

"Wait, what? When? I didn't know that!"

"I was too embarrassed. I told you I was going to a spa to get over Hank, remember?"

Hank, her second husband, the one with the Calista Flockhart fetish. They'd split after six years. I recalled her telling me she was going to Arizona or someplace, on Hank's dime of course.

"I wish you would have told me." I watched the huge gates in front of us open inward. We drove through them, and I tried not to gape at the massive mansions on either side of the road.

"Well, now you know."

"Where are you, anyway?"

"Um, it's Thanksgiving night, unless you've lost track."

I sighed and slumped back in my seat "I had, actually, but I had a nice one. I'll tell you about it later."

"Does it involve bumping boots with beardy brewery guy?"

"Well, almost. Anyway, we're here."

"Okay, I'll send a few links to some groups for families of anorexics. There are some decent rehab places down there."

"Do me a favor? Check out the options up in Michigan. I want to get her home."

"You sure? Maybe staying away from her triggers is a better choice."

"Maybe. I want to have all the information, just in case."

"You got it, babe. Hey, I'm here at the neurosurgeon's house. With his teenaged kids and everything. I think they like me."

"Great, Stell. I'm so happy for you. We'll catch up. Promise. You skipped your trip up to see me. My mom was pissed. She's not about to drive up on her own."

"I know. We talked. We're still planning on coming up for the holidays. I haven't seen snow on the ground on Christmas since God was a boy."

The driver signaled and turned left. We went through another gate and stopped in a circular drive in front of the biggest house I had ever seen. It was typical, Florida-style architecture but oversized. I had no spare time to be intimidated. My friend needed me. "Thanks."

"You're welcome. Here's my card. When you need to go anywhere, text that number." I took it, thanked him again, and got out with my suitcase.

After taking a moment to prepare myself for whatever I might find, I headed for the front door. No answer after repeated knocking and ringing and calling. I left my suitcase on the front porch and headed around the side, grateful for the security lights that flipped on every few feet so I could see where the heck I was going.

After trying every door I could find—and there were plenty of them—I sat at a patio table and called Michael. "Hey. I'm here. I'd say she's not if I didn't know better. House is locked up tighter than Fort Knox.

No lights on anywhere inside."

"Shit. Okay. Hang on. I used to have the garage door code. Maybe the door into the mud room is open."

I waited, tapping my foot, sensing deep in my soul that she was in there, somewhere. And in way worse shape than I'd thought.

"I don't have it anymore. I must have deleted it," he said.

I felt certain the volatile trajectory of Sloane and Michael's relationship could be traced by how many numbers, passwords, messages, and photos had been deleted between them.

"I'm sending you her mother's number. She can tell you what it is. Call me as soon as you get inside."

"Okay, got it." I hung up. While waiting for the number to come through, I made a decision. No matter how bad it was in there, I wasn't going to let on to Michael. I couldn't. The man was ready to jump on a plane right now. And I was convinced Sloane didn't need him here, hovering, making her backslide by making excuses about control, despite herself. I touched the number Michael sent, sweaty and clammy and exhausted as I waited for someone to answer.

"Hi, Mrs. VanAnsel, I'm Andi Rigby, a friend of Sloane's. I'm here at your Palm Beach place, and I can't get anyone to answer the door."

"The garage door code is five-five-eight-four," she said. "Do you mind terribly staying on the line with me until you find her?"

"Of course. Let me get into the garage." Once in, I ran to the door into the house, sending up a quick prayer that this would be—

"Unlocked. Thank God." I could hear Sloane's

mother breathing in my ear, which ramped up my stress. "Okay, Mrs. VanAnsel, I'm not going to hang up, but I need to put the phone down for a minute or two. Hang tight. I'll be right back with Sloane, and we can all stop worrying."

I set the thing on the first counter I came to before she could say anything.

"Hey! Sloane! Where are ya, girl? I came down early. Who'da guessed it?"

I flipped on every switch I could get my hands on, flooding the massive kitchen with light. It was neat and tidy with the requisite full fruit bowl on the island. The den was dominated by a wall-sized fireplace with huge mantel. The couches looked untouched, in pristine condition with their clever throw pillows and cozy looking light blankets.

I peeked into the dining room capable of seating twenty people and a formal living room with another fireplace. *Who needs all this fire anyway? Weren't we in Florida?*

I headed for the wide, center staircase. "Sloane? Honey? Give me a high sign or something. Where are you?" I opened every door in the upper hall, all of which were closed. I cursed at the sight of the fancy, unslept-in beds. Where in the name of all heck was she? That delivery kid said she was here yesterday.

I saw a set of double doors at the far end of the hall. Marveling at a house with no fewer than eight bedrooms for a family of three, I grabbed the handle, assuming she was behind them, sulking about Michael.

"Sloane?" But instead of shifting down and opening the door like the others had, this smooth, pewter colored thing wouldn't budge. "Okay, gosh darn

271

it, this isn't funny. Let me in." I knocked, then I pounded, panic skittering around in my chest. "Sloane, I'm calling nine-one-one. I know you're in there."

I glanced around, seeking something I could use to jam into the door, something that wasn't my shoulder, preferably. I ran around the house, evaluating items in the other rooms and discarding them based on fragility or the likelihood that I'd hurt myself using them. Finally, I spotted a heavy, wooden urn-like-container holding a few umbrellas in the front foyer.

"All right, you'll have to do." I dumped out the umbrellas and hauled it up the stairs. Without letting myself worry about damage to walls or anything else, I started whamming the umbrella holder against one of the doors. Deciding the weak point was where the doors joined, I slammed the heavy wooden thing into it one, two, then four more times before the lock gave way.

Breathing heavily, my heart pounding, I stumbled into the dark room. My eyes watered within seconds, and I covered my nose against the stink—rank and sour with sweat and what I'd swear was pee. The bed was unmade. There were clothes all over the floor. I peeked into the bathroom first, ignoring its opulence.

I found a bank of light switches and flipped them all on at once. I blinked, unused to the bright light.

"Sloane? Sloane? Where in the hell are y—" I spotted her hair first, an inky waterfall spilling down from a couch arm. I ran to it, crouched by the divan that faced a huge wall of windows. Something was hanging down on the front of couch. It looked like a pale stick. When I realized it was my friend's arm, I had to choke back a scream.

"Oh God. Oh Jesus. Oh…*shit*, Sloane." I hovered,

my hands held out in front of me, helpless in the face of this. Was she dead? Did I even want to know?

I let one hand rest on what I assumed was her hip. I took a few breaths of the fetid air, then tugged the blanket down so I could see her. Tears filled my eyes. She had to be dead. What in the hell was I going to tell her family? Michael was going to lose his ever loving…

"Mmm," the corpse said, rolling onto its back.

I screamed for real and dropped on my butt before scooching away toward the windows, my voice echoing in my ears and bouncing off the walls. I watched the dead girl blink and then stare at me and gave myself a moment to accept that she wasn't, in fact, a corpse.

I crawled to her, tears running down my face. "Oh, Sloane, honey, what have you done?" I touched her hair. When I removed my hand, long strands were stuck to my palm.

"Go 'way," she slurred. "I'm fine."

"Like hell you are." I scrabbled for my phone, remembered it was downstairs, and stood, frozen with indecision. "Can you sit up? We need to get you downstairs, or even better, to a hospital."

"No!" Her voice cracked as she tried to roll away from me. "Fuckin' juss…leave me 'lone."

"What? Are you drunk?" I hesitated another second. "Just…stay here, okay? I'll be right back."

I flew down the steps into the kitchen and snagged my phone. "Okay, Mrs. VanAnsel, I found her. She's alive. But I'm calling an ambulance. I think you should come down, like right away. But do me a favor. Don't let Michael know you're coming. He'll end up here, and she doesn't need that right now."

273

"Okay, thank you. Her father and I will—"

"No, no, sorry for interrupting. Just you. Do you understand?"

"I understand. Thank you for taking care of her. Let me know what hospital you end up at." I ended the call and dialed 911.

The forty minutes it took for the EMTs to show up were the longest of my young life. I sat on the floor, staring at her. I'd never seen anyone literally starve themselves, so I had no frame of reference for the scary way her bones stuck out of her skin, the alarming prominence of her clavicle, the deep sockets of her beautiful blue eyes, their whites gone a terrifying shade of yellow.

And the smell... It was like she'd been peeing herself and lying in it for days.

Her shoulders shook, but no tears fell. She smelled like piss and sweat and misery. I had never felt more helpless. "Don't cry, honey. It's gonna be just fine. Hang on, and we'll get you all fixed up. I promise."

"No Michael," she croaked out.

"No Michael," I swore. I knew it would be tough. James would want Michael to know what was really going on. So, I decided not to tell him either. I could gloss over it, get her home and into rehab. The poor starving, birdlike girl was desperate and crying out for help. This whole scene had triggered some kind of mama bear instinct in me I didn't know I possessed.

One thing was for darn sure. I had to keep Michael as far away from her as possible. Even if it meant lying to James. I'd also have to convince her mother to keep Sloane's father away. He was the original toxic trigger. Michael was his stand-in. And no matter how great a guy I believed him to be, I had to protect my friend—from herself, of course, which meant protecting her from him.

Chapter Twenty-Two

"No, no, I'm sure. She's fine. I mean, she's okay. Not great. But they're rehydrating her, and we'll probably be out of here in a few hours." I said all this while staring at my friend in her hospital bed, hooked up to monitors galore, including two IV lines snaking into her stick-like arms.

I turned away and headed into the hall. I'd determined not to reveal the truth, and I was sticking to it. No matter how hard it was to hide it from James, I'd made a promise to Sloane and to myself. It was time for the women to circle the wagons around one of their own.

I sat in a stiff waiting room chair and forced my voice to sound breezy and unconcerned, but it was harder by the minute. It wasn't like me to be sneaky about anything, and this outright lie I was perpetrating... While part of me knew it was necessary, another part was fighting with all of her might.

"Why am I having a tough time buying what you're selling," James said after I'd given him the whole "Relax, she's fine, and she'll contact him when she's ready. He can go back to work and stop worrying."

My face flushed hot. I jumped up to pace, gnawing the inside of my cheek to keep from blurting out the truth. "I don't know why, but I'm tired, so I'm gonna go…"

"Andi, wait. He's in the other room. Talk to me. For real this time."

"Dang it, James. I've told you everything I can. Cut me some slack, already. I've been awake for something like twenty-four hours straight."

"I know. I'm sorry."

Guilt flooded into my bloodstream. I stopped, pressed my forehead against the wall, willing him to let me end the conversation. "I'm sorry," I said in a whisper. "It's just…stressful."

"I'm sure it is. I'll fend him off, let you help get her sorted and back home, no sweat."

"Thank you." My heartbeat thumped in my ears. I was not a good liar. I never have been. But I kept at it, knowing Sloane needed serious space from the men in her life and accepting my part of that by continuing to downplay her condition.

"Talk soon." I ended the call and clutched the phone in my trembling hand, "Lord, forgive me and while you're at it, please make sure my friend's okay," I whispered.

"Um, Andi?" I looked up and straight into the eyes of a woman who could be none other than Sloane VanAnsel's mother. She was a tall, slender, healthier version of her daughter with identical eyes. Her hair was a nice shade of steel gray. She wore it stick straight, flowing to her shoulders. She was clutching her purse and a tissue to her chest.

"Yes, I'm Andi."

The woman grabbed onto me and held tight.

I patted her back, then peeled her off me. "She's in there, Mrs. VanAnsel."

"Please, call me Carolyn."

"Carolyn. Go in and see her. She was awake earlier, but I think she's sleeping now."

I walked with her to the door, knowing what a shock it would be to see Sloane in such a state. I pushed it open, ready to catch her when she fainted. I waited for her gasp, perhaps a cry. She stood in the door, staring at the skin-covered skeleton that resembled her daughter.

"Oh Sloane, not again."

"Excuse me, did you say again? She's been like this before?"

"The summer between high school and college. It was even a little worse." She blew her nose, her eyes filled with tears.

"What did you do? What happened to change…to fix…to get her to eat?"

"She went to an intensive rehab program. It's a little unorthodox, but it worked, or at least, it did for a while I guess." She fell into a chair. "I don't know. I can't explain it." She heaved a sigh. "She's my only child, you know, and I wanted a big family, so we poured everything we had into her. Too much. Too much attention can be worse than none at all." A tear slid down her pale cheek. "What am I going to do with her now?"

We sat together, next to the bed, my phone at the ready. "Do you have the number for the rehab place?"

Carolyn glanced over at me. "Grant, my husband, he…" Her voice broke, and she sobbed against my shoulder for a few minutes. "I'm so sorry, Andi. You shouldn't have to deal with this. I'll handle it."

I handed her a fresh tissue. "What about him? Your

husband?"

She slumped back in her seat. She wore a pair of skinny black jeans and maroon sweater under her down jacket. And it was boiling in this hospital. "It's okay. Never mind. Not my business. Why don't you take this off?" I moved to assist her with the coat. "I'll get you some water."

She let me help, then put her chilly palm on my hand. "My husband says he isn't paying for any more rehab. That she's a grown woman with her own money, which is the way she wanted it." She grabbed a fresh tissue and pressed it to her mouth. "I never understood those two. They butted heads from the minute Sloane was old enough to realize he was… Well, he's bossy and overbearing and a bit of an asshole."

I raised an eyebrow.

"But it turned her into this stubborn little…well, you know. She was an impossible teenager, and when she turned seventeen, she realized she could make him pay for being so demanding and unsupportive. That's when she stopped eating." Carolyn closed her eyes and swallowed. When she opened her eyes, she looked so defeated it made my throat tighten. "She played volleyball in high school, so she had to eat some. I made sure of it. But after graduating, she started staying out all night, drinking, smoking pot, the works. I caught her more than once having sex with some random kid or another in our house."

She bit her lip. We sat in silence a while, watching Sloane sleep.

"All of that I get, I can handle, and I did. But when she started wasting away in front of my eyes and refused any food I put in front of her, I knew we had a more serious problem."

At some point during her mother's monologue, Sloane's eyes fluttered open. She turned to look at us. "Andi?" I headed for her. "Mommy?"

Carolyn walked to the bed, gathered the girl into her arms, and held her while they both cried. I watched a minute, then headed outside. I needed a drink. Okay, several drinks. I was still flying on the adrenaline of finding and rescuing and the sick stress of not telling James the truth about Sloane's condition.

I sat and stared at the few squares of floor between my feet, sorting through the options. The doctor showed up and filled Carolyn and me in on the situation. Sloane's kidneys were his main concern. She'd gone into a diabetic state in the last day or two, which put pressure on her heart.

Carolyn blinked fast. "Will she be all right?"

"We hope so. We're keeping her at least three more days. She's responding well to the hydration and antibiotics for an infection in her ear, but we need to address a core issue."

"I'm getting her a place at a rehab program back home," I piped up, wondering how we might pay for it and deciding I'd worry about that later.

"Good. All right then, we'll work on getting her strong enough to go there. Deal?"

"Yes, thank you," Carolyn said.

Sloane had drifted off again, so we went to the cafeteria and sat with terrible coffee and a stale piece of banana bread.

"You've been a great friend to her." Carolyn kept her eyes down, fixed on her coffee.

"The feeling's mutual. Sloane saved me once, got

me a job and out of my existing crappy situation."

"I heard. I'm sorry you were treated badly at my husband's company." Her lips twisted as if she wanted to smile but couldn't manage it.

"It worked out fine. And I might never have had a good job, which led me to an even better job, if it weren't for her."

Carolyn exhaled a long breath and leaned back in her chair. "Are we still not saying anything to Michael?"

I put a bite of the bread in my mouth as a stalling mechanism. She sipped her coffee and stared out the windows, seeming not to care about my answer.

"I don't think it's wise," I said. "I mean, you've known about them and their, um, challenging relationship longer than I have, but—"

"Oh, I don't get it any more than I get her relationship with her father. Sloane's a giving, generous young woman. She'd hand you the shirt off her back, but she doesn't know how to have a healthy relationship with men. Not that her father and I are a good example of anything healthy, but still...I like Michael. He seems like a genuine, nice young man."

"He is. But I get you." I shoved the plate of banana bread aside. "My mother would weep over this nasty thing. Then whip up her version to get the taste out of all of our mouths."

Carolyn smiled. "She sounds delightful."

"She is. I mean, we don't always get along, but that's the nature of mothers and daughters."

"I suppose."

I leaned my elbows on the table. "So, I want to call this place in Ann Arbor and see if they have room for

281

her."

"It's expensive, Andi. I know Sloane made some money and she has access to her trust, but…"

"So she doesn't need her father to pay for it, right?"

"She gets full ownership of her trust in four years when she turns thirty. But he made me the co-signer so I can access the funds in an emergency."

I gaped at her. "Sloane's only twenty-six?"

"Yes, she didn't tell you?"

"It never came up. She struck me as older. Anyway, if you can release some of the money to her, it should be fine, I guess. I don't know from trust funds, but I assume it's a substantial amount."

"It is, but I don't want her to have to use it for this. We should be taking care of it. We're her parents."

"I think she'd just as soon foot her own bill."

"You're probably right. But I can't stand to see her like this. I don't understand it. I never have understood her."

I reached across the table and patted her hand. "I know. I don't understand it either. But we love her, which is pretty much all we can do right now. Be there for her."

Carolyn sniffled, nodded, and pushed her coffee away. "This sucks, too."

"Damn right it does."

"I'm calling Dwayne. He'll pick up something decent for us to eat."

I smiled, understanding her need to do something positive, something forward moving.

I left Carolyn waiting for her driver to bring some decent coffee and "a little snack" and headed back to

Sloane's room. As I'd hoped, she was awake, propped up in a sitting position. She had a cup of broth and some crackers in front of her on the wheelie table and was staring at them as if they were the enemy and her mission was to destroy them.

I sighed and sat next to her, picked up the spoon, dipped some of the broth, and held it to her lips. "Just a little, okay? If you eat, they'll let you out of here once your kidneys stabilize."

She opened her mouth and let me pour the broth into it. I did this twice more, then stopped, staring at her before I started laughing.

I was relieved when she joined me. "I'm sorry. You don't have to do that," she said, her voice still scratchy.

"I know. But I will if it's the only way you're going to eat." I picked up the cracker. "Try this next."

She made a face. "No. I can't. I doubt my body can process carbs anymore." She picked up the bowl of broth. "I promise to drink it all down like a good girl."

I watched her take small sips as I pondered how to break my next bit of news to her. "So, I'm going to be working at Burke. VP of Marketing and Sales."

Her wide smile looked painful, thanks to her cracked lips. "I knew it. You're perfect for it."

"I'm also calling the rehab program in Michigan for you and begging them to admit you."

Her eyes filled with tears. She set the bowl down and balled her fists on the thin blanket covering her. "I can't go there. It's for kids and teenagers."

I put a hand on hers. "Your mom says it helped you once. And you need help, Sloane. You can't do this on your own. Not anymore."

Her lower lip trembled. She looked more like a miserable nineteen-year-old than the grown woman she was. "I'm such a fuck up."

"You're not. And we're going to get a handle on this, dang it."

She pulled my hand to her chest. I tried not to fixate on how honest-to-God skeletal she looked.

"Thank you," she said. "I don't deserve you."

"Please. I don't know if I can ever repay you for hauling me up to Michigan. You saved me. Don't forget it."

She let go of me and squeezed her eyes shut. Tears leaked from them, which, I now knew, was a good sign about her rehydration. "Does Michael know about this?"

"Nope." I got up when I spotted Carolyn in the doorway, holding a tray with drinks and a bag with promising greasy spots on it. "And he won't know, either. Finish," I said pointing to the half empty bowl and trying to put on a stern face.

"James will tell him," she said before she took another sip.

"I didn't tell James. And I won't." I took a cup from Carolyn, grateful for it. It was approaching four in the afternoon, and I hadn't slept the night before. Exhaustion was sneaking up on me, big time. "I need to call this rehab place," I said, once I'd onboarded half the coffee and the caffeine started lighting up my nerves.

Carolyn sat by her daughter and held a cup of water to her lips.

"I need to sleep. You guys should go. Mom, I'm sorry. I really am. I don't know—"

"Don't be sorry, Sloane. Be strong and get better. You did it once. You can do it again." She brushed a lank strand of black hair away from her daughter's face. "I know you can."

I got the number from Carolyn and stepped into the hallway to make the call, unsure how to ask or what to say but bound and determined to make it happen. It only took fifteen minutes and seemed way too easy. When we got to the part where I had to provide a deposit, I asked if I could call them back with that in a few minutes.

"Yes, that's fine, Ms. Rigby. I see here that the VanAnsels paid the entire fee in advance last time. Do you anticipate it will be the same arrangement?"

"I'm not sure, but I'll call you right back once I find out. She's in the hospital right now. In Florida."

"I see. We look forward to hearing from you. I have Ms. VanAnsel's place reserved, starting a week from Monday."

I let go of the breath I'd been holding. "Thank you. Thank you so much."

Sloane was sound asleep by the time I stepped back in the room. Carolyn was standing over her, touching her face and hair and arm, as if convincing herself the almost-all-the-way-starved waif was in fact her grown daughter. "Should we find a hotel?"

"What? Oh, no, my dear. We can stay out at the house. It's much nicer than any hotel."

"Oh, um, well…" All I could picture right then was the shattered master bedroom door and the horrific mess I'd found behind it.

"Don't worry." Carolyn patted my arm. "Dwayne has already been out there and arranged for everything to be cleaned and the pantry stocked for us.

"Oh. Right. Great." I saw in an instant where Sloane got her organizational inclinations. Exhaustion smacked into me like a tidal wave, making me sway on my feet. "Sorry," I said as I stumbled forward.

"Oh my heavens." She gripped my elbow. "You poor thing, you flew down here overnight. I forgot." She put her phone to her ear. "Dwayne, please bring the car to the front of the hospital. We're ready to leave. Thank you."

I followed her as she tip-tapped down the hall toward the elevator. I barely remembered the ride back out to the VanAnsel estate. At one point, I thought she was on the phone, her voice raised in anger, but I didn't care. Her relationship with her asshole husband wasn't part of my problem.

"Ms. Rigby?" I startled and almost fell out of the open door onto the driveway. A strong hand caught me and helped me to my feet. "I've got your suitcase, ma'am."

"Thank you, Dwayne. I think Matilda has some dinner fixed for us. Be sure and stay to eat."

"Okay, thanks, Mrs. VanAnsel."

I let her guide me in—the front door this time— and up the crazy huge set of stairs. I glanced down to the end of the hall. A couple of workers were busy repairing the doors. I could see other people in the room, moving around, cleaning and removing any sign of Sloane's hermit-monk-starvation experiment.

"I told you, dear. We're taking care of everything. Don't worry. You did what you had to do, and I'll always be grateful to you."

"Bed? Room?" I managed to blurt out. I was

getting dizzy and thought I might faint. I hadn't eaten much of anything in the last twelve plus hours, either. But sleep was job one.

"In here." She opened one of the many bedroom doors. "Shall I turn it down?" She headed for the bed piled high with fancy pillows.

"Nope. No need." I swept half the pillows onto the floor, kicked off my shoes, and climbed under the duvet. I'm pretty sure I fell asleep while I was talking, thanking Carolyn for the hospitality, and reminding her not to tell Michael what was going on, no matter how insistent he might be.

Chapter Twenty-Three

Sloane slept through the next few days, which the medical types claimed was the best thing for her while they hydrated and fed her in between her naps, working to get her blood sugar and electrolytes back in balance. When she wasn't sleeping or trying to force food into her mouth, she was telling me to go, to enjoy Palm Beach, to relax.

I gave it the old college try. I'd managed to pack my laptop and Michael had given me access to their sales software, so I spent a lot of quality sunshine hours studying the screen, pondering trends, and developing my strategy. I kept my face mostly covered. I had too much of my mother's ingrained "a lady knows to stay out of the sun to avoid wrinkles" in me not to wear a wide-brimmed straw hat I'd found in the well-stocked VanAnsel mud room. But the rest of me obtained a decent golden glow from the weak, winter sun.

When I wasn't plowing through sales reports or profit and loss statements, I was weaving myself into a corner of lies about Sloane's condition. It was exhausting. I hated having to keep up the pretense she was home, sitting next to me in the sun, that we'd be back in a week, but she still needed time to herself and Michael should keep his distance.

"Andi," James said during one of our daily chats, the day before we were flying back to Michigan, a full

288

three days before I'd told him we were returning.

I was pacing up and down a stretch of beach, willing him to have to get off the phone so I could stop trying to make it sound like everything was hunky-dory.

"I think you should consider making your stout into an Imperial," I said, desperate to steer the conversation to work and away from Sloane. "We need a higher price point in the mix. Something to appeal to the snobs still out there, you know?"

"Whatever. Listen, I'm having a tough time convincing Michael everything is as fine as you say it is."

My guts roiled. I hated lying, and I especially hated doing it to a man I cared so much about. "It is fine. He's going to have to deal with the fact she needs some space."

He sighed into my ear. "Do you swear she's okay? Right there with you, her manicured PR Barbie toes in the expensive Palm Beach sand?"

I winced. "Sure, sure. Of course. Now about that Imperial…"

"I'll see you…when? Next week?"

"Yes, I'll be in the office on Monday."

"Uh, I didn't really mean the office, although Michael's carved out a sweet space for you. I could definitely see us getting busy in there."

I smiled, relieved he'd stopped asking about Sloane. Our interrupted encounter preyed on my memory, fueling sexy dreams, but something else had been trailing around the edges of my subconscious. Something about not falling back into relationships, about making my own way, about being a friend to

Sloane and a kick-ass marketing expert for a great brewery, first. Before I fell into bed with the head brewer and half owner of the dang place.

"Well, anyway…I should go."

He was silent long enough for me to sense his displeasure with my non-acknowledgement. I let that feed the tiny spark of anger in my chest. He had a nerve, getting all huffy when I wouldn't rise to his bait about screwing me in the office I hadn't even seen yet.

I glanced up at the house. Carolyn was waving at me. I waved back.

"Sorry, James. We…we're going out to dinner or something. I have to go. Bye." I ended the call before he could say anything.

I hated myself right then. The conflict choking my windpipe over him and Michael and Sloane, and the bigger picture was giving me heartburn, making me lie awake with the sliding glass door open, wishing the sound of the tide whooshing in and out would lull me to sleep. It never did. I walked up the long dock and met Carolyn at the massive, stone paver patio on the lower level of the house.

"Hey, Andi, the doctor just called. They're discharging her tonight instead of tomorrow."

"Great. I'll go get her."

"No, no, you stay here and enjoy the meal. I opened some wine. A lovely Bordeaux I found in the wine cellar. Forgot I had it." She'd gained some color too this week. She looked refreshed, revived. Reset. She gave me a quick hug. "I'll go with Dwayne and pick her up. I have her room ready."

"Only for a couple of nights, though, remember? We have to check her in the day after tomorrow."

"I know. I'll be glad to get her out of the nasty, germy hospital."

She left, her long, silvery hair billowing behind her. I sat in a lounge chair on the patio and accepted a glass of wine from the hovering Matilda. I sipped and realized it was, indeed, a killer vintage. The soft Florida winter air felt great on my skin. The wine was sublime. The fact I'd ended up on a Florida vacation, with a tan after all, seemed so strange, yet right at the same time.

But I'd lied to James. Flat out, straight up, bald-faced fibbed to him for a solid week. And it was making me physically sick.

I drained the glass and poured more from the decanted bottle. Matilda brought a plate of salad niçoise, complete with fresh grilled tuna on top. She set it in front of me with a smile, put a basket of warm sourdough bread between us, then took her seat.

We ate in silence at first.

"How long have you worked for the VanAnsels?" I asked Matilda.

"Twenty years, going on twenty-one."

"So you knew Sloane as a kid."

"Yes." She smiled. "She was a handful, but I loved her. We all did. I'm so sad she's fallen back into this mess."

"What do you do when they're not here?"

"I clean for five or six of the families out here," she said, leaning back in her chair. "But I love the VanAnsels. I'd do anything for them. Did you know Mrs. VanAnsel helped bring my daughter and her baby from Mexico? And she paid for my daughter's college tuition. She's a nurse now, my Gina. She makes very good money. She also helped Dwayne by hiring him when no one else would." She leaned toward me. "He was in jail, for pot or something. I don't know. But she trusted him, and he's been clean and doing well, driving for her and her friends ever since."

The largesse of the VanAnsel women was becoming more obvious by the day.

When we heard Carolyn call out "We're home!" Matilda raced into the house.

I followed her and found Sloane wrapped in her arms in the kitchen, Matilda crooning and rocking her while Sloane smiled and waved at me over the woman's shoulder. "I'm fine. I mean, I will be. I'm not right now, no. But um…I'd eat some bread pudding. I mean, if you'd make it."

Matilda cut loose with a torrent of Spanish, holding Sloane's arms out from her sides. When she let go of her and started slamming ingredients onto the massive slab of granite island, Sloane sat and watched, as if mesmerized. And we ate the most amazing, melt-in-your-mouth bread pudding for dessert. I had to say a silent apology to my mother, whose pudding was good but didn't even approach this one, as I ate my portion. Sloane ate almost six whole bites. The rest of us took it as victory.

****

As we circled the airport above Michigan, I started getting antsy. Something was off or wrong or about to go wrong. I could feel it in my bones. We'd laid out this plan, flying into the airport in the mid-morning, with a driver waiting to take us over to Ann Arbor where the rehab facility was located. Michael and James thought we weren't returning until Wednesday so we wouldn't have to face either of them. Sloane stayed silent, brooding, staring out a window the whole trip. Carolyn was talking too much, filling the air with nervous chatter. I was ready to leap out of my skin by the time we landed.

I spotted them inside the terminal when the glass doors slid open. Michael and James stood shoulder to shoulder, one in his typical bespoke suit, the other in dark jeans and a Burke Bros labeled button down. They both smelled of brewery—the malty, yeasty, hoppy essence that coated them from head to toe and soon would be my reality, too. At least, I hoped it would be. Considering.

"Holy crap on a cracker," I said, under my breath. "Hang on, let me handle—"

But Michael ran to Sloane, looked helpless a few seconds, and then demanded to know how anyone in their right mind would consider her "okay."

I stepped between them. "Sloane needs to heal, without you up in her face. So back off, buster."

He glared at me. I lifted my chin, figuring my shiny new VP job for a lost cause. I was in for a penny now. Might as well stay in for the whole dang pound.

"Sloane," he said, turning away from me. "Honey. Why…"

"Because I felt out of control, Michael. I was being manipulated by my father, your mother, and I thought by you, although I know better now. It doesn't change the fact I have to get my head on straight. Which means we're not going to be together, not for a while, maybe not ever. I don't know how to have a relationship with you, and until I can figure that out, you have to steer clear of my life."

We all stared at her.

"What?" she asked, shrugging. "When they admit you for anorexia, you're obliged to have twice daily psychotherapy sessions. I had a few breakthroughs." She focused on Michael who seemed to be leaning against James for support. "The bottom line is, until I can feel back in control of my life, you can't be in it."

He reached for her. "Sloane, please...don't do this." The sound of his voice—Michael Burke, master of his universe, about to break down in front of all of us—made my heart ache. I took a step closer to James, but he moved away from me and refused to meet my gaze.

The constant worry I'd been living with the past week morphed into legit panic. What had I done? I never should have lied to him. I really, *really* liked him. Now, all my misgivings and insecurities came rushing back, flooding my brain and reminding me that, maybe, just maybe, I'd created this crisis on purpose.

Perhaps I'd used the excuse of keeping my friend's condition a secret to preserve her recovery as a way to invalidate my own growing feelings for him. To self-destruct a future potential relationship.

My throat ached with words I couldn't say as I watched Sloane and Michael talking in low voices. James stayed near his brother's shoulder, tall and silent, like some kind of bodyguard, sunglasses on top of his head, his lips pressed together. Not looking at me.

Yep. I'd totally done a number on myself. Big time.

I sighed and motioned for Carolyn to follow me toward the exit. My energy level for shielding Sloane from the man who was at this moment begging her to listen, to understand he loved her, he wanted to help her if she would let him, was down in the low to middling range. I was already sweating my future with Burke Brothers the company, now that Burke brothers, the men, had outed my subterfuge. And not only my job, of course. My living arrangements were tied directly to my employment.

What had I been thinking?

Crap.

I was such a sucker, a fool, a naïve idiot.

And now, very likely, an unemployed and homeless one.

Carolyn's driver greeted us and took our bags. I slid into the backseat of the SUV, my mind blank, my heart encased in ice. Both Michael and James had every reason to be furious with me. I'd promised them I'd keep them updated on Sloane. I hadn't. And they'd gotten hold of our travel plans, somehow. I suspected her father. Not that it mattered at this point.

My face flared hot as I sat, staring straight ahead, prepared to be fired before I even darkened the door of the brewery. It was their fault anyway, them and their overbearing, pushy personalities.

Sloane needed to be responsible for her own happiness. But I suspected she and Michael were a tad too alike—high maintenance on the one hand, nurturers and efficient fixers on another—for it to work. Love... There was no accounting for it. I knew she loved him. He felt the same way. But she had to get this eating thing under her control, independent of his oversight or influence.

The door opened, and Sloane climbed in, shivering all over. "Jesus, it's cold here."

A tap on my window made me flinch. I hit the

button and it slid down. Michael was there, his expression stern. I steeled myself for the inevitable. "Can you come by the brewery today? After you drop her in Ann Arbor?"

"Yes, I can." I hated the weak sound of my voice, but it was the best I could do.

"Good. I want to go over a few things."

"Okay."

He knocked on the roof of the car and strode off, his camel hair dress coat flaring out in the wind. James was already at his truck, standing by the open driver's side door, looking everywhere but at me.

My heart re-froze. This was my doing. I'd have to live with it. The epiphany I had—lying on purpose while my subconscious mind went into self-preservation mode and initiating a sort of kamikaze mission on my budding relationship—took a firm hold.

Made your bed. Now lie in it. One of my mother's favorite sayings in her vast repertoire of them. I swiped at my cheeks, surprised to find I'd been crying.

Sloane put her leather-gloved hand on mine, which were clenched together in my lap.

I was shivering almost as much as she at this point. "He'll never let me work there now."

"Of course he will." She squeezed my hands. "I told him not to blame you. It was a hundred percent my fault."

"James wouldn't even look at me," I choked out, embarrassed, but relieved to reveal how bad I felt.

"I know. I saw." She let go of my hands. "I'm sorry, Andi. I've ruined something for you, and I never meant to do that."

Ruined? She thinks so, too? Dang.

"Go and have your meeting with Michael tonight. It will all be fine. I'm sure of it."

"I guess." I took the tissue Carolyn handed me from the front seat. "Thanks."

I had that thing torn into a zillion pieces of thin confetti by the time we pulled up in front of a large, Tudor-style house with a massive front porch, bedecked with Christmas lights and a big Hanukkah menorah.

"This is your miracle facility?" I stared at it, flabbergasted. I'd expected low, gray buildings with tiny windows and barbed wire fencing, which was stupid. She had anorexia. She wasn't a serial killer.

The driver pulled out her suitcases and placed them on the sidewalk. Sloane sat in the car, eyes squeezed shut, her still-dry lips moving as if she were praying.

I touched her arm. "We're here."

Her eyes flew open. "I know. I'm... It's hard to explain, but I have this mantra about food. I know what I'm heading into in there, so I gotta let that go." She smiled. Her blue eyes, which had lost the unhealthy jaundiced sheen and regained a bit of their deep blue color, were shining with tears.

"You sure as hell do." I got out of the backseat, walked around to her side, and opened her door. She got out, wrapped up to her nose in a heavy coat, a thick scarf, and a woolen hat tugged down to her eyebrows.

"Come on now, honey," Carolyn said. "They're waiting for you."

I glanced up at the porch. Two people stood there, the man's arm around the woman's shoulders. They looked more like a set of parents waiting for a naughty teenager to slink home than what I knew them to be, two board certified, M.D. Ph.D. psychiatrists, dedicated to battling the scourge of eating disorders, no matter what form they took.

I also understood, thanks to plenty of internet research, this thing Sloane lived with meant she would never have a normal relationship with food. She probably never had. But they could help her cope with it, normalize it so her organs wouldn't fail. And their twice-daily group sessions would force her to talk about what led her here—her father, her erstwhile boyfriend, her constant need to be perfect at everything, to set things right for everyone else, like she had for me.

She sighed. "Mom, would you mind if Andi walked me in? I don't want to hurt your feelings, but it feels less like an expensive do-over if I'm with her."

"Of course." They hugged. Carolyn drew away and put her palm on her daughter's cheek. "You're only here three weeks, right?"

"Yes. I'm going through the intensive version. Kind of a combination of control-alt-delete reset and insanity workout. It suits me better. The docs agree." She indicated the couple on the porch. "I should be done by Christmas. If so, I might go to Chicago, back to my place. I don't know yet."

"You don't need to decide any of that now. Go on. Get going and get better."

I took one of her suitcases, she took the other, and we walked to the steps, then to the porch. I handed her off, got my own tight, weepy hug, then climbed into the back seat for the drive to Detroit, carsickness be damned. It was the least of my problems now.

Chapter Twenty-Four

"Andi!"

I looked up from the large computer screen on my desk, shocked at the sound of Michael barking my name.

Yes, I had managed to keep my job, my house, the basic outlines of my new life. He'd told me flat-out he'd been ready to tear up the contract I'd signed when Sloane's father called him to ask if he were planning to meet our plane.

"That was a surprise, to say the least," he'd said. "Since you told James who then told me you were there another couple of days." His ice-blue eyes had been stormy. His face flushed.

I'd already sweated through the shirt I'd thrown over my Florida-appropriate T-shirt, jeans, and purple Converse high-tops. I could sense it beading on my upper lip but resisted the compulsion to wipe it. I kept my gaze fixed on his. I could take this. I deserved it.

But once he said his piece, including the fact Sloane had warned him cutting me loose before I could even start would be the dumbest move possible, I clasped my fingers together on the desk between us and cleared my throat. "Thank you for keeping me on, Michael. I appreciate it, and I assure you, you won't regret it. But I need you to know something first, before we go any further."

"Okay. What is it?"

"I realize I may have ruined things with James by lying to you both, but I stand by my decision. Sloane needed the space from you, time not spent worrying about what you were going to do when you found out, time spent focusing on her own issues. If I had to do it over, I'd do it the same way."

"Good."

I had my mouth open to argue but snapped it shut at his response.

"Contrary to popular, female opinion, I want what's best for her, not what's best for me." He held up a hand to stop me from responding. "Hang on, let me finish." He got up from his seat and headed for the glass wall overlooking the darkened brewery space. "I've known there was something unique about Sloane from the moment I met her. I mean, she's hot, don't get me wrong. And funny and smart and can hold her liquor better than most guys I know."

I walked over to stand next to him. He kept his gaze on the glass as he spoke as if the things he said wouldn't allow for eye contact, lest he lose his nerve. Something new for him, I imagined—the thought of losing his nerve.

"We had some incredible times together in Chicago. I'm sure she's shared some of…it with you." He glanced at me, then away again after I nodded. "I'm really glad you guys met. She needed a close friend, someone like you, someone real." He heaved a sigh. "I swear it's like we both fall into our crappy, familial roles when we're in Michigan, which turns us into people who can't stand each other." He pressed his palms against the glass. "But I love her. I know I do.

And I'll wait for her, as long as she needs me to."

"She's lucky to have you. She'll figure it out, I think."

"As for James," he said, turning to face me, his face grim. "I honestly don't know what to tell you about him right now. He's…not in a good place in his head. About you, I mean."

"I know. I get it."

"No, I don't think you do." His eyes narrowed. He looked angry again. I tensed, recalling their fraternal loyalty. "I don't agree with it, but he can't stop aligning what you did with what Tracy did to him. He's a trusting soul, unlike yours truly. He wanted nothing more than to make their pretty, fairy tale marriage work. Suburban house, fence, dog, two-point-five kids. The whole ten yards."

I swallowed the lump in my throat, formed at the sound of his ex-wife's name. I had no reason to be jealous of her, but I was, of course. It was a female thing, I supposed.

"He'd made our parents happy by marrying her and her older-than-Belanger-money family. Hell, best I could tell, he made her happy. But she cheated on him for a solid year before the divorce."

"Oh. Wow."

"Yeah, so…as you can imagine, trust is a thing for him. A thing he can't sacrifice or refuses to sacrifice, however you want to look at it." He tucked his hands in his trouser pockets. "You lied to his face. And even though it wasn't related to you or him or you guys together, it threw him, big time."

"I understand."

"Good. Okay, so, I'll see you in the morning? Your

office is all set up. It's across the hall. You get a view of the side street." He was grinning now, being the consummate, business-first guy he was. He knew I was going to bring it for Burke Brothers. I knew it, too.

I matched his smile, tucked away the pain that had set up house in my gut over James and how I'd treated him, how I'd *hurt* him.

"Yes, I'll be here. Are you free at nine? I want to go over the initial plan I've made for next year. It's gonna cost you, fair warning."

"Fine, good. Yes. We'll meet." He glanced at his phone. "Um, one more thing."

"Sure."

"She's, um, Sloane... She's all settled and whatnot? At the facility?"

"It's not really a facility, per se," I said, eager to put his mind at ease. "It's this giant house, in a neighborhood. They only take eight patients at a time. She has to share a room with two other women—girls really. She's definitely the oldest one there."

"How long will she be there?"

"She and the doctors who run the place think she'll be out by Christmas."

His expression brightened. "Oh, that's a lot sooner than I thought."

"It's a flexible program. The doctors decide with each patient when they leave. She's determined to work on herself. And we both know what happens when Sloane's determined."

He smiled and looked so much like a happy little kid at that moment, I had to stifle a laugh. I felt lighter, less stressed, ready to tackle the job he'd hired me to do. I'd have to let go of James. I'd done this thing, possibly even on purpose with a subconscious eye toward avoiding my own conflicted feelings about him. Ugh. Lame. But, at least, I had a job and one I couldn't wait to start.

And now, three weeks after that, on the Monday before Christmas, Michael was hollering for me from his open office door. He was dressed casually for him, in a pair of slim black jeans and a crisp blue shirt, open at the neck. His face was beet red, though, so I hustled myself up and across the hall.

"What's wrong?" My mind ran ahead, wondering if there'd been a bad batch—unlikely since James kept an iron-fist control over quality—or maybe some disaster in the brewery itself. Ever since he and James rejected the buyout offer, we'd all been working in manic mode. Michael and I were both here by seven every morning and stayed well after seven each night. James, I assumed, did the same. Our paths rarely crossed, and when they did, he found an excuse to leave the room.

The loans Carter had taken out in secret were like an anvil over Michael's head as he attempted to balance his need to make more money with his knowledge of how this business worked. He'd managed to gather a few small investors to help defray some of it, but only if they were willing to consider the investments loans and not in exchange for ownership shares. Since he'd fought off a powerful takeover bid, neither he nor James were inclined to give away any part of their family's company.

Of course, nothing happened overnight. I needed time to hire a crack sales team, half of which was already in place. I also needed money invested in, among other things, a better website, a staff person dedicated to building our social media presence, and a total redesign of our packaging.

It was no small amount of dough, and I heard about it a lot from my boss.

But I stayed on track with my own goals, between hiring, vetting web designs and developers, and narrowing the redesign concepts down to two. I could still sense Michael's stress growing every day, with each week's worth of sales reports not meeting his expectations. I kept pointing out the good parts and reminding him that James needed to expand our offerings, add that Imperial stout for one, and age something, anything in a bourbon barrel.

"He hates that shit, you know," Michael had said during our last translate-James-to-Andi-and-back-again session. "Bourbon barrel aging is for hipsters. And have you seen how much those damn barrels cost these days?"

"I don't care," I said. "It sells. And numbers don't lie."

"She's not getting out," he said now as I tried to understand what in the hell he was talking about. "Sloane," he said, his tone one of exasperated frustration.

"Oh, okay, um…" I dropped into the chair. "Why not?"

"Hell if I know." He ran fingers though his hair, something I'd never seen him do. The dude looked like he was gonna lose it, and the realization shocked me. "Can you call her?"

"How did you find out?'

"Her mother texted me."

"Okay, I'm on it." I jumped up, was dialing her number, had the phone to my ear when I ran smack into someone's chest.

"Michael, I need to talk to you about that— Oh, hello."

"Shit," I spat out. I had to watch it. I was picking up Michael's potty mouth.

James had a hand on my arm, his expression neutral.

"Excuse me." I jerked out of his grip, aggravated by his stubborn insistence that I didn't exist in his universe. The whole thing was getting old and borderline bad for business.

If the head brewer—the guy who made the decisions about what to brew—didn't ever directly communicate with the sales director—the woman who made the decisions about what he *should* brew—things were about as SNAFU as they got.

"Sorry," he said, moving out of my way.

"*Goddamn* it," Michael hollered. We both turned to face him, surprised by his outburst. "I'm sick of this shit. Both you need to grow the fuck up. We have a business to run. I don't care what issues you're having with each other. Do you get it? *James?*"

I glanced up at the man in question, really looked at him for the first time in almost a month. It hurt; I won't lie. He looked like warmed over *caca*. His beard was out of control. If his hair got any longer, it would be man bun worthy. His shirt was wrinkled and had a rip in the side. He was holding a computer tablet in shaking hands. No wonder, since he reeked of booze, as if he'd gone out to visit some whiskey and settled in for a vacation.

Guilt washed through me, but I fought it off. There had been plenty of time for him get things straight in his head. He didn't have to keep acting like a nose-out-of-joint adolescent. I was moving on, doing my dang job, not bothering him. He should do the same.

"I can't have the head brewer and the sales director using me as a go-between. We are not in fucking middle school. Go, have dinner or get laid or something, work it out between you. I'm over it, and I need you both to be over it, too." He looked at me. "Can you call her, please?"

"I will," I said, looking up at James's profile. He was clenching his jaw. "I'll let you know what I find out."

What I found out was Sloane wanted to leave, but her doctors weren't willing to release her yet. One of the hard and fast rules of the place was that you had to regain a certain amount of weight based on your body type, and she hadn't met the goal. She was five pounds away and livid that they were "treating her like a teenager."

"New Year's," she said. "I'll be out then."

Something hit me. "Hey, can you have visitors?"

"If I schedule it, why? You bored?"

"No, but I forgot to give you something. Something Michael wanted me to give you in Florida and in all the kerfuffle, I forgot about it."

"What is it?" She sounded wary.

"A letter, I'm guessing. It's a fancy envelope with his name embossed on the flap."

"Oh. Well, okay then."

"Can I come now on short notice? I need a break from this place."

"Sure. I'll let the docs know. Come on out."

****

I sat with Sloane in the cozy living room decorated for Hanukah, Christmas, and Kwanzaa, amazed at how much better she looked. She turned the envelope over and over in her hands while we had a cup of tea and I met some of the other patients, one of whom pregnant, which seemed odd. But who was I to judge?

I left after an uncomfortable hour. Sloane was embarrassed by the whole thing despite my insistence that she shouldn't be. As I was walking down the steps, she hollered for me, ran out, wrapped in a million layers, and gave me a fierce hug. "I love you," she said.

"I know. I love you, too." I needed Stella at that moment. I hadn't talked to her in weeks and required her special brand of reality grounding. "Read what he wrote you, okay?" She nodded. "He wants to see you. Can you leave for a few days at Christmas?"

"No," she said. "I'll call him. After I read this."

She buzzed me with a call as I was on my way back to Detroit.

"Oh, my, *God*, Andi!"

"What? Are you okay? What's wrong?" I almost skidded off the road so I could turn around and go back.

"It's Michael. He's so honest and open and vulnerable in this letter. It's like he had someone else write it. I can't even."

"Well, maybe you should."

"Will you tell him to call me?" Her voice sounded stronger than it had when we were face to face. "I'm going to make him come to some therapy sessions with me. See if we can't... Oh my God. I can't even believe the things he wrote."

"I take it you're happy about them."

"I am. So happy." Her voice had a dreamy lilt to it. The same one she'd used when they'd spent a few hours paperclip engaged.

"Okay, I'll tell him to call you."

Chapter Twenty-Five

I walked into Michael's office the next morning and relayed what I'd learned, leaving out the part about therapy sessions. She could tell him that part herself.

His face lit up like a kid's. I tried not to be Debbie Downer and remind him one sappy love letter does not a challenging relationship make. Like I was in any position to talk about relationships, challenging or otherwise.

"You'll be at the party tomorrow night, right?"

"Of course."

"I know this is tough, Andi, but I need you to try and get to where you and James can communicate at work."

"I'll try."

He held up his phone. "I'm going to call her. Would you shut the door please?"

I headed to my office. It was two days before the holiday, and I'd decided I had too much work ahead to prepare for the new year and all the changes I'd be initiating to travel anywhere. I'd paid for a plane ticket for my mom, but she was balking as I knew she would, claiming her church needed her, she didn't like flying, blah blah. In short, I was facing a dismal, lonely Christmas. With no one to blame but myself.

The last thing I wanted to do was attend a giant company holiday party. But I had to. Once I was there,

I'd have fun. But right now, sitting in my big leather chair and staring at the fanned-out stack of projects on the glass top of my desk, I wanted nothing more than to go home and crawl under my mom's quilt, turn on old movies, and hide.

I'd been doing nothing but making plans, interviewing, making more plans, forecasting, and handling budgets for almost a solid month. Added to the extreme avoidance thing that James was engaging in, I sustained a low-level brain ache almost twenty-four seven. I had tried some yoga stuff, bending my poor, unbend-y joints into unnatural positions for the past week, so my entire body hurt, too.

I was a big fan of Christmas. My mother always went as all out as possible. And since I had no frame of reference for anything else, December always felt magical to me growing up.

I loved everything about it—live trees dripping needles on the floor for weeks, cookie and candy-making sessions, mixed in with our nightly Advent calendar story. Parties for me and my small group of friends making gingerbread people and endless chains of green and red construction paper that left our carpet crunchy underfoot with sparkles and baubles for weeks. These were my happy, if simple, memories of the holidays.

As a bar and restaurant owner, the holidays were the time of year to make a profit, so I loved and dreaded them in equal measure. They always meant staffing nightmares, kitchen disasters, customer tantrums, all with a healthy dose of annoying music, twinkly lights, and overindulgence.

This year looked like one firmly in the crapulous

column.

Again, no one to blame but myself. I'd had him. And I'd tossed him away. In the meantime, Sloane was getting better, which had been the goal of my lies.

I endured a long morning evaluating the final website design, had a lunch meeting with my new staff, and fought off an afternoon slump with a cup of fresh coffee. After I reviewed the re-branding presentation boards for the millionth time around four p.m., I was over it. I sighed and spun my chair around a few times, trying to muster some holiday cheer-type energy. While my email dinged away, populating itself with various messages, necessary and not-so-much.

I glanced at my phone to check who was texting me. The triple take I did gave me serious déjà vu.

It also left me dizzy, breathless, and more than a little nauseated.

An email flashed on the corner of my computer screen.

"*Hey, Andi. I was wondering what you were doing for the holidays. I want you to know I'm thinking about you. Hell, I miss you. Send me an update sometime. Let me know how you're doing.*"

He had the unmitigated balls to sign it, "*Love, Matt*".

I stared at it, stunned, sick, curious, and then suspicious. Without answering it—because, like I'd do that—I tossed the phone down and tapped "Beer Wenches, Inc." into my google search bar. I hit "news" and watched as it populated my screen, all of it dated the day before and today.

My heart sank all the way to my feet as I scrolled through the top story, dated yesterday, from

Brewbound, a respected beer news blog. How I'd missed this, I had no idea other than I'd been focused on Michael, Sloane, and what a sad sack I was this holiday season. But there it was, in bold black and white. "BWI, once the most popular and successful locally owned beer bar to close after franchise deal and potential partnership falls apart."

I jumped up, pulse racing, and stared at the screen so hard it hurt my eyeballs. If pressed to do so, I don't think I could've pinpointed which emotion was more dominant. There were too many. I wanted to scream, to cry, to throw my fancy Mac computer out a window, but at the same time, an eensy weensy tickle of self-satisfaction heated me from the inside out.

I hated that feeling. I tried like heck to quash it, but as I leaned on my glass desk top and read more, my disbelief at the words in front of me rising ever higher, that self-satisfaction turned to blind rage.

"That *motherfucker!*" I screeched. "I will fucking rip off his useless Goddamned balls and…and…"

"Jesus, what's wrong?" Michael stood in my doorway, a couple of my new marketing assistants behind him, their eyes wide.

Tears clogged my throat. I opened my mouth but couldn't make sounds.

Michael ran in and took my elbow. "Andi, breathe. Now."

I shook my head. My autonomous nervous system was in full shut down. I made a peeping sound, like a sad baby bird.

Michael tightened his grip on my arms as my vision fuzzed out while the intense ringing in my ears deafened me. I was going to die, right here, in my new office, wearing a new suit and designer heels, in front of my boss, who was the brother of the man I loved and had disappointed so badly he wouldn't speak to me.

But none of that mattered. Not anymore. BWI—my baby, toddler, recalcitrant pre-teen, and finally semi-autonomous young adult—was, for all intents and purposes, dead. Killed by my shitheaded, douche-baggy asswipe of an ex.

"Andi!" Michael gave me a shake.

My neck made a weird cracking sound when my head snapped forward. My eyes flew open.

"Do I need to call an ambulance?" he asked. "Talk to me."

All I could do was shake my head.

"Hey, Tyler, is James still down in the old brewhouse?"

"I'll check," the goggling marketing intern said.

"He left already," Melinda said as she rushed in with a cold cloth and glass of water.

"Andi, please, look at me," my boss said. "Focus on my words." I nodded, but I wasn't sure how much longer I could stand there, not breathing. "Breathe in. Breathe out. Come on, do it with me."

I tried. And failed at first. There wasn't any answer for it, but I was going into absolute shut down. And it was Matt Fucking Rigby's fucking ass fault. Finally, I was able to suck in a breath. I coughed and spluttered.

"Now, breathe out."

I managed this, too. Michael eased me into my chair. Melinda held the cloth to my head.

He crouched by my arm, his hand warm on mine. The one spot of warmth in my entire, ice-cold body. "You heard about BWI, I take it."

I nodded. Breathing in and out took all my concentration at the moment. "He…he…he sent me an email," I finally managed.

"Your ex? He told you?"

"No." I threw the cloth on the floor and lunged for my keyboard. I was losing it. I never cussed, much less turned the air blue like this, but… "Goddamn him to fucking hell and back, that useless, limp-dicked, fucking…fucker!" I was screeching again. "Fuh… fuh…fuck…"

Michael motioned toward the door. Melinda shooed the gathered crowd away. He stayed next to me, his hand on my shoulder while I executed a breathtaking nervous breakdown. All the energy I'd spent not doing this when Matt stood in my bar and told me he'd stolen it from me, and oh, by the way he was leaving me for the skinny blonde next to him came rushing up and out, spewing all over my office in a massive array of I-don't-know-what-the-hell.

Oh God, it hurt. Bad.

I laid my head on the desk and sobbed like a baby. I didn't care who was watching. I heard people talking over me, around me, about me. But I was blind, and the pain was centered in my gut, hot coals that had been doused with lighter fluid, licking up into my chest and throat.

I don't know how long I did this. All I did know was, once I'd cried every tear in me, I lifted my head from the desk and saw my office was empty. I drank the water Melinda had left. Then I stared at the glass of expensive bourbon Michael left, next to the almost full bottle. I grabbed it. Threw it down my throat. Sloshed in another hundred dollar helping and shot that one back, too.

It hit the fire in my gut like a splash of gasoline. I groaned and put my head back down, slapped the glass-top surface until I could breathe again, then sat up. The computer screen was so bright, I squinted at it in the gloom. I had to find out what happened. So I rolled my chair closer and read all about it.

I dragged myself home, after ignoring everyone who hovered, worried, concerned and annoying, including Mikey Burke himself. It was snowing. Again. I mumbled curses under my breath all the way home. I was numb, sick, exhausted, and still, even after reading it, I didn't understand what had gone wrong.

I found my way to my overstuffed chair, wrapped up in a robe, clutching a cup of cold tea. I didn't recall getting from my car, up my snowy steps, into the house, undressed, de-makeup-ed. But here I was.

I stared down at the contents of my mug, then at the snow filling the picture window in front of me. A tear burned its way down my cheek. I swiped at it, furious that he still had any power over me.

Granted, it wasn't about him. It was about what he'd done to our business.

He'd run it into the ground, thanks to greed, assumptions about how much money he could spend to attract big dog investors, and, finally, because he'd fired Vincente to save money. I'd read between the lines of the various, semi-gleeful reports of BWI's demise. He'd failed two health department inspections in a row. So his money guys had faded, fast.

I stared down at the phone resting on the table next to me. I'd half expected James to call, since I'm sure Michael had told him about my full office freak-out.

But my phone stayed silent. I sighed, tried to sip the tea, then put it on the table in disgust.

This called for more bourbon. I grabbed a bottle of overpriced corn liquor, yanked off the top, stared at my collection of rocks glasses, then took a long drink right from the neck of the dang bottle. It burned, but I didn't care. I wanted to be drunk. The sooner the better.

And nothing could help me achieve my goal quite like bourbon.

Well, okay, tequila, but I hated that nasty stuff.

I flopped onto the couch, legs sprawled out in front of me, robe gaping open, revealing my too big tits, my soft tummy, my thunder thighs.

"Fuck it," I said to no one in particular before taking another slug when the doorbell rang. I jumped up, still holding the bottle, and yanked it open without checking who it was first. I knew it would be James.

"Well, look who's here to sympathize with me. How 'bout a…" I stared at the man in front of me, his hair and shoulders covered in snow. "What the ever loving…" I swallowed hard. "Matt?"

My failed attempt at marriage and business stood on my front porch in man-shaped form, his hands shoved into his pockets.

"Can I come in?" he asked. His voice was low, soft, a tone I recognized. "Please, Andi?" He held out both hands. "I need you."

"That right?" I turned from him, leaving the door open. "Well, come the fuck on in, then."

He followed me in and shut the door. "It's cold here."

"Yeah? Tell me something I don't know." I faced him, clutching the bottle in one hand. My robe was still gaping, but what the hell. It wasn't anything he hadn't seen before. "Like, oh, maybe something about why in the hell you lost my bar?" I was screechy. I took a drink. It went down like warm honey.

"I don't know, but I'm here because…because I know I made a mistake. And I want you back."

"You want me back?" I laughed so hard I doubled over and sloshed amber liquor onto the fake Turkish rug. "Oh, God, Matt, that is rich." I wiped my streaming eyes.

He plucked the bottle from my hand, took a drink, and handed it back to me.

"Why?" I said, my voice cracking. "Why, Matt. Why did you do it?"

"I fucked it up, Andi. But I know why now. It's because I was confused. Madison had me all tied in knots, you know? You and I weren't exactly intimate by then, in case you've forgotten. I'm a man. I have needs."

I slapped a hand over my mouth to try and contain the giggles, but they escaped. And how. "You…you…" I pointed to him, unable to breathe for the shock, dismay, and hysteria. "You're a shitty actor, you know that? You failed. Sexy Madison-pants dumped you. So you come running all the way up to Michigan, go out of your way to find me, and show up at my door the same day I find out that you killed our baby!"

"Don't exaggerate," he said, moving toward me.

I moved out of his reach.

"It wasn't a child, Andrea. It was a business. And I fucked up. So yeah, I'm here to ask you to come back. I have a lead on another place, and I need you to help—"

"Oh. Hell. No." I backed up more until my legs hit

the chair I'd been sitting in earlier. I sat, staring up at him. Something about this was too weird. Like it was calculated. It was how Matthew Rigby operated. He messed up one thing, and he found something else to screw with. I cradled the bottle to my chest. "Get out. Please."

He didn't move. "I love you, Andrea. I miss you and I need you. I—"

I held up both hands. The bottle, having lost its moorings, fell over and rolled to the floor at my feet. Luckily, it was empty. "Stop right there. Stop running your stupid mouth, you...you..." All the super creative, expletive-laden insults I'd tossed at him while in my office, losing my mind in front of the staff and my boss, failed me. "You don't love me. You never loved me. You loved what I could do for you."

"But..."

"You're here hoping I'll leap at the opportunity to ditch my new life, follow you like some kind of...abused puppy, and work my tail off for...what? So you can fuck your clients or your co-workers or whatever? No thanks. Hit the road. *Vamoose*. Get the ever-loving fuck out of my house."

"Since when do you swear like—"

"Fuck you and the fucking horse you rode in on, you...you...twat waffle." No food and three quarters of a bottle of bourbon, no matter how classy, was making me want to hurl. I figured I might do it right on Matt's shoes.

"I don't have any place to stay."

"Tough titties. Sleep in your car."

"Can I crash on your couch? I'll get out first thing."

"Giving up on convincing me to come back to you? I'm insulted, but not surprised." I stood too fast. Matt grabbed my arm before I tipped over onto my face. And, of course, he pulled me into his sickeningly familiar arms. But I didn't want to be there. Not even as drunk as I was. "Get off me!"

He let me go. "Sorry. Old habits."

"Yeah? Fuck your habits."

"You've developed quite the vocabulary."

"Eat shit. Sleep on the couch if you want, but don't talk to me, don't touch me, don't even look at me. Got it? And I want you out before I get up in the morning."

"Fine," he said from behind me.

And then, the doorbell rang.

I froze in mid-flounce to the kitchen.

"Want me to get it?" my sorry-excuse-for-an-ex-husband asked from the other room.

I turned but couldn't make my feet cooperate. Matt Rigby was in my house, in Detroit, acting like the useless waste of space he was. And now he was answering my dang door like he lived here?

"No," I said, but the word didn't manifest in time.

I rushed into the living room, robe flapping open, bourbon fumes filling the air around me. "Hello," Matt said to the tall, broad, bearded man filling my doorway.

"Hello," James said, looking from me to Matt and back again. "I heard about what happened and thought I'd come by." He was holding a growler and a bag of food with grease spots, my favorite kind. "But I see you're busy." He took a step backward. "Sorry to hear about the bar, guys. I'll leave you to your…meeting or whatever."

"No, James, Matt isn't… He's not… I mean,

it's…oh hell."

Matt was standing too close to me, looking smug. I elbowed him so hard he grunted and doubled over before I ran barefoot onto the porch, calling out to James' back as it disappeared into the snowstorm. By the time he'd driven away, my feet were almost frost bitten. I ran back inside, slammed the door, cussed Matt out once more, and bolted upstairs so I could scream and cry and warm up my feet in peace.

Chapter Twenty-Six

Matt was gone by six the next morning. I looked around, anticipating some passive-aggressive gift he might have left behind, like an unflushed toilet or something. But it was as if he'd never been there. For a horrified moment, I thought I might have drunk dreamed the whole thing.

But I hadn't. It had provided the final proverbial nail in the coffin containing what might have been my relationship with James. *Thank you, Matthew. Thank you oh so very much.*

I made it into work by ten, way later than usual, but it was company party day and Michael said he might not be in at all, since he wanted to supervise the final touches. The party was being held at the downtown club that had hosted Carter's service, which sounded stuffy and awful. I was already brainstorming a different location for next year.

James had the brewery on half-day production, so everyone could attend. It wasn't dressy, which flew in the face of the club's dress code, but James had insisted on it, since Michael had insisted on having it there. I heard through company grapevines that Amelia had intervened with the club's board, throwing her Belanger money weight around and getting the code lifted for one night.

We'd be taking up the bulk of the rental area

anyway. It wasn't like the place wouldn't be compensated. Who cared what we wore? I had planned to leave early, go home and shower, do something with my hair, put on different clothes. But as I sat at my desk, turning my chair back and forth the way I did when deep in thought, I was too exhausted to contemplate so much work.

I had on a basic skirt, blouse, and heels. My hair was fine. I had no one to impress. I'd already made my mark as an approachable but numbers driven VP of sales. Some folks liked and respected me. Others did neither, but that was the way of being in charge.

Oh, and that fun, funny, maybe even sexy reunion I'd been plotting for myself and James for the night... Yeah, that wasn't happening anymore. So why bother?

I finished up my formal recommendation report about both the website and the packaging. It wasn't due until January 15th, but I'd made up my mind already. The bubble I'd been operating in—work, home, food, sleep, work again—had thick walls. I didn't let anyone inside it, other than Michael and the two people I'd hired to work as sales ambassadors for the brand. It wasn't a healthy way to live, but it was all I knew right now.

Matt and his BS had pierced it yesterday. Had gone deep and been ejected. Along with any hope I had of reuniting with James.

"You coming, Andi?" Maggie, Michael's patient and loyal assistant poked her head into my office. "It's starting soon." She kept her distance. One never knew when I'd fly off the handle and get all sweary.

"Sure am." I got up and stretched. The kink between my shoulders I'd developed from hours spent poring over spreadsheets, forecasts, and industry trends never went away.

"See you there!"

I gathered my stuff—phone, purse, laptop and bag, water bottle—and flipped off the lights. It was already dark at five-thirty, and snow was falling. I wondered if it ever stopped falling here. I still wasn't acclimated to it. Where I was from, a few inches of the white stuff meant closed schools and cozy days at home with hot chocolate. Here, it was the norm. You put on your coat, gloves, and boots, got in your all-wheel-drive vehicle, and powered through it.

The parking lot had been plowed, and the service had wiped most of the windshields clean by the time I got to my car. But it was still coming down, relentless and silent and effing cold. I knocked my boots clean and got into the used SUV Michael had helped me locate. I'd purchased snow tires, to be extra safe, making me somewhat more confident about getting around to conduct my daily business in the white Michigan landscape.

The club had valet parking, so I took my time getting there. Traffic was light, even in the more congested areas. I made it in under ten minutes, climbed out, and gave my keys to the young man standing at the curb.

"Jeez Louise," I said when the snow came at me sideways, stinging the exposed parts of my face.

"Ah, this is nothing," the kid said. "It's supposed to stop in an hour."

"Tell that to me again when I'm standing in a foot of the stuff. This is more snow than I've ever seen in my life."

He smiled at my Southern silliness and handed me a pick-up ticket. I headed for the door. I recalled this building, of course. The memories I had weren't pleasant, but this party wasn't for me. It was for the rest of the staff. Food, drinks, chocolate fountain for dessert, a band, plus a visit from Santa, the works. Michael knew how to throw a party, and he was bound and determined that this year's would kick off a new era so he was putting a ton of extra effort into it.

I checked my coat and scarf, chatted with several people from accounting and James' two new assistant brewers in the cavernous foyer before we headed into the soiree. I snagged a beer and a plate of food—lamb sliders with blue cheese, bacon-wrapped something or another, some expensive, out-of-season fruit—and stood at a tall table with a few guys from production. It was nice, pleasant, although I felt positively pickled in my own misery.

One of the guys at our table went back to get us all more beers as the room filled and got noisier. Michael got up in front of the band's equipment on the stage and made a rah-rah speech, formally introduced me, all stuff we'd planned.

I couldn't help but look around, seeking James. I'd hoped we could at least talk. I wanted to explain why Matt had been in my house when I was in my flapping robe, empty bourbon bottle and all.

Ugh. I wouldn't listen to me explain that, either.

I spent an hour or so working my way around the room, accepting congratulations and welcomes, even though I'd been officially working for several weeks. I shivered when the band opened with *"Boogie Shoes,"* the last dance song we'd shared at my place on

Thanksgiving night. Thrown by this and mad at myself for being thrown, I retreated to an empty table with a bottle of water, my nerves humming with memory, my eyes seeking the one man I couldn't seem to locate in the crowd.

Finally, I heard him, or rather, his laugh. I followed the sound of it, keeping myself tucked into the darker edges of the room. I spotted him at one of the low tables, surrounded by three women, all of whom were staring at him with stars in their eyes. I recognized two of them—one was an intern brewer, the other an HR assistant. The third one, the one sitting closest to him, so close his arm was draped over the back of her chair, I couldn't place. But I'd seen enough. He'd obviously made his peace with the fact that we'd never be together. I wasn't going to act like a love-sick fool. No way, no how.

I hustled away, wondering how soon I could leave. I wanted to cry or scream or curl up under a table and drink. Instead, I aimed myself at the door and freedom from the reality sucker punch.

I'd almost made it when I heard my name called. I looked and had a knee jerk thought to bolt out the door and pretend I hadn't heard it.

"Andi?" Amelia Burke called out from her position near the bar. "Do you have a moment?"

I sighed. "Not really, Mrs. Burke. I need to go…"

"Where? It's snowing too hard to go anywhere."

I bit the inside of my cheek to keep from saying anything, lest it be something rude. Because rudeness was on the tip of my tongue. "Okay," I said. "What can I do for you?"

"I'd like to show you something. We can go out."

She pointed to the closed venue doors. "I know of several quieter places."

I wasn't in the mood to be railroaded. "No, here's fine." I pointed to an empty table near the back wall.

Her gray eyes flickered with annoyance. "All right. It won't take a moment."

I followed her over, snagging a beer on the way, figuring I might as well get closer to tipsy. We sat. She pulled something from her purse and slid it across the table to me. I took a drink and waited for backstory.

"Take a look."

I turned it over. Picked it up. Studied it. It was a photo. "It's James, right?"

"Look closer. You're a smart woman, someone who notices details."

I sighed and picked it up again. It was a color photo, but I could tell it wasn't from a digital camera. It had that slightly faded, grainy look of developed film. I took a closer look at the man in the frame. Broad-shouldered, full-lipped, green eyes alight. He had his arm around someone who was out of the frame, a dark-haired woman in what could be a swimsuit cover up, but she was less than a quarter visible.

The man—not James I'd decided—wore a black T-shirt that hugged his broad torso. He had on faded jeans and a style of athletic shoes that hadn't been made in years.

I looked at his face again, fascinated by his resemblance to the man whose raucous laughter kept clanging in my ears like a wayward cymbal. The people in the photo were in front of a lake and a beach. The man's hair was tousled and long-ish. His beard well groomed.

"Okay, I'll bite," I said, tossing it onto the table. "Not James. It's too dated. So who is it?"

"Jeff. Carter's brother."

"Oh, his Uncle Jeff. Amazing family resemblance. If that's it, Mrs. Burke, I need to—" I pushed myself up from the table.

She put a hand on mine. "We need to talk about James."

"I have no reason to talk about him other than how I'm going to repair our work relationship." Why I'd told her that, I have no clue. But I said it as I sat, as something hit me. She hadn't called him "James' uncle." She'd said, "Carter's brother."

I tapped the photo with my fingertip. "This man, Jeffrey Burke, is James' father." I didn't make it a question.

She nodded, took a sip of her lime-choked gin, and set it on the table. "Jeff and I were together for a summer. That's me, there." She touched the photo. "We were at my family's house in Petoskey."

"All right," I said, leaning back. "What am I to do with this news flash?"

"I need you to understand something about James." She tucked the photo back into her purse. My skin was tingling. My scalp prickled. I didn't want to hear what she was going to say, but I knew I had to. "He and Jeff were, are, gentle souls. They're artist types, you know? The whole brewing thing?"

I nodded, still shocked into silence. But something burst out of me before I could drag it back and squash it. "Why did you marry Carter?"

She pressed her lips together. She was, without a doubt, a faded beauty. I could imagine her as a young woman—rich, carefree, hanging out in her lake house, eager to experience life. "Jeff was a bartender at a local bar, not far from our house. I had a fake ID and would hang there when my parents were partying with their friends at other houses. I was obsessed with him. He was so handsome, so nice, so eager to please." She heaved a huge sigh. "I was eighteen. He was twenty-five. Carter was twenty-three. His job that summer was mowing lawns, cleaning out gardens, sweeping the beach. Physical stuff. He'd meet up with us when we snuck to the beach after Jeff's shifts at the bar. We'd drink, talk about their brewery dream, smoke pot…"

She smiled when I couldn't hold back a gasp. "Yes, believe it not, we oldsters had some fun, too. And the sex…" She propped her chin in her hand. I tried not to recoil. "Well, anyway, we were young and stupid, and I got pregnant. I figured it out after the summer was over. I tried to contact him, but he was already in Germany. He'd used five years' worth of tip money to pay his way to the brewing institute. It was in the days before internet or decent international phone options. I had no way to reach him."

I drained my beer while she toyed with her glass. "I found Carter. He was in grad school in Ann Arbor, finishing his MBA. We went out for coffee. I broke down and told him, made an awful scene." She put a hand to her throat. "And of course, you know how that ended. He asked me to marry him. I did. And now, here we are."

"That doesn't sound like a happy ending."

"It wasn't. Carter and I…we weren't compatible, but I didn't know what else to do. He was good at convincing me of almost anything, including providing the money from my trust fund to set up his and Jeff's brewery. He had this way about him."

She chewed her lower lip. "I thought our basic, physical attraction could or would transform into something else. Something like what I felt for his brother and never stopped feeling for him. It didn't. After I had Michael, Carter and I stopped being intimate. It was, I don't know, as if he'd targeted me, figured out what I had to offer, and set out to get it from me." She shrugged. "I'm no angel. I know that. I grew up rich and spoiled and acted like a fool that summer. But one thing I would not let Carter take from me was control of my sons' inheritances. They both have trust funds, thanks to my father's investment advising team. He tried to steal from them more than once. It never worked."

She hesitated as if deciding whether or not to tell me the next part. "James' fund will mature on the first of January, the year he turns thirty-five, Michael's the year after. Neither of them know about it. I made sure of that. In eight more days, James will be six million dollars richer."

I blew out a breath. "Wow." I pulled my hair free from the band and rubbed my scalp. "This is quite the news dump, Amelia."

Her lips twisted. I hesitated, afraid I'd pissed her off, then decided I didn't give a rip.

When the twistiness turned into a smile, I figured we'd reached a stalemate. "I know, I'm sorry to do it to you at what's supposed to be a fun party."

We both looked around us, taking in the increasingly drunken revelry. I spotted Michael at a tall table, chatting with people from three different departments. They all looked relaxed, not like the boss was making them uncomfortable at a party he'd paid for. He had that effect on people. Even with his killer business instincts. People trusted him with their livelihoods on many levels.

"Michael taking over was the best thing that has happened to the brewery. The only thing that saved it."

"Yeah. It sounds like it was a real mess."

She snorted. "To put it mildly. Carter had lost his damn mind. He'd run through at least five mistresses by then." She waved a hand at my look of dismay. "A story for another time, but suffice it to say I didn't care. I had him figured out by then. Jeff's death did a number on him, but he never admitted it. He was a cold, calculating asshole."

"Did Jeff ever marry?"

"He had a girlfriend at the end, but I don't think he ever forgave me or his brother and wouldn't allow himself to trust any woman after that." She met my gaze. "We were never together after I married Carter. He barely acknowledged my existence. But he knew damn well James was his son. It was hard to deny. Carter took out a lot of shit on James, as if it were his fault who'd fathered him. He could have all the girlfriends he wanted, but I never forgave him for that."

"Does James know?"

"No."

I sucked in a breath. I could hear him again, laughing, talking, although I couldn't make out the words. When I looked, he was on the dance floor, boogeying away with the sweet little number who'd been hanging off him earlier. My pulse raced. I started to get up again. I had to get out of here before I made a fool out of myself.

"Wait, Andi, just a few more minutes?" Amelia patted the seat I kept trying to vacate.

I sat. "I'm sorry, but I don't see how this has anything to do with me." I played with my empty glass, wanting more to drink. "We…we had a few nice moments, but I'm afraid I've messed it all up."

"Oh, my dear," she said, patting my hand and sounding exactly like Carolyn VanAnsel had if a tiny bit bitchier. "It has everything to do with you."

We took a minute to ponder James, dancing, flirting, teasing the girl who kept angling closer, hoping he'd kiss her. Primal, proprietary rage flared in my chest, burned my throat. She'd definitely sampled James' kisses or she wouldn't be working so hard for more while he was weaving, drunk, and showing off.

"I heard about what happened with Sloane. I'm not surprised. That girl is wound way too tight. I'm sorry for her. But it sounds like she's getting help."

"How do you…"

She pointed to James. "Bless him, he tells me everything. I knew about Tracy's cheating well before anyone else. He wanted to blame me for it, but I'd hoped she could provide him with some stability. Something I knew he craved more than oxygen. I was wrong." She shrugged. "I could kill that selfish little bitch for what she did to his psyche. She shredded him. And destroyed his ability to trust. Not too far off what I did to his father, if you're into those sorts of comparisons."

"I don't know. I mean, look at him. He's fine. He's got himself a nice new gal pal and everything. I'm leaving." I got up again.

"Sit, down, young lady. I know your type. And you know better than to take that kind of behavior at face value."

I glared at her and didn't sit this time.

"My life with Carter was absolute hell, utter misery, and I don't want my sons to have the same life. James loves you, Andi."

I rolled my eyes and made a scoffing sound, even as a tiny part of me fluttered, hopeful and eager to hear more.

She took my arm and pulled until I sat. I felt deflated, frumpy, sweaty, over dressed, unsexy as hell. "He loves you. Michael and I don't agree on much, but we agree on the fact that you'd be a great couple. Something tells me you know it, too."

I blinked back tears. This day had lasted way too long. I needed to go home, ponder this news, figure out my next steps. "I don't know what to do," I finally admitted. "I lied to him. He has every right not to trust me. And then, last night, oh jeez, it was such a mess."

Look at me, confessing my love life trouble to Amelia Belanger Burke. Boy, I'd come a long way.

"Fiddle," she said, making me smile at the echoing reference to my favorite jokey phrase when I wanted to downplay something. She drained her glass. "I made crappy choices, Andi. And I paid the price for years. I want to tell James about Jeff, but I can't seem to find the right moment to let him know the man he loved more than Carter was actually his father. That's on me. But the future, your future mutual happiness? That's on you."

While I watched James deflect the girl's increasing efforts to get him into a clinch, I rose, keeping my eyes on him and nothing else.

"We'll be wrapping things up soon," the band guy said from the stage. "So we'd like to let our best singer show her stuff with a song I think you'll all recognize. Grab your favorite partner folks. This one's a slow dance."

I kept moving toward him. The girl looked more than a little put out. James finished another beer. She tried to drag him off the dance floor. He resisted. The song began.

"At last…" the woman who'd been playing a guitar crooned into the mic.

Well, if that wasn't a hard shove from karma, I didn't know what was. I glanced over my shoulder. Amelia made "go on" motions with her hands. I swallowed the lump of fear in my throat, fixed my gaze on James and the unhappy woman. She was whining and tugging at him, and he was laughing and trying to grab someone else to dance with.

"Excuse me," I said, tapping the girl's shoulder. "This is our song."

She glared at me, then shrank back. I assumed she figured out who I was, but I didn't care. She faded into the general gray space around me, leaving me facing James.

He looked disheveled, out of sorts, and drunk. I held out a hand as the song got going and the lights dimmed. He took it, yanked me hard against him, his eyes flashing with something I couldn't identify at first. When I did, I figured my eyes showed the same emotion—intense relief.

We danced in silence. The song ended, but we stayed on the floor, staring at each other.

"Last set, people," the lead singer yelled into the mic. "Let's do this!"

An hour later, we were soaked with sweat, laughing and leaning on each other. We still hadn't exchanged a word, but we'd consumed a lot of water and we'd touched a whole lot. And I, for one, was ready to pick things up where we'd left them at Thanksgiving.

It was funny really, how hormones rule. Mine were on high alert and wanted one thing. This man. In bed. With me. I didn't care whose bed it was. I didn't even know where he lived and didn't care. During the last song, I put my hand around the back of his neck.

"Can we get out of here?" I said close to his ear.

"I thought you'd never ask." He took my hand, and we made a beeline for the door. But when we reached it, he paused and turned. "Crap. I can't go."

"Why not?" I was afraid he'd say he couldn't leave his date.

"I have to put on the Santa suit."

"Seriously?" I stuck my hands on my hips. He looked me up and down and licked his lips, which sent a jolt of excitement up my spine.

"Seriously. Hang on. Hold all those…thoughts." He cupped my breast.

I smacked his hand away.

****

James and I ran out into the snow, giggling like kids. "I don't have a Santa fetish, but I'm about to develop one," I said when he stopped and kissed me under a light in the parking lot while snow fell all around us. "Jesus, Lord, and all the saints, James, take me home, like right now."

"But have you been a good girl?" He touched my

nose with a cold fingertip. "I think not. What was all that with that weasel-faced ex-husband in your house last night, hmm? And you practically naked. What is a guy to think?"

I reared back. "He lost my bar, James. He...went and ruined it in less than a year." A tear slid down my cheek.

"Oh honey, I know. I heard. It's awful. But, in a way, maybe it's a sign that you're supposed to move on for real. You can let it go altogether." He touched my lips.

I grinned and bit his fingertip, then held on and sucked it into my mouth. I shocked myself with this. I was usually pretty reserved, but I had a feeling I'd be outgrowing my shyness real soon.

"Yep. You're on the naughty list, all right. Let's go." He waved for one of the waiting ride share cars. There was no way in hell either of us could drive. Figuring we'd pick up our cars the next day, we tumbled in. "Your place or mine," he said, pulling me so close I was almost on his lap.

"I don't care. Which is closer?"

"Mine, I think." He gave an address, then lifted my chin to meet his gaze. "I'm not interested in a one-off here, Andrea. You understand?"

I nodded.

"And you fucked with my head, twice over. Not sure I should give you the time of day, much less the orgasms I plan to bestow tonight."

"I'm sorry, James. You deserved better. But you know why I did it."

"It doesn't make it any less wrong."

I leaned over and sucked his oh-so-tempting full

lower lip into my mouth. He groaned and kissed me and kissed me and kissed me all the way to his condo, in one of the renovated historical buildings a few blocks from the club.

I broke from him, breathing heavily. "So we could've walked here." I smacked his shoulder.

"My brother already paid these driver guys," he said as he pulled a twenty dollar bill from his wallet. "But here's a tip for your trouble."

"Thanks. Have a great night."

"Planning on it," I said as James handed me out of the car and straight into his arms.

"Andi, Andi," he muttered into my neck. I stared up at the falling snow, blinking as it landed on my eyes, nose, and cheeks. "What would you say if I said I think I love you?"

"I'd say you're jumping the gun. You hardly know me."

"I make quick decisions. How about this?" He slid both hands up my shirt and cupped my breasts. "I know I love these. Will that work?"

"Sure will," I said. "Can we rewind? Back to the you want to make love to me moment?"

"Done," he said, picking me up and tossing me over his shoulder in front of the building. I tried not to laugh, determined to be insulted by this cave man move. I was a grown, modern, feminist woman. I wasn't about to be manhandled. He held onto me until we hit the elevator. I slid to the floor and stood, in the circle of his arms, staring up at him.

He touched my cheek. "I'm sorry. I overreacted."

"Maybe a little. But I get it, and I swear I'll never give you a reason not to trust me again."

"Can I kiss you?" His voice was raspy. "Please?"

"I'm gonna be mad if you don't."

"Far be it from me to make my woman mad. I hear she gets pretty bitchy."

I leaned away from him. "You lie."

He shrugged and put his lips near mine, hovering, teasing. "Just ask your boss. He'll tell you."

I shrugged. "Maybe, but I get shit done."

"That you do, my love. That you do." He kissed me then.

I shut out all the clamoring, clanging, insecure nonsense that was my near constant self-narrating companion. And I let myself enjoy…and enjoy…and enjoy some more, until we fell asleep, sweaty and exhausted and spent, tangled up in each other's arms.

Chapter Twenty-Seven

Needless to say, I did not spend Christmas Eve alone or lonely. I spent it naked as a matter of fact, which was lovely.

We met up with Michael and Amelia for dinner Christmas night at the club. I don't know if I'd ever get used to calling it that, as if it were mine. While we were waiting at the bar for our table, I asked Amelia if she'd told James anything yet. She said no and changed the subject. But I think she and I had found our common ground. We both wanted James to be happy. The dinner was pleasant, even with Michael stressing left, right, and center about Sloane and what she was doing today.

"Don't rush her, Michael," Amelia said over a slice of pumpkin pie.

"Mother, don't be a bitch."

"Oh, I'm not," she said, at the exact moment I said "Oh, she's not."

Michael's eyes widened. James' expression matched it.

"Well then," James said, finishing off his pie. "Glad that's settled."

I flushed. He patted my knee under the table.

"What I mean is, she'll need more time before she can withstand the Michael Burke full court pressure," I said.

"I don't do full court—"

He looked around the table at us, all eyeing him in the same way.

"Fine. I get it." He wiped his lips and held up his glass of sherry. We all raised ours. "To Christmas. And to new beginnings."

"I'll drink to that," James said. His hand was still on my knee. I'd never felt more loved, more secure, or happier. I didn't even think about shoes dropping.

We settled into a nice routine. My new year changes hit everyone, but since those same everyones knew they were necessary, it worked out. The website was launched. The packaging ordered. The ace young woman with the keen social media and IT savvy was hired.

James even agreed to make an Imperial stout but flat out refused to age anything in bourbon barrels. We fought over that, and the making up was sweet, plus we got to test his theory about my office having plenty of room for making up activity.

The next day he announced he'd sourced some rum barrels out of a small distillery in the Bahamas. They'd be shipped here and arrive in a month. Those he agreed to age his beer in. "Something different," he said.

By the first of February, things were humming along at the brewery. James and I spent almost every night together, usually at my place since it was bigger. We never once brought up the M-word. Neither of us was prepared to take the marriage leap. My life felt full, complete, and when Stella and my mom made it up at the end of the month, they gave full and enthusiastic approval to him. Why wouldn't they? He squired them around town to museums, dinners, the works. If I weren't so secure in my skin, I would have been jealous.

He usually spent Sunday mornings at the downtown YMCA, which gave me some space to sit and read or binge watch bad movies. I'd repeatedly declined his invitations to join him. I hated swimming and wouldn't touch gym equipment. Way too many germs. I took long walks and executed the odd yoga pretzel pose, which was plenty of exercise as far as I was concerned.

I was enjoying my final cup of milky coffee, reading gossipy garbage on my tablet, when I heard the meow before I heard the doorbell. I looked up. There were always lots of feral cats roaming around. I kept a dish of food and water on my back porch, which was always licked clean.

The doorbell dinged again. I opened it, unsurprised by what I found on the porch.

"Hi, Andi," Sloane said. She was smiling. Her face looked almost normal, her hair restored to its lustrous shininess. She had on a thick coat, hat, and scarf. And was holding…

"Is that a kitten," I asked, crossing my arms.

"Yes. Isn't he sweet?" She held him out to me. I had no choice but to take him. He purred and snuggled into my neck.

I frowned, still hanging on to the doorknob. "Is he a bribe?"

"Maybe." She twisted her fingers together. "Can I come in?" I saw her suitcase next to her. Then I saw Michael, standing at the foot of the steps to my porch. "For a month or so?"

I tried to be put out, but I couldn't fake it. I smiled and pulled her in, giving her a hug and making the kitten squirm between us. "Of course, you can."

Michael came up the steps with her second suitcase, set it in the foyer, and lingered on the porch. "I'll talk to you later?" His voice was soft, and his gaze never left Sloane.

"Thank you, Michael."

He left without another word.

I put the kitten down. He wobbled around then made for the pile of newspapers under the dining room table.

"I brought supplies and everything," she said, holding up a bag from a pet store. "Food, a litter box, and litter. We'll need more of course."

"Of course." I watched the little guy try to sharpen his claws on the papers. "What's his name?"

"Hoppy, naturally."

"Naturally," I repeated and turned to her. "You're better. You look way better anyway. How's your noggin?"

"Better," she confirmed with a nod. "Poor Michael. He's attended six therapy sessions with me these past few weeks."

I knew about them. He always returned from those sessions looking wrung out like an old kitchen rag. He'd hide in his office for an hour before he emerged, back to normal.

"We...um...well, we're going to give our relationship a try. The doctors agree we love each other, but we have some issues to get past. It's going to take time." She pulled out the box, poured some litter into it and found a corner for it in the back hallway. "He went right for it!" she exclaimed. "That's cool. Way easier than a dog."

"Yes," I said. I'd grown up with cats, but after our last one had to be put down, my mother had sworn off the expense and the ultimate heartbreak when they died. "I love cats," I admitted.

"I know. The Burke brothers gossip machine at work."

"So, then you know, James and I..." I blushed, recalling how "together" we'd been the night before. I was letting myself enjoy sex in a way I never had. And I'd discovered that I had a penchant for dirty talk. I mean, seriously nasty, dirty talk, which James was always happy to oblige.

"Oh yeah. I know. And I am so, so happy for you both." She stood in the middle of the living room, looking awkward.

"So, here's my deal. If you're staying here, I won't tolerate any BS with food. We eat in this house."

"Deal," she said. "I'm actually hungry now."

"I have some leftover pancakes. That work?"

"Perfect, thanks."

I warmed them up and set the plate in front of her with a pitcher of maple syrup. She poured a bit on the side. "I'm a dipper," she said, cutting a miniscule bite, touching it to the pool of syrup, then putting it in her mouth. "Mmm," she said.

I watched her do this five more times and felt, if not out of the woods, a heck of a lot better.

"You're just in time for our big meeting," I said, pouring her a cup of coffee.

"What meeting?" She picked up Hoppy the kitten and cuddled him to her chest. I took a quick inventory. Her fingers were still bony and her neck seemed too fragile, but overall, she looked good. Her cheeks were fuller, her frame sturdier.

"With Amelia."

"Why?"

"Because I called a meeting with her and us."

"Who us?" She stuck her finger in the syrup and tried to get Hoppy to lick it, but he turned up his nose

"Cats can't smell or taste sweet." I found a lidless plastic storage bowl and poured a helping of the kitten food into it. "Where did you get him?" I picked him up and carried him and the food into the kitchen. He crawled all the way into the bowl and started jamming on it.

"This probably won't surprise you, but when Michael came to pick me up, he had the little guy in a box in the passenger's seat. We stopped for supplies on the way here." She got a faraway look in her eyes. "We've come such a long way in a few weeks."

"I'm glad to hear it. He's a total pain in the ass at work when he's worried about you."

"All right, spill it, Rigby. Why did you call a meeting with La Belanger Burke?"

"You might be shocked to know that she and I get along pretty well."

"Not shocked. Jealous maybe." She played with another bite. I pointed to it. She ate it.

"She has some things to say to James and I want them said. I refuse to be part of a family that's keeping secrets."

"Secrets? Seriously? What?"

I chewed my lip, wondering if I should tell her. "Carter wasn't James' father. Jeff was."

"Oh, that." She waved a hand. "Michael's suspected that for years. He's so much like his Uncle and not only in looks."

"Also, she has to release his trust fund to him."

That got me a raised eyebrow. "Really."

"Really. A metric ton of money."

She got up to take her plate to the kitchen. "I can't stuff a bunch of food in me in one sitting," she said when I blocked her way. "I eat, like, eight times a day though. Smaller amounts. And how in the world do you know all of this juicy Burke family gossip?"

"Noted." I moved so she could put the plate in the dishwasher. "I know because the night James and I made up, she came to the company holiday party to tell me. All of it. The Jeff-is-the-real-daddy part and the trust fund. She wanted me to be thinking about the best way to handle it. She was that confident we'd get back together. We might not have, if she hadn't insisted I walk over to him and stake my claim, as it were."

Sloane whistled. "Impressive. I knew you were awesome. And now you've gone and conquered Madame Money Bags."

"You should talk."

"I know, I know."

"Michael has one, too…a trust fund. His matures this time next year," I said.

"She held onto them long enough. Typically, they mature when you turn twenty-one."

"She did that on purpose. She didn't want Carter anywhere near the money."

Her eyes got big. She grabbed my arm. "Oh shit, Andi. Do you think she offed him? Carter, I mean?"

"No. She didn't. But he sounds like a total asshole in addition to being a douchewaffle."

"Yeah. He was."

"Wanna come with?"

She pulled her hair back and fastened it with a comb. "No. Too soon."

"Okay. The guest bedroom is all yours."

I took a shower, dressed in one of my better work suits, and the pair of designer heels I'd treated myself to after my second paycheck. My inner thrifter made spending the money I now had at my disposal a challenge. I'd picked them up, walked to the checkout, set them down, walked out of the store, breathed into a bag a few minutes, then gone back in and plunked down my new credit card.

"Wow," Sloane said when I came back downstairs to grab my purse and keys. James had gone home after his workout and basketball game and was meeting us at the Burke family home. I had insisted on it, had told Amelia I'd break up with James if she didn't come clean. She had to tell him and Michael about the trust funds anyway. Might as well make it a two-fer.

"You look fahbulous, dahling." She blew on her cup of tea. "I'll figure myself out soon, I promise. And I'll pay you rent for the time I'm here."

"Don't be silly. Okay, I'm ready. And I'm sweating like a pig." I held the shirt away from my chest.

"Why? You're not the one with the major news flash to share. You're there for moral support."

"I guess." I took a few deep breaths and headed out. We'd had non-stop snow for weeks. James and I had shoveled the walk and steps over and over again and constructed a huge snowman in my front yard, complete with beer bottle lids for buttons and eyes…with an empty Burke Bros IPA can in his stick

345

hand. I smiled at it when I passed by. I still wasn't used to the ongoing bitter cold, which was the only thing keeping this from being a one hundred percent perfect day.

The snow crunched under my heels as I made my way to my SUV. I plugged the Grosse Pointe address into my phone and was there within twenty minutes. I sat, staring up at the imposing brick and stone edifice, wondering what I'd gotten myself into.

Fact of the matter was, I loved James Burke. While I wasn't positive how things would progress, I was content to let them do so organically. No rushing. No knee-jerk decisions about anything. But I wondered what James would do with the information he was going to get in a few minutes.

I headed for the double front doors. Before I could knock, it opened. James stood, smiling at me and holding a glass of water. "Come in, come in, but be warned, old money smells funny."

The house was as impressive inside as it was out. Art, carpets, fresh flowers, delicious cooking smells, two fireplaces both burning bright.

"Andi, is that you?" Amelia came out of the kitchen. We exchanged a quick hug. "It'll be fine," she whispered.

I nodded, my mouth too dry to speak. I'd set this in motion. I was prepared to see it all the way through.

An hour later, we were at the fancy dining room table, empty plates in front of us, aperitifs poured.

"I understand we're all here for a specific reason," Michael said. "Can we get a hint or are we playing twenty questions?"

Amelia sat up straighter, adjusted her perfectly

straight silverware, then took a long breath. "James, Carter was not your biological father."

My pulse raced so fast I felt dizzy. I sat next to James so I had to crane my neck around to gauge his reaction. Michael looked blasé, sipping his drink. James pressed his lips together. His jaw clenched. I put my hand on his leg under the table.

He grabbed it. "Mother, if you honestly think that's news to me, you're naive."

I looked at Michael, then Amelia, then back at James.

"It's okay," he said to me before putting my knuckles to his lips. "I'm okay. I know. I mean, I didn't know in any official way, but Carter hinted at it enough to me over the years. Plus, I've been known to look in a mirror, and I'm not blind."

"I'm sorry, James. I should have told you sooner. I should never have married Carter."

"Yeah, but then, what would I have done without that knuckle head in my life." He jerked his chin at Michael who'd remained silent throughout this exchange.

Amelia smiled and visibly relaxed.

"You said there were a couple of things. What else?" He lifted his glass.

"Your trust fund has matured. I've signed it over to you." She handed him a thick, fancy-looking navy-blue folder.

James spit wine all over the table. I smacked his back while he spluttered and swiped his streaming eyes. "My…what?"

"Yeah, mother. His what?" Michael chimed in.

"You have one, too, don't worry."

"I don't want your money," Michael declared.

"Shut up, Mikey." James stared at the folder like it was a poisonous snake. "I don't understand. How did you keep Carter away from this?"

"My father managed it, that's how. He and Carter got along on the surface, but that's about it."

James opened the folder, stared down at the top sheet of paper, then slammed it shut on the table. "Christ, Mother. Is this some kind of a joke?"

"I never joke about money, James."

"Give it to me," Michael demanded, turning the folder around to face him and slapping it back open. "Okay, let's see…." He made a few humming sounds and ran his finger down the top page. I couldn't see it, but I already knew what he'd find at the bottom. His eyes widened. He blinked, looked at his mother, looked at the paper, blinked again. "Holy. Shit."

Amelia sipped her wine, looking calm and cool and rich. "My father's investment team is very good."

"I'd say so." Michael closed the folder and sat back, his hand resting on the table. "What in the hell are you going to do with it?"

"I was thinking about handing it over to the only financial advisor I know," James said. He still seemed shell shocked. "Hopefully, he'll cut me a friends and family deal."

Michael blinked. "No, I can't. I have enough to do. But I know a guy…" He squeezed his eyes shut. "Fuck, Jimmy the tax ramifications on this are massive to the point of terrifying."

"I have an idea for some of it," I said.

They all looked at me, which the moment I knew I belonged here, with them, and their smelly old money.

"What about a foundation? A lot of the big breweries have them. They take applications for grants and stuff. Or we—I mean, you—could dedicate it to a specific charity or effort or something." I shrugged. "I don't know from trust funds and tax shelters, but I know you can use a lot of it to do some good."

"A foundation," Amelia said. "I like it. The Burke Brothers Foundation."

"I've been wanting to do something for women in fermentation businesses," James said, threading his fingers in mine and holding tight under the table. "Kind of like the Gates Foundation does, for women all around the world trying to work their way out of poverty, making everything from kimchee and pickles to crafting beer, cider, and wine."

"I'll get our attorneys working on it," Michael said. "I like this. I like it a lot."

"It will require an administrator. Someone, probably a couple of people, to create the application process, vet the applications, award the money, run the publicity," Amelia said. She smiled at Michael. "I know the perfect person."

He smiled back. "I do, too."

Chapter Twenty-Eight

Ten Months Later
Back in Denver

"I can't stand it," I said, gripping James' hand in one of mine, Michael's in the other. "How long is this gonna take, anyway?"

"I entered some crowded categories. We won't win," James said.

"Of course we will. Don't be a negative Nancy," Michael insisted.

I sucked in a breath. Talk about full circle. This time last year I'd been at this very Expo, seeking validation for my lousy life by finding any job I could, aware of the Burke Brothers Brewing Company on a basic level, nothing more. And now, here I was, dating one brother, working for the other, waiting for the results of the first World Cup of Beer contest they'd ever entered.

James liked to claim they were beauty contests, fixed, a waste of time and effort. I insisted otherwise long enough and loud enough, until he agreed to enter in three categories. We hadn't bothered with a pouring booth this year, but Sloane made sure we were a presence via our Burke Brothers Foundation booth, where she sat now, talking with other breweries and entities interested in setting up something similar.

It had taken six months to get it set up as a legal

non-profit, but once it was, Michael handed it over to Sloane. She now ran with it with the sort of organization and efficiency we all knew she would. To date, we'd given out four mini-grants to women-owned businesses here and overseas in Argentina, Brazil, and Senegal. Sloane jet-setted all over the place, establishing the foundation as a legit entity and verifying the applications she got.

The same investment company that grew the trust to six and a half million continued to manage it. Sloane took to the whole thing like the proverbial duck to water. James gave himself a small raise, plus bigger ones to everyone in production. Michael didn't draw a salary from the brewery since he could live off his investments and real estate profits, but he offered up an across the board ten percent raise to the entire administrative staff. Once his fund matured, he'd put it all into the foundation.

I still had some worries. One being the Burke Bros tap room retail space. They were losing opportunities to draw larger crowds, thanks to the lazy attitude of the guy in charge. I knew I couldn't go barreling in there and find a better person to run it. Not yet, anyway.

Michael tightened his grip on my hand, pulling me back to the present. "Hey, Andi, can I ask you a favor."

"Sure, what?" I wasn't paying attention to him, fixated as I was on the announcer sorting through his stack of winning envelopes.

"Will you and James join me and Sloane at Le Rouge after this?"

I glanced at him. "Yeah, I mean, whatever. That's fine."

"Good," he said, looking satisfied with himself.

Before I could ask him what was up, the announcer cleared his throat.

James' Imperial Stout and New England IPA both won gold, and his Vienna red lager won silver. By the time all the cheering, hugging, back slapping, and photographs were accomplished, I was drained. All the emotion in the buildup and my own nostalgia for "this time last year" culminating in such massive success left me wanting nothing more than to go back to our hotel suite and sleep.

"Le Rouge, remember?" Michael said as he broke away from us.

"Wait, where are you going?" James held two large trophies. I had the smaller, silver one.

"I gotta find Sloane. We'll meet you there, okay? Two hours? Don't be late."

"Okay, sure," James said. He looked stunned, like a deer in the headlights. He glanced down at his hardware. "This is all you. I never would have brewed an Imperial stout and I sure as hell would never have entered this contest."

I shrugged and blew on my fingernails. "I am awesome. Thank you for acknowledging it."

He shifted the trophies under one arm and yanked me to him with his other. "You're more than awesome, Andi. You're quadruple awesome."

"Aw, shucks, thanks." My face hurt from smiling, but I couldn't stop. I looked up at him. "I love you."

He reared back in pretend shock. "What's that? I'm sorry. My hearing's bad. Come again?"

"I said, I love you, you giant, bearded oaf."

"That's what I thought you said." He looked around, spotted more media coming at us. "Let's get out of here. Maybe take a quick…nap?"

"I'm game." But I was reeling. I'd said it. The words he'd been saying to me for weeks. I had resisted, guarding my heart, hedging my bets, waiting for the other shoe to drop. But those days were in my rearview mirror. "Hotel, and fast."

"Agreed."

We raced out into the warm Denver night, flagged down a cab and managed an intense quickie in the hotel room before we had to be at Le Rouge. Afterward, I sat on the couch, wrapped in a towel and sipping a beer while James finished his shower. I ran my fingers over the trophies, still zinging from head to toe, thanks to the James-induced orgasm. I smiled, recalling how he'd looked when he crawled up from between my legs, loomed over me, ready for more, but holding back.

"You're sure?" he'd asked, his voice breathy and low.

"I love you, James Burke. And I'm sure if you don't get inside me right now, I'm going to be super mad." I'd reached up with my arms and my legs and guided him to me.

He'd angled his hips and joined our bodies, slow, easy, perfect. "Far be it from me to make you mad. I hear you turn into a real bitch."

"Shut up, already and just…do…that."

I shivered. We were like a couple of teenagers and had maintained the heat level for almost a year. I wondered if it would taper off, then decided it didn't matter. I loved him. If he asked me right now, I'd marry him.

I sat up straighter, my ears ringing. I shouldn't have to wait for him to decide. I was a grown, strong woman who ran sales and marketing for a multi-million-dollar production company. I would take care of this myself.

I got up and marched myself into the bathroom. "Hey, lover boy," I said, rapping on the shower door.

"Huh?" He squinted through a veil of shampoo. "What's up?"

"Marry me," I said.

"Hold on a second." I watched him rinse off, climb out, and grab a towel. "Now I can hear better. What did you say?"

"I said…"

"Hang on, I think I know." He grabbed the edge of my towel and yanked it off, leaving me stark naked, a condition I was comfortable with for the first time in my life, thanks to him. "Do me a fav, Scarlett," he said, touching my light covering of red pubic hair.

"What?" I asked, already getting all quivery and wishing we had more time.

"Look in the drawer at the wet bar."

"What? Why?"

"Humor me." He turned me around and gave me a tiny push out the door.

I walked across the suite, still marveling that I felt comfortable doing so in my altogether. I'd always been modest to a fault, but my time with James had turned me into someone else entirely. He'd even coaxed me onto a bicycle this past summer, insisting he wasn't trying to change my body but seeking something we could do together he could consider exercise. He loved my body the way it was.

Well, he had *not* loved it when I let Sloane talk me into a Brazilian. Dude had been apoplectic over my lack of pubes. I had to swear to him I'd never do anything so drastic again.

I opened the drawer. "Do you need a corkscrew? A martini shaker? A cheese knife?" I pawed through the stuff. When I reached deeper into the drawer, my fingers touched something velvety. I pulled it out and noted the distinctive light turquoise color and the big "T" on top.

He was behind me now, his hands on my arms, my shoulders, in my hair. He kissed my neck as I stared at the box, afraid and thrilled and all of the above.

"Yes," he said, turning me slowly. "I will marry you."

The ring was a simple, round solitaire, set in platinum filigree. Old-fashioned, the way I liked it. I hesitated before sliding it onto my finger. "Wait, this isn't Tracy's hand-me-down, is it?"

He burst out laughing and pulled me close, pressing his lips to my hair. "No, but I did get a good deal on the trade-in."

I smacked his bare chest.

"Ooh, baby, hit me one more time." He grabbed my wrist and kissed his way down the inside of my arm to my armpit and around to my breasts. If James loved all my hair, he was downright obsessive about my tits. They were his favorite pillow, play toys, you name it. Luckily, my nipples were hypersensitive, so it was a win-win arrangement.

"We have to go," I whispered as he took my hand and pulled me back to the bed. "We promised your brother we'd... Oh, hell, yes."

We were late. But only twenty minutes, which I knew would make both Michael and Sloane insane as they were those types. Anything past early was late. When we ran up to the door of Le Rouge, giggling like naughty kids, the place was dark.

"How can it be closed?" He banged on the door while I tried to peer in the window.

"Nope. It's shut down tight."

"Damn it." James pulled out his phone. "Nothing. You?"

I shook my head, still mesmerized by the sight of the ring on my finger, the finger I'd once sworn would stay empty the rest of my life.

Who knew?

We stood staring at the locked door a minute. "Well, I guess we can…"

The door creaked open. "That you, James? Andi?"

We glanced at each other. "Yes, it is," I said. "Who're—hey!"

Two hands reached out and grabbed us each by the arm, hauling us into the pitch-black interior. "Michael warned me you'd be late."

"What the hell?"

"Oh, I get it," I said. "It's one of those sensory deprivation dinners, right? I've never tried one." It didn't strike me as the sort of thing Sloane would go for, but whatever. I was three orgasms and one diamond ring in so far. Nothing else mattered.

"Here," someone whispered in my ear. "Take these." They shoved something cold and stiff into my hand. I was struck by a smell I didn't expect, that of day lilies. I brought them to my nose and sucked in a breath.

"Here," someone said to James. "You're in charge of these."

"These what? What is going on here? Michael,

what the hell are…"

I heard the sound of a curtain being swept aside. It took a few seconds for my vision to adjust, but I could tell we were surrounded by candles. Hundreds of the dang things. Nothing but candles as far as I could see.

"…we…doing." James finished.

I looked at him. "Did you plan something special for me?"

"I, uh… Well, I mean, you got a ring."

I looked down at the bouquet in my hand. He held out his hand. I saw two platinum rings in his palm.

"Late for your own brother's wedding," one of the people who'd pulled us inside said, with an audible "Tsk, tsk."

"My brother's what?" James' voice raised by the end of the three-word question. It echoed around the room, causing fifty or so people to look back at us, confused by the interruption, not to mention the question.

"James. Look." I pointed to an area in front of a set of white chairs. There was an arch, threaded through with lilies and other fragrant flowers. A woman stood under it, in some kind of a religious robe, smiling at us.

"Holy…shit, Mikey!" He yelled even louder. "Fuckin' a man! Seriously?"

The entire room whirled around in unison and glared at us.

"Shh," I said, grabbing his arm. "I think we're supposed to be down there." I pointed at the officiant person.

"Ha! Nice one, dude. This is…"

"It's Michael and Sloane's wedding, Jimmy. Chill out and do your job."

He held out his elbow. I stuck my hand in it. He pulled it up and kissed it. "I love you, Andrea Rose. Now let's get my brother and PR Barbie hitched. Whaddaya say?"

"I say, yes. Let's do that."

Sloane was radiant in a simple cream sheath dress, her only ornament other than the light in her eyes, a drop sapphire pendant, surrounded by diamonds I'd later find out was her engagement jewelry. Michael looked ready to eat her up, sleep a while, and start over again. He was in a black suit, white shirt, his French cuffs perfectly ornamented with a pair of matching sapphire cufflinks.

I started sniffling the moment I saw her, my friend, marrying the man she fought for, fought against, found again, and loved. She walked down the aisle alone, no need for escort, although I'd spotted her father, uncle, and mother in the crowd. When she reached us, she turned and gave me at tight hug. Many tears were shed. I held onto her a second longer.

"Congrats, Sloane. I'm so happy for you. And nice secret-keeping by the way. I didn't think you had it in you."

"I know, right?" She glanced over at Michael who beamed like a schoolboy about to get his first kiss. James had a hand on his brother's shoulder. "They are special, aren't they?"

I let go and turned her around. "They are indeed. Go on, marry him, quick before you change your mind." I gave her a tiny push. The crowd chuckled. Michael took her hand and kissed it. And it was as if only he and she existed for the next few minutes.

Exactly the way it should be at any good wedding.

About the Author

Liz Crowe is a Kentucky native and graduate of the University of Louisville living in Central Illinois. She's spent her time as a three-continent expat trailing spouse, mom of three, real estate agent, brewery owner and bar manager, and is currently a social media consultant and humane society development director, in addition to being an award-winning author.

With stories set in the not-so-common worlds of breweries, on the soccer pitch, inside fictional television stations and successful real estate offices, and even in exotic locales like Istanbul, Turkey, her books are compelling and told with a fresh voice. The Liz Crowe backlist has something for any reader seeking complex storylines with humor and complete casts of characters that will delight, at times frustrate, and always linger in the imagination long after the book is finished.

~*~

Visit Liz at
http://www.lizcrowe.com

Thank you for purchasing
this publication of The Wild Rose Press, Inc.

For questions or more
information contact us at
info@thewildrosepress.com.

The Wild Rose Press, Inc.
www.thewildrosepress.com

www.ingramcontent.com/pod-product-compliance
Lightning Source LLC
Chambersburg PA
CBHW051130030726
47504CB00004B/793